Lyn Andrews was born and raised in Merseyside, the daughter of a policeman, and now married to one. She is the mother of triplets and has recently returned to writing after a gap of several years bringing up her family.

THE WHITE EMPRESS, the story of the big luxury liners of Liverpool, was published in 1989 and was enormously successful. It was followed in 1990 by THE SISTERS O'DONNELL, her second book since returning to writing.

Best Wishes
Lyn Andrews

Also by Lyn Andrews

THE WHITE EMPRESS
THE SISTERS O'DONNELL

and published by Corgi Books

LIVERPOOL LOU

Lyn Andrews

CORGI BOOKS

LIVERPOOL LOU
A CORGI BOOK 0 552 13718 9

First publication in Great Britain

PRINTING HISTORY
Corgi edition published 1991

This book is set in 10/11 Imprint by
Falcon Typographic Art Ltd

Corgi Books are published by Transworld Publishers Ltd., 61-63 Uxbridge Road, Ealing, London W5 5SA, in Australia by Transworld Publishers (Australia) Pty. Ltd., 15–23 Helles Avenue, Moorebank, NSW 2170, and in New Zealand by Transworld Publishers (N.Z.) Ltd., Cnr. Moselle and Waipareira Avenues, Henderson, Auckland.

Made and printed in Great Britain by
Cox & Wyman Ltd., Reading, Berks.

For my fellow Liverpudlians, especially
those who are now expatriates.

Author's Note

Earlier this century there lived in Liverpool a woman called M
Elizabeth Braddock. At least two generations of people, ev
Liverpudlians, may never have heard of her, but there are ma
who have and many who knew her well. 'Our Bessie', as she w
known, was a woman of the people. An ordinary woman who w
to become 'extraordinary' – a City Councillor and a Member
Parliament. When she died half of Liverpool attended
funeral.

The idea for this book was inspired by Bessie Braddock but i
not the story of her life. My characters are purely fictional, no
of them is based on any of 'Our Bessie's' relations or friends, ye
is set in the Liverpool she knew and loved.

St George's Church still stands at the top of the hill, Nor
umberland Terrace remains. It is still possible to get a wonder
view across the Mersey but the rows of 'back to back' terra
have gone, to be replaced by a landscaped park, new, mode
houses and a few tower blocks. But on a cold winter day with
wind whistling around St George's churchyard, if you close yo
eyes, you may hear the cries of laughter, sorrow and anger t'
once filled those streets. The voices of the ghosts of yesterda

Lyn Andre
1!

Oh, Liverpool Lou, lovely Liverpool Lou,
Why can't you behave just like other girls do?
Why does my poor heart keep following you?
Stay home and love me, my Liverpool Lou.

Liverpool ballad

PART I
'LOUISA'
1936

CHAPTER ONE

Louisa Langford turned on her side and for a brief second her eyelids fluttered open before she burrowed back down in the bed, beneath the blankets. It was still dark, the room was cold and the warming nest of the bed induced drowsiness. Then, as if her eyelids had been attached to an invisible spring, she opened her eyes wide as she remembered what day it was. It was Sunday and her Da was coming home.

She was wide awake now. It was the first time in five years that he had been home for Christmas. Why, she'd only been nine years old that time. The memory that occasion evoked sent a tingle of excitement right down her spine. Even though it was so long ago she still remembered what a wonderful Christmas it had been, but this one would be even better for she was grown up now. She'd left St George's School for ever, last Friday. By this time next week she would be a working girl, as would her cousin Evelyn.

Her vision had adjusted to the semi-gloom and she could see her cousin's figure curled up in a ball in the bed on the opposite side of the room, against the partition wall. She and Evvie – as everyone called her – were the same age. There was just a bare month between their birthdays. They had been brought up together – as close as sisters – by Aunt Babsey, her Da's sister, for her Mam had died of pneumonia when she had been three.

She lay still, thinking about her Mam and trying to remember her. Trying to picture her in her mind's eye, but, as always, she couldn't. There was just the blurred

11

memory of a pale woman with a quiet voice, devoid of the usual thick, nasal, Liverpudlian inflection. Aunt Babsey had always maintained she'd been too good for this earth and for Big John Langford, even though he was her only brother. Mary Talbot had suffered for her love of him. Disowned by her family who were far above his station in life. Left alone for months while he was at sea; unused and unprepared for the hard, relentless drudgery of life in the tiny house in Joshua Street. No, she couldn't remember her poor Mam, but she'd been christened after her. Mary Louisa Langford, but everyone called her Louisa.

Behind the heavy curtains the cold, grey December dawn was breaking and the room had become fractionally lighter. Louisa raised herself on one elbow and peered at the round, brass alarm clock that stood on the chest of drawers that separated the beds. Its face was dull and the black numerals were blurred, but the small hand looked to be on seven. She couldn't make out what number the large hand was pointing to. If she got up now and went to the top of St George's Hill, she could see right over the city and up-river. The *Berengaria* was a big ship, she wouldn't have much difficulty seeing her as she entered the Mersey and sailed majestically down the Crosby Channel.

Pushing back the blankets she shivered, the icy chill cutting through her nightgown. At least it was Sunday and everyone was still asleep. On a weekday morning at this hour the house resembled Lime Street Station, with all the activity and everyone getting in each other's way. Uncle Jim would just be coming home from the market and would be in and out to the cart. Aunt Babsey would be in the kitchen cooking breakfast, directing Uncle Jim's movements and trying to eye the Produce, while shouting to herself and Evvie to 'shift yourselves, sharpish!' Her cousins, Eddie and Tommy, would be getting ready for work and school respectively. Yes, she was glad it was Sunday. There would be no lecture from her Aunt about running out at this hour to stand in the freezing cold, when she ought to wait and go down to the Landing Stage later, with the rest of the family; after a good breakfast and dressed in her best clothes. She knew her Da wouldn't care what she was wearing, but Aunt Babsey would.

Slowly she eased herself out of bed, curling her toes on the rag rug. Cautiously she pulled open the bottom drawer of the chest and extracted a pair of thick stockings. Sitting on the edge of the bed she began to pull them on. Aunt Babsey was always going on about 'appearances'. They were 'different', she told them at least a dozen times a week. They were 'tradespeople' and that set them apart from the rest of their neighbours in the mean, narrow streets of back-to-back terraced houses that clung to the slopes of Everton Ridge, one of the highest points in the city.

There wasn't any need to be reminded of their 'different' status, she thought. The poverty was there, right under your nose, you couldn't ignore it, although Aunt Babsey seemed to. She herself didn't see that having a green-grocery shop on the corner of Northumberland Terrace and Bathesda Street made her any better than anyone else. She was 'different' but not 'better'; everyone worked when they could. The difference was that she was always well fed, well clothed and in winter there was always a good fire in Aunt Babsey's kitchen.

As she drew her nightgown over her head, then pulled on a flannelette petticoat, Evvie stirred and uttered a slight groan. Her head moved restlessly on the pillow for her sandy-coloured hair was twisted around rag curlers. Louisa ran her hands through her own thick, brown hair that curled naturally, marvelling that Evvie managed to sleep at all with her hair screwed up into tight knots like that. She knew it peeved her cousin to the point of open animosity that her own hair could be brushed around one finger to instantly produce the desired curls that Evvie suffered to achieve.

Evvie had taken Aunt Babsey's diatribes about 'appearances' to heart and now believed that she was 'different' and 'better'. Louisa sighed. Over the last three months

Evvie had become something of a pain in the neck. No longer had she sneaked out to play on the corner or up the Terrace with the others. At school she had studiously ignored those who turned up in their usual garb of ragged dresses and tatty cardigans full of holes. Evvie now averted her eyes from their feet, devoid of socks or stockings and clad in shoes or boots donated by some charity. Usually the League of Welldoers or the Police Clothing Association. Now Evvie looked down on her former friends and, despite their taunts, stuck to the likes of Edith Gouldston from the grocer's on the corner of Camlet Street, and Mavis Wills, the eldest of the Wills brood who had the chandler's on the corner of Neil Street. They didn't have nits in their hair or red blotches on their arms and legs from bug bites. But then Evvie missed a lot of fun too.

She'd lost out on the street games that had fostered and nurtured comradeship, forging kids from all backgrounds into a single group who forgot their often miserable lives for a few hours as their laughter and shrieks filled the soot-laden air, and the sound of their running, jumping, skipping feet echoed on the cobbled roads and dirty, narrow back entries or 'jiggers'. 'Kick the can', 'Lally-O', 'off ground tick' were the favourites of the older ones. 'Cherrywobs', 'ollies' and 'grid fishing' the pursuits of the younger set. The endless games of skipping or swinging with the aid of a piece of old rope, attached to the cast-iron arms of the street light. She sighed again and with nostalgia. Those days were over for her, too, now. But not from choice. When you started work you had to forgo such pastimes, you were supposed to have outgrown them at fourteen.

As she buttoned up her skirt and was about to pull on a thick, hand-knitted jumper, Evvie opened her eyes.

'What time is it?' she muttered.

'Shut up!' she hissed back in reply.

Evvie blinked owlishly and pulled the blankets higher up to her chin. 'Why are you up? Where are you going?'

As Louisa's face appeared through the neck of the

jumper she scowled at her cousin. 'I'm going up the Hill to see if I can see the *Berengaria* coming in. Does that satisfy you? Now shut up and go back to sleep before we have everyone awake!' This explanation was again delivered in a sharp whisper.

'You're cracked, that's what you are. It's freezing and it's the middle of the night, you won't be able to see anything and you'll be for it if our Mam catches you!'

'I don't care, it's a free country, isn't it? If I want to go out then I can!' She bent down and pulled her shoes out from under the bed.

'Well, your hair looks like a bird's nest. A right cut you'll look,' Evvie muttered, before turning her back on her cousin and wriggling down in the bed.

She knew it was childish, but she stuck out her tongue at Evvie's back, then she turned and crept towards the opening at the end of the partition wall.

When she reached the aperture she stopped and listened. In the other part of the bedroom – for that's what it really was – she could hear the regular breathing of Tommy who was two years younger than herself, and the heavier exhaling of Eddie who was eighteen and worked on the Docks.

The fingers of her free hand curled around the brick-work. The wall itself was a monument to Aunt Babsey's sense of propriety and 'appearances'. The living accommodation comprised of a large kitchen cum living room, behind the shop, a scullery, and two bedrooms upstairs. Aunt Babsey and Uncle Jim had one bedroom and the rest of them shared the other one. There was nothing remotely unusual about this; in fact many families all slept in one room. The old houses were damp and rooms were often unfit for use; it was the attempt to keep warm that frequently meant as many as five or six children sleeping in the same bed. Such arrangements Aunt Babsey wouldn't tolerate. First of all an old screen, painted dark green, had divided the room; that had given way to a long dark brown curtain and finally, against all the arguments Uncle Jim had put forward about cost, mess and invasion of privacy, Pat Crowley had been paid to build the wall.

The Crowleys were Catholics and Irish to boot and only the fact that Pat's estimate had undercut the others by half, had induced Aunt Babsey to allow him over her doorstep. In her Aunt's eyes all Catholics and especially those of Irish descent, were idle, slovenly drunkards and not above helping themselves to other people's belongings. She openly scorned and disapproved of a religion that, in her eyes, enabled its adherents to commit all sorts of sins, then go and confess to a priest, receive a telling off and a few prayers as a penance, then go back and do the same things all over again. It wasn't her idea of Christianity and the sight of many of them going straight from church into the pub only added to her contempt. While the wall had been under construction, they had all been threatened with dire consequences should they utter one word to its builder.

Louisa smiled at the memory. She'd found the big Irish bricklayer to be a jovial man, not at all inhibited by 'appearances' and 'proprieties'. He'd given her a toffee one day when no-one else was looking. She smiled again as her gaze settled on the outline of the 'put up' bed that she would make up later in the day for her Da.

Crossing the polished strip of lino, she opened the bedroom door and pulled it gently shut behind her, then crept slowly down the stairs. The fire in the kitchen range had been 'damped down' so the room was fairly warm. Silently she drew back the curtains from the window that overlooked the yard. Fingers of dull, grey light filtered in. The room was tidy. It was her Aunt's usual practice to see to this before she retired each night. The table was set for breakfast. The cushions on the horsehair sofa had been straightened, as had the one on Uncle Jim's winged armchair, set before the fire. In one alcove was a small dresser on which were displayed the blue willow pattern dishes. The other alcove was known, jokingly, amongst the family as Aunt Babsey's 'Office'.

She sat down in the winged chair and began to put on

her shoes, glancing towards the window and the leaden sky beyond, wondering whether or not her rubber wellington boots wouldn't be more appropriate. It looked as if it would snow again. Northumberland Terrace and St George's Hill already resembled a skating rink from the last fall two days ago, which had frozen hard.

Her coat and scarf were hanging on a peg behind the door with everyone else's and Uncle Jim's shop coat. She put them on, wrapping the scarf tightly around her neck. In one pocket she had stuffed her woollen tam-o'-shanter and her knitted gloves. The hat reminded her of Evvie's remarks about her hair and she peered into the oval mirror above the bog-oak bureau in the 'Office'. The image reflected there was that of a tall, slim girl with an oval face and large, blue eyes, heavily fringed with dark lashes. Her eyebrows swept upwards against her pale skin, giving her face an expression of being permanently surprised by and curiously interested in life. Her thick mass of dark chestnut hair, that in some lights threw out gleams of gold, was indeed a mess.

She turned, her gaze sweeping quickly over the dresser and the bureau, before she frowned in irritation. Aunt Babsey had a rule that no combs, brushes, hair clips or slides were allowed downstairs to clutter the place up. She pursed her lips and began to try to smooth down the untidy mane. Finally, exasperated, she gave up, gathered it back and twisted it into a knot and shoved it all up under the hat. At least it was tidy.

As she reached over to pick up her gloves from the top of the bureau, the sleeve of her coat caught the handle of the small key which was still in the lock. She stared at it. Aunt Babsey must have forgotten to take it up with her, something she rarely did.

She'd seen the bureau open many times and her Aunt bending over the writing top, surrounded by papers. She knew what all the pigeon holes contained and why it was called the 'Office'. Inside were receipts, invoices and lists of names and columns of figures and a large, stiff-backed ledger that was referred to by everyone as 'The Book'. She knew what was in that, too. Evvie had explained it all to her one day on their way to school, years and years ago, after she'd seen her Aunt and Mrs Unwin from further down, deep in hushed and urgent conversation in the kitchen, early that morning.

'She's come for a loan from Mam,' Evvie had replied in answer to her question.

'A loan of what?' she'd asked, innocently.

Evvie had stopped trailing her hand along the links of chains set between iron bollards that ran along the edge of the pavement and acted as a hand-rail, for the terrace was steep. Evvie's pale blue eyes had been filled with scorn. 'Money, of course! Stupid!'

'Aunt Babsey is going to lend her money?'

Evvie had raised her eyes to the blue sky. 'Honestly, you're as thick as the wall, sometimes! Mam lends money to people and they pay her back at so much a week, that's what "The Book" is for!'

Although generous, up to a point, with her own family, she'd never thought of her Aunt as being generous to other people. 'That's really good of her, Evvie.'

Evvie had made a sucking noise through her teeth. 'It's not good, it's business. She charges them a per . . . per.' Evvie had given up on the word percentage which she didn't really understand anyway. 'It's a service and people have to pay for it. Like she's always saying "You don't get owt for nowt". Mind, she doesn't loan money to just anyone; she's got to know they can pay it back. She wouldn't lend a penny to any of "that lot".' Evvie had jerked her head backwards in the direction of the Catholic school of Our Lady Immaculate at the bottom of the Terrace. 'They go to the pawn shop, if they've got anything worth pawning.'

'Why doesn't Mrs Unwin go to the pawn shop then?'

'How do you expect me to know that? Maybe she doesn't want all and sundry knowing her business, maybe she needs more money than old Rosenbloom will give her. Our Mam's business is "on the quiet" like. It's her rule.'

'We know about it.'

'We're family and you just remember that, our Louisa!'

They had walked for a while in silence while she'd digested all this. Evvie had abandoned the chain swinging and was concentrating on avoiding the cracks in the paving stones.

'But it's a proper business, like Mr Rosenbloom's, all legal, like?'

Evvie had stopped dead and had grabbed her arm and pushed her face close to hers. 'You shut up about that! Everyone is happy with the arrangements, as Mam calls them! We don't want no scuffers poking their noses in, especially not them that don't wear a uniform!'

It had been then that the first niggles of doubt about Aunt Babsey's business had started. For weeks afterwards she'd been half afraid that one night there would be a knock on the back door and the plainclothes police would be standing there. But no knock ever came and her apprehension had disappeared. Long ago she'd accepted the fact that the scuffers weren't liked in their neighbourhood. They were feared and some were even respected, but they weren't liked. People in their neighbourhood 'sorted' things themselves and, in turn, when there was the usual Saturday night punch-up outside the Northumberland Hotel, the police would turn a blind eye, unless things really got out of hand. And as for 'that lot', as Evvie termed the small Irish community, their parish priest had more influence over them than the scuffers did. So, 'Honest Babsey MacGann's' money-lending business had thrived. They actually owned the shop and the living accommodation – they were the only ones in the Terrace who did – and that was part of being 'different' too.

Louisa unbolted the back door of the scullery and stepped into the yard. Instantly the cold air cut her throat like a knife; the pale dawn seemed filled with ice, all pressing on her. It was as if she wasn't wearing a coat, hat, scarf or thick jumper; nor woollen stockings and stout shoes, for as she made her way over the slippery flags of the yard her feet were already beginning to feel numb.

The one small window of the wash-house was patterned with a delicate tracery of frosted feathering. The wooden fruit and vegetable boxes, stacked against the wall beside the privy, were covered in frozen snow. Against the soot-blackened bricks of the yard wall they looked like an old and awkwardly shaped piece of furniture that had been hastily covered with a white sheet.

The broken glass, cemented onto the top of the wall, glistened like pieces of fine, hand-cut crystal. They'd been put there to act as a deterrent to anyone attempting to climb the wall and make off with the boxes, which could be used for firewood, or, in the poorer homes, for furniture. Aunt Babsey wasn't having any of that. The door into the back entry creaked on its frozen hinges but she only needed to open it slightly, she was slim enough to squeeze through. Then she was out. With a bit of luck in about ten minutes she would be at the top of St George's Hill, her eyes straining for the sight of the red funnels atop of the huge black hull of the liner that was bringing her Da home.

Cicero Terrace ran parallel to Northumberland Street and at number twelve, Sally Cooper watched the grizzled light struggling through the curtainless window. She was wedged tightly between her elder sister Doreen, and her two younger sisters. She didn't notice that the flock mattress was lumpy and stained, she counted herself lucky to have a mattress at all. A pile of old coats and one thin, dun-coloured blanket covered them all and she was cold. Her Mam and Dad and young brother were all huddled together in the other bed. All she could see of her Mam was a strand of coarse brown hair. There was no other piece of furniture in the room and the floor boards were bare. On the walls and ceiling were large, brownish stains where the damp had seeped through. She didn't notice them, they'd always been there.

Her stomach rumbled emptily and she thought of the

half a loaf and the remains of the dripping downstairs in the kitchen. Half a loaf between seven of them; she'd be lucky if she even got a wafer thin slice of it. Doreen tried to turn over and in doing so her elbow stuck sharply into Sally's thin chest. Roughly she shoved her sister away. Now that Doreen was working at Bibby's and was contributing to the household, as she put it, she demanded a bigger share of whatever food they had. It was dirty, heavy work she was doing and she needed proper nourishment, she had stated. Her Da had been 'one day on the hook, the rest on the book' last week. That had just paid the rent, Doreen's money was all there had been left to live on.

Again she twisted her head and looked over towards the figures in the other bed. Poor Da, she thought. If only he could get regular work and didn't have to go down the Docks each day and have to fight to get taken on, even if just for half a day. It wasn't right that men should have to put themselves out for hire, like work-horses, and any man who even dared to think about opposing the system was likely never to get work. Anyone who spoke his thoughts aloud was branded a 'troublemaker' and besides, the blockerman didn't like her Da. If she had known words like 'degrading' and 'injustice' she would have applied them to the system, but she didn't, so she just thought it was a shame. A damned shame.

Her stomach rumbled again and she made up her mind. She didn't care how much of a row it caused, she was going down and get herself a crust spread with dripping, before they all got up. It couldn't be any colder down there than it was up here. They all slept in their clothes, except Doreen. In fact her Mam had sewn the little ones into theirs, just like she always did when the winter came.

With some difficulty she extracted herself from the tangle of arms and legs belonging to her sisters, but she almost cried aloud as her bare feet came into contact with the floor, it was freezing. Doreen had stockings, rolled up and stuffed under the mattress, but she didn't dare purloin them, besides, the initial shock of the cold boards was wearing off.

When she got downstairs she thought how wrong she'd been. There was no fire in the range and there hadn't been since late yesterday afternoon when all the rubbish that she and the little ones had collected from the surrounding streets, had been burned. The room was so cold that she could see her own breath. The loaf, covered with a piece of cloth to keep off the mice and other 'Jaspers' that shared the house with them, was now stale. She cut off a medium slice and spread it with the brownish-coloured fat. She couldn't see out of the window, it was iced up both on the inside and the outside. She munched slowly, wondering what she could do for the rest of the day. She'd have to go out, for once the transgression of helping herself to the bread was discovered, there would be an outcry and probably a belt from her Da. Perhaps if she went round to Lou's later, when they'd all gone to church, Mr MacGann might let her warm herself by their fire and maybe even give her something to eat. He was good like that, even though he wasn't a church-going man, and 'she' wasn't around.

Mrs MacGann didn't like her nor did she approve of her being friends with Lou, or Louisa as they all called her. Just lately their Evvie had gone all stuck-up too. She wouldn't even go near her now, said she had bugs. She had shrugged that off. Nearly everyone had bugs, even those better off than themselves. The men came and stoved the houses every now and then, but after a few days the bugs were back. Bugs hadn't bothered Evvie until lately. 'Yer'll all be goin' to live in Aintree next!' she'd mocked. Lou wasn't like that at all, even though she was soon to start work at Frisby, Dyke & Co, in Lord Street, which was a better job than Evvie's. Evvie was only going to work at Marks & Spencer, selling stockings. Lou was going to train in the millinery department of a much bigger store.

She looked down at her old plimsolls. The toe of the left one was completely out and neither had any laces. Next to them were Doreen's new boots. She was pure selfishness

22

through and through was Doreen. There was no food in the house and no fire; most of their clothes came from the fund the scuffers paid into and was all marked so it couldn't be pawned. That in itself was mortifying and it made her Da furious. They had to rely on the hated scuffers to put clothes on their backs and boots on their feet. But Doreen spent nearly all her wages on herself and she spent them before she got home, so Da couldn't force them off her. She'd even threatened to leave if any of her new things got pawned, knowing they couldn't do without her contributions. The resentment these thoughts provoked made her push aside her plimsolls and bending down, she pushed one foot inside one of the boots. It was lined with something warm and soft and it was heaven to wriggle her numbed toes against the warm lining. Doreen wouldn't get up until lunchtime and so she wouldn't miss them and anyway, she didn't care if she got found out. She'd get Lou to come back with her and Doreen never screamed or swore when Lou was there. She wriggled her toes again for re-assurance, then put on the other boot.

From a nail on the wall she took her old brown cardigan, her coat was still upstairs on the bed. Over that she wrapped her Mam's heavy, black shawl, pulling it close to her face, over her light brown hair. It came down to her knees. Silently she let herself out of the house.

She was startled to meet Louisa at the corner of Daniel Street. 'Lou! Lou! What yer doin' 'ere, at this time? Wait for me! 'Ang on a bit!' She slipped and slithered on the icy pavement in her haste.

'Is that you, Sall?' Louisa called to the strange little figure bundled up in the old black shawl.

Sall grabbed the top of an iron bollard and nodded, panting a little. 'Where are yer goin'?'

'Up to the top to see if I can see the *Berengaria*. Da's coming home today, don't you remember? I told you.'

Sall's face fell. She had forgotten and with Big John Langford home, there was no way Lou would go back home with her later.

'What's up now, Sall?'

Sall looked down at her feet and Louisa's eyes followed the direction of her head.

'Where did you get them?'

'They're our Doreen's. She got them down the market, yisterday.'

'She'll kill you!'

'I know,' Sall replied, miserably.

Louisa looked at the thin, pinched face. The hands, blue with the cold, that clutched the edges of the shawl, and at the bare legs, mottled blue and purple. She felt suddenly ashamed of her own warm clothes. Stripping off her gloves, she thrust them towards her friend. 'Here, put these on. I can put my hands in my pockets.'

'No, yer can't, you'll fall flat on yer back on this ice if yer don't 'ang on ter somethin'.'

'I won't! We'll go slowly. Put them on, Sall!'

As they made their way at a snail's pace up the steep slope that had been made more treacherous by a gang of lads from Grecian Terrace, using it as a slide the previous night, Louisa made up her mind to buy Sall some stockings and gloves with her first week's wages. Then she sighed. Sall had her pride. All the Coopers had pride, and they would view the gesture as patronizing. Sall had also left school on Friday, being the same age as herself and Evvie. 'Never mind, you'll be able to buy your own boots and things when you get a job.'

'Who's goin' ter give me a job, Lou? Half this city's out of work!'

'You can read and write and your arithmetic is as good as our Evvie's, better in fact.'

'Oh, aye, but your Evvie's got decent clothes, ain't she? Even if our Doreen would lend me somethin', which she won't, no-one would give me a job! I'd never gerra job in a shop or in service, would I?'

'They'd have you in a factory, like your Doreen.'

'Just brushin' the floor they might.'

Louisa knew this to be the truth and yet some factories

paid far better wages than shops, but the shops had a more 'respectable' image, at least in Aunt Babsey's eyes. 'After Christmas you come round and you can borrow some of my things, then you can go down to Tillotsons or Tates or the Match Factory and they'll take you on.' She didn't say she'd have to give Sall the clothes. For one thing she knew Sall would have refused and for another Aunt Babsey would have hysterics at the thought that they'd been worn by Sally Cooper. She got the de-lousing treatment and lecture every time she was seen with Sall.

'Do yer mean that, Lou?'

'Of course I mean it! I wouldn't have said it if I didn't!'

'What about . . . yer Aunt Babsey? Won't she create about it?'

Louisa shrugged. 'Not while me Da is there she won't, and you've got to get a job, Sall, just to help your Mam out.'

'It's not fair that, Lou! Me Da wants ter work an' 'e works 'ard, but that blockerman don't like 'im, so 'e don't get no work.'

Louisa frowned, she knew the system, and so did Cousin Eddie. He bought Alf Browning, the foreman – or blockerman as he was called – a pint nearly every night and Eddie was never out of work, even though he was a single man. Sall was right, it wasn't fair. After Eddie had 'turned up' his keep to Aunt Babsey, the rest of his money went on clothes, beer and woodbines, while the likes of Mr Cooper went home with coppers or often nothing and Sall went cold and hungry. The thought made her feel angry. Angry at the blockerman, angry at Eddie, angry at herself, though she didn't know why. 'Come on, it's not much further now!' she urged with a forced cheerfulness.

Panting and red-faced, they finally reached the top of the Hill and stood in the comparative shelter of the church wall, looking down over the sprawling city. Down over the grey slate roofs and black chimneys. Nearly all of them were sprouting smoke and this moved upwards to form a cloud under the already overcast sky. Beyond the rows of houses and shops were the tall, blackened buildings of the waterfront, the bonded warehouses, the three chimneys of the Clarence Dock Power Station – adding to the smoke. The five-sided clock tower and to the left the Royal Liver Building, known as 'the black house', the Cunard Building and the grand, domed building housing the offices of the Mersey Docks and Harbour Board. And then – grey and sluggish – the river itself. Its surface choppy for a cold wind was blowing in off the Irish Sea. And, as if they had strayed from the pack on its way northwards, a few snowflakes fell.

Louisa shaded her eyes with her hand and peered into the distance. Then she gave a little cry and grabbed Sall's hand. 'Look! Look, Sall! Right out there, beyond Perch Rock! There she is! There's the good old *Berry*! Da's on his way, Sall!'

Sall peered in the direction of Louisa's outstretched arm and saw the black hull that even at this distance looked huge, and wished her Da was coming home on the *Berengaria* for Christmas laden down with presents. Lou was looking forward to Christmas, while she . . . it could be any time of the year for all the difference it would make in their house.

CHAPTER TWO

Aunt Babsey was standing in the scullery supervising Tommy, who was making a great to-do about having to wash his neck again. He tried reasoning with his mother. He'd only had a bath in the tub in front of the kitchen range the night before, his neck just couldn't get dirty again so soon, it just wasn't possible.

'We have this performance every Sunday morning and if I have any more lip from you, meladdo, I'll box your ears! I've enough to do today without you playing me up!'

Louisa stood in the doorway, smiling at the familiar scene.

'And where have you been, Miss?' Aunt Babsey demanded.

'Up the Hill, Aunty. The *Berengaria*'s on her way in, she's just passed Perch Rock.'

'Were you born in a barn! Put the wood in the hole, you're letting all the heat out!'

Louisa shut the door while Tommy, his mother's attention diverted, grabbed the towel, rubbed his neck and face and darted towards the kitchen.

'Aye, well it will take her another hour to get berthed, then another couple of hours to get all the passengers off, then half an hour to get the crew off, and you know your Da is always one of the last, him being a greaser. He's lucky he doesn't have to stay on to take her into dock. Now get yourself upstairs and get changed for church!'

Babsey bustled past her and into the kitchen. She was a small woman, but wide-hipped and big bosomed, which made her appear larger. She had a swarthy complexion and dark hair, streaked here and there with grey, which she wore dragged straight back and twisted into a tight bun. Her round eyes, which could be likened to jet beads, were as bright as a bird's and missed nothing. Physically she had little presence but she made herself felt by her temper and her tongue and both were feared by every member of the household and most of the immediate neighbourhood.

As Louisa followed her into the kitchen she immediately sensed that there was something wrong, although everything looked normal enough. Uncle Jim, in his Sunday shirt and trousers, was sitting by the fire reading the newspaper. His glasses were perched on the end of his nose and his shoulders were hunched slightly. Evvie was arranging the results of a night's discomfort with some satisfaction in front of the mirror and Eddie was sitting eating his breakfast. But it was Eddie's appearance that caught her attention. He wore a clean shirt but with no collar or tie and his second best trousers, not those to his Sunday suit. Nor had his dark hair been slicked down with brilliantine. It didn't even look as though it had been combed.

Aunt Babsey whisked the dirty dishes from the table with the speed of a magician practising 'sleight of hand', including her eldest son's plate on which there still remained half a piece of fried bread. 'Are you going to get yourself changed then, Eddie?' Her mouth was set in a small, tight line.

'I've told you, Mam, I'm not going! Not this morning or any other Sunday morning!' He answered quietly, not looking at his mother.

Louisa looked across at Evvie who just raised her eyebrows and shrugged. For the past few weeks Eddie had been surly and reticent about their weekly trip to St George's.

'And that's it, is it? Your final word? A nice thing, I must say! Can't even give the Lord an hour of your time and after all He's given you!'

'It's not that, Mam, and you know it! I just feel that, well . . . I'm too old to be traipsed along to church. I feel like a "cogger" going to mass!'

28

'Don't you dare talk like that in my house! Don't you dare compare us to them! They *have* to go – for all the good it does most of them – we go from choice! Now, for the last time are you coming?'

Eddie stood up, towering over his mother but still refusing to look at her. 'No, I'm not!'

Babsey's chest rose and her chin jutted out as she turned towards her husband. 'Jim MacGann, put that paper down and speak to your son!'

Jim looked up with resignation. He'd seen this coming for weeks now and he didn't blame the lad. Not the way she marched them all up the Terrace together, as if to impress on the neighbours how much better they were. And why was it that when any of them did wrong, they were 'his' but on all other occasions they were 'hers' or 'ours'? He knew Eddie was getting ribbed by his mates. On the Docks there were few labourers who went regularly to church. Except some 'left footers', another of the epithets by which the Catholic-Irish were known. Work and conditions were hard and rough and the men who worked on the four miles of Docks were a tough lot; most of them real 'hard cases' who had little time for religion. They had their own code of ethics though, and were in the main what he called 'decent'. Eddie was eighteen, doing a man's job and it wasn't right that he should be treated like a fourteen-year-old lad.

He, himself, wasn't a church-going man, but in his own way he felt he was a good Christian. Aye, better than some who were running to church every Sunday. It wasn't often he dug his heels in with Babsey. He was placid by nature and let her have her own way for the sake of peace, but he'd stood firm over his own form of worship years ago and now he was prepared to stand up for his son.

'Now look, Babsey, he's a grown man. He works, aye and damned hard. He brings in a wage and he's a right to choose what he does with his time.'

'Not until he's twenty-one, he hasn't!'

He ignored that. 'He's a right to his views, just as everyone else has and whether he goes or not is a matter for his conscience. Now let's hear the end of it!'

Babsey knew she'd lost this battle. Jim could be cajoled, bullied or bribed – with subtlety – on most things, but when he decided to make a stand, she knew of old that nothing would budge him. Now he'd decided to take his son's side. 'All right, there's an end to it! You suit yourself Eddie MacGann, but don't think you can do as you like just because you work! I'll just explain to the vicar that you've "outgrown" God! Evvie, don't stand there gawking, give me a hand with these dishes! Do you intend to go to church in that old coat? If not, go and get changed, Louisa!'

As her Aunt and Evvie disappeared into the scullery, she glanced at Eddie. There was a smug expression on his face now and suddenly, as she remembered Sall, she decided that there was something new about Eddie. Something she didn't really like and he'd taken all the sparkle off the day. This special day.

'What's up with your face, Louisa? You got a cob on as well?' he asked pointedly.

'No. You do what you want. I couldn't care less if you never set foot in a church again, but did you have to choose today?'

'What's so special about today?'

Before she had time to reply, Uncle Jim raised his head, looked sharply at his son and said flatly. 'Big John's home today, that's what special, isn't it, girl?'

She threw her Uncle a grateful look.

'Well, there's no need for her to get all airyated!' came the cocky reply, now that his mother was out of sight and he'd got his own way.

'You'd start a row in an empty house, Eddie.' Uncle Jim sighed and returned to his paper.

'I'm sorry,' Eddie muttered, ungraciously.

She ignored his apology and went upstairs to put on her red and white dress and her best, dark-blue melton coat. Now Aunt Babsey would be cross and prickly all day. Eddie's defection had taken the edge off her excitement.

They all stood in the kitchen while Aunt Babsey inspected them as if they were a row of soldiers on parade. Before they would walk up the street and come under the scrutiny of the neighbours, not one hair had to be out of place. Aunt Babsey was dressed entirely in black, from her black velour hat, adorned with its bunch of artificial violets, her wool coat with the curled lamb collar, to her black stockings and rather old-fashioned, black, buttoned boots. Louisa had brushed her hair and caught it up at the sides and then secured her small-brimmed blue felt hat with a hat pin. Evvie looked neat in a dark green and white checked coat and a dark green hat which suited her fair complexion; Evvie took after her father in looks. Tommy was poking his finger between the starched collar of his shirt and his neck. He hated his tweed knickerbockers and jacket. They were 'scratchy' and smelled of mothballs. His unruly, spiky hair had been plastered down with a wet comb and he twisted his cap between his hands, looking thoroughly glum.

He'd received a sharp box around the ears and a short, succinct lecture on 'disrespect' after he'd come downstairs singing the latest version of the old carol 'Hark the Herald Angels Sing'. In his tuneless voice and at the top of it, he'd started 'Hark the Herald Angels sing, Mrs Simpson's pinched our King!' He'd got no further and his left ear was still red, for the Abdication was no joking matter in his parents' eyes. They, like the rest of the nation, were still deeply shocked.

'Right, put that cap on, Tommy, then we're ready!' Aunt Babsey announced, giving Evvie's hat a last pat and pulling Tommy's cap further forward. Then, without a word to either her husband or her eldest son, she led them out.

'It's cold enough for two pair of bootlaces!' Tommy muttered, wondering if there was any way he could possibly get out later and join his mates who would be sliding down the Terrace, using old tin trays or oven shelves as sledges.

It wasn't easy trying to walk with dignity up a pavement

that was almost a solid sheet of ice, Babsey thought, hanging on to the chain railings for support. She was annoyed with Jim for not supporting her and furious with Eddie, who had started to keep what she called 'bad company'. She had wanted something better for him than labouring on the Docks, but with the way things were he was lucky to have a job at all. At least he had the sense to keep his nose clean and keep on the good side of Alf Browning. He thought he was smart did Eddie, but it had been she who'd 'spoken' to Alf Browning and she who'd told him to see the blockerman 'right'. He wasn't smart, wasn't Eddie, but he was crafty and she'd have to keep her eye on him.

'Mornin' Mrs MacGann, looks like we'll be 'avin' more snow, don't it?'

The little group stopped as Babsey's deliberations were interrupted by two of her neighbours who, despite the weather, were standing on their doorsteps, gossiping.

'I hope not, we've had more than enough already and the Council should do something about these pavements, they're downright dangerous!'

'I was just saying that to you, wasn't I, Dolly? Downright shockin', they are!'

'Aye, an' those young hooligans from up Grecian Terrace haven't made it any better!' Dolly Unwin added.

Tommy's hopes instantly faded and he glared at Mrs Unwin from under the peak of his flat cap.

'Your Eddie not with you this mornin', then?' Mrs Gaskell asked, innocently.

'No. Got a bit of a cold,' Babsey lied, her gaze steady. Danny Gaskell worked with Eddie.

'Your Da's due in terday, Louisa, ain't 'e?' Mrs Unwin changed the subject.

'He is and we'll all be going down the Landing Stage later.' Babsey forstalled any remark her niece was about to make. 'It's all go. Never a minute to myself.'

'Oh, aye, it's that all right! I don't know how yer do it. I said ter you Flo, didn't I? "'Ow that woman copes with the business, the 'ouse an' everythin' else, I don't know!"'

32

Mrs Gaskell nodded.

'Mostly because I don't stand jangling on the front door step all day. Or spend all day Monday down the wash-house, jangling! I don't hold with taking the washing down there – never have!'

Dolly Unwin sniffed. Babsey MacGann had a wash-house in the yard, complete with a boiler, dolly tub and mangle. No-one else did.

'My washing is done and on the line before half of them are back!'

Nonplussed by this open criticism of them both, Mrs Gaskell beamed. 'An' it's a credit to yer, Mrs MacGann. I've never seen whites that bright. Do yer 'ave a special blue bag, like?' It paid to keep well in with Babsey MacGann, especially if you were hoping for a loan.

'No, just the usual "Dolly Blue".' Babsey's head moved slightly in condescending appreciation and she made to walk on for both Evvie and Louisa were shuffling their feet, Tommy was stamping his loudly, but Mrs Gaskell wasn't finished.

'Mind, yer should see the stuff them Irish take ter wash, I'd be mortified! Me floor cloth's in better shape!'

'What do you expect from the likes of them! Not even washed properly, never mind rinsed! I've seen it on the lines, grey it is, and not from the smuts either! Wouldn't know hard work if it hit them in the face!'

Dolly Unwin, who considered herself to be a fair-minded woman – now the last instalment of her loan was paid – looked thoughtful. 'It pains me ter say it, but some of them are real 'ard workers. Take that Maggie Crowley. Every time I see that woman she's step-dashin'. I said ter 'im once, only in passin' mind, "That wife of yours is never off her knees, she'll 'ave that step worn away!" And 'e laughed an' said "Sure, if it's not on her knees scrubbin', it's on her knees prayin' she is. I'll tell you this Missus, she's wastin' her time prayin' for our Mike to get the vocation to the priesthood. A fine young bucko is our Michael!"'

Babsey had heard enough. She had no interest in Maggie

Crowley or her son and she did not want to know about 'vocations'.

'Mam, my feet are so cold I can't feel them!' Evvie complained, tugging at her mother's sleeve.

'We'd better be off then, before we all freeze.'

As they resumed their journey, the two women wrapped their shawls more tightly around them and glanced at each other.

'It won't be no warmer in there an' yer wouldn't catch me sittin' listenin' ter "old misery guts" goin' on for an hour about "Hell and Damnation"; not when I can sit in front of me own fire,' Dolly Unwin said.

'Looks like their Eddie's church-goin' days are over. Looks as though 'e's finally stood up ter 'er. Our Danny said 'e was goin' to.'

'It's a brave lad that'll stand up ter that one!' Dolly Unwin pronounced.

Inside the church it was cold and smelled damp and musty, despite the pinkish hue of the local sandstone which gave an illusion of warmth. They sat in their usual pew and despite the chill, it did look nice, Louisa thought. Bright and cheerful with the candles and the holly and ivy that decorated the altar and window recesses.

She wondered idly if their Catholic neighbours decorated their churches like this. She'd never been inside one or knew anyone who had, but they must do. They had processions on their Saints Days, when they carried plaster statues draped with flowers and their priests were decked out in bright, silk robes. All the girls wore white dresses and veils, though where they got them from she didn't know, for they were all desperately poor. She couldn't concentrate on the Reverend Bailey's words, her mind kept wandering to the river and the Landing Stage. The *Berengaria* would be tied up now. The gangways would be down and the passengers would be coming ashore. There would be porters hurrying with luggage to the Riverside Station. Cars and cabs and waiting relatives and friends. There would be a happy sort of chaos. She wished impatiently that Reverend Bailey would get a move on, she wanted to see her Da. But when the service was over, Aunt Babsey would stand talking to the vicar, which would prolong the agony of waiting. Then she remembered Eddie. Perhaps this morning her Aunt wouldn't want to linger in the porch, making polite conversation and answering questions on the health and well-being of her family. She sincerely hoped not. She just wanted to see her Da.

She always spotted him first amidst the crush for he towered head and shoulders over everyone else. Aunt Babsey said it was from him that she got her height for she was tall for her age and still growing. She wanted to see his face break into the familiar grin when he saw her. He'd pick her up and hug her, even though she was 'grown up'. She'd hug him back while protesting 'Ah, stop it, Da! I'm too big now!' But he'd just laugh and say 'That's a nice thing to say to your Da after all this time!' It was always the same. Then they'd go home with her hanging on his arm all the way, and he'd start handing out the presents. He always did this, even when it wasn't Christmas. His case and old kitbag became an Aladdin's cave, but this time it was Christmas. The Reverend Bailey's voice intoned, 'Let us pray' and she bent her head dutifully, as if in prayer. In reality it was to hide her happy, glowing expression and the excited anticipation in her shining eyes.

When Sall had left Louisa she'd crept into the churchyard and leaned against an old gravestone. She often did this. She waited for the verger to open up, then she sneaked into the back of the church and would sit huddled at the far end of the pew and no-one noticed she was there. She would stay through early service and leave before the late morning one. Then she would go round to Lou's, after hanging around the corner of Bathesda Street to make sure they'd all gone.

It hadn't been much warmer inside the church this morning though and she'd sat shivering, her teeth chattering, and when she finally left and walked to the corner she'd thought they were going to stand talking to those two old biddies for ever; at last they'd moved on up the Terrace.

She knocked loudly on the scullery door as she pushed it open. 'It's me, Mr MacGann, Sally! Can I come in an' gerra warm, I'm perished?'

She was standing in the doorway to the kitchen before she realized that Eddie was sitting at the table staring at her. Her hand went to her mouth. She hadn't even noticed he wasn't with the others; she'd been too cold and preoccupied, wishing they would move on. She didn't like Eddie MacGann; there was something shifty about him. He never looked straight at you, not if he could help it.

Eddie turned to his father. 'What's she doing here?'

Jim MacGann looked at the shivering little figure and then at his son. 'Come on in, Sall, girl, and stand by the fire. She comes nearly every Sunday, don't you, Sall? She comes to see me, we have a good old jangle and what your Mam doesn't see doesn't hurt her,' he added in a lower tone.

Hesitantly Sall approached the fire and spread out her hands towards the warmth, her back to Eddie. She could feel his eyes boring into her back and it made her skin prickle.

'And how's tricks at home this week then? Your Da get taken on?'

She shook her head. 'Only fer one day. That blockerman don't like 'im,' she added.

'That's his own fault, he's a trouble-maker,' Eddie said.

She turned around. 'No, he ain't! He only said what everyone else thinks! An' 'e hasn't got the money ter buy 'imself a pint, let alone anyone else!'

Eddie's eyes narrowed. The hardfaced little bitch, he thought. So she came here every week, did she? Well, Mam would have something to say about that all right, even thought he wasn't exactly 'in favour' at the moment. As he stood up he intercepted a look from his father. A warning look. 'I'm going to get myself changed and you'd better do the same Da. She'll go mad it we're not ready to go down to meet our John when they get back.'

His father ignored him, so pushing past Sall he made for the staircase.

'I'm sorry, Mr MacGann, I shouldn't 'ave said that.'

'Don't you worry your head about him, girl. Have you had anything to eat?'

'I didn't think 'e'd be here. Ain't 'e goin' ter church no more then?'

'No. Now, have you eaten today?'

Again she shook her head and he got up, went into the scullery and in a few minutes returned with two thick slices of bread with a generous slice of cold meat between them.

She tried not to cram the food into her mouth. She felt much warmer now and she glanced furtively around, wondering if Eddie would come back. When she'd finished eating, she sat down on the floor in front of the range. 'Will 'e tell the Missus about me?' she asked.

'No, he won't, not if he knows what's good for him!' Jim MacGann answered with uncharacteristic grimness. 'I'll give you some potatoes and veg Sall, your Mam can make a pan of blind scouse. That'll fill you all up until Monday and keep you warm, too.'

'Ta, me Mam will be real grateful, but . . .'

'But what?'

She began to pick at the frayed edges of the shawl, then she looked up at him openly. 'We ain't got nothin' ter cook it on.'

He got up and went out through the scullery into the yard and came back with a small sack which he left by the scullery door. 'There's some wood and coal, take it with you.'

'Aw, you're real good Mr MacGann! Lou's good, too, like. She's goin' ter lend me some things so I can gerra job.' Jim MacGann smiled down at the earnest little face. He and Frank Cooper had grown up together, but Frank had always been a bit of a loudmouth and it had got him

37

into trouble more than once. And this one was like him. She could stand up for herself, could young Sally, like the way she'd had a dig at Eddie just now.

'That's good, and even if your Da isn't taken on, there's always the Christmas parcels.'

Her face lit up. She'd forgotten about that. They'd got one last year with oranges, tea, sugar, flour, a plum pudding and a turkey. They'd stuffed themselves so much that she'd been sick.

'And I'll send our Louisa and Tommy around with the sprouts and spuds and enough coal so your Mam can cook whatever they send. Now you stay there and thaw out. I'd better go and get ready.'

She smiled up at him and for a moment he thought that under the dirt and the rags, she was a pretty little thing.

He met Eddie on the landing.

'Our Mam would go stark raving mad if she knew *she* was round here! Her clothes are heaving up!'

To his surprise his father caught him roughly by the shoulder. 'You leave her where she is, she's doing no harm and your Mam is so obsessed with exterminating imaginary bugs, that the few Sall leaves behind won't survive more than a couple of hours!' He lowered his voice. 'You're getting too big for your boots, meladdo, and if you say anything about Sally Cooper then I'll be having a few words to say about some of the things you get up to, and she's already suspicious! Oh, I've seen you sloping off down the back of Cicero Terrace for Mogsey Green's Pitch and Toss school. You know how she hates gambling and illegal gambling, too! I took your part this morning over that church business because I happen to agree with you and because I know you're getting a rough time of it at work because of it. I'm not deaf nor bloody daft! But you step out of line, lad, and I'll put a stop to your gallop and don't think I won't! That poor kid's starving and so is the rest of the family, and if you put your twopenny 'orth in to Browning about Frank Cooper I'll take my belt off to you, big as you are! He's got a family to keep. All

38

you think about is booze, gambling and dressing up like a pox-doctor's clerk!'

Eddie shook himself free. 'I don't hear you going on when I bring you the odd bottle that fell off the back of a cart or any "'arry Freeman's" that I can get past the scuffers on the gate!'

'That mouth will get you hung one day, lad,' came the cold reply, before his father opened the bedroom door and left him standing on the landing.

Eddie shrugged. He was all talk, was Da. Besides, Big John would be home soon. He liked his Uncle. He treated him as a man and he liked that. You could talk to John Langford about almost anything, ask advice, he was a man of the world; as his mates would say a 'real good skin'. He straightened his tie and ran a hand over his slick hair. Of course Big John doted on Louisa. You'd think she was the Princess Elizabeth or the Princess Margaret Rose the way he treated her. Would he approve of her having friends like *that one* downstairs? You never could tell with Big John. He shrugged, why should he bother himself with Frank Cooper's dirty little brat, she wasn't worth it. When Louisa started work she'd make other friends and drop the likes of Sally Cooper, just as Evvie had done.

Sall got to her feet when he came back downstairs but he ignored her. He picked up the newspaper, pulled his father's chair backwards, away from her, then sat down, hiding his face with the paper.

She just stared at him. Sunday mornings wouldn't be the same now, not with him there. Loath though she was to leave the warmth, she picked up the bag containing the vegetables and went through the scullery, adding the small sack to her burden. She thought about Doreen and the boots, then she shrugged. The coal and vegetables would more than make up for wearing the new boots and so would the thought of the Christmas parcel.

CHAPTER THREE

John Langford cursed his big frame for the hundredth time. Six feet three inches squeezed into one of the cramped cubby-holes in the bow section of the *Berengaria* and shared with fourteen other men, was a definite disadvantage and a downright nuisance. These small crew's quarters were always untidy, except for the once weekly inspection by the captain, when everything was stowed away.

Even though the *Berengaria* was better than many ships he'd sailed on, little thought had been given to the comforts of the crew. When he'd first joined her he'd been a little uneasy, but he'd put that down to superstition. Originally she'd been the *Imperator*, the 52,226 ton pride of the Kaiser's merchant fleet and launched by Wilhelm II himself. He'd laughed when Harry Webster, the Chief Engineer, had told him that when told that all German ships over 16,000 tons were forfeited to compensate for Allied losses, the Kaiser's fury had been monumental.

'Serves the bastard right!' he'd replied, but he'd still felt uneasy. But it had passed.

Two rows of two-tier, iron-framed bunks left little space for a single table and two benches and the small, cube-shaped metal lockers that were totally inadequate. Now every bunk was strewn with half-packed gear. Suits and overcoats hung from the bunk ends and it was against one of these sharp projections that he'd once again caught his broad shoulder. He cursed aloud, picking up the small box he had dropped.

'Yer awkward bugger! Yer could wind the Liver Clock!' one of his mates joked.

He grinned back. His height had always been the cause for such comments and he was used to them. He pushed the box into his pocket and looked around, checking that everything was packed up.

'Going up top, John?' another asked.

'Too bloody right I am! I've had enough of being stuck down here. Mind your backs!'

'Duck, or 'e'll 'ave yer bloody 'ead off!' Taffy Davies yelled.

With some difficulty he swung his kit bag over his shoulder, tucked two brown paper parcels under one arm and picked up the battered case. With head and shoulders lowered he made for the doorway.

'Don't let the Chief see yer, all the "bloods" might not be off yet!'

'Sod 'em! Happy Christmas!' he called good-naturedly over his shoulder.

All the quarters of the lower ranks of the crew were below the waterline and after sweating for twelve or more hours in the bowels of the engine room, then sleeping like sardines in a tin, as he put it, he was eager to get the stench of unwashed bodies, stale cigarette smoke and beer, oil and grease out of his nostrils. And he knew they would all be waiting. He'd been lucky, this was his sixth trip on the *Berengaria*. Usually he'd go down to the 'Pool' and sign on for whichever ship he could get. There'd been many who'd been out of work in the early thirties, but he'd been fortunate. He'd also not been home for Christmas for five years.

Taffy had been right, he thought, as he reached the promenade deck. A few passengers had still not disembarked and so, with unusual stealth for a big man, he made his way aft and up to the boat deck. Then he slid behind one of the metal spars that held the lifeboats.

He breathed deeply as his gaze wandered over the waterfront, familiar to seamen the world over. It was more than his job was worth to lean over the side to look for his family in case an officer looked up and saw him. He'd see them soon enough. He took a packet of cigarettes from his pocket and lit one and leaned back against the davit.

It was dirty, sprawling and smoke-grimed; poverty and affluence stood side by side, but it was Liverpool and it was home. Even the dirty, grey water far below him was part of it. He loved his city and its river. That great, glaucous artery pumping out ships at the rate of ten or more a day. the gateway to the Atlantic and the world. Liverpool had a love affair with the sea which provided work for most of its population in one form or another, in good times. He'd heard the words 'It's in the blood' uttered by hundreds of men. Sometimes with pride; sometimes as an excuse to placate angry wives and sweethearts. He'd used the explanation himself, lamely, when Mary had shouted 'You love the sea and those damned ships more than you love me!'

He sighed, his forehead furrowing, his eyes darkening with the painful memory and he stubbed out the cigarette butt. Mary. Sweet, gentle, well-brought-up Mary. He still missed her, even after all this time. He'd had other women since her death, sometimes he'd even paid for them – he was a man after all – though lately the fire of desire burned lower. He found solace in books and music, though he was ribbed unmercifully by his mates for indulging in such pastimes. Mary had been responsible for introducing both into his life and had carefully nurtured that interest, until it had blossomed.

She'd been a passenger on the old *Mauretania*. An only child, her parents had died tragically in an accident in Canada. She had been returning to Liverpool to live with an Aunt and Uncle. He'd come upon her standing alone on the promenade deck, gazing at the black water far below. He'd come up top to breathe the fresh, salt air after twelve hours in the engine room. It was nearly two in the morning and at first he hadn't noticed her, she'd been standing so still. It was only when she'd moved quickly and he'd thought she was going to jump overboard, that he'd covered the few feet of deck and caught her by the shoulders, uttering quietly 'Come on, luv, it can't be as bad as all that!' She'd looked up at him. A slight, pale girl with huge blue eyes and a mass of dark, wavy hair. Then she'd collapsed against him, sobbing. It had started that night, after he'd slowly drawn the pitiful story from her. The brief, snatched meetings; the gentle kisses and embraces, until he knew he was hopelessly in love with her.

Together they'd faced the cold fury of her middle-class relatives who had finally washed their hands of her, when she'd persisted in marrying him. She'd been twenty-two so there had been nothing much they could do about it and he'd never been so happy in all his life.

Babsey had found them the house and, surprisingly, she and Mary had got on well, though they were as different as chalk and cheese. His happiness had been complete when Louisa had been born, but shortly after that Mary had started to complain about his absences. He'd tried then to explain to her that the sea was his life. That he earned more than he could have done ashore, if indeed he could have found work in the depressed city. He wanted to give both her and the child the best he could possibly afford.

After that she had stifled her resentment but when Louisa was barely three, on the last night of his leave, her resolve had broken and she'd shouted that he loved the sea more than he loved her. It was the first time he'd ever heard her shout and it was the last. Three weeks later she was dead. They were halfway across the Atlantic, after calling into Cobh in Southern Ireland on the outward trip and the Chief Engineer had sent him up to see the First Officer. He'd known then that something was wrong at home. He'd thought it was Louisa. He'd stood in the wardroom and heard the words, uttered with a depth of sympathy, and he'd dropped his great head and cried. He who had the reputation of being a 'hard' man. Big John Langford that few would care to tangle with, had wept openly and unashamedly.

She'd been buried by the time he'd got home and all the love he'd had for her had been transferred to his small daughter.

He pulled himself out of his reverie. He still missed her, his gentle Mary, but when he looked at Louisa he could never forget her. Louisa was the image of her mother. Over the years he'd placed her on the pedestal that Mary had once occupied. Nothing was too good for the child. Babsey said he spoiled her and she was probably right, but he knew it was his way of assuaging some of the guilt. Mary Talbot had given up so much for him. He patted the box in his pocket and smiled. She'd grown up had his 'Lou'. She was fourteen now.

The biting wind that was blowing down the estuary tugged at his cap and he pulled it further down over his forehead and ventured a glance downwards. The last of the stewardesses was disembarking and they were always the first to leave. Moving his gear towards the rail, he leaned over, his gaze scanning the crowds on the Landing Stage below. She'd seen him before he spotted her and was waving like mad. His face broke into a broad smile as he took off his cap and used it to wave back.

As soon as he had pushed his way ashore and through the crowds, he dumped his gear and swept her off her feet, swinging her around as he always did.

She laughed. 'I'm too big for all this now, Da!'

As he set her down on her feet he looked down into Mary's blue eyes and the familiar pain tugged at his heart. 'Aye, I suppose you are, and too grown up now to give your old Da a welcome home kiss!'

She laughed again, then reaching up, kissed his cheek. Fourteen or not, she'd always be his 'little Lou'.

Similar scenes were being enacted all around them as, after hugging Evvie and Babsey, shaking Jim's hand and slapping Eddie and young Tommy on the backs, he hoisted his bag onto his shoulder.

'Well, are we going home then or are we going to stand here and freeze? I can see these two are dying to see what I've brought for them!' He ruffled Louisa's hair playfully. 'But you're going to have to wait this time. No presents until Christmas morning!'

'Oh, Da!'

'Oh, that's nice, I must say! Aren't you glad to see your Da? Is it only what he brings you that you're interested in, Miss?' Babsey said, shaking her head with mild disapproval. 'That says a lot for the way I've brought you up, doesn't it?'

Big John laughed. 'Give over, our Babsey! You've done a great job, they're all a credit to you!'

Babsey smiled at her brother. She was proud of him; she always had been, despite the fact that her words were often sharp. She glanced at Eddie who was carrying his Uncle's case and parcels. 'Most of them are! There's one who's getting too big for his boots though!'

Eddie shot a glance at his mother. A look that was intercepted by his Uncle.

'They're all growing up, Babsey, and there's not much we can do about that.'

Babsey tutted, still annoyed with Eddie. 'Are we going on a tour of the Pierhead then?' she asked, suddenly realizing that they were all walking along the Landing Stage and not heading for the tram terminus.

'No. We're getting a taxi home.'

She turned and stared at him. 'A taxi! Have you been promoted or something? We'll get the tram like we always do.'

'No, we won't! This is a special leave – it's Christmas – we're going home in style!'

'Oh, can we get a taxi, Uncle John?' Evvie begged.

Babsey glared at her. 'You've more money than sense, John Langford! Besides, we won't all fit into a taxi, there's seven of us, and we're not having two taxis!'

'Our Eddie and Tommy can go on the tram,' Jim intervened. Always the peacemaker, yet this time he got some satisfaction seeing the smirk wiped off Eddie's face. He hadn't forgotten their earlier conversation.

'That's settled then. Don't worry, lads, we'll take the luggage.' Then, seeing Eddie's face fall, he added, 'I'll stand you a pint this afternoon.'

Babsey made a moue with her mouth. She strongly disapproved of Sunday drinking, classing it as 'common', but there was little she could say. Big John would just brush aside her complaints and arguments like he always did. 'And leave us women at home with the mess,' she muttered, but loud enough for him to hear, as they made their way to the taxi rank.

Taxis were almost never seen in the rows of narrow streets running down Everton Ridge and, by the time they had turned into Northumberland Terrace, there were quite a few ragged lads running alongside, as the black hackney made its way slowly up the treacherous slope. Mrs Unwin and Mrs Gaskell – amongst others – were on their doorsteps, summoned by the shouts of their younger children. They nudged each other and waved as the MacGann family passed.

Babsey, the extravagance now forgotten, waved back regally.

'You look just like Queen Elizabeth, Mam!' Evvie giggled.

'Don't be so hardfaced, Miss! What do you expect me to do, stare straight ahead and pretend I haven't seen them?'

Evvie poked her cousin in the ribs and Louisa looked down at her hands, her eyes dancing and her lips quivering. Aunt Babsey was enjoying every minute of it, her bosom thrust out with pride. It would be the talk of the neighbourhood for weeks.

'Jim, get rid of all those street arabs before we get out, or it will look like Fred Carno's Circus!' she instructed as they drew up outside the shop.

While Jim cleared the crowd of curious youngsters, Big John paid the cabbie. Babsey sailed across the pavement without looking right or left, but fully aware of the envious looks directed at her. She called out sharply for the girls to follow and not dawdle around, but Louisa had spotted an open-mouthed Sall on the opposite side of the road. She called to her and beckoned and Sall made her way across.

The taxi moved away slowly, taking its accompanying

straggle of kids with it, leaving Louisa and her father standing on the pavement.

'Hello, Sall. How's your Mam and Dad, girl?'

Sall craned her neck and smiled up at Lou's Da. 'All right, ta,' she answered a little shyly. She didn't know Big John very well and his height made her a little apprehensive.

'Sall's left school, too, Da.'

Big John shook his head. 'Has she now? Every time I turn my back, you all grow up. Tell your Da I'll be in the Northumberland later on. I'll buy him a pint.' Judging by the pinched little face, the dirty, ragged clothes and the chapped, blue hands, Frank Cooper was doing far from all right.

'Ta, Mr Langford. I'll tell 'im. Are yer comin' over later then, Lou?'

Louisa looked towards the open front door of the shop.

'Tell you what, Sall. We'll both be over. Tell your Da I'll pick him up,' Big John intervened.

Before either Louisa or Sall could answer, Evvie's head appeared in the doorway. 'Uncle John, Mam says are you coming in or are you stopping out there all day?'

Placing an arm around his daughter's shoulder, Big John called, 'Coming now, Evvie!'

Sall grinned at them both before turning to make her way back home. 'See yer later, Lou!' she called.

John Langford looked down at his smartly turned-out girl and a grim expression came into his eyes. He'd be happy to work until he dropped so that Louisa would never look like that poor child of Frank Cooper's. Then he sighed heavily. He, too, had been brought up with Frank and knew that his old schoolfriend would give his right arm just to have the chance of a job like his. He could only try to imagine how it must feel to see your children go cold, hungry and almost barefoot.

Louisa, too, had noted the bare, chapped legs and the feet now back in the old plimsolls. 'They're having it hard, Da. I'm going to give Sall some things so she can go for a job. Mr Cooper hasn't had any regular work for months now.'

'I guessed that.'

Suddenly the blue eyes sparked with fire. 'It's not fair! Eddie gets regular work! Someone should do something! Someone should change the system!'

'The Unions are doing their best, luv, but you're right, the system needs changing.'

'Then why doesn't someone *do* something?'

'Desperate men are afraid to speak up, they've got families to feed. It's no use you railing against it, Lou, it will be a long time before things are done fair and square on the Docks. Aye, and by the Council.'

'Then we should get rid of the Council! There should be people who care about Sall and Mr Cooper on the Council!'

He smiled down at her, surprised and proud of her fiercely caring little face. 'Maybe one day there will be. Come on in now or your Aunt Babsey will be slamming the door in our faces.'

Louisa laughed, the anger gone as quickly as it had come. 'She wouldn't do that, not to you!'

Despite his earlier statement, presents had been distributed after they'd all eaten. For Jim there was the 'docking bottle' of good Scotch. Big John had long since given up spirits but Jim liked a drop now and then, to keep out the cold after a long day in the shop. For Babsey there was a small cut-glass posy bowl. Eddie was slipped a carton of American cigarettes. For Evvie and Louisa there were small bottles of toilet water in fancy bottles. Tommy was excitedly poring over the American comic books which would ensure his popularity for weeks to come with his gang of 'hooligans' as his mother called his friends.

Surrounded by his family, basking in the cries of delight and thanks, replete with the good meal Babsey had put before him and with Louisa (her grown-up status forgotten) sitting on his knee, Big John Langford was a happy man. 'That was the best meal I've had in a long time, Babsey.'

'Don't they feed you then?'

'Oh, aye. But nothing like that. There's no-one can make pastry like you.'

Babsey glowed.

'You going to open your bottle then, Da?' Eddie asked, emboldened by the convivial atmosphere that now prevailed.

'No. I'm saving it for Christmas Day,' came the sharp reply.

'And I don't approve of you drinking spirits at your age!' his mother added, beginning to clear away the dishes.

Evvie put aside her present to help her mother, knowing from experience that Louisa would remain firmly by her father's side.

'You listen to your Mam. I've seen many a good man ruined by strong liquor. Stick to ale, lad.'

Eddie ignored the advice. 'Well, talking of ale, what about the pint you promised me?'

'You've not been in the house more than an hour and now you're all off down the pub!'

'Now Babsey, it's Christmas,' Jim intervened.

'And don't I know it! I'm rushed off my feet, what with the shop and all the baking and cleaning! Evvie, that reminds me, you can take the bunloaf down to the bakery tomorrow morning early, before it gets crowded. It's too big to fit into the oven.'

Evvie pulled a face.

'Don't you look like that! Not after all the mixing and stirring, to say nothing of the cost of the ingredients! You can decorate the tree as well, when it arrives. Tommy can do the paper chains, that will keep him out of mischief.' Babsey hurled instructions as she moved between the kitchen and the scullery. 'Where is he, anyway?' she asked, suddenly noticing the absence of her youngest son.

'He's taken his comics to show his mates,' Evvie volunteered.

'Typical! Sloping off when I wasn't watching. A right young devil he's turning into! Are you going out then?'

'Yes.' Eddie seized the opportunity.

Louisa got up. 'I'll get my hat and coat.'

'Have you lost your mind, our John? You're not taking her to no pub!' Babsey was outraged.

Big John threw back his head and roared with laughter. 'You're a case, Babsey! Of course I'm not taking her. We're going round to Frank Cooper's. I told young Sall I'd call for him.'

Babsey's dark gaze flitted from her brother to her niece and her lips were set in a thin line. 'I wish she'd find other friends!'

Eddie looked quickly at his Uncle. Big John Langford's reputation carried a lot of weight and he wasn't particularly anxious to spend the afternoon listening to Frank Cooper's ill-disguised barbs at himself.

'She can choose her own friends, Babsey.'

Eddie looked away; that boded ill for him.

Babsey sniffed. 'That's not what her Mam, God rest her soul, would say.'

'I'm just going upstairs, don't go without me!' Louisa moved quickly between her Father and her Aunt. Evvie was in the scullery and Uncle Jim and Eddie were preparing to don overcoats, caps and mufflers.

She ran upstairs and with Evvie preoccupied, she riffled through the drawers in the chest. Taking out a pair of stockings and a petticoat she stuffed them into a brown paper carrier bag. From the wardrobe they both shared, she took a blue wool skirt and folded it neatly, together with a plain, darker wool jumper that had become too tight. A pair of gloves and a knitted beret were added to the pile, but the problem of a coat caused her to pause. She had her best blue coat and the brown and white flecked one she'd worn for all other occasions. She bit her lip. Aunt Babsey would create enough about the skirt, jumper and other things, let alone a coat. She delved into the wardrobe again. Behind the two new black dresses with their small white collars –

the uniform of shop workers – was a short jacket belonging to Evvie. She fingered it then pushed it aside. Even though it was Christmas and her Da was home, she daren't take anything of Evvie's. It was the brown and white coat or nothing and Sall couldn't go looking for work in this weather without a coat! Hastily she rolled it up and shoved it on top of the other things. Then she looked down at her feet. Shoes! But Sall's feet were much smaller than hers.

Evvie's voice floated up to her, saying that everyone was waiting for her. Maybe Doreen could be cajoled into lending Sall the boots, or maybe Sall could get something from Rosenbloom's bargain table, if she'd accept a couple of pence.

She ran down the stairs and straight to the group by the door, so Aunt Babsey didn't have time to see what she had in her hand.

'You go on ahead, Jim, we'll catch you up. Tell Davey Whale to set up a round, I won't be long,' Big John instructed, taking the bag from her and shoving it under his coat.

There was a small, spluttering fire in the Coopers' range and the entire family huddled around it. A blackened pan and some dirty dishes were on the old deal table. The place smelled of damp and dirt.

'All right there, mate? You ready to come for a jar?' Big John said cheerfully as he entered the room, noting the obvious signs of dire poverty yet giving no hint of the knowledge.

Frank Cooper thrust his fists deep into the pockets of his greasy trousers and cleared his throat as he stood up. 'Good t' see yer, John. 'Ad a good trip?'

'Aye. Get your cap, mate, the ale will be getting warm! You're looking a bit peaky Aggie.'

Agnes Cooper gave him a wan smile and shot a cautious look at her husband who coughed again.

'I'll tell yer straight, John. There's more chance of the King buyin' yer a round than me, I'm skint!'

'Did I ask you to buy? How often am I home at Christmas? And if I can't stand my old mates a bevvie, then it's a poor do! Get your cap!'

Frank Cooper unbent, his pride appealed to. 'I'll just gerra quick wash then, sit down. Move over you lot, yer hoggin' the fire!'

John Langford eased his big frame cautiously down onto the old orange box that Doreen had vacated with none too good a grace. He was afraid to actually sit on it, fearing it wouldn't take his weight, and so he half squatted beside Agnes. The younger children eyed him curiously from the old, upturned paint tins they were seated on.

'Having a hard time, Aggie, and don't tell me you ain't,' he said quietly. He delved into his pocket and brought out a coin. 'Here, don't tell Frank. I know what he's like. Got his pride.' He pressed it into her hand.

'I couldn't! I couldn't, John!'

'Get off with you! Call it a Christmas present. Here . . .' Again his hand went into his pocket while with his free one he beckoned the children closer. 'You lot spend this on sweets or whatever you fancy.'

Three grimy little hands shot out as a silver threepenny bit was placed in each one.

Agnes uttered a small cry of gratitude.

'I've brought you the things I promised Sall,' Louisa interjected, to try to cover the noise of the smaller Coopers.

Doreen poked her head forward into the circle. 'What things?'

'Some clothes so she can go for a job. There's no shoes though. Could she borrow your boots, just for the day?' Louisa stared straight at the older girl, defying her to refuse.

Doreen's eyes shifted from Louisa's face to Sall's and finally to John Langford's. He was looking at her speculatively. She shrugged. 'I suppose so, just for the day.'

Sall looked triumphant. She knew Lou would best Doreen, she always did.

Big John saw the look and his fingers closed around the half crown he'd been holding back. 'Here, Doreen, this is for you. Get yourself something, and one for you, too, Sall.'

Doreen took the coin and a slow smile spread over her face. She'd get some make-up and scent and some beads and ear-rings from Woolworth's. She'd seen some really nice ones and she was fed up having to beg or borrow from the girls she worked with who all seemed to have far more than she had. 'Ta, Mr Langford.'

'Christmas present, Doreen. We should all share at Christmas.'

'What's goin' on in 'ere then?' Frank Cooper came back into the room, wearing a stained and shiny jacket and a greyish-white muffler around his neck to hide his frayed and collarless shirt.

'Just giving the kids a couple of pennies for sweets, seeing as it's Christmas. You're not going to get a cob on about that, are you?' He eased himself up from the cramped position. 'Come on, let's get off. They'll all be under the counter by now!'

CHAPTER FOUR

Sall had tried on the clothes with the aid of Doreen and Louisa; the younger children having disappeared and Mrs Cooper, after placing the sovereign under the chipped candlestick on the mantel over the range, had gone into the scullery to attack the dirty dishes. Doreen had chattered on about what she was going to buy from Woolworth's.

'You should buy me Mam somethin', she never gets nothin',' Sall had interrupted the flow.

Doreen ignored her.

'When I get me first wages I'm goin' ter buy 'er something' just fer 'erself. Somethin' daft, like scent or flowers.'

To ward off the impending quarrel Louisa made Sall put on the coat and hat to get the entire 'effect' as she put it. Sall's appearance was pronounced 'wonderful' and they had then spent a happy hour discussing what they would all do with their future wages. It was nearly dark when Louisa had finally returned home.

She'd helped Aunt Babsey and Evvie with the chores and had assisted in getting some supper ready when the men arrived back. Eddie somewhat the worse for wear, his condition prompting a long tirade from her Aunt about the evils of drink.

After saying it was all his fault and he took the blame entirely, it was with some difficulty that her Da and Uncle Jim got Eddie to bed. They'd all then settled down to a quiet evening, listening to the radio.

Christmas Eve dawned with clear blue skies after another heavy frost that increased the treachery of the roads. Straw

54

and ashes were liberally thrown onto the cobbles to aid the many horse-drawn carts which still formed a large part of the transportation on the Liverpool streets, but there were many accidents as heavy, iron-shod hooves struggled to maintain a grip.

Uncle Jim arrived home from the market red-faced and panting, after having pulled and coaxed the horse up St Domino Road and Northumberland Terrace. When he'd regained his breath, he'd complained that he'd had to walk most of the way holding the bridle and that he'd seen more than one animal that would have to be shot. 'The bloody Council should be horsewhipped! They're probably still snoring in their beds!' he finished heatedly.

The disappearance of the coat was discovered when she and Evvie had been instructed to help unload the cart, along with Tommy. Aunt Babsey, harassed by the increase in trade in the shop and her own numerous preparations, lost her temper and it was into a full blown row that Big John descended at half past eight.

'What the hell's the matter now? It's quieter in the *Berry*'s engine room than it is in here!'

Babsey placed her hands on her wide hips. 'She's only gone and "lent" Sally Cooper her coat, that's all! Lent! She knows full well that anything she "lends" doesn't come back into this house! It will be crawling with lice and God knows what else!'

'She *had* to have a coat, Aunt Babsey! She's got to get a job, you know how desperate they are for money!' she answered, knowing her Da would back her up.

'Oh, and we've got so much money that you can hand out good coats to all and sundry!'

Big John sat down at the table and looked calmly at his indignant sister. 'She's right, Babsey. They're in a right state over there. Frank's out of his mind worrying about them.'

'Worried enough to go drinking with you!' Babsey flashed back.

He just stared at her. Often, despairing men needed a

release from their worries, but she wouldn't understand that. Sometimes she was so hard, he thought. As hard as two pieces of anthracite, of which her eyes reminded him so forcibly. But she'd had to be hard; they hadn't always been so well off. They'd built up the business from almost nothing. Their parents had started with a handcart in Clayton Square. Babsey had always had that hard business streak and a moneylender with a soft heart would soon be out of business. She was fair in her own way. The interest she charged wasn't exorbitant, unlike some of the sharks he knew. And he owed her so much, he couldn't have brought up a child alone or given her all the things she had. 'I was going to buy Louisa a new coat anyway, for Christmas. I didn't see anything I fancied in New York.'

Babsey tutted loudly, indicating that she knew he was lying. Nothing he fancied in a great city like that! Did he think she'd come over on the last boat?

Undeterred he carried on. 'And I think she's old enough now to choose what she wants, so she and Evvie can go into town. Evvie can choose something, too. A new frock,' he added. In gratitude to Babsey he tried hard never to leave Evvie out.

'And who's going to help me while they go chasing off round town?'

'Me. I've nothing to do, besides, they won't be all day, will you?'

'No, we'll only be a couple of hours, Mam, honest!' Evvie put in, delighted at the prospect of going to choose something by herself, a novelty never before experienced.

Slightly mollified, Babsey heaved a large, square tin onto the table. 'You can take this down to the bakery before you go and you, John Langford, can give Jim a hand. They'll be fighting to get in the door soon, but before that you can get "drunken heels" up there up! I don't care if he's got a head as big as Birkenhead, he needn't think he's hanging round here all day moaning! He can get himself off to work, he'll get an afternoon in!'

'Oh, leave him where he is, it's not worth him dragging himself down to the Docks now and there won't be much work done this afternoon. Except exercising the elbow.' He flashed a grin at the girls and did an impression of throwing back imaginary pints.

Babsey threw her hands up in despair. 'This family is going to the dogs and most of it's your doing, our John!' She turned towards the door that connected with the shop. 'All right! All right, I'm coming Jim! Hold your horses!'

He smiled. 'I'll just give these two some money and then I'll be in to give a hand.' He had good reason to leave Eddie snoring upstairs. After he'd poured a few double rums down Alf Browning's throat, he'd had a quiet word with the blockerman and they'd come to an 'understanding'. Frank Cooper was to be taken on for Christmas Eve and for at least three days' work a week thereafter. He'd left Browning telling the entire clientele of the Northumberland Hotel what a good man Frank Cooper was; best man with a docker's hook this side of Seaforth! He handed a five pound note to Louisa.

'Now get something sensible. Something your Aunt Babsey won't go off the deep end about, do you hear me? No fancy, cheap rubbish! I'll get away for an hour and meet you at Bunny's Corner in Church Street. Twelve o'clock sharp!' Winking at them both, he turned and went into the shop to be greeted by cries of surprise and welcome by many of the customers.

'We'll go to Lewis's, there's an advert in the *Echo* for coats and frocks!' Evvie rummaged around and found the newspaper and quickly skipped to the appropriate page and began to read aloud. 'Especially for the Festive Season, Exclusive models at exceptionally low prices. In the newest fabrics and all for twenty-seven shillings. Some embroidered, some shot with gold threads . . .'

'No gold threads or flashy embroidery, your Mam will go mad!' Louisa hissed.

Evvie continued undeterred. 'Coats in all sizes and styles, forty-two shillings. Marina Green. Java Brown.

Victoria Plum. Some with fur collars and cuffs. The "Sybil" with cravat collar and toning lining, forty-seven and sixpence. The "Marguerite" with real Musquash collar, fifty shillings.'

Babsey rushed into the room. 'Haven't you two gone yet?'

'I was just reading Lewis's advert, Mam.'

'Well, put that paper down and shift yourself! You sound like Blackler's parrot! And don't come back here with cheap, gaudy rubbish, I don't know what your Da is thinking of, Louisa Langford, letting you two loose with a whole five pound note! There's many that have to live for months on that! He'll want some change, mind, so don't think you can go spending the lot and take care of it, there's enough rogues in this city that'll have it off you!'

Clutching the white five pound note in her hand, Louisa shoved Evvie up the stairs in front of her.

At five minutes to twelve they both stood at the corner of Church Street and Lord Street amidst the bustling crowds of shoppers. The Salvation Army Band was playing carols outside Henderson's in Church Street, adding to the already congested traffic. The shop windows glittered and sparkled with decorations and there was an atmosphere of excitement and bonhomie.

Evvie was clutching the box that contained the smart wool crêpe dress with the padded shoulders and box pleated skirt, in Marina green. The colour named after the beautiful and elegant Princess Marina, wife of the Duke of Kent. It was plain except for a small cluster of embroidered flowers on the right shoulder, which the sales assistant assured her was the very latest in elegance and not at all ostentatious or cheap looking. How could it be at twenty-seven shillings?

Louisa's box contained the latest 'swagger' coat in a bright, cherry red wool. She hadn't been too sure about the colour at first. 'It's a bit bright' she'd murmured, but encouraged by Evvie and two assistants, she'd bought it. Evvie had then said she didn't have a hat to go with it, her blue one would definitely clash and would look tacky. So she'd been persuaded to buy a black velvet beret from Val Smith's and had then felt terribly guilty about only having one pound and one shilling change to give her Da.

'He won't mind!' Evvie argued.

'But I do! I know he's already bought my Christmas present and he works so hard for his money, stuck down in that stinking engine room for hours on end! I feel awful!'

'You should have thought of that before you gave your coat to Sally Cooper!' Evvie, too, was beginning to feel guilty.

Louisa said nothing. There was nothing she could say to that.

'Just don't tell Mam how much the hat cost or she'll go on and on about it!'

'She'll see the box and she knows you don't get cheap hats at Val Smith's.' Louisa began to crane her neck to see if she could see any sign of a tall figure pushing through the crowds.

'We could have gone home by ourselves, we're not ten years old,' Evvie began to grumble.

'There he is!' Louisa cried as she spotted him, dodging between the trams, cars and carts that were all virtually at a standstill.

He weaved as he approached. 'Spent up then?'

They exchanged uneasy glances.

'I'm sorry, I didn't mean to spend so much, really I didn't.' She handed over the remaining money.

'Why the face? It's made round to go round.'

'But you've already spent so much on me!'

'How do you know what I've spent?'

'Because I know you, Da!'

'I'm not standing here to be told off by my own daughter! We'll go to Lyons and have a cup of tea. Then, Evvie, you'd better get home. Your Mam's going to be tearing her hair out soon. When I left she was trying to help your Da peel half a ton of potatoes and keep Tommy from setting the place on fire. He was "testing" the candles for the tree, besides, I want to talk to Louisa. You don't mind, do you?'

Tucking the box more firmly under her arm, Evvie beamed at him. 'Course not, Uncle John. I got the most beautiful frock in Marina green.'

'Good. You can describe it to me over a cuppa.'

When Evvie had departed on the tram, clinging tightly to her precious box, Big John took Louisa's boxes and with his hand resting on her shoulder, guided her through the crowds. They walked up Lord Street, past the Victoria Monument and down James Street, then across the cobbled setts of Mann Island to the Pierhead. The sunlight danced and sparkled on the river and the wakes of the ferry boats, dredgers and tugs crossing to and fro. At the Landing Stage the Isle of Man boat and the old Canadian Pacific liner the *Duchess of Richmond* were tied up. The old ship dwarfed the beige-coloured hull of a tug with a decorated fir tree strapped to its masthead.

'Look, Da, it's the Christmas boat for the Bar Light-ship!'

The red-and-white clothed Santa Claus waved from the bridge and she waved back. Encouraged by her gesture some of the choir boys on board also waved, until the chaplain, his long robes stirred by a slight gust, called them to order and they began 'Silent Night'. Every year, despite the weather, a tug went out with mail, turkey, pudding and other Christmas fare for the crew of the Bar Light.

The river was almost as busy as the streets leading from the waterfront, she thought, as she waved again as the tug pulled away. Then she sniffed, taking in a deep breath of salt- and soot-tinged air as they stood just behind the chain links at the edge of the Landing Stage. 'It's just like a busy road, isn't it?'

He looked down at her and laughed. 'Aye, it is.'

Suddenly she tugged at his arm. 'Shall we go for a sail, over to Birkenhead and back, we don't have to get off?' Aunt Babsey had often taken them across to New Brighton during summer months, but they'd only been once last summer.

'All right. It's years since I've been on the ferry. I spend most of my life at sea and yet I hardly ever see it.'

She smiled ruefully. 'I don't suppose you do, being stuck down in the engine room all the time. Come on, the *Mountwood* is just about to leave!'

They hurried along the stage as quickly as they could and paid the twopence fare and clattered across the wide, wooden-slatted gangway with a few other people, before the shore hands began to heave on the ropes that pulled the gangway up. Then they climbed the steep, narrow stairs to the upper deck and sat on the wooden seat while the engines throbbed into life and an eddy of dirty grey foam was churned up at the stern. She pulled her coat collar higher around her neck and watched the Liver Building diminish in size as the ferry pulled away. A stream of black smoke rising from its funnel into the blue sky high above.

'You love the sea, don't you?' she said quietly.

He nodded.

'So do I. I love to come down and watch all the ships.'

He placed an arm around her and she dropped her head onto his shoulder. She understood him, he thought. She bore no resentment against him for being away for so long. Although he'd been away for so much of her childhood, there was a close bond between them which had strengthened over the years. She'd never hung back or been awkward with him when he first arrived as many children were and he'd taken to treating her almost as an adult over the last year or two. Theirs was a special relationship, for despite the rest of the family, he felt she was the only person he was really close to and it was the same for her. They shared these quiet, precious moments and talked of all their hopes and dreams.

'I'm really sorry I spent so much. It's not fair of me; Evvie was right, I shouldn't have given my coat to Sall.'

'I don't begrudge you a single penny, Lou, you know that.'

She smiled. Apart from Sall, he was the only person who called her Lou and then only when they were alone, which wasn't often. 'Sall calls me Lou, I wish you would – all the time. I like it better than Louisa, it's such a mouthful.'

'Louisa was your Mam's choice.'

'I know. But I don't think she would have minded.'

'You didn't know your Mam, luv,' he replied with a catch in his voice. 'She was a lot like your Aunt Babsey in some ways. Well, about things like that.'

'About "proprieties" you mean? But I do remember her and what Aunt Babsey said about her.'

'That's why I wanted to talk to you today – alone.' He took his arm away and she looked up at him.

'What's the matter?'

'Nothing. I wanted to give you this, Lou.' He handed her a small box, covered in black leather.

She took it and opened it slowly. Inside was a gold locket on a chain.

'Oh, Da!'

'Open it.'

She did as she was bid and inside there were two photographs. One of himself and one of a sweet-faced young woman with a cloud of dark hair and sad-looking eyes. The teardrops sparkled on her dark lashes and her hand crept towards his arm. 'Oh, it's . . . beautiful!'

'I thought you should have it now. It belonged to her, it was your Grandmother's, the one who died in Canada.'

'But you only had that one clear photograph of her, the one you carried in your wallet!'

'I don't need a photograph, Lou, her face is as clear in my mind as if it were only yesterday . . .' He fell silent.

'Put it on for me, please?'

Almost reverently he took it from the box and fastened it around her neck.

She patted it gently as she smiled up at him.

'Promise me one thing, Lou?'

'What?'

'That no matter how desperate you may be for money,

at any time in your life, you'll never sell it or give it away?'

The tears welled up again. 'Oh, Da! How could you even ask? I'd never, never part with it!'

'You don't know what lies ahead, none of us do and one day you may be on your uppers. Hungry, cold . . .'

She caught his hand. 'No! No! I'll never let it go, never!'

He wiped away a solitary tear from her cheek with his index finger. 'You're as pretty as she was. I'll be fighting the lads away from the door soon and there's not one of them that's good enough for you!'

She laughed. 'I don't want to be bothered with boys yet! I've got you.'

It was his turn to laugh. 'Oh, you'll soon change that tune, Miss! One will come along and then you won't give your old Da a second glance. You just wait and see.'

The ferry shuddered and lurched against the thick rope bumpers of the Birkenhead stage and the passengers hurried off, leaving them alone on the top deck, looking out across the river towards Liverpool.

She fingered the locket before tucking it inside her coat, then she leaned her head against his shoulder again. 'Sing *my* song, Da! Go on, there's no-one up here listening.'

'You always could twist me around your little finger, couldn't you?'

'Go on, please? It's ages since you sang it to me. You used to sing it to me when I was little and I'm not *that* grown up.'

He looked around quickly, then, in a surprisingly good baritone, he sang quietly,

> 'Liverpool Lou, lovely Liverpool Lou
> Why can't you behave just like other girls do?
> Why does my poor heart keep following you?
> Stay home and love me, my Liverpool Lou.'

CHAPTER FIVE

Christmas Day and Boxing Day passed in something of a blur. A seemingly never-ending round of large meals and the attendant washing-up and visiting friends and neighbours bearing gifts.

They had all gone to church on Christmas Morning, even Uncle Jim and Eddie, prodded along by both Babsey and Big John who tried to pay his sole annual visit no matter which port he happened to find himself in. Although sometimes it was a service on board if they were on the high seas.

On Boxing Day Louisa had gone to Sall's and had found the Coopers in far better circumstances than on her last visit, with the remains of the Christmas parcel and the extra things Agnes had been able to buy. Frank's one day's pay had been spent on coal and a penny toy for each of the three youngsters. Sall had proudly shown her the string of shiny black beads that she'd bought for her mother with the half crown John Langford had given her.

'The feller said they's real jet!' she announced with pride.

Doreen was decked out in an amazing collection of bright, cheap jewellery and her lips were painted with bright scarlet lipstick.

'We don't need no Christmas tree with 'er done up like that! She only needs a fairy on 'er 'ead!' Sall had remarked tartly. Only Louisa's present to Sall of a pair of woollen gloves with a Fair Isle pattern on their backs, had scotched the imminent quarrel.

As traditionally on Boxing Day, all the men of the family

had gone to the football match, including Tommy. And, just as traditionally, this had caused the usual rivalry. Everyone except her father followed Everton. Big John had always supported Liverpool Football Club. Such comments as 'He'll never be as good as our Dixie!' 'Go back to Stanley Park' and 'The last time the Blues scored more than two was when Jesus was playing full back for Nazareth!' were bandied about the kitchen, although this last Aunt Babsey had declared was going too far. It bordered on blasphemy in her opinion and John Langford should have more sense! A fine example he was setting!

Young Tommy, puffed up with excited anticipation and draped in a hand-knitted, blue-and-white scarf, sporting a rosette almost the size of a football, had darted into the scullery to escape his mother's heavy hand for sniggering openly.

All that was behind them now, it was Thursday and both she and Evvie were to start work. Sall – decked out in her 'new' things and Doreen's boots – was going to Bryant & May's matchworks.

Under her blue coat, now relegated to her 'work coat', Louisa wore the new black dress with the crisp white collar. Evvie wore beneath her coat a grey skirt and jumper, for a green overall would be provided by Marks & Spencer on her arrival.

They caught the tram at the bottom of St Domingo Road and both alighted in Church Street with most of the other passengers, all hurrying to work.

'I'll meet you here just after six, Evvie. Wait for me in case I'm late,' Louisa said as she prepared to walk the short distance to Lord Street where Frisby Dyke's was situated.

Evvie nodded. 'I'm scared stiff!' she admitted.

'So am I! See you tonight!'

She was taken to the millinery department by Miss Hamell, a middle-aged lady who took charge of all the young, female members of staff. First, she'd been shown where to hang her coat and had been provided with a tiny locker in which to place her handbag, and a key, with the strict instructions that she must *not* lose it! It was impressed upon her that she was very lucky to have somewhere to keep her bag. In other shops all such items had to be handed over to a senior member of staff who locked them away until the end of the day. Of course the lockers could be searched at any time, to deter pilfering.

Miss Hamell introduced her first to Mr Hughes, the floor walker whose dark morning suit and starched, winged collar made him appear very important and forbidding. Then to Miss Fox, head of ladies millinery, who in turn introduced her to the rest of the staff whose names she couldn't remember. She was put to work with a girl a few years older than herself who had short, blonde, curly hair and a doll-like face.

'I'm Annie Cronin, but you'll have to call me "Miss Cronin" or her Ladyship will throw a blue fit. What's your name?'

'Louisa. Louisa Langford.'

'Oh, that's nice!'

'It's a bit of a mouthful!'

'Miss Langford's better than Miss Cronin. Some of the others call me Miss Moanin' when *she's* not around "Mornin' Miss Moanin'"!' she mimicked.

She decided she liked Annie. 'What do we do now?'

Annie pulled a face. 'Dust all the show-cases, then sort and straighten out the trimmings. Then *she'll* come and show you how to put on a ribbon band and attach feathers and flowers and veils. Feathers are all the rage at the moment. You'll be sneezing your head off by the end of the day and your fingers will look like pincushions.' She pushed a plump hand forward for Louisa to examine. The tips of the fingers were punctured with tiny pin marks.

Louisa followed her example and began to dust the show-cases with a clean mutton cloth, gazing around at the hats displayed on models and shelves. She'd never seen so many hats of all shapes, sizes and colours.

'I'm lucky they kept me on, I was sixteen last week and

66

quite often they get rid of you then and replace you with someone younger – like you.'

Louisa was incredulous. 'Why?' She'd thought that once you obtained a job, unless you did something really awful, your position was secure.

Annie carefully poked a corner of her mutton cloth under the wooden trim of the case. 'Money. They have to give you a rise when you're sixteen, then eighteen, then twenty-one – if you last that long!'

'Oh, I see.' It was obvious that it wasn't only on the Docks that unfairness existed. 'How much do you get now?'

'Seventeen shillings a week.'

'I'm to have fifteen.'

'They're not bad here. Not like some places. Course you don't get paid when you're sick or for holidays, when you're entitled to them.'

'Miss Cronin, you're not paid to talk and if I were you I'd watch my step!' came the sharp tones of Miss Fox, and conversation ceased as that lady walked over and took a plain straw hat, obviously much used, and a length of Petersham ribbon from a cubby hole behind the counter and beckoned for Louisa to follow her.

By the end of the day her fingers were sore but she'd completed the tasks set her by Miss Fox with a certain degree of neatness and dexterity which had drawn a nod of approval. She didn't have a watch but she guessed it must be nearly closing time by the gradual departure of the customers and the flurry of tidying up by the other girls. As the last customer departed Miss Fox clapped her hands and Annie and three other girls disappeared into a tiny cupboard, re-appearing with a small carpet sweeper in each hand.

'You take this one and do all the bits around here.' Annie swept a hand over the immediate area of carpeting. 'You'll have to shove it hard, it doesn't pick up much. It just gives the fleas a headache!' She grinned impishly. 'And mind it doesn't empty itself, it's got a knack of doing that!'

When the carpet had been vigorously cleaned and Miss Fox had inspected everything, she looked over her spectacles at them all and said, 'Good night, Ladies. You may go now!'

There was rather a crush in the small staff cloakroom, but, after retrieving her bag from the locker and putting on her coat and hat, Louisa called 'Goodbye' to Annie and went out into the crowded darkness of Lord Street. As she pushed her way towards Church Street, through the throng of home-going workers and shoppers, she felt tired but quite elated. It hadn't been too bad. She wouldn't get the full fifteen shillings on Saturday because she hadn't worked a full week and she had to work a week 'in hand', but she felt a new confidence and independence. Now she *was* a working girl.

Evvie was standing outside the window of Marks & Spencer's so as not to get mixed up with the people waiting for the trams, but as she caught sight of her cousin she stepped forward and joined the end of one queue.

Louisa joined her. 'How did it go?'

Evvie shrugged. 'Not bad. It's a bit boring, just selling stockings though and they wouldn't let me use the cash till. I just had to keep tidying the counter and helping the customers.' She frowned. 'Honestly, Louisa, some of them are so rude! It was only my first day, so how was I supposed to know that there are different shades of fawn and brown and different thicknesses! They're all rayon stockings to me!'

'Don't you like it?'

'I expect I'll get used to it. The supervisor told me that they'll train me to use the cash till and help with the stock. Train me to use a cash register! Me, who's been helping Mam out since I was eight!' She lowered her voice. 'I don't think they trust you at first. With the money, I mean. I think they wait and see how you shape up. There's all kinds of rules, too. You can't roll the sleeves of your overall up no matter how hot it gets, in case you hide money in the folds! You can't wear lace-up shoes, in case you put money

68

inside them! You have to give your bags in and you don't get them back until the end of the day!'

'They certainly don't trust anyone, do they? Mind you, I suppose in a way they're right and the lockers we put our bags in can be searched at any time.'

Evvie brightened. 'At least I got a nice hot dinner for a shilling. Three courses. Soup, meat pie, mashed potatoes and carrots and steamed pudding and custard and a cup of tea, that's really good for a shilling. How did you get on?'

Louisa told her, showing Evvie her reddened finger tips. 'But the girl I work with – Annie Cronin – is nice. We got told off for talking though. She's older than me, she's sixteen. But we have to take our own lunch or buy something from a cafe,' she added.

A tram had arrived, half full, and, although the conductor pushed and shoved and shouted 'Move along down there, there's others waitin' ter ger 'ome, too!', there hadn't been room to squeeze another person on and it moved off, bell clanging loudly, and they had to wait for the next one.

It was getting colder and they were both tired and hungry.

'The girl I work with said it's murder on Saturdays, you need half a dozen pair of hands and eyes in the back of your head. I'm not looking forward to it much, and all for sixteen shillings!'

'Stop complaining, Evvie! It's a shilling a week more than I'm getting and we'll probably be just as busy. I wonder how Sall got on? Oh, I hope she's got something, she'll be so disappointed otherwise.'

'I don't know why you bother with her!' Then, seeing the look on Louisa's face, Evvie added quickly, 'Oh, she'll be all right! If their Doreen can get a job then I don't see why Sall can't. That Doreen is the laziest piece I've ever seen!'

The conversation and Louisa's reply were cut short as another tram appeared and the crowd surged forward, pushing and shoving; eager to get home to warm kitchens and waiting suppers.

Sall had been lucky. She'd been taken on making match boxes, as no less than three of the other girls had failed to return to work after the holiday. She learned from the foreman who took her into the large room where she was to work with about thirty other girls, that it wasn't uncommon. She also learned that if she was late more than once without a good reason, then she'd be sacked on the spot. She was expected to work quickly for it was 'piecework' and they were paid by each hundred boxes they managed to assemble. Each section depended on all the girls working on it to pull together and ensure a good rate.

She'd watched the flying fingers with something akin to horror, thinking she'd never keep up with them. But Maisey, who sat next to her, was a good sort and showed her how to make 'short cuts' in preparing the wood and making the boxes. The smell of the glue was noxious and towards dinner time she had felt quite sick. The work wasn't hard but it was fiddly and at first the sticky, foul-smelling adhesive had stuck to her fingers and hampered her efforts. It had stuck to Lou's blue skirt too, she thought depressingly. It was a good job Lou had insisted on her keeping the clothes because the skirt was now rather messy.

"Aven't yer got an overall, luv?' Maisey asked as they sat on the low wall that bounded the factory yard, the watery December sunlight giving no warmth to the day.

She shook her head.'This is me only good skirt.'

'Well wear an old pinny of yer Mam's termorrer. Ain't yer got no "carryin' out" neither?'

'No. I were that scared this mornin'; I fergot an' besides, I didn't know if I'd be took on.'

Maisey handed over half a 'doorstep' of white bread spread thinly with margarine and jam.

'Ta. I'll give yer some of mine termorrer.' She munched slowly. The fresh air had dispelled the nausea caused by the glue fumes. ''Ow much can yer earn?'

'If yer real fast about four shillings a day, but that's if yer all really quick an' pull tergether, like. It's not often we get that, more like three.'

Sall made a quick mental calculation. Six days at three shillings a day – eighteen shillings a week! That was more than either Lou or their Evvie were getting! She'd never expected so much and determined there and then that by the end of the week she'd be working as fast, if not faster, than the rest of them. What couldn't she do with eighteen shillings! What couldn't her Mam do with eighteen shillings, regularly! 'I'll bring an old pinny termorrer, too!'

The blaring of the hooter put paid to any further conversation as, brushing the crumbs from her lap, she stood up and followed the others back inside, determination stamped on her pale little face. The fortunes of the Cooper family were on the mend, she'd thought.

All too soon it was Saturday and the *Berengaria* was due to sail again. It was what was known as a 'quick turn round' and because Louisa was working she wasn't able to go and see her Da off, as she'd always done before.

They'd said their 'goodbyes' on the Friday night, after she'd come back from Sall's. He'd met her on the corner of Cicero Terrace and they'd walked up St George's Hill and had stood looking down over the darkened city.

'You know I don't like you being out by yourself at night, Lou,' he'd said when they'd met.

'I'm not. I'm with you,' she'd replied, tucking her arm through his and regaling him with tales of Sall's good fortune as they walked.

'And what about your job, are you happy there? You seem to be.'

'Yes. It's quite interesting. I like trimming hats and Miss Fox said today that I've got a good eye for colour.' She raised her eyebrows and adjusted an imaginary pair of spectacles on the bridge of her nose. 'Which is more than can be said for Miss Cronin!' She mimicked Miss Fox's high-pitched voice. 'Annie and I laughed when she'd gone.'

His lips twitched and his eyes crinkled in a smile but the darkness hid the expression. 'You keep your nose clean,

Lou! I want you to have a trade in your fingers. That way at least you'll always be able to earn some kind of a living.'

'And it's certainly in my fingers! They're sore!' she joked.

'You know what I mean.'

She sighed. 'I know and I'll behave, Da, I promise. I don't think it's right though, the way they get rid of some girls when they're sixteen just because they have to pay them more. There should be a Union.'

He laughed. 'For shopgirls? That'll be the day! But I'm glad you're happy because your Aunt Babsey has been to see that Miss Hamell about that. She was livid when you told her.'

'When?' she cried, mortified at the thought of Aunt Babsey tackling the all-powerful Miss Hamell and wondering if she would be sent for – for complaining. Had she already earned the name of 'trouble-maker'?

'Today! Now calm down, Lou, I didn't know she was going!' He'd felt her pull away from him and, although he couldn't see her face clearly in the badly lit street, he knew she was staring up at him. 'She said she was very civil to her. You're to be properly trained, she said. Your Aunt Babsey pointed out that you came from a respectable family – themselves in trade – and that you were used to dealing with people and working hard. Miss Hamell said she'd been told that you were a quiet girl and a good worker and she understood your Aunt Babsey's concern. There will be no question of your being dismissed as long as you continue to work well and there is no gross breach of conduct.'

'She should have told me, Da!'

'She was just thinking of you. You're not *that* grown up, Miss!'

'Oh, don't be cross, not tonight!' She patted the collar of her coat. Under her dress she wore the locket and it reminded her that he was going away again.

He patted her hand. 'I'm not. All I'm saying is that she's

got your best interests at heart, like I have. I want my girl to do well.'

'I will.'

'Good. And I want you to save too. Everyone should try to put a few shillings away for a rainy day.'

'You sound just like Aunt Babsey! But I will, if it will make you happy.'

He'd laughed and they'd stood at the top of the hill, watching the lights on the ships moving up and down the black surface of the river, until she'd begun to shiver and they'd turned their steps towards home.

Now she was exhausted after a day when the pace of work had been frenetic, for Annie had been seconded to the group of girls preparing stock for the January Sales. She'd been left to do most of the trimmings by herself.

Evvie had fared no better. She'd complained that her head was buzzing, her back was aching and her feet were killing her and that Marks & Spencer's on a Saturday was like being in a lunatic asylum. She was fit to drop and she never wanted to see another pair of stockings, fawn, brown, black or any other colour!

Neither of them had had the energy to hold much of a conversation on the way home and, after Evvie had finished her meal, she'd sat with her feet in an enamel bowl full of hot water and Epsom Salts, declaring she was fit for nothing but her bed.

Louisa had helped Aunt Babsey to wash up, for Uncle Jim was tired out, too. Only Eddie and young Tommy, who'd spent the day collecting empty bottles on which there was a halfpenny for each one returned, seemed to have any energy. Eddie, as usual, was going out. Dressed up in his best suit, clean white shirt and a new and rather gaudy tie and with his hair gleaming with brilliantine. Apparently he was going to a dance, after he'd found some courage in a pint glass in the Northumberland.

Although she was tired she felt strangely restless and bored and eventually decided to go to the top of the

Hill to see if she could just catch a last glimpse of the *Berengaria*'s lights.

'Don't you be long! I don't like you wandering the streets in the dark!' Aunt Babsey said, irritably.

'I won't,' she replied as she donned her coat and wrapped her scarf around her neck.

She retraced the steps she'd taken the previous night, until she stood in the inky-black shadow of St George's Church. It was cold but the sky was clear and twinkled with a thousand stars. There was a milky-white rim around the moon which foretold of more frost. You could smell it in the air already, she thought. She thrust her hands deep into the pockets of her coat and looked out across the rooftops that gleamed like polished pewter in the candescent light of the moon.

The street lights below looked like fireflies in the dusk of a summer evening and beyond, interspersed with the white lights, were the green and red starboard and port lights of the ships on the river. The river itself looked like a necklace set with tiny rubies, emeralds and diamonds, she thought. A broad collar set around the neck of the Wirral peninsula. She strained her eyes, trying to pierce the curtain of darkness that was the mouth of the estuary. She was too far away to see the Bar Light, but there in the distance she could just make out a faint string of lights that seemed to be moving like a strip of narrow, fluorescent ribbon. She sighed deeply. She could only guess as to whether or not they belonged to the *Berengaria*. It could be another ship, perhaps on its way in.

Standing alone in the darkness, as though detached from the world about her, she suddenly felt very small and very alone. It would be nearly a month before she saw him again and in winter the North Atlantic could be wicked. She'd heard of waves, whipped up by howling gales, that were bigger than even the *Queen Elizabeth* and the *Queen Mary* and they were the biggest ships in the world. What chance would any ship have in seas like that?

It wasn't often she thought like this. Seldom did she put

her fears into a conscious thought and never did she speak them aloud. The terrifying fact that one day he may never come back. That she would wait here in vain for the sight of a black hull edging its way across the Mersey Bar. She shook herself. She was tired and now she was depressed. She should have stayed at home.

She walked slowly, her head down, lost in thoughts that pressed in on her. The streets were unusually quiet, the only sound seemed to be that of her own footsteps crunching on the frozen snow of the half-cleared pavement. She was halfway down the Hill when she felt uneasy, as though she was being watched. She turned around quickly. She appeared to be alone, there was no-one in sight, but as she continued the feeling persisted.

Just as she reached the bottom of the hill a figure stumbled out from Priory Mount. Her hand went instantly to her throat and she stepped back, her heart beginning to beat in quick little jerks. 'What do you want? Who are you?' She tried to keep her voice steady.

'Who are *you*?' came the slurred reply.

She could see him more clearly now and she breathed a little easier. It was Tatters Remmey. Regularly, once a week, Aunt Babsey chased the old, meths-drinking tramp from the back door, but she knew Uncle Jim sometimes gave him a few coppers.

'I've got no money Tatters! Now go on, get out of my way!'

He didn't move. 'I know who you are, girlie. Just a few coppers so old Tatters can buy a drink?' he whined.

She backed away. He'd obviously been drinking already, his foul breath made her stomach turn over. 'I haven't got any money! Now go away or I'll yell for my Uncle Jim!'

He lurched forward and grabbed her arm and she was surprised by the strength of his grip. Her heart lurched as the dirty, bewhiskered face with bloodshot eyes and blackened stumps of teeth was pushed close to hers.

'Let me go!'

'Just a copper, girlie? 'Aven't had a drink all day!'

75

He could obviously sense her fear, she thought, as the grip on her arm tightened. She moved her arm in an attempt to fling it off.

'Leave me alone! I'll scream! I'll have the scuffers on you!' She began to struggle in earnest now, trying to keep the filthy, smelly body covered in layers of old clothing and sacking, away from her. She'd almost succeeded in freeing herself when her feet slipped from under her on the icy pavement and she fell hard, jarring her back and bumping her head. She gasped as the wind was knocked out of her by the old vagrant stumbling and falling on top of her. The smell of drink, dirt, rotting teeth and urine enveloped her, choking her and she began to thrash about wildly. Nausea was overtaking her and with it a queer faintness. He was suffocating her! She was beginning to sink into unconsciousness! As panic surged through her she lashed out with all her strength, then she heard a voice and felt the weight being lifted. The air that filled her nostrils smelled clean again. She struggled to rise and realized that strong hands were helping her and she looked up into a face that was vaguely familiar.

'Are you all right? I've seen that old drunk off, give me your hand. Slowly now.'

She took the strong, outstretched hand and clutched it tightly. Then she was slowly and gently helped to her feet. 'Thanks!' she managed to gasp.

'Nothing broken? Here, lean on me until you get your breath back. He's getting to be a real nuisance lately, poor old sod. The scuffers will take him soon and then it'll be the asylum, God help him!'

She was feeling better as she leaned for a few minutes against the broad shoulder. 'I don't think he meant any real harm, but he wouldn't believe me when I said I had no money and then I slipped and fell and he must have gone down with me. I . . . I couldn't breathe!'

'Take a few deep breaths to steady yourself. It's all right now, I'll see you home.'

She looked up into a pair of dark eyes filled with concern.

His cap was pushed to the back of his head and under it was a thick mop of very dark hair. He looked to be about the same age as Eddie, but he was taller and of a much heavier build. She managed a weak smile. 'Thanks, but I think I'm all right now.' She drew away from him, realizing that she was clinging to a complete stranger.

'Sure?'

She nodded.

'Better give me your arm anyway, these flags are like glass and you're still shaken up. We don't want you falling again.'

With a shy smile she clung to the proffered arm. Her back was sore and she felt a little unsteady, but apart from that there didn't seem to be anything seriously wrong with her.

They walked a short way in silence and she cast a surreptitious glance at him from beneath her lashes. She'd seen him around the neighbourhood, but not frequently. He was a good looking lad, she thought.

'What are you doing out by yourself anyway?'

'I went to see if I could get a last glimpse of the *Berengaria*, my Da's a greaser on her. They sailed this evening.'

'I know. You're Big John Langford's girl, aren't you?'

She was surprised. 'Yes, do you know him?'

A broad grin split his face, revealing white, even teeth. 'Everyone around here knows him, or knows of him. He's got the reputation for being a hard man.'

'He's not. Not really. Not any more.'

'Well, he wouldn't be with you, would he? Treats you like a princess, so I've heard.'

She shrugged that aside. 'He's never mentioned you.'

'That's because he doesn't know me.'

'I thought you said . . .?'

'No. I said I knew *of* him.'

'Then you don't really know him?'

'No, but you know my Dad.'

She looked puzzled.

He grinned again. 'He came to build a wall, I believe. Pat Crowley's his name and I'm Mike and you're Miss Louisa Langford.'

She made to pull her arm away but her foot slipped again and she was forced to hang onto him. Her eyes widened. Mike Crowley! She was walking down Northumberland Terrace hanging onto the arm of Mike Crowley – a Catholic!

He laughed. 'Don't look so horrified, I'm not going to sprout horns and a tail!'

'It's . . . it's . . . just that . . .' she stammered, looking around quickly.

'I know. I'm a "cogger" and you're a "proddy" and if my Mam sees me she'll take a broom handle to me and beat me half to death!' He laughed again, unconcernedly. 'Would you sooner I left you rolling on the ground with Tatters Remmey crushing the breath out of you?' he asked more gently.

Despite her predicament she felt a little ashamed and shook her head.

'I won't eat you. I don't know what tales you've heard about us, but we're human too, you know. We haven't got the Irish Tricolour or "Sod King Billy" tattooed on our chests!'

'I'm sorry. I haven't even thanked you.'

'There's no need to. I'd have done the same for any girl.'

She shot him a timid glance. He wasn't that bad, she thought, remembering the tart comments on the characters of their Catholic neighbours that Aunt Babsey frequently used. Then common sense prevailed. 'I'm nearly home now. I think . . .'

He stopped and looked down at her. 'I know. You'd better go the rest of the way by yourself. We don't want to cause war to the death, do we, with not even the excuse of it being Saint Paddy's Day or the "Glorious Twelfth"?'

She smiled, thinking his words weren't far from the truth. Open warfare regularly exploded between the two communities on both of the days he'd mentioned. 'No, we don't. Well, thanks again.'

'My pleasure. Now off you go, Miss Louisa Langford, and if I see you again I'll pretend I've never met you!'

She ducked her head with a sudden surge of embarrassment and muttering 'good night' walked slowly towards the shop.

He watched her for a few minutes, then he turned and walked away smiling. He wondered how Big John Langford would have reacted if he'd seen them? He'd probably have both his legs broken by now, aye, and an arm as well!

CHAPTER SIX

Babsey wasn't much given to throwing parties, or 'dos' as they were known. She considered them a total waste of money, but this one was different and the excuse was three-fold. There was the fact that Big John was home, that her twenty-first wedding anniversary was imminent and then there was the acquisition of the piano. Also to be taken into account was the fact that she could engage in a bit of match-making.

In the summer of 1938 John Langford had left the *Berengaria* for she was an old lady of twenty-five and was due to be scrapped in Jarrow. He'd been lucky, he'd signed on with Shaw Saville & Albion on the *Ceramic* which plied between Liverpool and Sydney. Consequently he'd been away for months instead of weeks but was due back in mid September.

'Can't we have a bit of a "do", Mam, to celebrate?' Evvie had asked, after Louisa had read out part of his last letter and given them the docking date.

'Do you think we're made of money?' Babsey had replied shortly.

'It's not such a bad idea, luv,' Jim had interjected. 'It's our twenty-first anniversary soon . . .'

'And there's the new piano,' Louisa had added, smiling to herself. It was something of a status symbol to own a piano and Babsey had bought one after Evvie had said that Mrs Gouldson had a lovely upright grand, even though no-one could play it. That had been enough for Babsey. She'd gone down to Cane's and bought the most modern piano they had in stock. It had meant that the furniture had had to be shuffled around a bit and the room was even less spacious, although the bureau had been moved upstairs. But it had been the opportunity to show off the piano that had finally won Babsey over.

Evvie seemed to spend a lot of time over at the Gouldsons', Babsey had noticed. Ostensibly the excuse was to visit her friend Edith, but she'd noted that Evvie took special care with her appearance before each visit. Evvie was as transparent as a sheet of glass and she couldn't hope to fool her Ma. Well, young Arnold was considered by many to be the best catch in the neighbourhood. He was a quiet, polite, young man who would one day take over the shop and the Gouldsons' were 'tradespeople' like themselves. Yes, Arnold Gouldson was quite suitable, if that's what Evvie wanted. And a party would help matters along. A few drinks might make Arnold a little less reticent. A party would also enhance her social standing. To be able to splash out on a really grand 'do' always impressed the neighbours, though few would be invited, and once persuaded no expense had been spared.

It was originally intended that just family, the Gouldsons and the Wills were to attend, but then Evvie had wanted Letty, her friend from work, to come. Eddie had thereupon protested, saying he should be allowed to have his mates. So Mogsey Green and Tad Buckley had been invited – under sufferance. Seeing that everyone else was having their friends, Louisa was allowed to ask Sall and Annie and, after much argument, Tommy was allowed to bring one friend.

'If we go on at this rate we might as well have it in the street!' Babsey had stated, after Tommy complained that everyone else was having two friends.

There were still too many people to fit into one room, Babsey thought, as she surveyed the table and doubted the wisdom of laying out her best china and glasses. She'd just have to watch that nothing got broken. She wasn't having Florrie Gouldson making detrimental remarks to Mary Wills about the MacGann's tableware. 'Evvie, bring

81

some of those tea towels in from the scullery and put them on top of the dresser! Someone's bound to spill something and we don't want a fuss about finding something to mop it up,' she directed.

Evvie, dressed in a short taffeta dress of dark turquoise and green, disappeared into the scullery.

'And I don't want you and that Mercer lad stuffing yourselves like pigs, our Tommy!'

Tommy grimaced. She was always treating him as though he were a kid, even though he was now an apprentice shipwright and bringing in a wage, albeit a very small one.

John, who had arrived the day before, was leafing through a dozen or more copies of sheet music that lay on top of the gleaming new piano. 'What did you buy all these for Babsey? There's only Jim can play and he plays by ear.'

Babsey sniffed.

'He's right, Babsey. Don't expect me to try any of those, I can't read a note!'

'Mary Wills can and I'm not having her ask and us have none!' She fixed them all with a granite stare. 'And I don't want any wet glasses put on top of the piano! Louisa, put out plenty of beer mats.' She nodded with satisfaction. Everything looked just splendid. She'd put on a good spread. The wine and spirits were set out on the draining board in the scullery. A barrel of beer reposed under the sink so any slops would go on the flagged floor and the carpet had been rolled back, so she didn't need to worry about that. No-one could say that Babsey MacGann didn't know how to throw a good 'do'.

Louisa began to set out the cork beer mats that her Da had cadged from Davey Whale at the Northumberland. Her dress was one she'd bought specially from Blackler's for the occasion. It wasn't as fancy as Evvie's, but then she wasn't trying to catch Arnold Gouldson's fancy. It was a cornflower blue rayon with a softly pleated skirt, Peter Pan collar, and sleeves that puffed at the shoulder then tapered to a cuff just above her elbow. She'd brushed her hair up into a roll that showed off the silver filigree ear-rings her Da had brought her. Around her neck – as always – she wore her gold locket.

The Gouldsons were the first to arrive, followed closely by the Wills family and, on their heels (as if by a pre-arranged signal), Mogsey and Tad. Letty, Annie and Sall arrived almost simultaneously and some minutes later Tommy's friend edged his way shyly into the crowded room.

At first the atmosphere was a little strained until the drink took the edge off everyone's inhibitions and Jim was persuaded by John to 'Give us a tune on the new Joanna!' After that things livened up considerably.

Eddie was trying to impress Letty with his 'man of the world' attitude and Mogsey had made a bee-line for Annie, plying her with drinks and sandwiches. Louisa caught her eye and bit her lip to stop herself from laughing, for Annie was trying to look interested and amused by Mogsey's rather banal conversation.

The room was becoming increasingly hot and stuffy.

'Looks like we're stuck with each other, Sall, let's go and sit on the back step. At least it'll be cooler.'

'It's no use going out there, Lou, your Evvie's finally got Arnold cornered. I saw them sitting in the yard on two orange boxes. Best leave the lovebirds alone.'

'We'll sit on the stairs then. Bring your drink.'

Holding her glass slightly out in front of her so as not to slop her drink down her best yellow-and-white print dress, Sall followed. She'd filled out although she was still small and slight. Good, plain food had seen to that and regular trips to the public baths, plus a few nice clothes, had transformed her into an attractive, pert young girl.

'What were they doing out in the yard?'

'Well, Evvie was doing all the talking. He was just sitting there. He looked a bit gobsmacked if you ask me.'

They settled themselves on the stairs to watch the party gather momentum.

'I don't know why she's set her cap at him, he's so boring! He can't even string two words together, but he's got no chance now she's got him out there. I bet she finishes up asking him to take her out!'

'Oh, she's not soft, isn't your Evvie! She'll get her own way with him and he'll get the shop one day and, besides, your Aunt Babsey likes him,' Sall replied sagely. 'Oh, just look at that Mogsey, he'll be standin' on his head given half the chance! The big show-off! Don't you think you should go and rescue Annie? He's a real pain!'

Louisa laughed. 'She just looks helpless but she's not! She could buy and sell him any day! She'll give him the brush-off when she's had enough! Was Harry upset that he wasn't invited? I tried but Aunt Babsey said if we had any more it would look like the Employment Exchange on a Monday morning!'

Sall had started to 'walk out' with Harry Green, Mogsey's younger brother. 'Not really. Not after I explained that it would probably be dead boring and he'd have to put up with their Mogsey making a show of himself! Harry doesn't get all bitter and twisted about things like that, not if you explain.' She sipped her sherry and pulled a face. 'This stuff's horrible! Do you think they'd mind if I had a shandy?'

John Langford appeared at the foot of the stairs. 'Drink it up, Sall, and we'll have a dance. You look like a pair of wallflowers sitting there.'

'And what about me?' Louisa cried, feigning indignation.

'You're next! Sall's a guest!'

'Oh, get him!' Sall laughed as she was led through the crush.

She watched them as they shuffled around the crowded room, a smile of amusement on her lips. They looked so odd. Her Da so tall and Sall so tiny.

'They look like a comic act, don't they?'

She turned to find Tad Buckley leaning on the bannister beside her.

She returned his smile. 'I was just thinking that, too.'

'Mind if I join you?'

She shrugged and he sat on the stair beside her. The space was narrow and somehow his close proximity was having a strange effect on her. She glanced sideways at him from beneath her lashes as she toyed with her half-empty glass. He was a handsome lad with dark brown wavy hair and hazel eyes. She sipped her drink.

'Mogsey seems to have hit it off with that friend of yours.'

'Um,' she replied. She'd begun to feel a little light-headed, must be the sherry, she thought.

He studied her closely. She'd certainly grown up this last year. She was a good-looking girl and, although she was younger than himself, the way she spoke and acted made her appear older. Nor did she simper or giggle the way other girls did and he was an expert on girls. He was quite proud of his reputation. He was known as a 'bit of a lad'. Usually he had no trouble 'chatting up' the girls but she didn't appear to be very communicative. She seemed pre-occupied, aloof.

'Would you like another drink?'

'No thanks, I think I've had enough already.' She was feeling shy which was stupid, she thought. She'd known him for years but she'd never really noticed him before. She'd never noticed how his hair waved onto his forehead or the way his eyes crinkled at the corners when he smiled or the strong hands that rested lightly on his knees. No, she'd never really *seen* him – until now.

'Do you want to dance then? If you can call all that shoving and pushing dancing.'

Uncle Jim had launched into another medley of popular tunes and Sall was now dancing with Mr Wills. Before she had time to reply her Da appeared half-carrying Tommy and they both had to move whilst Tommy was got upstairs.

'Nice state he's in, your Aunt Babsey's livid! He's been

knocking back the whisky on the sly. Still, we all have to learn, eh, Tad! Mind, I wouldn't be in his shoes in the morning!'

Tad laughed before catching her arm. 'Come on, Louisa, let's dance! We'll get crushed flat against the wall otherwise!' he urged.

Everyone was packed into the middle of the room and they were forced together, their bodies pressed close. She glanced up at him and smiled before dropping her gaze again. He squeezed her hand and gripped her more tightly around the waist. Her heart had begun to beat jerkily and she couldn't think of a single thing to say to him.

When Uncle Jim paused to finish off his pint and asked for a refill, Mogsey shouted, 'How about something more lively?' She caught Annie's speculative gaze and she felt herself blush. She made to turn away from him but he caught her hand and held it tightly.

'It's as hot as the hobs of hell in here, let's get some air?'

'Evvie and Arnold are in the yard,' she replied, cautiously. What was the matter with her? Why had she suddenly become tongue-tied and a bit wary of him?

'No they're not. Evvie's piling Arnold's plate up with food.'

She looked across the room and saw Evvie smiling archly at a rather red-faced Arnold and she let Tad lead her through the scullery and into the yard. She arranged her skirt demurely over the orange box. He sat beside her.

'That's better, at least we can breathe out here!' He loosened his tie. 'You're not cold are you?'

She shook her head and they sat in silence for a few seconds.

She was certainly different, he thought. She looked so young and so beautiful in a serene sort of way. He'd never thought of anyone as being 'serene' before. In fact the word surprised him. He must have heard it somewhere; he was sure he'd never learnt that one at school. 'You're a strange girl, Louisa.'

'Strange?'

'Yes, you don't talk much. You don't giggle and act daft like lots of girls do. You're not afraid of me, are you?'

'Of course I'm not!' She began to toy with the locket around her neck.

'That's nice. A present, was it?' He pretended to peer closely at the locket.

His face was very close to hers and the strange, giddy feeling was back. She looked up into his eyes and was powerless to drag her gaze away. It was as though she was hypnotized. Then he gently cupped her chin in his hand and kissed her on the mouth.

Even if she'd wanted to she couldn't have pulled away, but she didn't want to. She felt as though she was cocooned in a bubble of elation. That she was drifting off on a cloud. The music and laughter from inside receded and they were the only two people in the whole world and all that mattered was that he go on kissing her and holding her!

At first he'd looked on her as a challenge but as he kissed her he was experiencing something new, something vibrant. It had never been like this with any of the others. She was 'special' and he was gentle with her. Slowly tasting her lips, caressing the back of her neck and instead of letting his hands wander down over her shoulders, he found himself drawing away from her. 'Oh, Louisa! You're so beautiful! Say you'll come out with me, please?'

She was still floating on her cloud as she whispered 'Yes! Yes! Tad!'

They'd stayed in the yard, talking quietly, her head on his shoulder, until Eddie had barged out pulling a giggling Letty behind him.

'Oh, aye, and what are you two up to?'

She'd stiffened and Tad helped her up.

'Nothing! I could ask you the same question!' Tad had sounded annoyed, but Eddie had only laughed and they'd gone back inside.

Even though it was well after midnight when everyone

had gone she had helped clear up. Her eyes were shining and she'd sung softly to herself.

'I saw Tad Buckley making up to you!' Evvie said coyly.

'So? I saw you and Arnold Gouldson sitting in the yard!'

For once Evvie didn't pursue the subject. She'd smiled. 'Then we both had a good time, didn't we? Are you seeing him again?'

She nodded.

'Arnold's asked me to go to the cinema with him.'

She smiled back. There was nothing that could dispel the euphoria that had claimed her and she'd already begun to count the hours until she would see him again.

'What are you two whispering about?' Babsey asked, counting her glasses.

'We were just saying that we've enjoyed ourselves,' Evvie answered.

'I think it went off very well – apart from our Tommy disgracing himself! I'll see to him in the morning!' A smile hovered around Babsey's lips. 'Well, did Arnold find enough courage to ask you out or not?'

'Oh, Mam!'

'Well, did he?'

'Of course he did!'

'At least I've achieved something tonight then and Florrie said what a lovely couple you make and it was about time their Arnold got himself a "nice" girl! And Mary Wills said what a beautiful piece of furniture the piano was, though I'm not sure quite what she meant by that! So I think we can say it was a successful night!' And with that she turned her attention to instructing her husband and brother to roll back the carpet and move the furniture into its rightful place.

'You don't believe all the stories about me, do you, not really?' Tad asked, the following night as they stood under the street light outside the shop.

He'd taken some ribbing from Eddie and Mogsey, neither of whom had managed to make any real progress with either Letty or Annie. When Mogsey had started his usual 'patter' Annie had put him firmly in his place. Eddie had fared worse. After getting Letty into the yard and 'trying it on' as he put it, she'd slapped his face and called him a 'creep'. 'She'll run a mile when she hears about all the girls you've had!' Mogsey had jibed, winking at Eddie. He'd just laughed but he'd felt annoyed. He didn't want her discussed in the same tone as all the others. He felt differently about Louisa Langford, so he reasoned he'd better tell her himself and put the record straight. She looked up at him with such trust in those clear blue eyes.

'I don't listen to gossip, Tad, but sometimes . . .'

'Oh, Louisa, you know the way they talk around here! Everything gets exaggerated! They're not happy unless they've got someone to pull to pieces! I'm not going to lie to you and say I've been as pure as the driven snow. I've been out with a lot of girls, but you're different, Louisa. I want us to start out with no secrets! All that's behind me now, I promise! You're the only girl for me! Will you be my "steady"?'

She slipped her arms around his neck and buried her head on his shoulder.

He kissed her ear. 'Will you?'

'Of course I will, Tad,' she replied, feeling as though she were the happiest girl in the whole world.

He gently traced the line of her cheek with his finger. He hadn't been giving her his usual line about being special. He meant it. What he felt for her was nothing like he'd ever felt for any of the others. Most of them had been 'easy' and you couldn't respect a girl if she let you do anything after a few kisses. It was as if he was placing her on a pedestal above the crowd, just as her Da did. And that was another thing, you didn't play fast and loose with Big John Langford's girl.

'I don't care what anyone says about you, Tad! We'll show them we don't care! We'll show them how . . . how much we mean to each other.'

'I love you, Louisa! I mean it!' He'd blurted it out before

pulling her to him and kissing her to hide his embarrassment. He hadn't meant to say it, it had just happened, but for the first time he uttered the words and meant them.

Of course no-one approved of their liaison. Eddie said scornfully that he didn't know what Tad saw in her, she was just a kid. Evvie said he was all right for a night out, but she must be mad to get serious about him. Aunt Babsey sat her down and started to point out all his faults.

'What's so awful about him?' she demanded, defensively, determined to stand up for him.

'He's a spendthrift and no better than he should be!' Babsey replied firmly, noting the stubborn set of Louisa's chin. 'And he's got a reputation!'

'What for – spending money?'

'Don't come the innocent with me, Miss! You know what I mean! He's been out with every girl in the neighbourhood and a good few from other neighbourhoods as well! He's a "Womanizer"! This is for your own good, Louisa! I'm not having you classed as another of his "conquests"! Love them and leave them is Tad Buckley's philosophy, but he's not making a laughing stock of you!'

'You're not being fair, Aunt! I know all about the . . . others. He told me himself!'

'Well, he'd have to, wouldn't he, seeing as you've known him for years. He couldn't get away with the "you're the only girl for me" line, now could he?'

She felt rebellious and resentful. They weren't being fair to him! 'That's all over now! It is! It was just "wild oats" and I believe him!'

'Is that what he calls it? Well, he needn't think he's going to do any "sowing" around here or your Da will be turning into the "Grim Reaper"! He's got his poor Mam heart-broken, has Tad Buckley!'

'He's changed, Aunt Babsey! He has! We talked about it. He said he wanted to start afresh, that I was different and that all . . . all that was over and done with now! It's not fair to judge him on gossip and rumour!'

Babsey sighed deeply. Louisa was smitten. It was useless

to try to talk sense into her. She'd fallen head over heels for his slick talk. He was too old and far too experienced for Louisa but she could see she was wasting her breath. The child was infatuated with him. 'I can see it's no use, but I just don't want you to get hurt!'

'I won't! Tad wouldn't do anything to hurt me, he wouldn't!'

Babsey sighed heavily as she watched her niece go upstairs.

Even Sall had been amazed and had told her to be wary of him. 'Lou, how can you believe anyone who's been out with our Doreen and most of her mates?'

'Oh, Sall, don't you start! I've had all that from Aunt Babsey. I thought you'd understand!'

'I do, Lou! I just don't want to see you get let down!' Sall had replied earnestly, shaking her head.

It wasn't just out of sheer perversity that she'd gone on seeing him. Her whole world now revolved around him. She was hopelessly in love with him. And her Da knew it. Before he'd sailed he'd tried to talk to her, as Babsey had urged.

'Da, I'm sick of saying this, but he's settled down now! He's promised!'

'It's about time then.'

'He hasn't so much as looked at anyone else since he started taking me out and it's nearly a month now.'

He'd looked down into the upturned face and had seen the happiness shining from her eyes. He'd felt a pang of jealousy, loneliness and longing. He knew how she felt, he'd felt like that once. But she was so young, so vulnerable, so trusting. He wanted to protect her, but it was impossible. She'd grown up and the more they tried to separate her from Tad Buckley, the more tenaciously she'd cling. The best thing to do was to say nothing or at least very little and just hope that it was infatuation and that she'd tire of him. He quite liked Tad, but not enough to allow him to court his daughter. He'd also realized that anyone she went out with would never be good enough for her. Aye, best to say nothing and hope it would just be like summer lightning. A first love, brief and beautiful. He'd patted her hand. 'Maybe you're the right girl for him, Lou. Maybe he'll settle down now.'

She'd clung to his arm. 'Oh, he will, Da! It doesn't mean that I love you any less, it's just . . . different.'

'It's just as it should be, Lou. As long as you're happy, then I'm happy,' he'd answered, hoping that by the time he returned it would all have fizzled out. He'd smiled ruefully. He'd have to get used to this. Tad Buckley was probably the first of many boyfriends.

CHAPTER SEVEN

Three weeks later she was surprised to see him waiting for her when she got off the tram on her way home from work. Evvie raised her eyebrows and made a moue with her mouth.

'What's he doing here, he should be at work? Arnold won't be very pleased if he hears I walked home with him!' Her romance with Arnold was blossoming. 'I'll walk on ahead, don't mind me!' she said curtly.

'Had a bad day, Evvie? Customers playing up?' he asked genially.

Evvie ignored him. She didn't like him. She thought him loud and common.

'Leave her alone, Tad. Stop teasing her.'

'Sorry, but she really gets my back up with the airs and graces she gives herself!'

'I know, but it's no picnic working there on a Saturday.'

'What about you? You work just as hard. I thought I'd come and meet you.' He pointed to the box she was carrying. 'What have you been buying?'

'A dress . . . for Sunday. We are still going to Southport, aren't we? I know I'll have to wear a coat over it, but . . . I want to look smart, for you.'

'We'll go to a tea dance, if you like. You can show it off there. They have them in all those posh hotels.'

'We couldn't go to a place like that!'

'Why not? Our money's as good as theirs!'

'It's too expensive and besides, I'd feel awkward. Anyway, why aren't you at work? Are you all right? You're not sick or anything?'

'Fit as a fiddle! Finished early, that's all. We only had a half empty freighter to unload. The rest of them went to the pub.'

The concern left her eyes and she smiled. How could Aunt Babsey keep going on about him being feckless. He could have gone with the others and she wouldn't have been any the wiser. Instead he'd forsaken his mates to come and meet her. She felt the warm glow washing over her. 'What time shall I meet you?'

'About seven? Hasn't Babsey calmed down yet? I hate having to hang around on corners waiting for you. I should be able to come and call for you! Everything open and above board, like.'

'I know, but she's still dead set against you. She'll come round in time. I know she will.'

'I'm doing my best!'

'I know and her bark is worse than her bite!'

'Don't you believe it!'

Evvie had disappeared and they'd reached the corner of Neil Street.

'I'll see you later then, we'll go and see that Cary Grant film *Gambling Ship*. It's on at the Popular.'

She nodded and he bent and kissed her. 'Now they'll all be talking. Dolly Unwin's peeping from behind her curtains, I saw them move,' he whispered as he drew away.

She turned her head and felt a bubble of defiance rise up. She didn't care if they were all gossiping. She raised her hand and waved deliberately towards Mrs Unwin's window. The curtain moved again and she laughed. 'Now they'll all be saying what a brazen hussy I am! I don't care!'

'Let's give them something to talk about.' He caught her to him and kissed her again. A long, lingering kiss that made the sky spin and her whole body feel shaky until she drew away from him, breathlessly. 'See you at seven, under the lamp,' she whispered, pulling herself reluctantly from the circle of his arms.

She walked the short distance with her head held high,

looking neither right nor left. He loved her, so let them talk as much as they liked. She didn't care!

After she'd hung up her jacket she went upstairs to hang up the new dress. Then she put on her pinafore and started to help her Aunt with the supper. Babsey looked cross and she knew that Evvie had faithfully reported the meeting. Sometimes she could kill Evvie, she thought. She was so smug! It was 'Arnold this' and 'Arnold that' until she felt she could scream and that no-one could possibly be such a paragon of virtue as Arnold Gouldson – or as incredibly boring.

'What's he doing home so early?' Babsey finally asked curtly, buttering the bread with a speed and dexterity that was truly amazing and virtually throwing the slices onto the plate.

'They finished early but he didn't go down to the pub with the rest of them, wasting money, he came to meet me!' she replied, just as sharply.

Babsey glared at her. She was getting right hardfaced lately! Ever since she'd taken up with *him*. And Eddie was sitting in the pub was he, she'd have something to say about that! He was getting too fond of his beer and he was mixing with some fast pieces! That Doreen Cooper and her friends! Painted, brazen madams all of them and from what she'd heard, well on the way to causing a scandal.

The atmosphere over supper was strained although Evvie seemed not to notice and chattered on about work. She'd been moved to ladies knitwear which was far more interesting than hosiery and Miss Bellamy, her supervisor, said that she was doing so well that in time she may even be made up to a deputy supervisor. Of course that wouldn't be for years and she may get married before then. She'd paused, her expression expectant, but no-one seemed to be taking any notice. Arnold would, she thought, pursing her lips in annoyance. Arnold hung on her every word, although sometimes this irritated her. Occasionally she wished he would be more outspoken, more outgoing, more . . . dominating. Still, you couldn't have everything. He was the best catch in the Terrace and he saved his money did Arnold. She shot a glance at Louisa. Not like Tad Buckley. Arnold was 'careful' but that was because he had plans. Plans for the future of the business, for their future, too. She smiled smugly to herself.

When the meal was over the two girls began to clear away the dishes.

'You can dry, I'll wash,' Evvie said when they were both in the scullery and the dishes were piled into the sandstone sink.

Louisa nodded. She knew it meant that she would have to put them away, too, but she wasn't going to give Evvie the excuse for an argument.

'Are you going out then?' Evvie asked.

'Yes. Are you?'

'Arnold's taking me to the pictures.'

Louisa shot her a guarded look. 'Which one?'

'The Popular in Netherfield Road, it's a Cary Grant film. Where's *he* taking you?'

Groaning inwardly she answered. 'The same place.'

Evvie looked up quickly and then attacked a greasy plate. 'Just don't sit anywhere near us! Arnold doesn't like Tad Buckley any more than I do!' she hissed.

'Oh, you and your precious Arnold! We wouldn't sit anywhere near the pair of you!' That's all she needed, she thought. Evvie twisted her head around to see what she was doing so she could report back to Aunt Babsey. They always sat at the back with the other courting couples and they usually didn't get to see much of the film. It was one of the few places where there was a chance to kiss and cuddle. In the darkness where prying eyes couldn't see and censor.

The last plate had been dried and Evvie had wiped the draining board and wrung out the dishcloth. She decided she couldn't stand much more of her cousin's company.

'I think I'll go round and see Sall for a few minutes. You can have the bedroom to yourself to get ready.' She hung her pinafore on the nail on the back of the door.

'I don't know why you bother with them – especially that Doreen!'

'I don't go to see her!' she retorted at Evvie's disappearing back.

As was her habit, she entered through the ever-open front door, pushing past the young Coopers and their motley group of friends who had congregated on the door step, arguing over a collection of tatty cigarette cards and match-boxes.

'It's only me Mrs Cooper, is Sall in?' she called as she walked down the tiny lobby and into the kitchen.

Sall was just clearing the table and she looked up and grinned. Doreen was putting on her lipstick, a bright, garish red, with the aid of a cracked mirror balanced on the overmantel. As usual, her clothes were cheap and gaudy, Louisa thought. She had two bright red combs in her hair and from her ears dangled red ear-rings that reminded Louisa of cherries. The lipstick made her look pale and a bit drawn, Louisa thought. It seemed to have drained all the natural colour from her face.

'Oh, it's you! I thought you'd be off out with "him"!' Doreen said with thinly disguised scorn.

'You watch your mouth, our Doreen!' Frank Cooper reprimanded from behind the evening edition of the *Echo*.

Sall made a face at her sister's back. 'Come into the parlour, Lou,' she urged. Both Sall and Mrs Cooper were extremely proud of the fact that the front room now boasted a rug and two winged chairs and a plant table, on which reposed a large aspidistra. All bought on the weekly 'cheque' system, although they were not yet paid for.

'Take no notice of her, she's just jealous!' Sall said, plumping herself down in one of the chairs. 'What's up?'

'Oh, only our Evvie! Sall, I get so tired of all the nasty remarks about Tad and of hearing how wonderful Arnold is!'

'He's "respectable". Bloody boring, but respectable! Not like Tad nor Harry either for that matter.'

'The sooner she gets married and shuts up the better!'

'Don' let them get to you, Lou!'

'I try not to. He met me off the tram tonight rather than go down the pub with the rest of them but even that didn't seem to impress Aunt Babsey! Can't they see he's trying?'

'They don't want to, Lou. They want to believe everything they've heard about him and your Eddie doesn't help much, not the way he's carrying on!' She still didn't like Eddie MacGann and she certainly didn't trust him. His Mam might not know it but he was in on every fiddle going, she'd heard her Da say. But he was crafty enough not to get caught. Only last week they'd been stopped trying to get some smoked hams out of the gate, but Eddie had been quick enough to give his to poor Jimmy Frazer who was a bit slow. Jimmy had been caught, sacked and was up before the magistrate next week. Anyone else would have dumped the stuff rather than get a mate into trouble. But not Eddie MacGann! 'Aren't you and Tad going out?'

Louisa nodded. 'I just couldn't stand any more of Evvie so I said I'd come over here while she got ready. Are you off out, too?'

Sall shook her head. 'No. Harry's skint. Their Mogsey talked him into playing cards and he lost.' Her pointed little face suddenly became animated. 'I hate that Mogsey! He's never satisfied until he's got the few bob Harry has for himself, one way or another! I said I'd pay, my treat, but he wouldn't hear of it. Got really mad he did. Said if he couldn't pay then we weren't going out! He's coming round later though. We'll probably go for a walk.'

Louisa sighed. Mogsey had always been sharper and more streetwise than Harry who was what Uncle Jim called a 'plodder'. He was a quiet lad who worked hard and would get there in the end, but slowly, in his own time. They were a bit like the tortoise and the hare, were Harry and Mogsey Green, she mused. Sometimes she wondered why Sall was attracted to Harry. Sall was like quicksilver; always dashing here and there, always busy, always chattering. She still worked at the match factory. The other girls liked her and she was one of the fastest workers they employed; which probably accounted for half of her popularity.

'I'd better be going. It doesn't take me long to get ready.'

'It takes our Doreen hours to paint her face.' Sall uttered a cutting laugh. 'Mind you, with a face like that it needs hours and all the help it can get!' There was still little love lost between Sall and her sister for in her opinion Doreen was totally selfish. She refused to 'turn up' any more money, although she'd had a rise. It was her money, she said, and she wasn't going to pay for furniture for a room no-one used. She didn't understand how proud it made her Mam feel to be able to tell people she had stuff in the parlour. It was a sign of their increased fortunes and status. It meant a lot to her Mam did this stuff. She'd promised that as soon as it was paid for they'd get a nice gate-leg table and some dining chairs and some new curtains and maybe even a real cut glass vase.

Sall saw Louisa to the door and watched her walk up Cicero Terrace. Lou was happy, she thought, and she was glad for her. Couldn't they all see that and leave her alone? Couldn't they give them both a chance? She sighed as she turned away. Knowing the MacGanns they wouldn't – with the exception of Mr MacGann of course. He was a nice bloke. How he ever came to have such awful kids she'd never know, although Tommy wasn't bad – yet! She was lucky she supposed. Her Mam and Dad liked Harry nor did they expect miracles of her like Babsey MacGann expected of Evvie and Lou. A smile flitted across her face. But they hadn't bargained on Lou's stubborn determination, had they? The smile had gone as she went back down the lobby towards the kitchen. She wished Harry would stand up to Mogsey more, show a bit of gumption sometimes.

By the time she'd changed and run down to meet him and they'd walked to Netherfield Road, there was a queue outside the cinema and she frowned as she caught sight of Evvie and Arnold standing near the front.

'Has she been getting at you again?' Tad asked. He

looked very debonair in his new sports jacket and grey flannel trousers. His cap at a rakish angle.

'I'm not letting her spoil my night.'

He put his arm around her waist and she smiled at him. He was so very handsome, she thought. She'd seen the envious glances of the other girls standing in the queue. Evvie was welcome to nondescript, spotty, boring Arnold Gouldson and his damned shop.

There was a burst of raucous laughter from behind and they turned around. Doreen Cooper and two of her friends had joined the end of the line. Louisa quickly turned away. Doreen and Evvie all in one night was straining her patience.

'Shall we go somewhere else?' she suggested.

'What for?' He jerked his head backwards. 'Because of *her*?'

She nodded.

'It's not like you, Louisa, to take any notice of the likes of that one. Don't let her get you down!'

She smiled again as he squeezed her. 'You're right! Who cares about her?'

She'd just finished speaking when Doreen came and sidled up to her. She turned her head away.

'Can I speak to you?'

To her surprise the question was uttered in a quiet voice and she turned to see Doreen looking past her and straight at Tad.

'I've got nothing to say to you! Go back to your mates! Clear off!'

'I want to speak to you! It won't take a minute and she won't mind, will you?'

'Yes she will! Now clear off!'

The commissionaire was advancing towards them, trying to keep the line in some sort of orderly fashion and chase off the buskers who were trying to earn a few bob by entertaining the waiting crowd.

'Go on or I'll get you moved! Annoying people!' Tad said loudly.

The couple in front turned around and Louisa felt her cheeks going red.

Doreen glared first at Tad and then at her before tossing back her head, the ear-rings clicking together. 'I'm going! No need to get all airyated and show me up! You had your chance, Tad Buckley, don't say you haven't! I'm going to see that you get what's coming to you!' she called over her shoulder as she walked back to her girlfriends.

'What did she mean by that?'

'Take no notice, she was just trying to cause trouble! She's good at that! Cheer up, we're starting to move.'

She hadn't enjoyed the film. She hadn't been able to concentrate. A feeling of foreboding had settled on her and she couldn't get Doreen Cooper's remarks out of her mind. The incident had spoiled the evening. She'd even been self-conscious when he'd tried to kiss her, feeling that she was being watched by Doreen and sniggered about.

'What's the matter?' he asked as they stopped on the corner beneath the lamp.

'I don't know. I must be tired, Tad. I'm sorry.'

'It was that slut, wasn't it? She's nothing to me, I swear! I took her out a couple of times, that's all. It was ages ago, before I came to my senses and saw her for what she really is! Louisa, look at me! I mean it! She doesn't mean anything to me!' He cupped her chin in his hands and tilted her face upwards until she had to look into his eyes.

She felt guilty. 'Oh, Tad, I'm sorry! I'm just being stupid, getting like everyone else. I suppose I'm . . . jealous. I hate to think about all the . . . others!'

He drew her closer. 'Louisa! Louisa! There's nothing to be jealous about. You're the only one I love! I never loved any of them, not the way I love you and I've never lied to you – have I?'

She knew it was the truth. He'd never tried to hide his past from her, yet all his assurances didn't seem to help. It was a part of him that she couldn't obliterate from her mind. She *was* jealous of Doreen Cooper and all the rest and she didn't want to be. Oh, she'd just have to stop being so stupid and look forward to the future, not keep dwelling on the past. Nor should she give anyone the satisfaction of knowing that that part of his life upset her. Aunt Babsey would be the first to say 'I told you so!'

'We'll go into town next week. Get away from here and all the nosy, interfering no-marks! Cheer up now, it's you I love!'

She pushed the evening's event to the back of her mind; she was being foolish. He loved her and it was now and tomorrow that were important. She slid her arms around his neck as his head bent towards hers, his lips caressing her and all her doubts faded.

She'd only been in a short while when there was a loud hammering on the back door.

Uncle Jim looked up from his newspaper and Aunt Babsey, who was doing her accounts, tutted loudly and said. 'In the name of heaven, who's that at this time? Louisa, go and open it, luv.'

Evvie was not yet in and so she went and pulled open the back door. Sall was standing there, an old cardigan thrown around her shoulders, her face white and strained.

'Sall! What's the matter? Come in.' She ushered her into the kitchen.

Aunt Babsey put down her pen and her eyes narrowed with suspicion.

'I had to come out! I had to! Da was going on something awful!'

Louisa pushed her down onto a chair by the table. 'What's the matter with him?'

'Oh, Lou, he's really mad! I've never seen him madder and it's all her fault! Mam was crying and the kids were whingeing and he was threatening to leave her black and blue! He took his belt off to her!'

'Doreen?'

Sall nodded.

'What's she done now?'

Sall looked up at her friend and suddenly realized what a fool she'd been to come here. She just hadn't thought

– really thought! She'd run to the only haven she knew. Tears welled up in her eyes. She shouldn't have come here, it wasn't right! How was she going to tell Lou, her best friend . . . She began to sob.

Aunt Babsey got up. 'Pull yourself together, girl! What's that madam been up to now?'

Sall's sobbing increased and Babsey and Jim exchanged glances over the top of the weeping girl's head.

'She's in trouble, isn't she?' Babsey, stated flatly.

Sall's head moved slightly, her shoulders still shaking.

Jim let out a long, slow breath. 'No wonder he's mad!'

'If he'd taken his belt off to her before this she wouldn't be in this state! What's she going to do?' Babsey demanded.

Sall wiped her sleeve across her face. 'Me Da says she's got to marry him! He'll *make* him marry her! He won't have no . . . bastards in our family! Oh, poor Mam's in a terrible state, Mrs MacGann!' She became incoherent again.

Louisa put her arm around Sall's thin shoulder. 'Don't upset yourself, Sall, please! Don't cry! It's not your fault!'

'So who is the father?' Babsey demanded. She had little sympathy for the Coopers. This was what happened when parents failed to discipline their children.

Sall shook her head and appeared to choke.

Babsey was scandalized. 'Doesn't she know?'

Sall took a deep, shuddering breath and raised a tear-streaked face. 'She knows! Da is taking her over there now! He was dragging her out the front way as I ran out the back door! Oh, God!' She began to cry again.

'Who is it?' Babsey asked coldly.

Sall covered her face with her hands. 'Oh, Lou . . . I'm sorry! I'm sorry!'

'What's it got to do with our Louisa?' Jim asked quietly.

The voice was muffled but the words were as clear as if they'd been shouted aloud. 'Tad Buckley, Mr MacGann! It's Tad!'

It was as though she hadn't heard the words. As though the whole scene was part of a dream. A nightmare she was watching unfold before her eyes, peopled with characters she didn't know. It couldn't be true! It couldn't! Her incredulous gaze swept all their faces. Sall heartbroken. Aunt Babsey grim. Uncle Jim pitying. She turned and rushed from the room, through the scullery, across the yard and out into the back entry. Leaving every door behind her wide open. She looked wildly around, ignoring the shouts coming from the house. Everything looked strange; nothing looked even remotely familiar. Then she started to run, not knowing, not caring where.

She ran blindly on until at last she was fighting for breath, her chest constricted painfully as though her ribs were crushing the air from her lungs. Her heart beat so loudly that the thudding echoed in her head. She leaned against a wall. It couldn't be true! He loved her! What was it he'd said? None of them had meant anything to him, but he and Doreen Cooper . . . She cried aloud at the pictures that forced their way into her defenceless mind. Of him and . . . her! She remembered Doreen's words. So that was what she had meant! Oh, God! No! NO!

She stumbled on, her feet slipping on the refuse lying in the gutter that ran down the centre of the narrow entry. No matter how hard she ran she couldn't seem to leave the pain, the shock or those images behind. There was no escape from them! She stumbled and fell hard, but dragging herself up she staggered on again. Then she turned a corner and fell against something warm and soft.

'What the bloody hell! Holy Mother, it's you! What's the matter? Who's done this to you?' Mike Crowley looked down at the tear-streaked face, the loose, tangled hair, the stained and torn dress and the scratched and bleeding arms.

Tears blurred her vision but, at the sound of his voice, she collapsed against him, sobbing.

He smoothed back the soft, tangled curls. 'Who was it? Who was it, Louisa?'

She couldn't answer him. Her throat felt as though it

was burning and again she was fighting for breath. Deep, shuddering sobs racked her.

'Calm down! Calm down, girl, and tell me what happened?' He soothed, holding her trembling body closely.

Gradually she quietened a little as he continued to stroke her hair and soothe her, using the words his mother had used to get him to sleep when he'd been a child. When the sobs had almost subsided he gently lifted her face. 'Are you hurt?'

She shook her head, still unable to speak.

'Then no-one's . . . harmed you?'

'No,' she managed to whisper.

'Then what in the name of all the Saints is the matter? Is it your Da?'

This time her head moved vehemently and the tears welled up again.

'I think I'd better get you home.'

'NO!' The word was wrenched from deep inside her. She never wanted to go back there!

'All right. All right! We'll walk for a bit and you can tell me all about it.' With one arm around her waist he supported her but her steps were halting. The pain still gnawed at her heart, she still felt hurt, betrayed and lost but she drew a little comfort and a measure of calmness from his firm grip and his silence.

He'd tried coaxing and cajoling but he couldn't get it out of her, but at least no-one had molested her. He'd seen her on a few occasions since the night he'd rescued her from old Tatters Remmey, but they'd never exchanged more than a cursory greeting. He'd heard that she was courting one of Eddie MacGann's mates. That no-good, skirt-chasing Tad Buckley. A no-mark if ever there was one. Brains in his trousers. He found it incomprehensible that a man like Big John Langford had allowed his girl to associate with such low life. That thought struck him forcibly. Was that the reason why she was so upset? Had Buckley thrown her over for someone else? Decent girls shouldn't get mixed up with the likes of Tad Buckley, he thought savagely and the fierceness of this reaction surprised him.

'Is it Tad Buckley?' he asked abruptly.

The question brought on a renewed bout of sobbing and he was sorry he'd mentioned him. Obviously that's what had happened. Someone should sort that bastard out! No doubt one of these days someone would – probably Big John Langford.

She clung tightly to him, not fully realizing who he was, just that he was someone to cling to, someone to hold out some comfort.

They were half-way along Grecian Terrace and he wondered if he should take her home. She didn't appear to be aware of where she was and he couldn't leave her wandering the streets in this state. Suddenly his shoulder was gripped tightly and he was spun around, pulling her with him.

'Get your filthy hands off her! I'll break your bleedin' neck if you've touched her!' Eddie MacGann spat at him.

She uttered a cry, realizing where she was.

Mike shook off the grip and glared back at Eddie. The gesture was one of contempt. 'Go and ask your mate Tad Buckley why she's so upset! I found her running the streets, half demented! She could have been raped or run down by a tram! And don't you ever lay a finger on me again MacGann or it'll be your bloody neck that gets broken!'

Eddie's eyes narrowed as he stared at Louisa.

'Go on, take her home! Or can't "you lot" look after your own? Fine mates you've got, the morals of a jigger cat and you're not much better, you knew what he was like!' Mike was openly sneering. 'Tarred with the same brush, the pair of you! No sister or cousin of mine would get within ten feet of a cheating, whoring no-mark like that!'

Eddie's face became puce at the taunts and he grabbed Louisa by the arm and dragged her away from Mike Crowley. 'You watch your bleedin' mouth!'

'Take her home!' came the contemptuous reply. Eddie MacGann was as low as a sewer rat in his estimation.

106

Louisa began to cry, she hated them both! Fighting and arguing when her life was in fragments! Neither of them cared about her.

'Let's get home, Louisa! Mam will sort this out!' Eddie put an arm around her shoulders and began to pull her away. 'I'll get you Crowley! No red-necked Papist touches any of us, do you hear me! I'll get you!'

Mike laughed scornfully. 'I'll be waiting MacGann! But you'd better bring all your so-called mates with you. You're not man enough on your own!'

None too gently Eddie pulled her away and pushed her towards home, ignoring her protests. If Crowley thought he'd finished with him, he was mistaken! He'd see that arrogant sneer wiped off his face – by a boot! 'What the hell's all this about?' he growled at her.

She just shook her head and let him lead her across the yard and into the house.

Evvie had gone to bed with the strict instruction that she wasn't to utter even one word to Louisa, tonight or any other night. She'd gone upstairs feeling very apprehensive and curious. She'd never seen her Da look so mad. Her Mam's face had been set; her dark eyes flashing sparks at her husband. There had been a terrible row and Jim had sworn that if Babsey even mentioned that blackguard, he'd raise his hand to her for the first time in his life.

'She's heartbroken! She's devastated and if you start on her Babsey, with the "I told you so", then so help me God, I'll hit you! It's maybe best that it has happened. He's no bloody good, never has been, never will be, but right now she doesn't need you telling her that! Or anyone else either. When she comes in, you say nothing, do you hear me? Just try and comfort her, it's what John would want.'

Babsey was shocked into silence by this tirade and it had been then that Evvie had come in. Before she'd had time to open her mouth Jim had laid down the same rules to his daughter.

'Just wait until our John gets home, that's all! He'll break that little toe-rag's neck!' Babsey had exploded, crashing the breakfast dishes down on the table.

'Well I for one won't blame him! I might even give him a hand!' had come the grim reply. 'I'll go round the block again to see if I can see her, I'm getting worried about her. You go to the shop door and have a look.'

'I'm not standing on the front step at this time of night, giving the neighbours something else to talk about! When our Eddie comes in you can both go out and look for her, if she hasn't come in by then. She probably just wants to be alone, I don't suppose you'd thought of that, had you?' Babsey shot back, glowering.

Before Jim could reply Eddie pulled Louisa into the kitchen and Babsey, tutting, guided her into the scullery to bathe her face.

'So, you found her then? I suppose you've heard all about it. You and your bloody friends!' Jim took off his jacket.

'I didn't find her. The cogger, Crowley, found her! I'll kill him! He had his arm around her as though she were some slut of an Irish slummy!'

'You couldn't even do that! You're useless Eddie! It doesn't matter who found her, only that she's safe!'

'It matters to me! What's wrong with her anyway? What's all this about my mates?'

'That no-good, skirt-chasing, lying Tad Buckley has got Doreen Cooper pregnant, that's what's wrong with her! Frank has dragged Doreen over to the Buckleys to make sure he does the right thing by her and marries her! After he'd given her the hiding she should have had months ago! Your Mam was right about that!'

'What's that got to do with me? It's not my fault! I can't help what my mates get up to!' Despite the outward bravado Eddie felt sick. He'd gone with Doreen Cooper himself. She could have named him! He felt his mouth go dry.

'If you hadn't brought him around here then he'd never have set his cap at her, would he? Changed, my foot! Poor, innocent little lamb like that, what chance did she stand and you're not without blame! You knew what he was, but no, you sided with him, didn't you? "He's settled down now. Give him a break. He's been a bit wild, but all lads are!"' Jim mimicked his son's voice. 'If you'd had any feelings for her, any respect, you'd have fought tooth and nail to keep him away from her!'

Eddie's cheeks flushed redder. That's what Crowley had said. 'You can't blame it all on me! How was I to know she would get all serious over him? I'm not her keeper, it's not my fault!'

Jim looked at his son with contempt but he supposed he should blame himself for the way Eddie was turning out. He realized that keeping quiet for the sake of peace had its price and although Babsey was aware of most of Eddie's failings, she wouldn't hear a word said against him. He was *her* son. Her pride and joy. 'You know what you are Eddie MacGann? You're a bloody coward! A creeping, sneaking little coward! God, that I should have to say that to my own flesh and blood! But I've learned from the mistakes I've made with you and I'll make damned sure our Tommy doesn't turn out like you and I don't care what your Mam says! Oh, I heard all about that poor dimwit, Jimmy Frazer, and now you're washing your hands of your part in this . . . fiasco! Well, meladdo, you're not going to be the "blue-eyed boy" when Big John finds out, are you?'

The colour drained from Eddie's face and he was shaken. Although he'd never seen his father so angry and he was smarting at his taunts, he was terrified of what his Uncle would do and say. He sat down suddenly. 'She'll have got over it by the time he gets home,' he muttered.

'I don't think so,' Jim said quietly. Eddie was a fool, but he wasn't stupid. Why waste any more breath on him? Better to leave him to stew; to worry and wonder about what his Uncle would say. He sighed heavily and sat down, staring into the fire. It was better that she'd found out now. Better that it was all over, but it tore at his heart to see her so upset. She was young and young hearts mend quickly. Despite himself he felt the frustrated anger boil up again. They should have put a stop to it – all of them! They should all have tried harder, they were all to blame, not just Eddie. Even Big John Langford, furious as he would be, could have stopped it. He got to his feet and tried to smile as Babsey brought her back into the room and guided her to his vacated chair. Eddie got up quickly and went upstairs.

'Here, luv, sit down. Your Aunt Babsey will make you a nice, strong cup of tea and I think a drop of whisky wouldn't go amiss.' He placed an arm around her shoulder and nodded over her bent head to his wife.

Babsey pushed the kettle onto the hob and then opened the cupboard at the bottom of the dresser to bring out the whisky bottle. He patted her hand helplessly. 'After you've had that you get off to bed. I'll go to Mr Gouldston's first thing and ask him if I can use his telephone. You won't be fit for work tomorrow,' he added firmly, glancing up at his wife.

She'd sobbed herself quietly to sleep, burying her face in the pillow so as not to wake Evvie, although she really didn't care whether her cousin was asleep or not. Over and over she'd repeated to herself 'Why? Why did he lie to me? Why did he tell me he loved me?' The almost physical pain gnawed at her. Doreen Cooper! She could see the red lips and those red ear-rings as she'd tossed her head! Oh, why did it have to be her! That painted, common trollop who'd flitted from man to man like a bee from flower to flower, sucking up all their goodness! Why? Why? Why? And without him – what point was there in life at all? She'd never, ever be happy again. Her head was thumping and she felt cold and stiff and her knee hurt where she'd grazed it when she'd fallen, but what was that compared to the misery that now faced her? 'Oh, Da! Please come home, I need you so much!' she'd sobbed into the pillow.

A very subdued Evvie and an equally silent and furtive Eddie had gone off to work. Tommy had been told that Louisa was sick and that if he clattered and thumped about the house his head would ring for a week with the clout he'd get. And from now on he was to stop hanging around street corners with those hooligan friends of his. Life looked pretty grim and it all had something to do with Louisa. He knew something bad had happened to her, he wasn't daft, and it was something to do with Tad Buckley. He'd heard his Da yelling at Eddie last night and Louisa had cried half the night. Both his Mam and Da were in terrible moods and he decided that it wasn't the right time to tell them that he wanted to give up being an apprentice and go away to sea. He brightened. He'd have a talk to Uncle John, he'd understand. Then he frowned. If Louisa was upset then it stood to reason his Uncle would be too. He'd not get much help from that quarter, not until Louisa was all right again. When she'd got over whatever it was that was wrong with her. He collected up his 'carry out' and went quietly out the back way, meeting Mrs Cooper who was on her way in. He thought that was odd, too. For her to be coming round at this time in the morning. He shrugged. She must want a loan.

Tommy was right in his assumption. Agnes Cooper, having spent the night crying, had told Frank that she would go and see Babsey MacGann for a loan. How else could they afford to pay for the wedding, she'd argued tiredly? Even though it was to be quiet, hadn't Doreen brought enough shame and disgrace on them without Mrs Buckley looking even further down her nose and saying they couldn't even afford to 'rig' the girl out and give her a bit of a 'do', so people wouldn't be even more scandalized. The furniture and the rug weren't paid for yet and if they didn't pay, then they would come and repossess them and they'd still have to pay for them. No-one had bothered to read the small print on the credit agreement. Reluctantly Frank had agreed with her. He was bitterly hurt and angry that Doreen had shamed them all. Well, she'd made her bed, now she could lie on it and thank God, Mrs Buckley, who'd been equally horrified and stunned, had agreed that Tad and Doreen could live with them.

Mr Buckley, as he'd shown Frank to the front door, had closed the kitchen door on his weeping wife and mutinously sullen son, had shaken his hand. 'Don't worry Frank, lad, he'll stand by your girl even if I have to drag him by the scruff of his scrawny neck up the aisle! Take no notice of him! He won't marry her! He'll bloody well do as he's told or I'll kill the young bugger! Any more of that and I'll put his eye in a sling! He'll stand by her! Serves him right! I warned him time and again about messing around with all those girls! "You'll come a cropper, meladdo, one day" I told him! He laughed. Well he can laugh the other side of his face now!'

'It takes two, Danny, and our Doreen's no angel! God Almighty, what a bloody mess! The pair of fools! Aggie's right cut up about it and I'm sorry Doris is too! Selfish, thoughtless pair!'

'Aye, well, Frank, no use cryin' over spilt milk now and no use us all rantin' and ravin' and fallin' out, either. The least we can do is present a united front.'

'You're a good skin, Danny, I'll say that for you and there'll be enough janglin' goin' on already! Bye, there's some who'll fair wear their jaws out over this – bloody neighbours!'

Danny Buckley had shaken his head as he'd closed the door. Agnes was right, Frank thought morosely. There'd been enough fingers pointed without giving them more fuel by not having the obligatory 'do'.

In answer to the timid knock, Babsey pulled open the back door. 'Oh, it's you! You've got a nerve coming around here!'

Agnes Cooper twisted her hands helplessly. 'Mrs MacGann, no-one is more sorry, aye, and shamed as me! Me own girl! Oh, yer don't know how bad I feel! I've had no sleep all night! Norra wink! But what's done is done an' he's goin' ter marry her.'

'And so he should! Thank God my poor Louisa found out about him before it was too late!'

'Can I come in? I'd like ter talk to yer, private like?'

Babsey looked at the thin, careworn face and knew what she'd come for. She felt no pity for her. They were feckless, like most of her neighbours. As soon as they got a bit of money they spent it on things they couldn't afford instead of saving it for emergencies. Then they came to her. Mentally she shrugged. If they were so stupid that they couldn't see their own mistakes, who was she to complain? It was more business for her. 'You'd better come through then.'

Agnes stood by the table until Babsey indicated that she should sit down.

'I was wonderin' if you could see your way clear ter let me have a loan? For the wedding. We've got to give her a bit of a "send off" like, though she don't deserve it! She deserves nothin'! Doris Buckley is goin' to let them live with her. We've got no room, not with the four of them still at home. At least she's only got him and her girl. Oh, it's bad enough havin' the shame of it all without folk janglin'!'

'They're going to talk anyway, it's all so sudden. You can't hide that!'

'I know, but what else can we do?' She gestured helplessly. 'Oh, Mrs MacGann, she's always been a handful, that she has! Not like our Sall. She's a good girl is our Sall but *that* one . . . I said to Frank many a time that a good hiding was what she wanted but he'd never listen. Too wrapped up in his own worries he was!'

Babsey went upstairs and returned with 'The Book' and her cash box. 'How much do you need?' she asked, opening the ledger and writing COOPER in large, black letters on a new page.

'Could you manage about six or seven pounds, please? I'd be ever so grateful. There's the stuff on the "cheque" you see. The things in the parlour and we'd still have to pay for them, even if they took them back.'

Babsey tutted. She didn't approve of the system of cheques either. They were issued by finance companies so the recipients could go to allotted stores and buy goods, then pay it off weekly. On the 'never-never' she said to herself. It wasn't called that for fun. You 'never' managed to pay for them; they'd usually worn out before then, being of an inferior quality.

She opened the black cash box and took out a white five pound note and two sovereigns and handed them to Agnes. 'You know my rates and I expect the payments to be regular or I'll have to make arrangements to recoup the loan.'

Agnes nodded as she folded the note and slipped it with the coins into her apron pocket. She understood what recoup meant. Babsey MacGann could be a hard woman – especially where business was concerned. As she looked at her with her 'no nonsense' hairstyle, her hard, black eyes and grim expression she shuddered involuntarily. She looked like a black crow. There certainly wasn't much charity in her. 'You'll get it every Saturday, I promise! I'm ever so grateful. You've got to give them a bit of a start, haven't you? Marriage is hard enough without startin' off like that.' She glanced at the staircase and lowered her voice. 'How is she taking it? Our Sall was heart-broken for her! Heart-scalded that she had to be the one to tell her, she thinks the world of your Louisa, does Sall.'

Babsey's expression hardened. If she'd had her way Louisa would never have got mixed up with the Coopers – any of them! 'How do you think she's taking it? She's really cut up, but she'll get over it. I'm a plain speaking woman as well you know, Agnes Cooper. I speak as I find and I'm glad she's found out what he is!' She closed 'The Book' firmly. 'And in my opinion your Doreen's welcome to him – he's no bargain! They deserve each other!'

Agnes got to her feet. There was nothing she could say to that and so, thanking Babsey again, she let herself out.

Louisa opened her eyes to see Aunt Babsey staring down at her. The light streaming in through the window hurt her swollen eyes and she turned her head away, a leaden feeling in all her limbs.

Babsey sat down on the bed. 'How are you feeling now, Louisa?'

The tears welled up again. She'd thought she couldn't possibly cry again. That there wasn't a single tear left, but she'd been wrong. 'Oh, Aunt Babsey, I feel . . .' She reached out and clutched Babsey's arm.

Babsey patted her hand. 'There now, luv. It's all over and done with. You'll forget all about him. I know you won't think so right now, but time has a way of healing and one day you'll be able to smile and put the whole . . . episode down to experience.'

How could Aunt Babsey say such a thing? How could she be so blind and stupid. Couldn't she see that she'd never, ever smile again? 'But why? Why? I've been asking myself that over and over again.'

Babsey frowned, remembering Jim's warning words. 'Because . . . because some men are like that, Louisa. It's in their nature, they can't help it, I suppose.' She had to pick her words carefully. 'After all the . . . others, I suppose he looked at you, a lovely, respectable, gentle girl and . . . Maybe he meant everything he said to you at the time! But the past has a way with catching up. Forget him! It's all for the best.' There, she'd said it without saying 'I warned you'.

Louisa looked up slowly. Now as well as the sense of shock and loss, a feeling of betrayal was washing over her. 'Oh, Aunt Babsey, I feel such a fool! How could he do this to me? Everyone will know and they'll all be laughing and talking! How could he treat me like this? I can't ever go out again! I can't!'

Babsey felt the anger surge through her veins. She could cheerfully strangle Tad Buckley and Doreen Cooper with her own bare hands! 'No-one is going to do any laughing or talking, I'll see to that!' There were too many people around here who were indebted to her and therefore could not enjoy the luxury of openly criticizing any of her family. But they'd snigger and gossip behind their own front doors all right. She brushed a strand of dark hair from Louisa's hot forehead. 'You're to stop all this, right now! You're going to make yourself ill and he's just not worth it! Put it all behind you and you walk down this street with your head held high, do you hear me? You're a Langford, just you remember that!'

At these words a fresh spasm shook Louisa and she clung to her Aunt. 'I want my Da! Oh, Aunt Babsey, I want my Da!'

'Don't you fret,' she soothed, her dark eyes filled with rage. Oh, it was a good thing for Tad Buckley that John Langford wouldn't be home for a while yet!

In the saloon bar of the Derby Arms at the bottom of Everton Valley, Eddie, Mogsey and Tad sat in the corner. The empty pint glasses on the table evidence that they'd been there for over an hour.

'Can't you talk to her, Eddie?' Tad asked for the third time.

'I've told you I can't, and you've about as much chance of talking to the King!'

'But I've got to explain to her! That I didn't lie! That I really love her and, God help me, I do!' he said in an emphatic whisper. The regulars of the Derby didn't engage in conversations like this.

'You should have thought of that before you started "dippin' your wick",' Mogsey sniggered, finishing his drink. 'It's your shout, Eddie!'

Eddie pulled some coins from his pocket and placed them on the table. 'You go and get them, bucket gob!' Mogsey wasn't exactly known for his tact.

'Now I've got to marry the bitch! I told my old feller it could have been anyone! It could have been you!'

'Shut your bloody gob! Don't drag me into it!'

The drink had given Tad some courage. He'd spent the last two days in a daze. 'I've a good mind to dump her, refuse to marry her! I don't want to be stuck with her for ever! I can't stand her, fat, lazy bitch!'

'You'll do as you're told! Your old feller will see to that!' Eddie warned. He wasn't going to let anyone try to put him in Tad's shoes and Danny Buckley was a riveter at Cammell Laird's shipyard in Birkenhead and years of driving home

116

the white-hot rivets with a heavy hammer had given him a physique that most men respected.

Mogsey had returned with the drinks. 'That's your "future intended" you're talking about,' he grinned.

'You're looking for a belt!' Tad shot at him. He felt trapped and utterly helpless to do anything to alleviate his predicament and he did love Louisa. When he compared her with Doreen his blood turned to ice and he was going to be stuck with Doreen and Louisa was lost to him for ever.

Mogsey ignored him. 'You'd better marry her. As a married man and with her "in the club" Big John Langford might only break your arm and not your neck!'

'Oh, Christ Almighty! When's he home?'

'Not for ages. You'll be wed by then.' A sly grin crossed Eddie's face. He was making sure that as little blame as possible fell on his shoulders.

Ted gulped his beer, visibly shaken.

'You'll be all right, mate! Once she's had the kid she'll be happy enough and besides, they're all the same. Put a sack over their heads and they're all the same!' Mogsey tried to inject some hope into the conversation.

'Oh, an' you're the bloody expert on women now, are you!' came the bitter retort. 'And we've got to live with me Mam. Life won't be worth livin', not with the two of them naggin' me day and night! It's not bloody well fair! I thought the old feller would have at least tried to stand up for me! But no, he was rantin' and ravin' along with Frank Cooper.'

'Put a sock in it, Tad, you'll 'ave me crying in me ale next!' Mogsey was becoming tired of the whole affair. It was bad luck of course, Tad getting caught with *that* one, but he was getting morbid about it. 'Can't we change the subject of Doreen Cooper and all her effin' relations?'

Eddie leaned his chin on his elbows. 'There's one thing we can do!'

'Oh, aye, what's that then?' Mogsey was interested. Eddie usually came up with something interesting.

'That effin' Mike Crowley!'

'The cogger?'

'Walking along with his arm around our Louisa! I swore I'd get him! Said I couldn't look after my own and he'd break my neck if I laid a hand on him! Said we've all got the morals of a jigger cat and that I'd better bring me mates, I wasn't man enough to sort him on my own!'

'Bleedin' pape!' Mogsey growled.

'So, we'll sort him out – good style! We'll wait for him, round the back of their church. He won't be expecting us there! I've been making some enquiries, sent out my spies. Our Tommy and his mates will do anything for a few pennies. I know what time he gets off the tram and where and which way he walks home!'

Mogsey looked a little apprehensive. 'What if he ain't on his own? They're a hard lot, them papes.'

'Listen to the big man! Frightened of your own shadow, Mogsey?' Eddie mocked. 'You needn't come if you're scared. "Takes a man, norra shirt button"!'

'Count me in! I'll purra flukes gob on the bastard!' Tad interrupted. Here was a welcome diversion and a chance to work out some of his frustration.

'You in or not, Mogsey?' Eddie asked.

'Yeah, I'm in!'

'Put your hand in your pocket then, Rockefeller, and get the ale in!'

CHAPTER EIGHT

The three of them were waiting on Thursday night behind the church of Our Lady Immaculate at the bottom of St Domingo Road, knowing Mike Crowley would come this way to cross Wye Street into Beacon Lane. This knowledge had been readily supplied by Tommy for a price of twopence, which Eddie had grudgingly paid, telling his brother he'd go far in business, it was nothing short of extortion. His grumbling had been silenced when Tommy had asked the reason for this sudden interest in one of 'the opposition'. They were all a little uneasy, they were well into the small Catholic enclave of the area, but there was no help for it. Eddie fingered the flick knife in his pocket, thinking of his father's taunts. He'd show him he was no coward and he'd teach Crowley to speak to him like that!

Mogsey balled his hands into fists in his pockets and Tad was poised like a taut spring, ready to vent his anger and frustrations. The forthcoming nuptials were only seven days away and then his life would be over! Or as good as. He'd be saddled with a wife and child and the thought of meeting Big John Langford in a darkened street. Crowley was going to pay for all that and more.

The sound of footsteps made them all shrink closer to the wall and Eddie dropped his cigarette butt and ground it out. It was Tommy and one of his mates.

'Boo! That scared you lot!' Tommy laughed.

'Bloody 'ell! What's he doin' here!' Tad hissed.

Eddie aimed a blow at his brother but Tommy dodged quickly out of reach, still laughing. 'Clear off, you young sod! Go on! Bugger off!'

The two lads ran off smirking.

They settled down to wait.

Mike was tired. His broad shoulders slumped and he walked slowly, his heavy, steel-capped working boots ringing on the cobbles. Carrying a hod full of bricks up and down the ladder all day to his father had wearied him. He'd even refused the offer of a pint to get the dust of the site out of his mouth. He still wasn't finished with work. He didn't intend to be a bricky all his life. One day he wanted to work for himself, start his own firm and for that he needed qualifications. So it was off to evening classes three times a week at the Technical College in Byrom Street. He wanted his supper and a bath first and his Mam would have both waiting.

He looked up quickly as he turned into Wye Street, thinking he saw a movement from the back entry. He shrugged, probably a jigger rabbit on the prowl. Then he felt a sharp pain in the back of his head and bellowing he turned to see Eddie MacGann, Tad Buckley and Mogsey Green standing in a semi-circle around him. He put his hand to his head and felt the warm, stickiness of his own blood. His Irish temper boiled up. The sneaking, yellow bastards! He ploughed into them, fists flying. His right one caught Mogsey full on the chin, sending him sprawling back down the entry. Then the blows started to rain down on him and he staggered backwards. Under the street light he saw the dull flash, then he felt the stab of pain in his side. Roaring like a wounded bull he swung around and grabbed Eddie's wrist, holding it in a vice-like grip. Eddie yelped and the knife dropped from his hand. He should have realized that Crowley would be strong. The muscles of Mike's shoulders rippled under the coarse jacket and still hanging onto Eddie, he swung his free hand and caught Tad across the cheekbone, sending him down onto the floor. Eddie tried to jump on his back and get his arm around his neck, but Mike just shook him aside as though he were a fly, turning his attention again to Mogsey who had lurched forward. Another blow sent Mogsey sprawling, face down in the filth, and a well directed kick caught Tad, who was struggling to rise, full in the ribs. Putting him down again, cursing with pain.

Eddie scrabbled about on the ground looking for the knife. Fear was now replacing his bravado. He'd made a serious error in judgement. Crowley was a born fighter. He seemed to fear nothing, but he'd stick him, that would slow him down! He grasped the handle of the knife and twisted it in the air in a semi-circle, the light catching its blade.

Bloodied and dirty Mike faced him again. 'Come on, proddy! Come on and have a go!' he taunted.

Eddie lunged forward, blinded by fury, but Mike was too quick for him. He'd shrugged off his jacket and he threw it at Eddie. Surprised, Eddie desperately tried to tear away the folds of material that obscured his vision. He caught a blow on the side of his face and staggered, losing his footing. Then an excruciating pain shot through his right hand as the heavy, steel-capped boot crushed his fingers, releasing his grip on the knife. He heard himself screaming and then came the sound of running feet and he knew the other two had left him. He was crawling and rotten with fear. It oozed from every pore. It wouldn't be long now before he'd hear other footsteps, the noise they'd made would have half the Catholic-Irish in the neighbourhood down on him!

'Even with your mates you're still pathetic, MacGann! You'll never use that hand to hold a knife again, you yellow sod!'

Holding his mangled hand against him, Eddie began to crawl away from the figure that now towered over him. His hand was badly broken, he was certain of it and the pain and fear were making him feel faint.

'Go on, sneak away like the rat that you are! Crawl after your mates – they've gone! It's just you and me now, if you've got any fight left in you!' Mike's head was thudding, his side was burning and his skinned knuckles were smarting and he felt a little dizzy.

Eddie had managed to get to his feet and he cowered against the wall, looking like a rat in a trap, expecting to see a horde of Irish navvies come pounding down the alleyway.

Mike managed to laugh, 'Crawl off home! I wouldn't soil my hands with you! Break my neck, wasn't that what you said? You and who's bloody army, Eddie MacGann? Rock Steady Eddie, isn't that what they call you on the docks?' He laughed again, grateful that the darkness hid the pain that suffused his face. 'Nerves of steel, except when it comes to carrying the can or fighting fair! Get home to your Mammy!'

Clutching his twisted hand, Eddie broke into a trot and headed up the street, Mike Crowley's mocking laughter ringing in his ears.

The sweat was pouring down his face and the pain of his crushed fingers contorted his features as he stumbled through the back door.

'Oh, my God!' Babsey cried, jumping up as she caught sight of him. He was covered in blood and dirt. His jacket was ripped and an ugly bruise was forming on his cheek.

'Crowley!' he gasped, thrusting his mangled hand towards his mother.

'Pat Crowley?'

'No. Mike Crowley. They were waiting for him!' Tommy supplied before he suddenly realized what he'd said and what implications it would have for him.

'Jim, get the police! Don't argue with me, this is a matter for them!' Babsey gently took her son's right hand and tried to turn it over.

Eddie yelped in pain. 'No! No! Mam. No scuffers! It's all right!'

'It's not all right! It's broken!'

Tommy sidled out into the scullery.

'No scuffers!' Eddie shouted.

'What the hell have you been up to now?' Jim asked. He'd heard Tommy's words even though Babsey appeared

122

to have forgotten them. 'What quarrel have you got with the Crowleys?'

'Louisa! I told you, he was bringing her home! Had his arm around her!' he gasped. 'So we . . . Ouch, for God's sake, Mam, be careful!'

'So you thought you'd pay him back! You and who else?'

'Jim! Forget about the damned Crowleys! Look at his hand!' Babsey shouted.

'You and who else, Eddie? I can ask Tommy, he seemed to know something about it.'

'Mogsey, Tad . . .'

'Don't you ever learn, Eddie! After all the trouble that Tad's caused in this house . . .'

'Never mind all that now, Jim! We'll have to get this hand seen to! Get your coat on and take him down to Stanley Hospital! I'll clean him up a bit first. Get your coat on, do you want him to be crippled?'

Jim looked at his son and then turned away and took his jacket from the peg behind the door. Three onto one wasn't his idea of a fair fight. No wonder Eddie didn't want the scuffers involved. He'd been right. Eddie was a coward and a bully and somehow he couldn't but feel admiration for young Crowley.

When they'd gone Louisa came downstairs. She'd heard all the shouting. It had penetrated her still fogged mind that Eddie and Mike Crowley had been fighting, about her. For the first time she thought about Mike Crowley and how gentle he'd been that night. It was the second time he'd come to her aid. Eddie never had.

'Aunt Babsey, what's the matter?'

Babsey passed her hand across her furrowed brow. 'Oh, it's our Eddie. He's been fighting with that Crowley lad. Your Uncle Jim's taken him down to the hospital. I think his hand is badly broken.' She looked at the wan face of her niece. 'He said it was all to do with you.'

She went over and laid her hand on her Aunt's shoulder. 'I'm sorry, Aunt Babsey. When I ran out . . . the other night

. . . he found me. He brought me home but Eddie saw him and they quarrelled. It's all my fault!'

'Now stop that! It's not your fault. It's not Eddie's fault – not all of it, anyway. He was only trying to help. It's just a pity he doesn't choose his friends more carefully! It's all that . . . Buckley lad's fault. Come and have some soup, you've not eaten properly for days,' she coaxed. 'I don't know what this family is coming to lately, I don't, and our Tommy knows more about all this than he's letting on!' She sighed heavily, setting a bowl of home-made chicken soup on the table.

Louisa pushed her spoon around the dish and took a few mouthfuls, before pushing the bowl away. 'I can't eat it.'

Babsey looked harassed. 'Maybe you'll fancy it later. I'll heat it up again and there's enough for those two, when they get back.'

It was almost three hours before they did get back, Eddie with his hand heavily bandaged and in a sling.

'Well, what did they say?' Babsey cried, putting down her mending and getting to her feet.

Jim took off his jacket and hung it up. 'It's broken in about half a dozen places. The thumb and two fingers and some small bones on the back are crushed too. They don't think there's much they can do about those, or the tendons, but they've done the best they can. He's to go back in two days. They gave him some tablets for the pain. Aspirin, I think.' He placed a small, brown bottle on the table.

Eddie, his face ashen, glared at Louisa. His hand was throbbing unmercifully and it was all her fault! he thought unreasonably.

'He won't be able to work for a while,' Jim added.

Babsey put three bowls of steaming soup on the table. 'Well, when he feels up to it, maybe he can do a bit in the shop. He can still use his other hand and his brain. What a week!'

Louisa got up. 'I'm just going for a walk.' Then seeing the look of alarm on her Aunt's face she added, 'I'm all right! I won't do anything stupid. I just feel I need some

124

air.' It was the truth, she couldn't stand the atmosphere or the way Eddie was glowering at her. She felt guilty, as though in a way it was all her fault. It wasn't. She was the one who had been hurt and humiliated. If Eddie wanted to go fighting with Mike Crowley it was his own fault if he got hurt. As Mike had said, it should have been Eddie who should have looked after her.

'I'm not going, Mam, and that's final,' Sall said stubbornly, glaring at both her sister and her mother.

'You tell me Da about her, Mam, when he gets home! How's it going ter look if me own sister won't come to me wedding?' Doreen wailed.

'I don't care how it "looks"! Lou's my best friend and if I go then she'll think I don't care about her! It's bad enough having you for a sister and having everyone smirking and saying "That's that Doreen's sister! You know, *that* Doreen Cooper!" I'm not going and me Da can beat me black and blue, but I won't go!'

'Sall, haven't I got enough to cope with with her? But she's right, how will it look?' Agnes pleaded.

'Mam, I don't care! I hate her! I do! We'll be well rid of her and look at the debt she's got us all into! And all she does is whine and complain! I'm *not* going!'

Agnes sat down heavily and covered her face with her hands. She just wished they would all disappear in a cloud of smoke. She was sick and tired of all the worry and the arguments.

'I'll be glad to get away from you lot! At least I'll have me own room and it's not like a mad house over there!' Doreen shot back.

'And good riddance!' Sall yelled.

'Will you two stop it! Half the street can hear you and they've got enough to jangle about as it is! Your Da will speak to you, Sally Cooper, when he gets home! Now take these things down the wash-house, I'm worn out!' She shoved a large bundle, tied up in a sheet, at Sall.

'But Mam, I'm going! Harry's calling for me!'

Agnes lost her temper. 'You'll do as you're told, girl! You can take him with you! I'm not having you finish up like her!'

Sall snatched up the bundle. 'It's not fair, Mam! I'm not like her and you know it! You like Harry, you said so! You've never liked Tad Buckley!'

'Don't stand there arguing with me! Get a move on or you'll feel the back of my hand, my girl!'

Sall slammed the door behind her with so much force that it shook the window frames and scattered the ever-present crowd of kids, dirty faced, some with jam-ringed mouths forming an O as they gaped at her. Damn their Doreen! A fine way to spend a Thursday night – down the bag-wash! But she wasn't going to the wedding and that was final! She would go round and sit with Lou, thereby letting everyone know how much she disapproved of her sister and how much she thought of Lou. It had hurt her to hear her Mam say she wasn't having her end up like Doreen. She'd never been like her. She'd always tried to help her Mam, turning up most of her wages to help with the housekeeping and the payments on the furniture. And now there was the loan for this wedding! She didn't see why Doreen should be given anything. She'd never considered her Mam, not even when her Da had been all that time out of work. Now Doreen was to be 'rigged out' with new clothes and there would be boiled ham and tongue and shop-bought cakes. A fancy wedding cake and beer and whisky, just so the Buckleys and the rest of the neighbours could say what a good 'do' they'd given Doreen! And she'd have to help pay for it! Well, they could stick their 'do' – she wasn't going!

Half-way down the Terrace she met Harry, his face scrubbed, his hair slicked down and wearing his best suit from the Fifty Shilling Tailors.

'I thought we were going out?'

'I've got to take this to the bag-wash! Mam's got a terrible cob on and it's all *her* fault! Mam's taking it out on me because I won't go to her damned wedding!'

126

'Why not? Shame to waste all that food and free ale.'

'Don't you start, Harry Green! What would Lou think of me if I went? A fine friend!'

Harry fell into step beside her and shrugged. 'So, we're not going out then?'

'Does it look like it?' she snapped.

He looked down at his highly polished boots.

'I'm sorry. Now I'm taking it out on you and it's not your fault!'

He smiled. 'I'll wait for you. We can go for a walk after you've finished and get some fish and chips, if you like?'

'It will be too late, it will take me ages to do this lot.'

'I don't mind,' he said cheerfully.

She felt rotten. He had enough to put up with with his Mam and their Mogsey without her taking out her temper on him. 'All right, I'll be as quick as I can. I'll have to go home and get changed though, I'm not walking out in this old frock!' She paused. 'Harry, can we go to your house? I don't want to start fighting with her again and I will.' She would even put up with his ever-complaining mother who had every illness known to medical science and who was always on the point of collapse.

'I suppose so, though our Mam's had one of her "turns" over our Mogsey.'

'What's up with him now?'

He grinned. 'He's been fighting. Got a lovely shiner and a lip the size of a manhole cover!'

'Who's he been fighting with then?' She was interested in anyone who could blacken Mogsey Green's eye although she knew Harry was exaggerating about the lip.

'That Crowley lad. You know, them coggers from Beacon Lane. Him and Eddie MacGann and Tad Buckley.'

'What! Three onto one?'

Harry chuckled. 'Me Da said the three of them are about as much use as a man with no arms! Couldn't punch a hole in a wet *Echo*. But he's a bad 'un, that Eddie. He had a knife!'

Sall's eyes widened. 'Gerroff!'

'It's true! Didn't do him no good though, Crowley broke his hand, stamped on it with his hobnailed boot! Our Mogsey said he screamed like a stuck pig and he and Tad legged it while they could!'

'That was dead brave of them!' she said caustically, but it got better, she thought. Serves Eddie MacGann right. There was no harm in a clean fight. One to one. But three to one and knives were bad news.

'Something to do with Lou and Crowley.'

'Lou said he'd brought her home that night and that their Eddie had started yelling at him, calling him names.' Thinking of Lou brought back the impending wedding. 'That's why I'm not going to the wedding. Lou would never forgive me, especially as it was me and me big mouth that told her about . . . them. I still feel awful about that. You do understand, don't you, Harry?'

Harry wasn't like his brother. He was a little slow on the uptake sometimes, but there was no harm in him. 'I think so. Do you think your Da'll make you go?' He was full of admiration for Sall's staunch loyalty to Louisa but he was a bit dubious as to whether she could maintain her stand against Frank Cooper.

'He can't! I'll leave home first and they can't do without my money now!' She brightened. 'I know, we'll go round and see Lou when I've done this lot. Let's get her something to cheer her up! While I do this you go down to that little flower shop next to Pobjoy's on Walton Road, they stay open late, get her some nice flowers.'

Harry looked at her with undisguised horror. He might be a bit backward at coming forward, as his Da put it, but he wasn't going to no flower shop. If his mates saw him walking back up with a bunch of flowers, he'd never live it down and Mogsey's comments would make his hair stand on end! 'Ah, eh, Sall! Not flowers!'

'Why not? What's wrong with flowers?'

'Nothin', but I'd feel a right twit!'

'Well what then?'

'Can't you think of something else?'

She smiled. 'You big dope! Get some sweets. She likes chocolate drops.'

'Eh, what do you think my name is then? Moneybags?' he asked, but she'd already disappeared through the doors of the wash-house.

Despite all her protestations and threats Sall had been forced to go to the wedding and the night before she'd gone over to see Louisa, feeling utterly miserable and despising herself.

Babsey and Eddie both glared at her as she followed Louisa upstairs.

She sat down on Evvie's bed facing her friend. 'Oh, Lou, I feel really rotten! They're making me go! I've got to "stand" for her, be her bloody bridesmaid! I tried, Lou. I really did, I even threatened to leave home!'

Louisa fingered the locket, wishing her Da was home, as she'd done every day since that Saturday night. 'You've got to do as your Mam and Dad tell you, Sall. It's no use you getting into trouble over it. I don't mind. I know you really don't want to go.'

Sall stood up and twisted her hands helplessly. 'It's the bridesmaid bit that really makes me mad! I hate her! I really hate her! I've let you down! A fine friend I am!'

Louisa reached out and caught her hand. 'You're a good friend, Sall, and you haven't let me down. You haven't! I understand!' Despite her understanding words and her attempts at cheerfulness, she still couldn't console Sall.

'At least I've stuck to my guns about not taking the whole day off, just the morning!' They'd need her money, she'd argued and that was one argument that had not fallen on deaf ears. 'Tell you what, I'll come over after work and we'll go out, you and me? That will show everyone that I don't care about *her*! They needn't think I'm staying for the "do" in the evening!'

Louisa managed a smile. 'All right, Sall, we'll go out. You'd better get back now, your Mam must need some help.'

Sall sighed. Lou was right, her Mam was fussing over dishes and things. 'She will and she'll get none from our Doreen! She's too busy putting curlers in her hair! Seeing her with a head full of screwed up curling papers will soon make him sorry! Oh, me and my big mouth! I'm sorry!'

Louisa shrugged.

'Come down and show me out, Lou. Your Aunt Babsey and Eddie were giving me looks fit to kill! You'd think I was responsible! Oh, I wish I was anyone's sister but hers!'

The following morning in the chilly, sombre atmosphere of St George's the wedding group assembled in the front pews. On one side stood Tad, looking pale and browbeaten. Beside him stood Mogsey who was to be his best man. Mogsey was still sporting faint purplish marks around one eye. In the pew behind Mr and Mrs Buckley stood with their daughter, Alice. Mrs Buckley dabbed at her eyes with a handkerchief and Alice gave an occasional sniff. Mr Buckley looked as though he was carved from granite.

On the opposite side stood Doreen in a pale pink two-piece, a small pink hat with an open-mesh veil over her teased and frizzed hair and clutching a small posy. Frank Cooper stood beside her looking ashamedly bitter while Sall stood beside him, her expression openly mutinous. She had on her best coat and hat. She'd flatly refused to buy anything new despite Doreen's protests. Next to Sall stood her mother, dabbing her eyes like Doris Buckley. The younger Coopers had been packed off to school. Even all done up in the new finery Doreen looked a mess, Sall thought. The suit was too tight, emphasizing the large bosom and the slight bulge of Doreen's stomach and, in her opinion, the hat looked as though it was on back to front!

Tad looked at the girl who, on the vicar's instruction, had moved to stand beside him and felt a wave of despair rush over him. He wanted to run as far away as possible but he was afraid of his father and he hated himself for that too. And now there was Doreen smiling up at him with her painted lips and rouged cheeks, her frizzy hair protruding from beneath that ridiculous pink hat. He noticed, with a queer detachment, that the top button of her jacket looked about to burst open and reveal the white flesh of her bosom and just as detachedly he wondered what the vicar would do if it did. She looked like a great pink and red blob, he thought, the despair deepening almost to panic. Any minute now he'd have to speak aloud the words that would make her his wife and his life would be over! For a brief instant he thought of Louisa. He saw her face, heard her laugh, thought he felt the touch of her hand. He looked down to see the Reverend Bailey's hand on his and he began 'I Tudor Buckley . . .'

Doreen was the new Mrs Buckley when Big John Langford arrived home after Christmas. For Louisa it had been a miserable holiday. Life had lost all its sparkle and she missed her Da terribly, thinking how happy she'd been the last Christmas he'd been home. Annie had persuaded her to go to a dance but she hadn't enjoyed it and had left early, but strangely she found that there were times when she didn't think about Tad and that those times were becoming more frequent.

John had got the story first from her and then from Babsey and Jim. It was Jim who had restrained him from going round and giving the new husband a good hiding.

'What good will it do now? It's done and she's starting to get over it. She's started to go out with that girl from work, Annie Cronin. You'll do more harm than good going round there and causing an uproar! Think about it, man! She's been hurt and hurt badly. Her pride's been wounded.'

'Aye, her pride and mine! By God, Jim, I shouldn't have been so lax! I should have gone and warned him off!'

'And do you think she'd have thanked you for that – then? Of course she wouldn't! We can all blame ourselves but it won't do any good, not now. Nor will it do any good to drag it all up again and give everyone something else to talk about!'

Babsey sided with her brother. 'He's shamed us all!

Dragged our name through the mud! He deserves to be taught a lesson!'

'Leave it Babsey! It was a five minute wonder, they've all forgotten about it now, you know what they're like.'

'Oh, I know just what they're like! All of them! Can't wait to find something about us that they can make a meal of! They're as jealous as hell of us all!'

'I said leave it alone, Babsey! I don't care what any of them think, it's our Louisa I care about! Leave it be, John! Don't go upsetting her and don't sink to their level!' Jim had glanced meaningfully at his wife.

So he'd stayed at home and they'd walked and he'd let her talk it all out. All the hurt, all the anger, all the humiliated pride, but inside he'd fumed. He was hurt. Hurt because she'd been so upset and he hadn't been there when she'd needed him.

'And then there's Eddie's hand.' She'd finished at last, her arm through his, as they reached the boating lake in Stanley Park. 'It's not healing the way it should and he's blaming me, I know he is although it wasn't my fault!'

They'd sat down on a bench and watched a line of ducks swim slowly across the water.

'Of course it's not your fault, Lou! I want a few words with Eddie. I hold him partly to blame.'

'No, Da! I wouldn't have taken any notice of him. If anything I'd only have clung to . . . They all told me, Da, but I wouldn't listen! Even you warned me but I was such a fool! I think that's the worst part now. Feeling such a fool!'

He patted her hand. 'Forget it, Lou. Get on with your life now.'

'I'll never trust another man!'

He laughed. 'Oh, yes, you will! Believe me! You'll be more wary, more cautious, but you'll learn to trust again, Lou.'

'Maybe.'

'Look to the future and leave Eddie to me.'

'Don't go on at him, Da. It looks as though his hand

won't ever be right and that will be hard for him. In a way, he only has himself to blame. He had a knife.'

'A knife! Your Aunt Babsey said nothing about that!'

'I don't think she knows. Don't upset her by telling her, Da. It's all over now.'

'Was Crowley badly hurt?'

'I don't think so. I didn't hear. Oh, leave it, please! I'm just so sick of it all!' she pleaded. Watching the ducks leave the water and settle down in the reeds, she wished sadly that they'd never got that damned piano.

CHAPTER NINE

There was going to be a war and everyone knew it. All that summer the dark clouds had been gathering over Europe. Yet there were many who hoped and believed, like Mr Chamberlain, the Prime Minister, that it could be avoided. Early in September hope was a commodity that was in short supply as the thunderheads loomed over Poland.

Babsey, too, had tried to be optimistic but she'd also started to hoard food. She remembered the last war and its attendant shortages; they'd have been in the desperate plight so many others had found themselves in, if it hadn't been for John and the stuff he'd managed to scrounge and bring home. Babsey hadn't forgotten. The cupboards in the dresser and in her bedroom were stacked with tinned foods. In the larder and in the cellar were air-tight biscuit tins filled with tea, sugar, flour and baking ingredients. It wasn't against the law although the Government had been urging people not to hoard, but Babsey always looked after her own. She'd also begun to cultivate other tradesmen. Saving the best produce for them, giving them that bit extra without charge knowing it would pay good dividends.

She'd served her last customer and had pulled down the window blind and put the CLOSED sign on the door, then she drew three tins of canned fruit from behind the stacks of paper bags underneath the counter.

'What've you got now, Mam?' Eddie asked, leaning on the brush.

'Ask no questions and you'll get no lies, Eddie!' Then she smiled. 'Just a few bits Mr Hilliard gave me.'

He grinned conspiratorially and began to brush up. His hand had not healed well and consequently he'd lost his job on the Docks. Now he helped out in the shop and he'd learned that there were other ways of making a few bob on the side.

He'd learned a lot by watching his Mam and by listening to people's conversations. He still had his 'contacts' on the Docks and in the pubs and he'd found that for every commodity there was a buyer. Frequently he had customers before he even had the goods. If you wanted something but didn't want to pay full price, then Eddie MacGann was the feller to see. His father didn't approve of course, so the least he knew the better. His Mam was different. Oh, she'd warned him half-heartedly saying 'I won't have any of that stuff in the house and just make sure you're careful!' But, as he'd explained, he had to 'earn' a bit somehow. It was a matter of pride. He had a small lock-up on the other side of town that he rented, so nothing was brought into the house, not for long anyway.

He manoeuvred the brush deftly with his left hand, seeking out the debris that had collected in the corner around the sacks of potatoes. He'd never forgiven Crowley for making him a cripple. He'd get even one day.

'Will you finish up here, Eddie, I've got to go out?'

'Anywhere important, Mam?'

Babsey's expression changed. 'Yes.'

Eddie closed the adjoining door to the back of the house. His Mam had begun to confide in him lately. She discussed things with him that were not for other ears. His Da was in the kitchen as were Evvie and Louisa. 'Well?'

'I had my doubts about that Baxendale woman when she first came round here. You learn a lot about people when you lend them money, there are certain signs, characteristics, and she was . . . just too "cocky".'

'Having trouble getting the payments?'

'Aye. She's come up with all the usual excuses. He's been off work sick. She'll pay me double next week when she gets her Panel money. He's been sacked but she'll pay me off in full next month, they've got an insurance policy due! Insurance – that one! What kind of a fool does she think I am? But she's run out of excuses this time! I want my money!' She lowered her voice. 'I don't want you telling anyone where I've gone, understand?'

'Do I ever say anything?'

'No. You've got your faults, Eddie, but you've got a good business head, not like the rest of them. You're learning all the time.' She smiled at him. One day she'd turn her business over to him, when he was older and more mature. Not yet.

When he'd finished, Eddie put away the brush and shovel and checked that the door was locked, then he put out the light before going into the kitchen. It was what his Da called 'hair washing night'. The scullery and kitchen were cluttered with towels, brushes, hair pins and curlers. His Da had taken refuge in the yard to see to his hens. He didn't blame him. The hens had been another of Babsey's ideas and he'd helped his Da to prise up some of the flagstones to make a run for them. Any spare eggs they sold.

Louisa was sitting in his Da's chair rubbing her wet hair vigorously with a towel. Evvie, with a towel around her head, was reading out the instructions from the back of a bottle of setting lotion. God but they were a boring pair, he thought. At least Louisa went out, usually with that Annie that she worked with and sometimes with Sally Cooper. She'd got over that 'episode' with Tad. What a bloody fuss about nothing that had been and he still felt resentful towards her. Strangely Tad was the one who mooned about it; said he still cared about Louisa, but that was probably because he was stuck with Doreen. But Evvie! Oh, Evvie was a real drip! She hardly ever went out, except to the Gouldsons. She and Arnold were saving up to get engaged. God, what a prat of a brother-in-law Arnold would make! He wouldn't touch anything that was a bit 'suspect'. He'd once offered him some stuff, dirt cheap. All he'd received for his pains was a stony stare and an ungracious remark. Well, he'd never get rich like that, wouldn't Arnold. Slaving away behind that counter in that shop until all hours, for buttons!

'I wouldn't put that stuff on your hair, Evvie, it smells like fish paste!' he jibed.

'It's not half as bad as that grease you put on yours – that stinks to high heaven!' she shot back dismissively and turned back to Louisa. 'Do you think it will give it "bounce and body?" she read from the label.

'You can only try it. Why don't you have a perm, Evvie, that would give it body? Annie's just had one and it looks great and she's got fine hair like you.'

'Arnold wouldn't like it. He says Marcel Waves look "artificial and cheap".'

Louisa caught the look in Eddie's eye and smiled as he mouthed the word 'Misery-guts' before disappearing into the scullery to have a wash.

'Anyway, it would be a waste of money. Those awful gas masks they've given us would ruin it.' Evvie began to twist a strand of hair around a pipe cleaner. 'Do you think we'll have to use them?'

'I don't know, Evvie. I don't want to talk about it. I don't want to even think about it, it's . . . terrible!'

'Tommy said if we do have a war, he's going to join the Navy.' She paused, comb in mid-air. 'Will Arnold have to go? Oh, I'd never thought of it affecting . . . us!'

'I don't know but I suppose he will.' Louisa gave her hair a last rub. 'Don't let's talk about it. It's all everyone seems to think about. I can't understand them – the lads I mean. It's as though they actually *want* it to happen! That they *want* to go dashing off with a rifle as though it's some sort of picnic!'

'Da looks worried and sort of . . . sad when he listens to the radio.'

'That's because he's got sense.' She started to brush out the tangles in her hair with brisk strokes of the hairbrush. Her Da had been worried too . . . The last time he'd been home she'd come into the kitchen and seen him talking to Uncle Jim. Quietly and seriously. So engrossed had they been that they hadn't noticed her for a few seconds. She'd caught the words convoy, U-boats and *Lusitania* and she'd gone cold. Everyone knew what had happened to the *Lusitania* in the Great War. She'd been the first merchant ship to be attacked and sunk by a U-boat and there had been anti-German riots in the city. Then they'd noticed her and had changed the subject abruptly, but those words still had the power to make the hairs on the back of her neck stand on end.

'Arnold's here!' Jim announced as he entered the scullery, two eggs in his hand.

Evvie uttered a shriek and headed for the stairs. 'He can't see me like this! Keep him out there!'

'It's not you he's come to see, it's Louisa.'

'Me?'

Arnold appeared behind her Uncle. 'There's a phone call for you. I said I'd come and get you. It's that girl you work with and she sounds right cut up about something.'

'Annie?'

Arnold nodded.

Wrapping a towel around her head, turban-wise, Louisa followed him out. Annie had never phoned her before so it must be something really urgent. Something that wouldn't keep until the morning. 'What did she say, Arnold? Did she give you a hint or anything?'

'No. She sounded as though she was crying.'

'Crying?' she echoed. She'd never seen Annie even close to tears.

Nodding politely to Mrs Gouldson and apologizing for the intrusion, she then picked up the telephone receiver, turning her back on Arnold's mother who obviously had no intention of leaving her alone to take the call in private. 'Annie? What's wrong?'

A choking sound came from the other end.

'Annie! Stop crying and tell me what's the matter, please!'

'Oh, Louisa! I . . . I got the sack!'

She was stunned. 'Are you sure?'

'Yes! Miss Fox called me back tonight . . .' With an effort she fought to control herself. 'She said that . . . my work and behaviour weren't satisfactory and that . . . Oh, Louisa!'

'But didn't you say anything? You're a good worker!'

'I tried to, I did! She said they . . . they would pay me for this week and that I'm to collect my cards on Saturday!' She began to sob noisily again.

'They can't do that!'

'They can! I'm not going in any more! I've told Mam they can keep their money . . . It's not fair! It's not because of my work, I'll be nineteen at Christmas and they don't want to have to pay me more money! I heard they were cutting back because of this war and a girl from footwear got stopped too and she's the same age as me!'

Louisa was stunned and then slowly anger began to replace shock. 'Annie, that's so unfair! I'll go and talk to Miss Fox in the morning!'

'No! Don't! You can't do anything! It's done now! I'll have to go, I've got no more pennies left.'

'Annie! Annie, wait . . .' There was a click and the line went dead. She replaced the receiver on its cradle.

'Not bad news, I hope?' Mrs Gouldson asked pointedly.

'Yes. Annie, my friend, has been sacked.' She was still too dumbfounded to notice the woman's avid curiosity.

'Really?' Florrie Gouldson probed.

'Thank you for letting me use the phone, Mrs Gouldson. I'm sorry to have disturbed you.' Still in a daze she let herself out but she didn't go straight back. She stood in the entry outside the yard door. It just wasn't right! It wasn't fair! Annie had worked there ever since she'd left school and she was good at her job! Just because they were going to have to pay her more money . . . Intense indignation bubbled up. She'd go and see Miss Fox in the morning! There must be something she could do! She wouldn't be impudent, she'd be calm, very calm. She'd remind Miss Fox that Annie was a good worker and a good time-keeper too and suggest, politely of course, that wouldn't it be more beneficial for the company to keep on a trained and proven girl, rather than another junior? Surely they'd listen to reason, it made sense. Then Annie would get her job back. She shivered. It was getting chilly and her hair was still damp. She opened the yard door and prepared to have to explain it all to Evvie. It was no use trying to fob her off. She'd told Mrs Gouldson about Annie.

Babsey was quivering with rage. Her face was set and she gripped her handbag tightly with shaking hands. She'd never been so insulted in all her life! Oh, she should have known! She should never have lowered herself by going there! She should have paid Jed Leach to go round and 'have a word'. It wasn't often she had to resort to such tactics because she had to pay him and pay him extra not to use violence. She never resorted to violence, it could cause untold trouble, damage her reputation and she'd never found it necessary. One visit from the ex-boxer usually worked wonders. Everyone knew he was half-mad. Her black eyes glittered with anger and outrage. That hardfaced bitch had been drinking, she'd smelled it on her as soon as she'd opened the door! And she'd had the gall to laugh in her face!

'You can sod off Babsey MacGann! You're getting no money from me! You fat bloodsucker! Go on, bugger off! You're a fat, old, money-grubber!' Nelly Baxendale had shouted at her. Thank God she'd gone around to the back door and not the front or the whole street would have been up! And that Alfie Baxendale had just stood there leering at her, a half-empty gin bottle in his hand. And he'd laughed too as she'd stormed off. Well, he'd laugh the other side of his face soon! This time she'd be paying Jed Leach to do more than just talk! No-one treated her like that and got away with it, and it had a bad effect on her customers!

'Mam! Mam, what's up? You walked right past me!' Eddie caught her arm and looked down at her. He'd never seen her so livid in years. Her eyes blazed in her colourless face and her lips were set like a steel trap. The hands that clutched the black bag were white-knuckled. 'Trouble?' he asked.

She nodded curtly. 'I've never been spoken to like that in my entire life! That pair of . . .'

'Nelly Baxendale? No money?'

Her head moved twice.

'What are you going to do?'

'Oh, I've got ways and means, Eddie! No need to get bothered on my account, I'll make sure I get what's owing!'

He knew all about Jed Leach but he wasn't going to have her insulted by riff-raff like the Baxendales or have to pay out more money. 'I don't like to see you so upset or leave yourself open to insult, Mam! I don't know what's wrong with Da letting you go round there alone in the first place! He should have gone with you!'

'Don't you say a word to your Da, Eddie! He doesn't really approve of my business, but that's between me and him.'

He was going to say that his Da didn't complain about the benefits it brought and which he enjoyed, but he thought better of it. 'Are you all right? Sure?'

'Of course I am!' she snapped, then her expression softened. 'You're a good lad, Eddie.'

'I've got to see someone in the Derby but I'll be back and I'll bring you a bottle of good port to calm you down, like.'

She patted his arm. 'Not a word to your Da now?'

'Sure, Mam, if that's what you want.'

'I do. I'll see you later.' She turned away and resumed her journey and he watched her walking slowly up the Terrace. A small, plump figure bristling with indignation. As she reached the corner of Bathesda Street she turned and raised her hand in a wave.

He grinned and thrust his hands in his pockets but as soon as she'd disappeared the grin was replaced by a grimace. He wasn't having her insulted. He'd show the

141

Baxendales that the MacGanns were not to be scorned or shamed. Mam wouldn't let his Da do anything about it, but he would! Why throw good money after bad? Who needed Jed Leach when he could do the job, with some help. And it would show her that he wasn't prepared to let such insults pass and that she could rely on him in future.

Mogsey and Tad were already standing at the bar in the Derby, Tad staring morosely into his beer. He tried to 'drown his sorrows' as often as he could these days. He was a father now. Doreen had given birth to a little girl but he hadn't been exactly overjoyed by the event. In fact he suspected, deep down, that the child wasn't even his. Charlotte, the name Doreen had insisted on giving her, didn't look in the least bit like him. And as Mogsey said, with his usual tact, 'It's not as if you can take a girl to the footie match or kick a ball around the jigger with her, not the way you can with a lad. And then you'll be moidered to death when she grows up and starts hanging around with lads!' He could truthfully say life was bloody miserable. Doreen was basically lazy and as her pregnancy had advanced she'd taken to lying in bed half the day and had become slovenly in her appearance. To his relief she'd spent a lot of time around at her Mam's. That was a relief to his Mam too, they didn't exactly hit it off. His Mam made no bones about the fact that she considered her daughter-in-law to be a slattern and she constantly derided him for 'ruining his life'.

Then there was the other side of the marriage – the physical side. She repulsed him with her pendulous breasts, her sagging stomach and her stupid, arch innuendoes. All his former appetite for sex had mysteriously disappeared. The times when he claimed his conjugal rights were few and over quickly. As soon as his need was satisfied he would turn his back on her and fall asleep. Yes, life was a dreary, hopeless existence. Work, the pub, the odd game of pitch and toss and the odd scrap to relieve the frustrating vortex he was caught up in.

Eddie nodded to them both before joining a shifty looking man sitting alone in a corner.

Mogsey and Tad took their pints to their usual table where Eddie joined them after concluding his 'business'. 'What's the latest, Mogsey? Is it definite that there's going to be a war?'

Mogsey was reading the paper, scanning the headlines. 'Looks like it. That 'itler's asking for bloody trouble!'

'Good!' Tad interjected with some bitterness.

'What?'

'I said good! I'll join up and get away from her and the baby. I'd sooner join the Army than put up with her any longer! Always bloody naggin' and moanin'! "I've got no money, Tad! I owe your Mam half a crown. Charlotte needs some things, she's growin'!" That's all I get! Money! Money! Money! That and bloody Charlotte!'

'So, you'd sooner go and get your balls shot off then?' Mogsey said, sceptically.

'He'd have been better off if he'd have had that done last year,' Eddie put in, smirking.

'You've always got to get a dig in, haven't you? Right bloody smart-arse!' Tad replied. He was envious of Eddie. Even though he was gammy-handed and couldn't do 'proper' work, he was never short of money and he always had sharp clothes. Was always wheeling and dealing, free as a bird.

'So, if there's a war you're going to join up, for definite?' Eddie said. 'Want to get some practice in then?'

'Practice?'

Eddie glanced around and lowered his voice. 'You know the Baxendales?'

'That Alfie Baxendale from Media Street? He's always pissed.'

'Right, Mogsey. They owe Mam some money and won't pay up and I'm not having her insulted by them!'

Mogsey rubbed his chin thoughtfully. 'It won't be like the last time, will it?'

Unconscious of the gesture Eddie rubbed his twisted hand, scowling. 'No, it won't! And don't think I've forgotten that bastard either. I'll have him one day!'

'So, we're going to pay Alfie and Nelly a bit of a "social call" then?' Mogsey brightened.

'Yes.'

'I don't go in for hitting women, you've got to draw the line there!' Tad said firmly.

'If we "duff" him up we won't need to touch her, she'll pay up!'

'What if she goes for the scuffers?' Mogsey hissed.

'Don't be bloody daft! I know for a fact that they're on their list of habitual drunkards, they'd chase her!'

Mogsey finished his drink. 'Are we right then?'

'Mam's got a right cob on! I wonder what's upset her?' Evvie neatly folded her clothes for the following morning and placed them on top of the chest.

Louisa was still burning with indignation and jerked back the bedclothes. Annie's dismissal had been overshadowed because when her Aunt had come in she'd made them clear up and take themselves off to bed and she'd snapped at both Uncle Jim and Tommy. 'Then that makes two of us! I just can't get over what they've done to Annie!'

'Oh, stop going on and on about it! And don't you go opening your big mouth and putting your foot in it! It won't do any good!'

'It might.' She pummelled the pillow.

'If you worked for a decent company things like this wouldn't happen. They never do anything like that at Marks & Sparks, they're very fair.'

'Oh, shut up about Marks & Spencer, Evvie, you sound like a walking advertisement!'

Evvie snapped off the bedside light. 'Well, don't say I didn't warn you,' she muttered, sanctimoniously.

Jim had gone to bed and Babsey was just finishing tidying up when Eddie came in. She looked at his untidy appearance and the scratches on his face and knew immediately what had happened.

He pulled out a pound note and some coins from his pocket and placed them on the table.

'Don't worry about the rest of it, Mam. You'll have it by the weekend.'

Although she was pleased, she was annoyed at the same time. 'Eddie, you fool! I didn't want you getting involved. You should have left it to me, I told you I have my methods.'

'They weren't getting away with it, Mam, and why waste money paying Jed Leach?'

'Because he can keep his mouth shut! When things get this bad it's best not to involve family. Then no-one can prove anything.' She lowered her voice. 'What if they go to the police?'

'They won't.'

'But just say they did?'

He shrugged.

'I don't like having to resort to violence, Eddie. It always spells trouble in the end. I made a mistake, a serious mistake, it won't happen again! I want you to promise to stay out of anything . . . like this in future. I know you were only doing what you thought was best . . .'

He felt deflated. 'So, that's all the thanks I get . . .' he began.

'I'm only thinking of you, I don't want you getting into trouble. I don't want this family's name plastered all over the front page of the *Echo*. Here, sit down and let me see to those scratches. You'll have to think up something to explain them away.'

'A jealous girl will do,' he answered, slightly mollified.

'Who else was with you?'

'Mogsey and Tad.'

'Oh, rent-a-mob, is it now? I would have thought Tad Buckley at least would have had more sense!'

'Ouch!' Eddie winced as Babsey dabbed TCP on his face. 'He said he's going to join up, if there's a war, to get away from her!'

'Out of the frying pan and into the fire! It's no picnic! At least I won't have to worry about you being away.'

'No,' he answered bitterly.

* * *

The next morning, with quiet determination, Louisa went to see Miss Fox and asked to see her in private.

The departmental head raised her thin eyebrows and then ushered her into the stockroom that boasted a tiny office.

'And what is so important, Miss Langford?' Miss Fox asked sharply as she closed the door behind Louisa.

'It's about Annie . . . er Miss Cronin. She telephoned me last night and she was very upset, Miss Fox. She said you had given her her notice.'

'I'm not at liberty to discuss other employees with you, Miss Langford, you should know that.' Miss Fox took off her glasses and cleaned them carefully with her lace-edged handkerchief.

'She's my friend, Miss Fox! You know that. I care about her and she was in a dreadful state! Is it true?'

The older woman's gaze darted around the room, then she looked over her spectacles at the young girl standing before her. 'And what if I were to say that such is the case?'

'Then I'm sorry if I'm speaking out of turn, but I don't think that's very fair!'

Miss Fox's pale eyes became glacial. 'It's not your place to question company policy, Miss Langford, you are indeed meddling. In fact I would go so far as to say you are walking on very thin ice! I think it best if this conversation is terminated right now!'

She'd told herself she would be polite and calm but, despite a certain trepidation, she could feel the anger rising. This cold, prim woman just didn't care! All she cared about was her own position. Her own, puny, limited power. That thought gave her courage. 'Is it company policy to sack someone rather than pay them more money? Money that is due to them?'

Miss Fox blanched visibly and her mouth twitched. 'That's enough, Miss Langford!' The words were uttered in a low, suppressed hiss. 'Go back to your work at once

146

and I don't want to hear another word about Annie Cronin or any of . . . this!'

She couldn't control the flood of angry words. They just spurted forth. 'It's not fair! She was a good worker and you know it! She won't find it easy to get another job – not after getting the sack! But you don't care about that, do you? It's not right! There should be a Union or something to stop you doing things like this to people!' Her hands were tightly clenched and she was shaking.

'How dare you speak to me like that, you impudent girl!' Two bright red spots of colour had appeared on Miss Fox's cheeks. 'I will see what Miss Hamell has to say about your insolence and all this talk of Unions! Get back to the sales floor immediately!' She flung open the door and Louisa walked out, her own cheeks flaming. She hadn't meant to lose her temper. She hadn't meant to say all those things but Miss Fox's cold, contemptuous dismissal of Annie's plight had caused something inside her to snap and she hadn't been able to stop herself. Someone had to speak up for Annie!

CHAPTER TEN

Half an hour later she was summoned. Miss Fox came over and told her to go straight to Miss Hamell's office and the triumphant, supercilious gleam in her pale eyes boded ill for Louisa. She'd calmed down a little and had begun to wish she'd never let Miss Fox's manner goad her.

She knocked on Miss Hamell's door with a sinking feeling in her stomach and was instructed to 'enter'.

Miss Hamell was seated at her desk and she indicated that Louisa should sit down. She sat, hands clasped on her knee. But she reminded herself that this wasn't Miss Fox. Miss Hamell had always appeared to be more approachable. On the odd times she'd seen her she'd always smiled and said 'good morning' or 'good afternoon'.

'Now, what is all this that Miss Fox has been telling me, Miss Langford?'

'I lost my temper, Miss Hamell. I'm very sorry, but I was upset. Annie Cronin is a good friend and she was very upset when she telephoned me last night.'

'I realize that, Miss Langford, but as Miss Fox has already made quite clear, we do not discuss other employees or their predicaments. It is very unethical.'

She nodded.

'But because you seem to be very concerned and very . . . involved, I will, on this occasion, clarify the situation. For your information, Miss Cronin was dismissed because her work has not been up to standard for some time and her behaviour has left a lot to be desired in a young woman of her age!'

She looked up into Miss Hamell's calm face with its

stern, superior expression and wondered with incredulity how she could sit there and tell such bare-faced lies and think her so gullible that she'd believe them! She took her courage in both hands. It was no small thing to do to contradict such a person as Miss Hamell. 'Miss Cronin said she was not warned. That Miss Fox had said nothing to her at all. She said it was because she will be nineteen this year and that another girl has been stopped too, from ladies footwear; and that you are cutting back because of the threat of war . . .'

Miss Hamell's eyes narrowed. 'I am not interested in what Miss Cronin said to you, nor do I have to give you any explanations! I see now that Miss Fox was right! You are indeed both impertinent and insolent! Miss Fox said you even dared to mention the need for a Union or some such organization!'

Despite the fact that her hands were clammy the injustice was too much for her. 'Yes, I did, Miss Hamell. I don't think Annie Cronin has been treated fairly at all! And the only way I can see of stopping these . . . things is to have a Union. How is Annie going to get another job after getting the sack, without a reference?' With an effort she'd managed to keep her voice steady and her tone quiet, even her manner was deferential, so she thought.

'I don't know but it's something you are going to experience for yourself, Miss Langford. I consider your behaviour a gross breach of conduct! You can collect your cards and any money due to you from the wages office now! Then you can go and console your friend, Miss Cronin! Please leave my office at once!'

She sat staring at Miss Hamell in total disbelief, then as that lady indicated the door with a sweep of her hand she felt as though she'd been punched in the stomach. She'd been sacked, on the spot! Slowly she got up and let herself out.

She'd thought she'd been doing so well! She'd been stupid enough to believe that she'd even put her case quite eloquently. Stupid enough to think that Miss Hamell

149

would even view her utterances with sympathy! She hadn't helped Annie at all, all she'd succeeded in doing was putting herself out of a job. She'd be branded as a trouble-maker now and she'd never get another job either!

She went back to her department and collected her locker key. She refused to even look at Miss Fox but the other girls shot her sympathetic looks. No doubt her behaviour and its consequences would be held over their heads to ensure their obedience.

She went along to the wages office and knocked on the glass window. It was pulled back and an envelope was thrust at her before it was slammed shut again. She didn't see the person the hand belonged to. In a daze she went to the cloakroom and got her bag, leaving the key in the locker, and put on her coat and hat. Still bemused she left the shop and stepped out into the sunshine in Lord Street.

She stood there, irresolute and dejected while the crowds of shoppers passed by her. At last she turned her steps towards James Street and the Pierhead. Now she was just another number on the dole register. She was angry with herself. Angry with Miss Fox and Miss Hamell. Angry with the whole world that was pushing past her – not caring. And why should they? She was just another girl without a job.

Her steps were slow and her mind in turmoil. She couldn't go home yet, Aunt Babsey . . . suddenly she felt sick! Aunt Babsey would be furious, especially as she'd gone and spoken to Miss Hamell herself when she'd first started. She had been assured that, unless there was a breach of conduct, she would be kept on. Now she had just committed that cardinal sin and Babsey would be livid! Oh, she must have been mad! What had possessed her? She was a stupid, naïve girl of seventeen with an unpredictable temper!

'You're going to get yourself run over if you don't look where you're going!'

'Oh, I . . . wasn't thinking!'

'That's obvious and this is getting to be a habit! Every

time I bump into you there's something wrong. What is it now?' Mike Crowley had just come from India Buildings and he was feeling very pleased with himself. He'd just passed the first part of his examinations in structural building.

She attempted to pull herself together, realizing who she was speaking to. 'I've just lost my job.'

The grin vanished from his face. 'Oh, bad luck! What happened?'

She shrugged.

'Are you going for a tram?' He had fallen into step beside her.

'No. I was just trying to . . . sort things out, in my head.'

'Do you want a cup of tea, you look as though you need one?'

She nodded. She was in enough trouble so she couldn't care whether she was seen having a cup of tea in Lyons with him.

He took her arm and guided her across the road, then ushered her to a table and asked for a pot of tea for two.

'So, what happened?'

She looked down at her hands and told him of the events of the morning and the previous night. 'And I told them I didn't think it was fair!' she finished.

'Did you, begod!' he said, admiringly.

'I said it wasn't right for them to treat people like that! That there should be a Union . . .'

'God, but you did go in with both feet, didn't you!'

'Oh, I could scream! I was so stupid, I thought . . .'

'No. You were damned brave, Louisa Langford.'

'It didn't do me much good though, did it?' she shot back. 'And now . . . Well, I'm not looking forward to going home.'

'I don't suppose you are.'

The teas arrived and she sipped hers miserably. 'I won't get another job, I've no reference.'

He leaned back and studied her. They'd hardly seen each

other over the months, but he'd often thought about her and wondered how she was getting on. She was a gutsy girl. He understood how she felt. In the building trade there was just as much injustice and discrimination. An idea came to him; she deserved a chance, there was more to her than just a pretty face and a pleasant manner. 'Seeing as how you argued the Union cause, so to speak, why don't you go and ask them for a job?'

She looked up. 'Them?'

'The Union.'

'Which Union?'

'The Transport and General Workers' Union. They have an office. You could manage a clerking job, couldn't you?'

'I couldn't do that! I don't know anything about Unions. Besides, I don't think I could just walk in and ask for a job.'

'Why not? You don't have to be a walking text book. You'll learn as you go along.'

She took another sip of the tea. All the courage she'd managed to muster in Miss Hamell's office had drained away and she felt as though she just couldn't summon up enough nerve to go looking for work right now.

'I bet you've got enough qualifications.'

'I got my School Leaving Certificate.'

'Well, go and see them. Tell them you lost your job trying to stand up for your friend's rights.'

'I couldn't! Anyway, why are you bothering about me?'

It was his turn to look uncomfortable. 'I don't know. Except, I suppose, that I seem to be in the right place at the right time. A sort of guardian angel.' He pulled a wry face. 'She called me after the Archangel and she had a right cob on when I told her there wasn't a chance that I'd be a priest.'

'I don't think we'd better talk about . . . religion.'

'Maybe not. Let's stick to your problem. A job is a serious thing, no joking matter.'

She traced the pattern on the saucer with her finger-nail, feeling embarrassed. Remembering the way she'd sobbed and clung to him that October night. 'Were you all right after . . .?'

'You mean after cousin Eddie had a quick stab at me? It was only a scratch.' His manner changed.

'I'm sorry I caused so much trouble. I didn't mean to.'

'It wasn't your fault. I heard his hand hasn't healed.'

She shook her head, feeling very gauche. She looked around quickly. She'd better go. She didn't want to cause any more trouble, she had enough on her plate as it was.

'I'm not sorry I did it. He could have killed me. I know he's your cousin, but . . .'

'Do we have to talk about Eddie?'

'No. Will you go then?'

'Where?'

'To the Union, for a job.'

'I don't think so, not today.'

'Best to go now. Maybe it won't be so bad if you go home and tell them you've got the prospect of another job, now will it?'

It made sense, she thought, and yet . . .

'Tell you what, I'll walk there with you. No arguments. I know Joe Doran quite well.'

She was surprised.

'You're not the only one who cares about other people and their rights.'

As they walked out into Dale Street she asked him why he wasn't at work.

'Just a bit of business. Oh, well, you might as well know. I've passed the first stage of my exams in . . . building I suppose you'd call it. I don't want to be a bricky all my life.'

'Oh! Congratulations.' She was learning quite a lot about him.

'Thanks.'

They walked on for a while in silence and Mike thought he must be mad. They could never be friends; in this city it wasn't possible – or was it? Just occasionally a brave and determined couple took on all the bigots and won. But there had to be something really special between you to do that. You became outcasts. Totally ostracized by family and friends and church. A perfidious schemer who had lured an 'innocent' into the enemy camp and therefore an object of hatred. He wondered if one day it would all change. The world was rapidly changing; any day now it would be thrown into chaos if the news was anything to go by.

The cry of the newsvendor standing in the soot-blackened gateway of Exchange Station brought him back to reality and he stopped and bought a copy of the *Daily Mirror*.

He scanned the headlines, his forehead creasing into a frown. It looked as though there was no going back now. Hitler had been issued with an ultimatum. Get out of Poland by eleven a.m. tomorrow – or else! He wondered if she'd thought about the implications this war would have for her Da. So far from home. So far from safety.

'What does it say?' she asked.

He read it out to her.

'Oh,' she said, flatly.

He was thankful that they'd reached their destination. He didn't want to have to answer the questions that would inevitably follow. Instead they climbed the three flights of dark, narrow stairs until they came to a dimly lit landing.

'What will I say?' she asked as they stopped before a half-glazed door on whose frosted pane were the letters T & GWU Office.

'Just tell them what you told me.'

'I . . . can't!'

'Coward!'

She straightened her shoulders. Coward indeed! She'd braved the wrath of Miss Hamell, she could manage this! 'I'll go in myself, thanks!'

He looked sceptical. 'You sure you won't burst into tears and run out?'

Her chin jerked up. How dare he make cheap inferences to their last meeting? The colour rushed into her cheeks. 'No! I can manage to speak up for myself!'

154

He shrugged. 'I'll wait for you.'

'There's no need! I don't think I'll get lost, I can find my own way home!'

He grinned. The ploy had worked. 'Suit yourself! Good luck!'

She watched him turn and walk away, whistling. She'd show him! She opened the door and went in.

There was a young boy sitting behind a small reception desk.

'I'd like to see someone about a job.'

'What Union are you with – us?'

'No. I've come here to get a job.'

He looked astonished. 'We . . . er . . . don't . . .'

'Just tell me who it is I have to see,' she said, firmly.

'It's not that easy.'

She began to lose patience with him. She could certainly do his job better than he seemed capable of doing it. 'Stop wasting my time! Just go and find someone I can talk to.'

He got up and looked at her askance before scuttling behind the wooden partition that divided the reception area from the rest of the room.

She picked up a few leaflets that were laid out on the counter and began to read them. As she'd said, she knew nothing at all about Unions but then she'd not known much about millinery either when she'd started at Frisby Dyke's.

She turned around as the boy came back, followed by an older man in a slightly wrinkled suit. Taking a deep breath she smiled and extended her hand. It was now or never. 'I'm Louisa Langford.'

The grey eyes showed a depth of cynicism but the handshake was firm. 'And I'm Mr Doran. What can I do for you?'

She glanced at the avidly curious youth. 'Can we go somewhere a bit more private?'

The bushy grey eyebrows rose a fraction. 'Follow me, Miss Langford.'

His office was a tiny space separated from the main

room by glass and plywood. There was an old desk, covered in papers. A chair and an open-fronted book-case jammed with books. He sat down. 'Shall we start again?'

'Until this morning I worked for Frisby Dyke's as a trainee milliner and sales assistant. I got my cards Mr Doran, for telling them that the way they treat people is unfair. They sacked my friend yesterday, because they would have had to have paid her more wages. Do you think that's right?'

'No, it's not.'

'So, because I spoke up for her and for having a Union I was dismissed on the spot. I think you owe me the chance of a job, don't you? I won't get another one. All of a sudden I've become a trouble-maker.'

He leaned back in his chair and studied her. 'You've got guts, I'll give you that Miss Langford.'

'I need a job, Mr Doran. I could manage filing or some-thing like that. I got my School Leaving Certificate.'

'It's not as easy as that. We can't give a job to everyone who gets the sack, unfortunately.'

'I can understand that but don't you think I've got a point?'

'Most definitely but we don't employ girls.'

'Why not?'

'It's not deliberate . . . we don't have the facilities. Our resources are very limited.'

'But I can do what the lad on the desk does. Probably better than he can. I'm used to dealing with people.'

'Would you put him out of a job?' The question was asked with mild reproach.

Her resolve was slipping away. 'No, of course I wouldn't! Haven't you got anything at all?'

'Not at the moment, although you may well be able to have his job in the near future.'

'Why?'

'Don't you read the papers? We've issued Germany with an ultimatum. Tomorrow we could well be at war.'

She remembered Mike's words. She'd forgotten everything except her own predicament. She thought about her Da and she felt a little light-headed.

Joe Doran got up. 'Here, luv, are you all right? I didn't mean to panic you!'

'It's all right. I knew . . . that it was expected, but it's my Da . . .'

'Is he in the forces? Regular, like?'

'No. He's in the merchant navy and he's on this way back from Australia and I'm afraid for him. I keep thinking about . . . U-boats and the *Lusitania*.'

Joe Doran nodded sympathetically. 'Aye, I had a cousin that went down on her. But cheer up, Herr Hitler might take the warning seriously.' He tried to sound hopeful but failed. It was impossible to sound convincing when you knew that time had nearly run out. The man was a bloody maniac. He'd take no notice of Chamberlain's threats, nor after his appeasement policy. Still, he shouldn't have frightened the kid. 'How old are you?'

'Seventeen.'

'And what's your first name?'

'Louisa and I live in Northumberland Terrace, Everton.'

'Well, Louisa, as soon as we get a vacancy it's yours. That's a promise. I admire guts and conviction and you've got both.'

'Do you really mean that?'

'I do! I'll write down all your details and I'll be in touch.'

'How long do you think it will be?'

'I don't know and that's the truth.'

She held out her hand. 'Thank you Mr Doran.'

'Call me Joe, everyone does.'

She smiled. 'I don't think I can, not yet. After all . . . you'll be my boss, won't you?'

'You're very formal, Louisa.'

'I expect I'll get over it.'

As he opened the door for her she remembered Mike Crowley. 'Do you know Mike Crowley?'

'Aye, a good lad, Mike. Make a good shop steward one day. Is he a friend of yours?'

'Sort of. He told me to come here. Actually, he brought me here.'

Joe Doran laughed. 'He would! It's the kind of thing he'd do!'

'What's the matter? Are you ill?' Babsey cried as she walked into the kitchen.

'No. I got the sack.'

'You what!'

She sat down at the table and took off her hat. 'I know you're going to be mad at me and I'm sorry! They dismissed Annie yesterday and I went in to try to . . . stand up for her.'

Babsey gasped. 'How could you be such a fool, Louisa?'

'She phoned last night, she was so upset, Aunt Babsey!'

'Why didn't you tell me last night?'

'Because you were upset and cross and chased us off to bed.'

Babsey slammed the iron down on its stand and grabbed another shirt from the pile in the basket. 'You mean to tell me that you've been sacked on account of that Annie Cronin?'

Louisa nodded.

Babsey attacked Eddie's best shirt with a vengeance. 'You've got to think of yourself in this world. How often have I told you that? No-one else will. And after me going to see that Miss . . . Whatshername and telling her you were the very essence of respectability! What's got into you?'

'I don't know! I couldn't let them fling poor Annie aside like that and with no reference!'

Babsey ironed the collar again. 'They can do what they like! Have you no sense at all? Shop girls are two a penny! Now what are you going to do? I don't suppose you've got a reference either! Oh, the disgrace! Getting the sack!'

Louisa got up and faced her Aunt. 'I've got the promise of a job. An office job.'

Babsey stood the iron on end and whisked the finished

shirt onto the clothes horse. 'Have you indeed, and where is this wonderful job coming from?'

'The Union. I went to see them because it was partly because I said there should be a Union that I got dismissed. So I reasoned they owed me a job.' She didn't dare mention Mike Crowley or his part in the affair.

Babsey's face turned an ugly shade of puce. 'The Union! That shower of . . . Bolsheviks! You went and asked them for a job?' she spluttered.

Louisa backed away, shocked at this unexpected outburst. 'What's wrong with them?'

'What's right with them!' Babsey cried. 'Anarchists! Socialists! You lowered yourself to go and ask *them* for a job! I'm shocked, Louisa, I really am! I thought I'd brought you up decent! With enough sense not to go mixing with . . . trash like that! Putting yourself on a level with all the no-marks around here! We've always voted Liberal, always! Don't think you're going to take any job they offer, because you're not!'

She was hurt and angry. 'Aunt Babsey, stop it! The man I saw was very nice, very respectable! It's a proper office and if it's being a Socialist to try to get fair treatment for people, then I must be one!'

'Dear God, listen to her! Your poor Mam would turn in her grave! She was a real lady and I've tried to make you into one! You're a child! You don't know what these people are like! I remember the General Strike! I remember the Police Strike and the riots that followed – that was the fault of your Unions! Just you wait until your Da gets home, he'll talk all this nonsense out of your head!'

'Da isn't against Unions, I know he isn't!'

'Then he should be! Nothing but a bunch of Anarchists all of them!'

She felt very near to tears. She hadn't expected this onslaught on top of the disastrous events of the day. Oh, she'd heard her Aunt muttering about Socialists before, but she'd never taken much notice and it had only been

159

muttering. It hadn't been anything like his outburst. 'I'm going out.'

'Oh, no, you're not, Miss! You can get upstairs until supper time! I'm not having all and sundry asking why you're home at this time on a Saturday!' Babsey yelled at her as she fled upstairs, totally defeated.

She wouldn't come down for her supper even though Evvie came up twice.

'I'm not hungry.'

'What did you go and do that for? You must be mad! Losing a good job like that and all because of *her*!' Evvie hissed.

'Oh, shut up, Evvie! You're too selfish to understand!'

'You've gone and put Mam in an even worse mood now! She's going on and on about Bolsheviks and stuff that happened years ago and Da's looking dead serious about this ultimatum thing. Why did you have to go and make things worse? Come down.'

'No! Oh, go and annoy Arnold and leave me alone!'

Tommy brought up some sandwiches and a cup of tea on a tray later on. 'Mam says you're to eat these, she's not having you getting ill.'

'I don't want them.'

'Can I have them then? I couldn't care less if you never ate anything.'

'Please yourself,' she answered, ungraciously.

He sat on the edge of Evvie's bed and ate the sandwiches. 'Don't you think it's exciting, Louisa? There's going to be a war! I'm going to join the Navy, I'm going to sea at last! I want to sail on a battleship!'

'Stop it! It's not exciting at all! It's terrible and if you can't see that then you're a fool, Tommy MacGann!' she snapped.

He shrugged and got up. He'd be glad to get away from them all. They were like bears with sore heads the lot of them, even Eddie. He had scratches on his face, some girl he said. Served him right, they were little better than tarts the girls he went out with.

At seven o'clock Sall came upstairs. 'Lou, are you asleep?' she called softly.

'No. Come in, Sall. I just couldn't stand going down there.' She switched on the light. It was almost dusk.

'I know what you mean. They all look as though they've lost a ten bob note and found a tanner. Your Evvie told me you'd got the sack and that your Aunt Babsey's livid!'

She nodded.

'Never mind, you'll get another job, Lou.'

'I'll have one, if she lets me take it! The Union said I'd have the next vacancy in their office, but you'd think they all had horns and tails, according to her!'

'Oh, you know what she's like! She's always thought she was better than anyone else round here and she wants you all to be the same. I got something to tell you, Lou.'

'What?'

'Harry and me, we've decided . . . we're getting engaged!'

Louisa's expression softened as she jumped up and caught Sall's hands, her own predicament forgotten. 'Oh, Sall! That's wonderful! When?'

'Next week, because of the war. Harry says we might as well do it now. Of course we haven't got much money. I'll have to have a second-hand ring from Stanley's on Scotland Road, but I don't mind. Oh, Lou, I'm so happy and Mam is too. She started crying when we told her, after Harry had asked Da, all proper, like. She said, because our Doreen disgraced us, that I can have a real posh wedding! That I deserve the best. I think she wants to show everyone that at least I'm going to do it properly and I am!'

Louisa hugged her. 'You are a good girl, Sall, and a good friend and I'm so happy for you! I like Harry. At least something good has happened today.'

Everyone had been up early that morning and St George's had been packed to capacity. As they'd walked up the Terrace, Uncle Jim and Eddie included, Louisa had thought that a blanket of silence had fallen on the city. Even the ships on the river seemed to move slowly, sedately and their sirens were muted. She'd seen tears in the eyes of many of the older parishioners during the Reverend Bailey's sermon. Now everyone was grouped around the radio set.

Because they didn't have one, Frank and Agnes Cooper and Sall had joined the MacGann family. There was a brooding, nervous atmosphere. The kind that made the butterflies dance in the pit of your stomach, she thought. The events of the previous day and the arguments were forgotten; overshadowed by the threat that hung over them.

She and Sall stood together by the table. Evvie stood close to Babsey who was sitting on the edge of the sofa. Uncle Jim and Frank Cooper were huddled over the set. Eddie and Tommy sat, fidgeting, alongside their mother, while Agnes stood near the door, as though waiting to escape. The wireless crackled a few times and Jim twiddled with the knobs and then they heard the voice of the Prime Minister, its tone incredibly sad. 'Peace in our Time' was over. They were at war with Germany.

The silence was deafening in its intensity until Babsey rose and turned to Evvie. 'Put the kettle on, Evvie, we could all do with a cup of tea. You'll stay and join us, Agnes, won't you?' For the moment all past animosity was forgotten.

Trying to busy themselves with the mundane, normal ritual of making tea, Babsey, Evvie and Agnes tried to lighten the mood. Jim was shaking his head sadly while Frank was talking quietly about becoming an Air Raid Precaution Warden. Eddie and Tommy had their heads together and there was an air of nervous excitement about them that only Louisa and Sall seemed to notice.

Sall reached out and grasped Louisa's hand. 'I wonder what it's going to be like? What will happen? We've all got gas masks so they must think . . . Oh, Lou! I didn't want it to happen!'

'No-one did, Sall. I suppose we'll just have to get used to it and . . . make the best of whatever . . .' Her voice trailed off.

'Mam wouldn't send the kids away to be evacuated. She said . . . whatever happens, we're going to stay together. I wonder if all the men will have to go?'

Louisa looked over towards her cousins. 'I don't know. I wish Da was here, Sall, and not out there . . . somewhere!'

'He'll be home soon, Lou!' Sall tried to sound optimistic.

That night was the first of the blackout. A total blackout, but such was the mood that people were not keen to go out, besides the cinemas and theatres were closed. The trams trundled along streets plunged into total darkness. Their headlights hooded, their windows covered with wire mesh. And the siren sounded for the first time. It was a false alarm and people stumbled out of shelters, trying to joke about it. As the all-clear sounded the regulars of the Derby straggled in in twos and threes.

'Make the most of it, it'll be on ration soon enough I shouldn't wonder,' the barman said glumly as Mogsey carried the pints to the table.

'Well, I'm off first thing in the morning to the recruiting office,' Tad said with the first hint of enthusiasm they'd heard in his voice for months.

'I hate to put the mockers on your dash for freedom but Da says they may not want you – at first. They'll need all the dockers they can get. The first convoy sails on Tuesday,' Eddie informed them.

Tad's face fell. 'Just my bloody luck!'

'We can try anyway,' Mogsey added. 'You goin' to try, Eddie, it's the best bit of excitement we've had for years!'

'What use would I be with this!' He thrust out his twisted right hand. Never had he hated Mike Crowley more than he did that moment. He felt cheated and useless. 'They'd really have to be scraping the barrel before they'd take me.'

'You could try the ARP,' Mogsey suggested, cursing himself for putting his big foot in it – again!

'That's for old men like me Da and Frank Cooper!'

'Don't even mention that name!' Tad muttered.

'Oh, shut up! You'll get away from her soon.' Mogsey, as usual, was irrepressible.

CHAPTER ELEVEN

As the weeks went by, punctuated by false alarms, people began to wonder what was going on. What was happening? Nothing much as far as anyone could tell. It was a 'phoney' war they told each other. There had been no air raids and the blackout restrictions were being eased. The theatres opened again and children who had been evacuated came back home.

Jim was proved right. Tad and Mogsey were turned down because they were in reserved occupations – much to their disgust. However, the sergeant at the recruiting office had told them to come back again next month. Eddie hadn't even tried. He knew it was useless and his rancour increased.

Louisa had received a letter from Joe Doran and, much to Babsey's fury, she'd gone for the interview. As Joe had predicted, the young lad she'd seen on her first visit, had joined up. He'd offered her the job as clerk/receptionist and at the going rate. There was no discrimination because she was a girl. It wasn't his policy to differentiate, he told her, although it was an acknowledged fact that all other employers did. He'd then outlined her duties and introduced her to the two other men, both in their early thirties, who worked there too.

'This is Ronny and this is Sid. Louisa, our new receptionist,' he'd said.

'She's an improvement on Jimmy,' Sid had joked as he'd shaken her hand.

Ronny grimaced at the cliché. 'Take no notice of him, he's a bit of a joker. If you get stuck or want to know anything, just ask,' he'd offered, pleasantly.

She'd begun to feel less anxious, more confident about coping with the complexities of the index and filing systems and the horrific-looking copying machine that looked like a large drum covered in sticky, black ink. 'It's a bit messy until you get used to it,' Sid had confided.

On her second morning she was sitting behind her desk checking the index system and she looked up to see Mike Crowley opening the outer door.

'So, you got it!'

She smiled at him. 'I only started yesterday. Jimmy joined up but Mr Doran had promised me a job. What can I do for you?'

'It's Joe I've come to see.'

'He's got someone with him at the moment, if you'd care to wait.'

'You sound very "official" or should that be "officious"? I'll wait. I can talk to you. How's your Da?'

She sighed. 'He's still not home yet.'

He looked a little uncomfortable. 'He's not on the *Athenia* is he?' He'd been careful not to say 'wasn't on the *Athenia*'. She'd been sunk a few hours after war had been declared with the loss of many of her crew.

'No. Why?'

'Nothing. Just curious.'

'I heard about it, but thanks, anyway. He's on the *Ceramic*. They're due in at the end of the week. I would have thought you'd have joined up?'

'I have. That's why I've come to see Joe. He's an ex-Royal Navy man. I thought he could give me a few tips. I'm off to Chatham at the weekend for training. Had my medical at Renshaw Hall, if you could call it a medical! The Doctor lined us all up, told us to strip off, asked us to cough and that was it! Fit as fiddles – or supposed to be.'

'What will you do after training?'

'Submariner – only I'm not supposed to tell anyone.'

'What's that?'

'Submarines. U-boats.'

She shuddered. 'I hate that word!'

'I know but I look at it like this. Two can play at that game and I'd sooner go hunting their ships than have them chase me. Somehow I think I'll feel safer under the sea than on it. That's Irish isn't it, but then that's what I am – or at least Mam and Dad are. It's bound to have rubbed off.'

She laughed. 'I'll be sorry when you've gone.'

He leaned on the desk top. 'Will you now, Louisa Langford?'

She laughed again. 'Who's going to come to my rescue next time I'm in some sort of . . . bother?'

'Oh, I'm sure you'll find someone. Has anyone told you that you're a very attractive girl? Probably hundreds, with my luck!'

She felt herself begin to blush. 'Oh, get off with you! You've got the gift of the blarney all right! Mr Doran's free now, go on through,' she finished in a very prim voice and smiled at the man who was just leaving. Joe Doran called out to Mike to join him.

She did like him, she thought. She wished they could be friends, real friends. She was in Aunt Babsey's bad books already and besides, there could be no future for such a friendship. He was a Catholic.

At the beginning of November the *Ceramic* arrived safely in Liverpool to the relief of everyone, particularly a large number of families in Bootle. She was known locally as *The Relief of Bootle* because there were so many men from that area who sailed on her.

Louisa was at work and was unable to go down to the Landing Stage but when the office door opened and Big John Langford stood filling the doorway, she uttered a cry and flung herself into his arms. 'Oh, Da! Da! I've been so worried about you!'

'What for? You know me! Bloody indestructible the lads call me! Have you nearly finished here?'

166

'Yes. Just a few letters to put in the envelopes and then I'm ready.'

He watched her as she bustled about. She appeared happy enough and she looked to be coping efficiently. She had even gained confidence. He'd never thought she'd get an office job. Almost the minute he'd set foot in the house he'd been the target for a long and heated diatribe from Babsey, warning him that she would be 'brainwashed' by those Bolsheviks she worked for. At first he'd been annoyed with her for being so foolish as to get sacked from what would have eventually been a trade, but on his way to meet her he'd had time to consider the situation and he had to admit that he did admire her for sticking to her principles; besides, the middle-aged man now coming towards him – hand outstretched – looked a decent enough bloke.

'Mr Doran, this is my Father, John Langford.'

Joe Doran shook the big man's hand warmly. 'We've got a real little treasure here, Mr Langford. I don't know what we'd do without her.'

'You'll be making her head swell going on like that, but I'm glad she suits.'

Louisa had sealed the envelopes and was sticking on the stamps, her head down to hide her relief. At least it didn't look as though her Da was going to demand that she give it up. 'I'll just get my coat and hat. I'll post these on the way home.' She disappeared behind the partition to collect her things.

'Aye, young Crowley did us both a favour, I meant what I said. With nearly all the young men gone or going, there'll be just her and me soon to run the place.'

'Crowley?' John questioned. Babsey had said nothing about him.

'He brought her here. Told her to ask for a job. You've nothing against the lad, have you? He's in the Royal Navy now – subs, I believe.'

'No, I've nothing against him.'

'I take it you're a Union man?'

Big John laughed. 'Recruiting, Mr Doran?'

'You're not anti-Union?'

'No, but I'm a seaman. My allegiance lies there.'

Louisa reappeared. 'Ready. Good night, Mr Doran.'

'Night, Louisa. Nice to meet you Mr Langford. I hope I'll see you again.'

'Bound to, as long as you keep her here.'

They shook hands again.

As they walked down the steep, narrow stairway she tucked her arm through his. 'I wish you'd got home sooner, especially after we heard about the *Athenia*. I do worry about you, Da.'

'That was a bad do, the *Athenia*. But it's just the luck of the draw. You won't go until your time comes and, besides, only the good die young, Lou, or so your Aunt Babsey says.'

'The Almighty doesn't want the weeds in His garden – that's why he leaves them here to torment us!' she laughed, mimicking her Aunt. It was one of Babsey's favourite epithets.

'Don't mock, Lou! And don't worry either. I came through the last war, why shouldn't I come through this one?'

She smiled.

'Now, there's something I want to talk to you about,' he said solemnly as they finally walked out into the winter's night.

'What? Is it what Aunt Babsey calls "Bolshevik brainwashing"?'

He laughed. 'No.'

'Then what is it?'

'Not here. We'll go to the Hole in the Wall in Hackin's Hey.'

'It's a pub!'

'You can have lemonade. I think I'm going to need something stronger.'

The pub was not crowded. Most of the office workers had hurried home and it was still a bit early for what evening trade there was. Beer and spirits were in short supply.

168

He ordered the drinks at the bar while she sat at a table in a booth, looking around her. It was the first time she'd ever been inside a pub but the feeling of excitement was marred by the ominous tone her Da had used.

'It's nice in here. Sort of old and cosy,' she said, sipping the lemonade.

John Langford frowned. 'Mr Doran just happened to mention that it was young Crowley who told you to go for that job.'

'He did.' She kept her eyes downcast.

'So, what's going on, Lou?'

'Nothing! I promise, Da!' She explained how she'd come to meet him again. 'And I saw him once more before he went away. He came into the office to see Mr Doran,' she finished.

'Is that all?'

'Yes!'

'Lou, I've seen you get hurt once and I'm not going to let it happen again. There can never be anything between you and Mike Crowley, you know that, don't you?'

She started to interrupt but he held up his hand to silence her.

'I've nothing against the lad, I don't know him well enough to pre-judge him, and I'm probably more tolerant than most. A lot of the men on the *Ceramic* are Catholics. Just don't get involved, Lou! It can only lead to heartbreak and misery. Stick to your own kind. You'd have to contend not only with religion but with a different culture as well. Your Mam and I had our troubles, God knows we did. We had the difference in class against us. In fact we never did overcome that. They disowned her. They never even came to her funeral. But at least there were no arguments over religion, Lou!'

'Da, how many times do I have to tell you, there's nothing like that between us! I hardly ever see him! It's just pure coincidence that I've met him when I've been in some sort of trouble!'

'As long as that's all it is, Lou. Your Aunt Babsey would

169

sooner see you dead than getting fond of him – especially after Eddie's hand. Oh, I know it was partly Eddie's own fault, but she won't see it like that!'

'Da, please! I'm not getting "fond" of him! He's not even a close friend! If I see him in the street I just say "hello" and that's all!'

'All right! All right! No need to get off your bike, as Tommy would say!'

'I suppose Aunt Babsey went on and on about my job? She's convinced they are revolutionaries but they're not! We try to help so many people. I really enjoy it, you won't make me leave, will you?'

'No, of course not! I have faith in Unions, Lou.'

'I wish you'd talk to Aunt Babsey.'

He laughed. 'It wouldn't do any good, she's too set in her ideas. So the less said about it the better. At least the stuff I brought home has calmed her down a bit. By the time I leave she'll have a list as long as your arm for me to bring back on the next trip. Especially now that Evvie and Arnold have decided to get married next June and that's a turn up for the book too! I thought Arnold was so cautious that they'd be engaged for years and that everyone would be poking fun and saying "Eh, up! Here comes Marks & Spencer" – quite appropriate that!'

Her eyes sparkled with amusement. 'I don't think Arnold had a great deal to say in the matter. You know Evvie, old bossy boots!' She grimaced. 'But I'm so sick of hearing about it already! A week she's been engaged, that's all, but it seems like years! There was an argument over it.'

'Didn't your Aunt Babsey approve?'

'Oh, yes, but she wanted to wait until you got home and have a proper party and put it in the personal column of the *Echo*.'

He smiled. That was Babsey all over.

'But Evvie said all that was a waste of money, which isn't like Evvie at all. She's getting like boring Arnold! I think she was tempted over the bit about the *Echo* though, but Mrs Gouldson sided with Arnold. She said seeing as they were getting married so soon it was a bit extravagant to have two dos, especially with the war.'

'I don't suppose your Aunt Babsey could say much to that.'

'Sall's engaged too, Da. She and Harry hope to get married at the end of May. Evvie is furious about that because the way things are going, Sall's wedding is going to be every bit as grand as our Evvie's. Harry's in the King's Own Lancashire Fusiliers and he looks really grown up in his uniform.'

'How is Frank going to afford all that? Has he won the football pools?'

'Aunt Babsey, of course! Sall told me she didn't want her Mam to get another loan, but she's insisting. She said Sall should save all her money for her own home. She wants her to start off with good things. They're getting a rented house in Melbourne Street. Her Mam says they can pay the loan off with no trouble now. There's plenty of work for Mr Cooper. I'm feeling a bit left out – there will only be me left soon.'

'Don't you be in any rush, Lou. There's plenty of time. Actually, I'm surprised at your Aunt Babsey. In my opinion Evvie's far too young. They should wait a year or so.'

'Oh, Da! Don't say that! I couldn't stand it! Besides, I'll have a bedroom to myself when she goes, they're going to live with the Gouldsons. Arnold's waiting to be called up.'

'You're a hard little madam, Lou!' he joked.

'I know!' she laughed.

'Drink up and we'll go home and don't tell your Aunt Babsey we've been in here or my life won't be worth living!'

She chuckled as he helped her on with her coat.

He did leave with a list of things Babsey wanted him to bring home. Things that were getting harder and harder to obtain and Jim predicted that by next Christmas everything would be rationed. There had been a few false alarms but no bombs had yet fallen on Merseyside and the convoys continued their increasingly hazardous journeys across the oceans of the world.

Before he sailed again John took Jim, Eddie and Frank Cooper out for a drink and while Jim and Frank discussed the latest news and their duties as Wardens, John took Eddie aside.

'Are you finding it hard, lad?' he asked, sympathetically.

'Hard?'

John Langford stared pointedly at Eddie's hand.

'No. Not really.'

'I mean about not being able to join up.'

Eddie swigged his pint. 'Sometimes. Sometimes I get mad when I see my mates in uniform and know I'll never be able to join them, to share . . .' His words died and his expression became brooding and bitter.

'Look, lad, it's no picnic! I've been through it once already and so has your Dad. Take no notice of them when they start going on about the excitement and the larks they get up to. They're bloody idiots and they'll learn soon enough! If they survive.'

Eddie looked at his Uncle and some of his frustration diminished. Big John Langford was no fool and if he said they were idiots then they must be. Then he thought of Crowley and the black anger flooded back. 'There's times when I could kill that bastard, Crowley. I hope he catches a bullet!'

'Understandable, but it will more likely be a depth charge from what I hear. He's in the Royal Navy. A submariner.' He signalled the barman to refill their glasses. 'You're not without blame Eddie. I know about the knife.'

Eddie shrugged. All that was history now.

John decided to change the subject. 'So, what are you up to then?'

'I've got a few things going. I do a bit of buying, a bit of selling.'

'You've got your Mam's head for business then?'

Grinning, Eddie nodded.

'Good luck to you, but be careful. They come down hard on black marketeers in war time.'

A guarded look crossed Eddie's face. 'Who said anything about the black market? I only sell stuff people want, there's no law against that!'

'Not yet, but if your Da's right and everything goes on ration, there will be. Keep your nose clean, Eddie.'

'I will, you can bet your life on that!' He was smart enough not to get caught, he thought confidently.

'And don't get too cocky, that's when you make mistakes!'

'You're getting to sound like the old feller. Can't we change the subject?'

The drinks arrived and Eddie insisted on paying for them.

'What are the rest of rent-a-mob, as your Mam calls your mates, doing?'

Eddie laughed. 'They've both joined up. Tad couldn't wait to get away from Doreen. I think if they'd refused him he would have joined the French Foreign Legion or even Gerry he's that desperate! They're both down south training. I've had a letter from Mogsey but I heard that Doreen's telling everyone who will listen that she hasn't had a word from Tad, only a pittance of an allowance. She should get off her fat backside and work, for a change. Doris Buckley would mind little Lotty.'

'Louisa had a lucky escape there.'

That, too, was history now, so Eddie ventured a laugh. 'And she's got more sense than our Evvie or Sally Cooper. Those two are racing to get to the altar! I tell you there'll be some fireworks between our Mam and Aggie Cooper, they're trying to out-do one another.'

'That's a bit ironical, isn't it? I mean our Babsey will really be paying for both weddings.'

'Ah, but she'll get the cost of the Cooper wedding back, with interest, won't she, and it will provide more business for me? So we're keeping it in the family, like.'

John finished his pint. Eddie had a point there.

Eddie made a mental note to suggest to his Mam that they charged the Coopers a higher rate of interest this time.

CHAPTER TWELVE

May arrived with a burst of early sunshine that induced a profusion of blossoms to cover the trees in all the parks and gardens. The churchyard of St George's became an oasis of delicate pinks and greens in a fuliginous desert of narrow streets and dilapidated houses. It was hard to believe that across the Channel Hitler's armies were sweeping through Holland, Belgium and France and pushing the British Expeditionary Force back towards the sea until they reached the beaches of Dunkirk. Then the little ships went out in their hundreds to bring home the beleaguered Army, and the Mersey ferries went too; following the wake of the *Iris* and the *Daffodil* who'd seen action at Zeebrugge in the Great War, earning the title 'Royal'. Merseyside was proud of her ferries.

As the month progressed, the ominous news formed a background to the forthcoming wedding preparations in both households. As John Langford had predicted there was open rivalry between Babsey and Agnes Cooper and the neighbours had something to take their minds off the war.

Babsey was incensed that the likes of the Coopers, whom she considered to be 'common', were hellbent on giving their daughter a wedding that would at least equal that of her own daughter. She wouldn't admit that it may even outshine Evvie's nuptials. And to fuel the fire of her chagrin, she herself had provided the money for the spectacle. She insisted on calling it that. They were making a thorough spectacle of themselves with all their newfound airs and graces, she remarked tartly to Jim who was sick and tired of all the fuss. All he wanted was a quiet life, he kept on telling her. Only Eddie provided her with some comfort, she thought. Eddie was learning fast. He was *her* son all right.

'Just think of it like this, Mam,' he reasoned. 'We'll both have the last laugh because, in the end, when it's all over and done with, we're the ones who will come off best. You with the interest and me from the proceeds from all the stuff they've bought, and there's plenty of it. I've been thinking, Mam, why don't you charge a higher rate of interest?'

She looked interested.

'Tell them that the bigger the loan, the more interest they'll have to pay.'

She considered it and then nodded. 'You're right, Eddie. I will. And it will take them years to pay for it all and for what? Just so they can say their Sally had a grand do and have an album of photos to show off.' She sighed. 'Mind you, Florrie isn't helping matters and neither is Evvie.'

'Why?'

'Florrie's moaning and complaining. Saying it's much too extravagant for a war-time wedding, especially with things looking so bad. I told her that that was just the point. Everyone needed cheering up, but she wouldn't have it. Then Evvie is insisting that she's only having Louisa and Edith Gouldson as bridesmaids!'

Eddie looked puzzled. 'So?'

'So that Cooper girl is having our Louisa, her two younger sisters, a girl from work . . . Mavis or Maud I think she's called, and that married sister of Harry's as matron of honour!'

'It will look like a May procession,' Eddie commented, laconically.

'And they've invited the whole of Cicero Terrace! I ask you! Everyone! Oh, it will be a proper fiasco!'

Eddie refrained from informing her that both Mogsey and Tad would be home and that he'd heard that there had been a terrible row because Sall had refused to have

176

Doreen as either a bridesmaid or a matron of honour. Doreen had retaliated by saying she wouldn't go at all, but when Sall had said, 'Suit yourself, you won't be missed!' she'd muttered sullenly that she wouldn't 'show her Mam up' by staying away. 'Just as long as you don't show yourself up!' Sall had shot back.

Agnes was determined that Sall should have everything that she and Doreen had not had. Even if, as Frank complained, they had to put their souls in hock to pay for it. Sall's dress had been bought from Lewis's bridal department and had been altered to fit her petite figure. It was made from yards and yards of white satin, edged with lace around the stand-up collar and the cuffs of the tight fitting sleeves. The skirt was plain but billowed out at the back to form a long train. The coronet of artificial orange blossom, to which was attached a full-length veil, had been purchased from Val Smith's, Liverpool's foremost millinery establishment. All the bridesmaids were to be clothed in pale pink satin, which suited everyone's colouring. Similar coronets of apple blossom were to adorn their heads and the whole effect was to be complemented by large bouquets of pink and white carnations with masses of trailing smilax.

Frank had put his foot very firmly down over the matter of the dress suits. He wasn't dressing up like a bloody penguin for anyone! He would wear a dark suit that could be worn again and the rest of them could wear their uniforms.

'You've taken leave of your bloody senses woman!' he'd finally yelled when Agnes had suggested a cheap champagne for the toasts. 'You'll have Yate's Australian White and like it! There's a war on, though listening to you two you'd never think it!'

Agnes knew when she'd gone far enough.

'He's only thinking of the expense, Mam,' Sall had intervened.

'I only want the best for you, Sall. Evvie MacGann will probably have champagne!'

'She won't! Aunt Babsey is complaining now about having to pay for other people to drink themselves stupid!' Louisa had interrupted. She was over for the final 'trying on'.

'Mam, I've told you, I don't care what Evvie MacGann has! In fact I'm beginning to wonder if all this fuss is worth it. We could have gone and got married quietly. Harry's a nervous wreck! He said he'd sooner go through his training again than all this!'

'Oh, that's nice, isn't it! It's not everyone who gets their wedding dress from Lewis's and their head-dress from Val Smith's!'

Louisa had tugged at Sall's sleeve in an attempt to distract her. Everyone's nerves were becoming decidedly frayed. 'Put your outfit on Mrs Cooper. Go on, I've only seen it in the box,' Louisa urged.

'I look a sight and just look at my hair!'

'Never mind that, Mam! Put it on for Lou. She looks like a film star, Lou, she really does!'

When Agnes had gone up to get changed Sall had sunk down in a chair. 'I'm only going through with all this for her sake. I think I'll go stark, staring mad before I get up that aisle, but she's loving every minute of it.'

'I know.'

'I keep telling myself it's the biggest moment in her life. I just hope our Doreen doesn't spoil it.'

'Don't worry about her, Sall,' she'd said firmly, although she still couldn't really forgive Doreen.

Agnes appeared and Louisa and Sall both made the appropriate exclamations of approval and amazement. Louisa had admitted to herself that never in a million years would she have dreamed that faded, worn-out Agnes Cooper could look so smart. The outfit took ten years off her age and she had caught a glimpse of what a pretty girl she must once have been.

It was a coat and dress in a buttercup yellow slub rayon that gave the appearance of moire. The hat was a small pillbox of black velvet that sported a veil covered in tiny black, velvet spots.

'Go on, Mam, give us a twirl!' Sall encouraged and Agnes had turned around slowly.

Louisa dreaded to imagine what it had all cost but it would certainly put Aunt Babsey in the shade. She had a pale, biscuit-coloured crêpe dress that was devoid of any trimming except the small cluster of embroidered flowers at the neck. Her hat was of a plain bronze straw and her accessories were bronze too. The whole outfit was to be completed with her much treasured fox fur, complete with head and claws and tail, worn draped around the shoulders, even though it would be June and probably warm.

'Oh, Mrs Cooper, you look just like someone straight out of the pages of a fashion magazine! What a pity the photos won't show up all the colours.'

'Our Doreen's going to be bright green with envy!' Sall said, gleefully.

'I just hope she doesn't go showing us all up! I told her to get herself something smart.' Agnes had taken off the soft leather gloves and had smoothed them reverently between red, work-worn hands.

'Smart! She doesn't know the meaning of the word! You know what she's like, Mam. She'll get something that will look like the Botanic Gardens on legs and a hat with half a dozen dead parrots stuck on it!'

Agnes was not amused. 'Don't you start, Sall! There's been enough trouble already.'

Sall shrugged. 'I'll walk round with you, Lou, I'm going on to Harry's.'

'I thought it was his stag night tonight?'

'It is. I'm going to warn him to watch what he drinks. I don't trust their Mogsey. I wouldn't put it past him to slip him a Mickey Finn, he'd think that was dead funny! And if he doesn't turn up tomorrow I'll kill him and their Mogsey!'

Louisa laughed. 'He wouldn't dare not to Sall. Not after all this expense, your Da would kill the pair of them!'

'Don't bet on that, Lou. He's going with them.'

'Then you've nothing to worry about, he'll watch them.'

'I just don't trust Mogsey, Lou. They're getting some stuff off your Eddie and he's as bad!'

'Stop worrying, Sall, everything will be just fine. It will be a day to remember.'

It was a day to remember for a number of reasons and not all of them pleasant.

Louisa was round at Cicero Terrace bright and early only to find that utter chaos reigned. Frank was still in bed nursing a hangover. Agnes was frantically trying to keep the younger Coopers calm and clean but did not appear to be having much success as they were all over-excited and kept running in and out, yelling and fighting. Sall was standing in her long petticoats bemoaning the shambles to her friend Mavis who still had a head full of curling papers, covered by a scarf.

Instantly, Louisa took charge. She made a pot of tea and dispatched Mavis upstairs with a cup for the bride's father, working on the assumption that the sight of a strange girl in his bedroom would soon stir him from his stupor. Then she told the young Coopers that if they could sit still and say absolutely nothing, not a single word, for ten whole minutes, she'd give them each a threepenny bit. She pushed Agnes down into the chair by the range and handed her a cup of tea and then set about tidying up a bit.

'I don't know what I'd have done without you, Lou. My head is thumping!' Sall wailed.

'You can have a cup of tea, too. Let's just all calm down!' She'd barely got the words out when there was a loud hammering on the front door and Sall started to struggle to her feet.

'Sit down! It will only be the post or something like that.' She went to the door and returned laden down with flowers. 'Where shall I put them?' she asked.

'Give them to our Lily, she can put them in the yard, there's no room anywhere else,' Agnes instructed.

Lily was duly told to take the bouquets, one by one, and

put them carefully in the yard, without standing on the trailing fronds of greenery.

Mavis appeared. 'Well, that worked! He's up. Looks a bit green, like, but he'll be all right.'

Sall was feeling better. 'Right. Mam, you go and get yourself ready because you'll be going first.'

'What about this lot?' Agnes asked, indicating her brood who were sitting in a row on the sofa with their lips pressed together, trying not to laugh. They were pushing and poking one another though, the deal hadn't included that.

'I'll get them ready,' Louisa said firmly. 'Any messing about and there'll be no threepenny joeys! Now get dressed and I'll do your hair and fix your head-dresses and then you don't even blink an eyelid! Sall, we'll get you dressed and after that Mavis and I can concentrate on ourselves. We've got an hour still.' She looked at the brass alarm clock on the mantel. 'Where's Bessie?'

'She's getting ready at her Mam's. She said it would be quieter – she's no fool!'

Despite some last-minute panics, everyone was ready on time and for the first time in all their lives the Cooper family travelled to church in style. In black hackney cabs decorated with white ribbons. The whole of the Terrace turned out to see them.

When they arrived at the church, Louisa, Mavis and Bessie helped to spread Sall's train out in all its glory. Louisa noticed that Sall had gone very pale and she gave her hand a quick squeeze and smiled. 'You look absolutely gorgeous! He won't believe his eyes! Now go on and try to smile!'

As she followed Sall and her father down the aisle she caught sight of Doreen at the end of one pew. Sall's descriptive forecast hadn't been far wrong, she thought. Doreen's overweight form had been squeezed into a black dress overprinted with huge, scarlet poppies and she wore a bright red, straw hat with a large spray of black and red feathers attached to one side. Beside her stood Tad in his uniform. She averted her eyes as she drew level, fixing her gaze on the gleaming satin of Sall's train. She could feel his eyes on her and it felt strange. Of course she'd known he would be here, but she hadn't really thought about it. Strangely she felt nothing. Nothing at all.

The ceremony went without a hitch as did the wedding breakfast, held in the community hall. Everyone got on very well as they were already well acquainted with one another. There was no division of the respective parties, something that often happened. The bride's family at one end of the room and the groom's at the other. Even Mogsey appeared to be on his best behaviour. He even looked smart and dignified in his uniform. If that word could ever be applied to Mogsey Green, Louisa thought.

She did feel a little sorry for Eddie as he stood with his mates. He was the only one of their age group in 'civvies'. Looking at him made her think of Mike Crowley and she wondered where he was and what he was doing. Was he hundreds of feet below the ocean, dogging enemy ships? That train of thought automatically led her to think of her Da and, as always, she uttered a prayer that he would get home safe and sound.

The first thing to go wrong was the gradual disappearance of all the men. The young ones sidled out first, to be followed by the older ones until only Harry, Frank Cooper and Mr Green were left. The latter two looked miserable, their glances straying to the door.

'Where've they all disappeared to?' she asked Sall who was sitting with Agnes, her new mother-in-law, Doreen, and a collection of aunts and cousins and who was looking less than pleased. Harry was standing dutifully behind Sall's chair.

'The match,' Harry answered. 'Of course I didn't want to go.'

'If you'd have gone this would have been the shortest marriage ever!' came the tart reply from his wife.

'You don't mean to tell me they've all gone off to the football match? I didn't think there was one. It's a bit late isn't it?' Louisa was incredulous.

182

'It's the reserves and it's a friendly, to raise money for the war effort,' Harry supplied.

'Isn't it just typical! I suppose if there hadn't been a match they would have kicked a ball around Stanley Park themselves! All this food and drink going to waste!' Agnes cried.

'It won't go to waste, they'll be back. They've not emigrated!' Frank said glumly.

'I wish they had! No bloody use, any of them! All they're fit for is swilling ale and stuffing their bellies and . . .'

'Shut up, Doreen!' Sall snapped.

As Frank had predicted they all returned at six o'clock in a very convivial mood that was temporarily quelled by the acid comments of their womenfolk. They immediately attacked the sandwiches and bridge rolls and began to argue the merits and demerits of Everton Football Club's reserve team and the vanquished visitors. To them there was no such thing as a friendly. You went out to win! The bandiments went on until the band arrived and they were dragged off to dance with their long-suffering wives, mothers, sisters and girlfriends.

As the evening wore on it was obvious that Doreen Buckley was becoming the worse for wear; becoming morose and argumentative. She hated her life, she told Mavis whom she'd managed to corner. She was too young to be stuck with a baby, a nagging mother-in-law and a husband who didn't give a damn for her! She should be out enjoying herself. And she hadn't had a do like this. It wasn't fair that their Sall should have all this when she'd had to nag and scream at her 'loving' husband for a few bob to buy this outfit! She couldn't let the side down, could she?

Mavis agreed that she couldn't and looked around for someone to rescue her, but she was stuck.

And their Sall wouldn't have her as a bridesmaid or matron of honour, but she'd had that Bessie. She was her own sister, her own flesh and blood, but that hadn't mattered. Then there was that Lou Langford, all done up and looking like Vivien Leigh in *Gone With The Wind*, in that satin dress. She thought she was better than everyone else, did that one. She could tell Mavis a few things about Lou Langford!

Mavis disentangled herself on the pretext of getting them both another drink and made a dash for the opposite corner of the room.

Tad had gone outside, wishing now he hadn't worn his uniform. It was uncomfortably hot even with his battledress jerkin off. He mopped his damp brow and leaned against the wall. At least he'd managed to escape from Doreen for most of the day. He grinned to himself. Trust Eddie to know about the football match. It had been better than hanging around all afternoon being bored stiff by all those women. Eddie seemed to be doing all right for himself, but then he didn't have Doreen round his neck like a millstone. God, but she looked awful in that outfit. It was something a high-class tart would have worn. She looked loud and cheap beside Sall's delicate, white purity and Louisa's soft, pink, femininity. Oh, Louisa! Louisa! Why did he keep on tormenting himself? She'd barely glanced at him and he could have curled up and died when Doreen had dragged him onto the dance floor and draped herself over him. God, he hated her.

A movement caught his eye and he turned his head and sucked in his breath. Louisa was standing a few yards away from him. Her head was tilted back as she drew in deep breaths of night air. She'd taken off her coronet and her hair fell in thick, soft waves around her neck. A dim shaft of moonlight filtering through a crack between the houses that backed onto the small yard, caught the pink satin and turned it into a sheath of rose-tinted crystal. Just looking at her made him ache.

'Louisa!' It was little more than a whisper.

She turned. 'Who's that?'

He moved forward, out of the shadows.

'Oh. It's . . . you!'

'Louisa, don't go in! Not yet, please!'

'We've nothing to say to each other, Tad.'

He stepped towards her, his eyes pleading. She looked just the way he'd imagined her in a thousand dreams. 'I did want to see you and talk to you! I wanted to explain, but everything happened so fast!'

She shook her head. 'Tad, it's all over. What we had has gone. I've just put it down to bitter experience.' She half smiled. 'As Eddie said then, I was just a kid. It's over Tad. I don't blame you now. I don't feel anything for you any more, except perhaps . . . pity.'

'Oh, God! Louisa, don't say that! Not . . . pity!' All the suppressed frustration and anger burst forth and unintentionally, he caught her by the shoulders and shook her gently. 'I hate her! I loathe her! She trapped me, I swear she did!'

'Stop it, Tad! Stop it!' She shook off his grip and stepped backwards.

'Don't go, Louisa! Listen to me! Lotty's not mine, I know she's not! She doesn't even look like me! I'll divorce her, I will!'

'No!' She was shocked and angry. 'How can you say such things about a child . . . a baby? You divorce Doreen if you must, if you hate her as much as you say you do. That's your affair. Just don't do it for me, Tad Buckley! It's over! Get that into your head once and for all! I don't love you any more and I never will again!' She pushed past him and moved towards the open doorway, but he caught her arm and clung to it, following her into the room.

She stopped dead as she saw Doreen standing, swaying a little, a few feet from her. She paled as Doreen's finger pointed at her and she began to scream obscenities. Her hands went to her mouth as she realized that the buzz of conversation and laughter was diminishing. Only the band continued to play, then the musicians, too, fell silent one by one and the discordant melody died away.

'Look at her! Look at her! She's still carryin' on with my husband! My husband and he won't even look at me

185

because he's too bleedin' hot for her! You can all see what she is! She's his tart, his fancy piece. His whore!'

'Shut your bloody mouth!' Tad yelled, pushing his way towards his wife but Frank Cooper got there first. The sound of his hand as he struck his daughter across the mouth, sending her sprawling to the floor, was like a rifle crack. He glared at Tad. 'Get her out of here and keep her out! And keep her out of my house, too! She's no daughter of mine!'

Louisa's gaze flitted over the sea of faces that surrounded her and she felt faint. Then Sall was beside her and Harry was urging the band to strike up again and Mogsey and Eddie were shouting, 'Come on, let's get the party going again!'

'Oh, Sall! I'm so sorry. I didn't know he was out there!'

'It wasn't your fault, Lou. I should have known she'd try to spoil things. I shouldn't have invited her in the first place. I didn't want to.'

'It doesn't matter about me. I don't care what she called me, but I didn't want anything to ruin your day!'

'It hasn't! Really! Look, everyone's forgotten about her already. Come on, Harry will get us both a drink.' And looping her now rather dusty train over her arm, Sall guided her back into the centre of the room.

Eddie stepped forward and said firmly that they were going to dance.

'I only went out for some air. I didn't know he was there! Oh, I could have died of shame!'

'He should keep her under control! Hold your head up, Louisa, and smile. You've nothing to be ashamed of. I'll fix that bitch one of these days, so help me God!' Eddie muttered.

She spent the rest of the night dancing, a fixed smile on her lips. Her facial muscles aching from the permanent stretching.

CHAPTER THIRTEEN

Evvie's wedding was a much more sedate affair. To Louisa's delight her Da was home and to the relief of Babsey he'd managed to get almost everything she'd requested. Of course she'd made much of Doreen Buckley's behaviour and said that thankfully there was no-one in either their family or the Gouldsons who would disgrace themselves. Eddie had been told that Tad was definitely not welcome, a sentiment endorsed by John who had heard of the unfortunate episode from Louisa. Babsey also stated that there would be no disappearing to football matches or dog races or anything else. She wasn't having Evvie's wedding turned into a circus. So the whole affair had been very dignified, if a little stuffy.

On the 22 June the *Ceramic* sailed again as the news came through that France had surrendered.

'Oh, Da, do you have to go? Can't you say you're ill?' Louisa begged.

'No, Lou, it's my duty. We're on our own now and we need all the supplies we can get.'

'Not even just one trip?'

He shook his head. 'I have to do my bit, just as your Uncle Jim is doing his.'

'But he's not done anything yet! There have been no raids!'

He didn't want to alarm her but he was certain now that the long-expected air raids would soon materialize. He didn't want to leave her, to leave any of them. He hated being away, but there was no help for it. 'Now, Lou, it's not like you to act like this!'

'I get frightened, Da! I don't want to be left alone and if anything happened to you . . .'

'You're not alone. You've got the family. Cheer up and give me a hug. I'm one of those "weeds" remember!'

She'd tried to smile as she'd waved him goodbye.

With only the English Channel separating the protagonists, the full force of the Luftwaffe was used to try to destroy British air power to facilitate an easy invasion. All through the summer months the Battle of Britain raged in the skies above. Sometimes German planes got as far as Woodvale, near Southport, and the citizens of Liverpool watched them buzzing angrily overhead and cheered when the RAF's Spitfires scored a hit.

The first bombs fell on the night of 8 August on Prenton on the Wirral side of the Mersey. Wallasey and Birkenhead suffered on the 17th and at midnight on the 19th the first incendiaries fell on Liverpool. There were a few sporadic raids throughout the rest of the month and on the 31st the phoney war came to an end. Night after night the sirens wailed and then, huddled in dugouts or Anderson shelters, under stairs and in cellars, the terrified population heard the heavy, double-throated throb of the Luftwaffe's heavy bombers.

On 2 October, when the raids had begun to become something of the norm, the *Ceramic* sailed into the Mersey at the head of Convoy 184. After ascertaining that Babsey and the family were safe and well, John Langford took the tram into town to meet Louisa.

As on previous occasions he talked with Joe Doran while she finished up and got ready to leave.

They walked out into Dale Street just in time to see a bus trundling towards William Brown Street.

'Come on, Da, we'll catch it if we run! Heaven knows when the next one will be along, or the next tram for that matter!'

Hand in hand they ran and John jumped onto the platform, hauling her up with him. Both were red-faced and panting as he fished in his pocket for the money for the fares.

'Good job you're fit, mate! Here you go. Two to the Rotunda.'

'Fit!' John gasped. 'Fit for nothing more like! Any room upstairs?'

'Might be. None down here though.'

They both climbed the spiral staircase to the upper deck and found two vacant seats.

'Your Aunt Babsey tells me the Luftwaffe's paid us quite a few visits.'

She nodded. She didn't want to talk about it. She didn't want him to know how she'd sat on the cellar steps gripped by fear, her hands over her ears, trying to shut out the noise of the bombardment. The yard wasn't big enough for an Anderson shelter and Babsey refused to go to the large public shelters. If she had to 'go', then she was 'going' in her own home, not herded in a pen like cattle, she'd stated emphatically.

'Still, it hasn't been as bad as in London, so I hear.'

'What about you? Anything . . .?'

'Not a thing. A clear run all the way home.' He made light of the hardships and the constant anxiety. 'What the hell's that!' He cocked his head to one side and listened.

She couldn't hear anything over the buzz of conversation. 'What's the matter?'

Other people were beginning to twist around in their seats and then she heard the sound. 'Da, what is it?'

They heard the conductor shout and turning around she uttered a scream before John pushed her roughly down onto the floor, covering her with his body.

She'd glimpsed the plane and she could still hear it, louder now, then there was a rapid, sharp, pinging sound, like giant hailstones hitting the roof of the bus. She screamed again and was thrown violently across the aisle as the bus swerved, weaving backwards and forwards across the road. Then she was hauled to her feet and bundled down the stairs. She lost one shoe and her knee was grazed on the metal treads and all the time the whine of the plane's engines and the rattle of bullets continued.

Hanging on to her Da's arm for dear life she jumped off the bus and ran beside him across the pavement.

'Run, Lou! Run!' he yelled at her, his legs taking massive strides, pulling her along with him.

The driver had got them as close to a shelter as he could but the bullets bounced off the pavements around them. At the entrance to the shelter the helmet was suddenly knocked from an auxiliary fireman's head and he, too, dived for cover. All three of them landed in a heap on the floor.

'Bloody hell! That was close, must be my lucky day!' The man managed a grin as they disentangled themselves. She was shaking so much that her teeth were chattering and, after he'd hugged her, Big John Langford laughed.

'You see, Lou! Bloody indestructible, they call me!'

'Oh, Da! Da!' She was laughing and crying at the same time.

To Louisa's disappointment the *Ceramic* sailed again seven days later and the weeks dragged by. Everyone was tired for there were few nights when sleep was not interrupted. She found, like everyone else, that she was becoming used to it. That she could gulp and manage a smile and say 'That was a close one!' whenever there was a direct hit in the area. Nerves were frayed but everyone tried not to show it and after a bad night people emerged for work the following morning, tired but still cheerful.

Ronny and Sid had been called up, so there were only herself and Joe Doran to attend to the Union business and try to help the relatives of men who had been killed or who had been bombed out of their homes. There was no central agency that these unfortunates could go to and, in their shattered state, they didn't know where to turn.

Groups of women arrived with children clinging to their skirts, begging for help and all she could do was make out a list of all the organizations they would have to visit to obtain help with housing, clothing, documents and money. Often she gave them the bus or tram fare out of her own purse and she knew that Joe Doran did the same.

It was nearly five o'clock on the Saturday before Christmas and she'd seen to the last family who'd come for help.

'I think we'll shut up shop, luv. I'm beat and I'm on duty tonight.' Joe, like all the other men, was a volunteer in the auxiliary force of wardens, firemen and police.

She smiled at him. He looked tired and despondent. 'It's all so pointless! There's no proper organization! God help them, they shouldn't have to go traipsing all over town dragging the kids with them. Not after what they've already been through! That poor soul only had the clothes she stood up in and she'd been passed from one department to another all day. She hardly knew what day it was. Why can't they get organized?'

'That's bureaucracy, Louisa.'

'Can't we do something? Talk to whoever runs all these departments and maybe get them to let us handle some of the work. Get everything in one place, establish an emergency centre?'

'You've still a lot to learn. You'll never cut through all the red tape that easily. It's a good idea but they'll never agree to it. Go on, finish up and get off home for what's left of the weekend.'

He went back into his office and she began to clear her desk.

She heard the door open and was about to say, 'I'm sorry but we're just closing' but the words died on her lips. It was Mike Crowley.

'I thought I'd find you here.'

'A few more minutes and I wouldn't have been. Look who's here!' she called out to Joe.

'It's the proverbial bad penny! Good to see you, lad!' They shook hands.

'Home is the sailor . . .' she quipped.

He grinned and jangled the coins in his pocket.

'And rarin' to spend his pay by the sound of it,' Joe laughed.

She thought how smart and how much older he looked in his uniform.

He held out his right arm proudly. 'Been promoted.' He pointed with his left hand to the row of brass buttons that ran around the edge of his jacket cuff. 'Chief Petty Officer.'

'You're a bit young, aren't you?' Joe queried.

'I suppose so, but it's a case of dead men's shoes.'

She shuddered.

Mike laughed. 'They put these buttons on to stop us wiping our noses on our sleeves,' he joked. 'I came to see if your clerk here would like to come dancing at the Grafton with me?'

She was dumbfounded.

'Well, Louisa, aren't you going to answer him?' Joe urged.

She didn't know what to say. He'd really put her in a quandary. 'I don't know if I should.'

Mike was leaning on the desk top staring at her, almost defying her to refuse him.

'Why not?' Joe asked.

'It's . . .'

'It's a case of the Orange and the Green,' Mike replied.

'Oh, get out of here, the pair of you! There's a war on. Enjoy yourselves and to hell with religion!'

'You heathen!' Mike laughed.

'I'm an agnostic and I'm not going to apologize for it.'

'What's that?' she asked.

'I'm not convinced there even is a God, a Supreme Being or anything mystical at all and as for formal religion . . . look at all the trouble it causes. You two are a prime example! Go on. Go dancing. Enjoy yourselves.'

She was still very apprehensive. She wasn't dressed for dancing, she stalled.

'What's the matter with that dress? You girls! "Vanity, vanity, thy name is woman"!' Joe quoted.

'I'll have to get a message home. They'll be worried if I don't turn up.'

'Phone your Evvie.' Joe was being very helpful.

'What will I tell her?' She appealed to them both.

'Tell her you're going dancing with a friend.'

'She'll ask who. Sall's married and Annie moved away and I don't see much of her now.'

'Then tell her it's a boyfriend! Does she have to know every single detail? Don't you have any privacy?' Mike said.

'There'll be murder!'

'She doesn't have to know it's me and who's going to see us anyway? Nearly every man there will be in uniform, I'll be just another sailor. Besides, this time I want you to enjoy yourself. I don't want you to be in the throes of some disaster!'

She had to smile at that and agreed.

On the way there she related to him the episode of the attack on the bus, something that had made the headlines in the *Echo*. She laughed as she finished, 'I didn't think it funny then though. I was scared to death!'

He told her of life in a submarine, laughing at the hardships and the danger and at a newly discovered fear. That of small, cramped spaces. He didn't tell her that there were times when he had to fight down the sheer panic that overtook him in those first few minutes when they heard the order, 'Dive! Dive! Dive!' Yet despite all this he did feel safer beneath the sea. Nor did he tell her of the hits they'd scored. It was at times like that when he thought of John Langford and all the other men he knew on the convoys and their escorts. He'd quickly learned that war was far from exciting. It was sickening.

'It's ages since I've been here. The last time I came it was Christmas, too. I came with Annie but I left early.'

'Then I hope you enjoy tonight.'

She'd handed her hat and coat to the cloakroom attendant and he'd handed in his uniform cap. He'd been right, she thought, glancing around the foyer. There were uniforms everywhere. It was a common sight these days. She still felt uneasy, remembering what her Da had said about 'sticking to your own kind', but she tried to shrug it aside. It was just a dance, that's all. He was home on leave and wanted to enjoy himself. Yet the doubts persisted. There must be other girls, Catholic girls, he could have asked. Oh, what did it matter. Joe Doran was right. There was a war on and they shouldn't let bigotry interfere with their lives.

They made their way onto the dance floor and she thought how festive they'd managed to make the place look with paper chains and balloons. The big glass sphere, suspended above the floor, caught the light as it revolved, showering everyone with multi-coloured prisms of light. The band was in an alcove and Mrs Wilf Hamer was conducting.

He took her hand and led her into a waltz on the packed floor. 'If I stand on your toes, don't blame me! There's hardly any room to move.' He smiled down at her.

'I'm glad you're in the Navy and not the Army then. Not with those great, heavy boots they wear.' The smile on her lips died and she froze in his arms as the rising wail of the siren drowned out the music. People around them also stood still, uncertain what to do. As the doleful notes died away the band played on gallantly and, taking their cue from them, the dancers resumed as did the chatter of voices. Attempting to drown out the throbbing drone of the approaching aircraft.

The next few minutes were terrifying. The Olympia Theatre next door received a direct hit and the force of the blast ripped off half of the roof of the dance hall. A hail of shrapnel tore through the remains of the plaster ceiling. Suddenly, Mike thrust her away from him and forced his way through the crowd. She pressed her fist into her mouth to cut off the scream, her eyes riveted to the huge glass ball that was swaying gently. The scene enfolded so slowly, or so it seemed, yet it could only have taken seconds. The glass sphere falling, Mike launching himself bodily at the stunned couple clinging together, the sudden backward surge of the crowd and the crash as the ball shattered into a thousand shards.

Then she was pushing her way forward, ignoring the cries and the hands that sought to restrain her. She couldn't see him! She couldn't see him! She started to scream his name and then he was there beside her. She flung herself into his arms. 'Mike! Mike! I thought it had hit you! I thought . . .'

He held her to him. 'It's all right, Lou!' he soothed.

She raised her head and looked at him through a blur of tears and tried to smile. She must try to calm down. What would he think of her? She began to wipe away the tears from her cheeks with the back of her hand.

'Here, use this.' He was smiling and offering her his handkerchief.

This time she did manage a smile. 'What were you saying about being in the throes of some disaster? Trouble seems to follow me.'

He squeezed her hand. 'Don't say things like that! It's not true and I'm the one who is supposed to be superstitious. We're going to enjoy ourselves.'

Those injured by flying glass and debris were quickly attended to and the dance floor was cleared. Within three-quarters of an hour and with the searchlights sweeping the sky now visible overhead, Mrs Hamer emerged from under the piano and gave the signal for the dancing to begin again.

He held her closer and she buried her face in his shoulder. Inside she was still shaking and it was so comforting to have strong arms around you and a broad shoulder to lean on.

Mike too was shaken, although like every other man there, he gave no outward sign. He wasn't used to hearing the earth-shaking explosions or the mayhem that ensued. His was a quiet world. His battlefield was the cold, dark water of the Atlantic. His was an almost silent war compared to this and for the first time he realized just what people at home, people like Louisa who was still shaking in his arms, had to suffer.

Towards midnight and with no let-up in the bombardment, a group of men set up a large microphone on the bandstand and one called, 'Quiet! Quiet, please!' The dancers slowly fell silent.

'This is the BBC Home Service. Tonight we've been broadcasting from all over the city and we're ending with a message to London.' He then indicated that Mr Munro, the manager of the ballroom, speak into the mouthpiece.

That gentleman cleared his throat and then said in a clear, crisp tone, 'Hello, London. I am speaking to you from the Grafton Ballrooom, Liverpool. I have to tell you that the theatre next door got it a few hours ago and we've lost half of our roof, but everyone here is enjoying themselves!' He waved his arms in a circular movement and the crowd responded with a loud cheer, accompanied by a fanfare from the band. He went on, 'So, if you can keep it up, then so can we!'

His words brought another cheer before the BBC. man waved them into silence again. The speaker crackled and then a voice came through as clear as a bell. 'We can keep it up all right, and we're proud that you, Liverpool, are doing the same. So, stick it Merseyside, it's worth it!'

This again brought a cheer and the band struck up with 'Rule Britannia' but there were tears in many eyes.

It was five a.m. when the all-clear sounded and everyone collected their coats and went out into the cold dawn. West Derby Road was a shambles. Fires were still raging, all the tram lines were down and sparking as water from broken mains seeped over them. The road was a sea of shattered glass and rubble.

'Oh, dear God!' Louisa gasped, clutching Mike's arm.

'It's a mess all right and it looks as if we're going to have to walk home.'

'What time is it?'

'A quarter past five.'

Despite the traumas of the previous hours she looked horrified. 'Aunt Babsey will kill me! I've never been out this late, it's . . . morning!'

'She won't. She wouldn't expect you to have tried to get home in the middle of a raid now would she? They've probably been in the shelter all night too.'

Fear clutched at her heart. 'She won't go to the shelter. Oh, I hope they're all right!'

'We'll find that out as soon as we get home. If we go at a brisk pace it won't take that long.' And putting his arm around her shoulder he guided her between the rubble.

He left her at the bottom of Northumberland Terrace, giving her a chaste peck on the cheek. 'Goodbye, Louisa, and thanks for a . . . memorable evening. I can't say "wonderful" can I?'

She smiled up at him. 'Not really, but I enjoyed it. I'm glad I let you talk me into it.'

'Can I talk you into coming out with me again?'

She looked quickly up the Terrace, a frown creasing her brow.

'I don't mean this leave, next time?'

'Do you think we should?'

'Why not? It's only a dance, we can't get up to much with about another couple of hundred people there, can we?'

Cautiously she nodded, feeling confused. She liked him, he was fun to be with and she felt safe with him, yet a warning bell sounded in her mind. She ignored it and smiled.

'See you next time then?' he said as he watched her walk away. He was a fool, he told himself. He shouldn't see her again, it wasn't being fair. He was becoming fond of her and that only spelled trouble and she had enough to contend with. Besides, his Mam – small as she was – would belt him all around the kitchen if she thought he was seeing a Protestant girl. Joe was right. Religion caused more problems than it solved.

To her relief everyone was safe although tired. She was

197

surprised to see Evvie in the kitchen with everyone else. Uncle Jim, covered from head to foot in dust, grime and soot, was gulping a cup of tea before going back out again. He'd been out all night.

'I'm sorry, I couldn't get back because of the raid. I thought it would never end.' She sat down at the table and nodded her thanks for the cup of tea Babsey put in front of her.

'We realized that, but we were worried just the same. Where were you?'

'In the Grafton. We . . . I walked home, all the tramlines are down. Half the roof was blown off, you should see West Derby Road, it's terrible!'

'No thanks, there's been enough damage round here. I'm off now,' Jim said.

'Drink that up and then you'd better get some rest. Evvie, you'd better get back now.' Babsey was bone weary.

'Why aren't you at home?' Louisa asked her cousin.

Evvie looked a little shamefaced. 'It got so bad and I was so scared, so . . .' She shrugged.

Louisa nodded. She didn't blame Evvie. If she hadn't had Mike to calm her down she would have run home too. Raid or no raid.

'Who did you go with, you've never mentioned anyone special?' Tired though she was, Babsey was still curious.

'It wasn't anyone special. Just someone who comes into the office now and then. I saw him tonight and he asked me out.' She hadn't told any lies but she got up. 'I'm going to get changed.' It was best to go now, before Aunt Babsey had time to question her further.

The following night the raid was concentrated on the north end of the city and Bootle, but the main target was Manchester. Despite this Der Fuehrer's Christmas present to Liverpool had wreaked havoc on the town hall, municipal offices, central police offices, food warehouses in Dublin Street, Princes Parade and Landing Stage, the Adelphi Hotel, the Dock Board offices, the list was endless. In Bentinck Street, beneath the five railway arches, a direct hit had brought down tons of masonry on top of the crowds sheltered there. As well as the Olympia Theatre, Webb's chemical factory in Hanover Street went up like a ball of flame. Huge fires burned in Hatton Garden, St John's Market and Hoickenhall Alley. St George's Hall was hit and the Law Library completely destroyed. The Royal Infirmary, Mill Road Infirmary, St Anthon's school, it went on and on without adding the heavy damage sustained by housing. On the night of the second raid, Liverpool's Parish Church of Our Lady and St Nicholas that had been on the waterfront for centuries, was completely gutted. All that remained were the walls and the tower. As she trudged to work amidst the piles of smoking rubble, the fractured water mains, the trailing telephone and tram wires, Louisa began to think that maybe Mike was right. Maybe it was safer to be hundreds of feet below the ocean.

CHAPTER FOURTEEN

The New Year of 1941 came in quietly enough. Since the awful carnage before Christmas the raids had been spasmodic. Both Harry and Arnold came home on leave. Sall had changed her job and had volunteered for war work and then wished she hadn't. She worked in the munitions factories out at Speke which meant long and often interrupted journeys, hard, messy and dangerous work and long hours.

'I'm sorry I bothered now, but I feel as though I've got to do my bit seeing that Harry is doing his.'

'I don't think I'll be long with the Union myself. I hear they're bringing in a sort of conscription for women. I've got fire-watching to do and I'm to be trained to use those stirrup pump things for the street fire-fighting. I suppose you'll get roped in for that too.'

'Probably. I don't know how I'll manage to fit it all in, not with the house as well.'

Louisa glanced around the tiny house. Sall didn't have much but what she did have was polished to death and you could have eaten your dinner off the floor.

'Have you heard any more from . . . you know who?' Louisa had confided in Sall about her date with Mike Crowley. Sall had already vehemently echoed John Langford's warning.

'No. I don't suppose I will either. I mean he can't write to me, can he? They'd throw a blue fit.'

'Then you'll have to wait until he turns up at the office again. Maybe it's best that you will be moving from there, he won't know where to find you and no-one round here is going to tell him!'

'Joe Doran will.'

'Not if he's got any sense he won't.'

'He's just a friend, Sall, that's all!'

Sall shook her head. 'Just make sure you keep it that way, Lou! It just won't work, you know that!'

'It's nothing serious, he's taken me out once!'

Sall shook her head again and made a gesture of despair. 'Lou, I hate to throw you out, but Harry and me are going out and I'm not even washed yet.'

'Where is he?'

'Round at his Mam's, trying to cadge a bit of tea. By the time I finish work I'm always at the end of the queue and whatever they had has gone. Ration book or no ration book!'

'I'll be going then.'

'If your Evvie can get me a tin of something I'll pay over the odds for it,' Sall said as she showed her to the door.

'It's not Evvie you want to see for that, Sall, it's Eddie. He's the one with all the right contacts.'

'Bloody spiv! I wouldn't pay his prices, not even if I was starving! He'd better watch himself or he'll end up in Walton Jail!'

Louisa sighed. 'You know Eddie, he's too crafty for that.'

'He'd sell his own Mam he would.'

She laughed. 'He'd have a hard job with Aunt Babsey! She'd sell him first and get the better bargain.'

The winter months were miserable for everything was rationed, but at least it had its good side, Babsey said. It was bad flying weather and the Luftwaffe was grounded. In March Evvie announced she was expecting and both Jim and Babsey were delighted at the prospect of becoming grandparents. It was the only bright bit of news that month, for the raiders returned. Life was a tedious round of work, housework and queuing for everything. The nights were spent fire-watching. As she had expected, Louisa had been informed that she was to transfer to the Petroleum Board at Dingle Bank but the conversation she overheard between Babsey and Jim had made her smile.

'Why couldn't they leave her where she is? That place is just behind the Herculaneum Dock and it's a death-trap! If it gets hit you'll be able to see the flames in Manchester!'

'Babsey, there's no use you arguing, there's . . .'

'I know! "There's a war on." I've never been so sick of a saying as I am of that one! But she's happy working at the Union.'

Jim had laughed. 'That's not what you said when she went there!'

'I know, but we never thought we'd have to suffer anything like this, did we? We never imagined that girls and women would be fire-watching!' Then seeing her husband's face she cried, 'Don't say it again, Jim MacGann, or I'll scream!'

Joe Doran had been sorry to see her go and the feeling was mutual.

'I'll need you back when this is all over, you know.'

'And I'll be happy to come back. I've enjoyed it. I feel as though I've been doing something worthwhile.'

'You have. You've got the knack of organization and of getting things done. You'd make a good city councillor some day.'

She laughed. 'Me? I couldn't sit there in the town hall with all the bigwigs, I'd be terrified!'

'You'd be terrified, after all we've been through?'

'Oh, you know what I mean. Here, I feel secure. I know what I'm doing. I'd be out of my depth doing something like that. Besides, they're all educated people and they speak . . . properly.'

'So what? It's the people of this city they're supposed to represent. And what the people need is someone from their own class who understands their problems and can get something done about them.'

'Oh, stop it! I won't be able to get my head through the door next, the way you're going on!'

'Just bear it in mind. When all this is over we're going to need good people.'

She hugged him. 'I'll miss you.'

'I'll miss you, too. What do I tell Mike when he comes looking for you?'

The smile vanished from her face. 'I don't know. I really don't!'

He looked perturbed. Was it wrong to encourage them? What future would they have? He smiled cynically. What future did anyone have? Did anyone indeed have the right to even dare to think of the future? 'If he asks me, Louisa, I'm not telling him any lies.'

'Did I ask you to?' she said, smiling.

On Thursday 1 May she was getting ready for bed. She was tired and she was finding the work for the Petroleum Board tedious and utterly boring, though she knew it was necessary. She'd even considered applying to transfer to the munitions factories but Babsey had very firmly quashed that idea.

'With your skills! You'll do nothing of the sort! You've never worked in a factory and you're not going to start now! Your Da would never forgive me!' And that had been the end of that idea.

It was a couple of minutes to eleven and she could hear Aunt Babsey still downstairs, setting the table for breakfast. She smiled to herself. Nothing changed her Aunt's routine. Tommy was already asleep in the other half of the room.

She'd just turned back the covers when the siren went, its wail rising like that of the Banshee, and she groaned. Oh, not again! When would she ever get a decent night's sleep? She pulled on her clothes over her nightdress and snatched the pillow and quilt from the bed and followed a bleary-eyed Tommy downstairs.

Babsey had blankets under her arm, a biscuit tin filled with sandwiches and the kettle in her hands. Mattresses, candles and a primus stove were kept in the cellar. Jim was shrugging on his coat and grabbing his tin hat from behind the door and Eddie was doing the same. He was on fire-fighting duty and she thanked God that it wasn't her turn on the street rota.

'How anyone is supposed to get any sleep is beyond me!' Babsey muttered in annoyance. 'You two take care, don't go doing anything foolhardy! I'd sooner have a live coward than a dead hero!'

'For God's sake, Babsey, don't say things like that!' Jim snapped at her.

'Oh, you know what I mean! Come on, Louisa, let's get down into the cellar and let's hope they bloody well go home early!'

By midnight they knew 'they' weren't going home early and that the raid was a heavy one. Above them the night air was filled with the menacing, droning throb of the Heinkels. The screaming and whistling of bombs, incendiaries and landmines and the earth shuddered and vibrated as hundreds of hits were scored.

Jim and Frank Cooper worked side by side, sweat pouring down their faces, induced by the heat from the flames and their exertions, as they risked life and limb to drag people from beneath their devastated homes. They were oblivious to the danger that surrounded them as fire engines screamed past and the police and specials worked frenziedly with ambulance crews.

Eddie had started out at the bottom of the Terrace but had worked his way down towards St Domingo Road. He, too, was sweating and the dust, dirt and smoke burned his eyes and throat. He could manage the stirrup pump quite well by hooking it around his right hand and pumping the handle with his left. Like everyone else he was surrounded by total chaos.

The pump was soon empty and he flung it away cursing. It would take time to refill it and besides the Fire Brigade had arrived, so he concentrated on trying to shift some of the rubble that was blocking a doorway. He strained and pulled at a solid piece of masonry until it moved slightly. In the light cast by the flames, he caught a glimpse of something shiny and black, lying half covered by debris.

He bent down, scrabbling in the rubbish and at last his fingers closed over it and he drew it out. It was a cash box, similar to the one his Mam had. He opened it and his eyes lit up as he caught sight of the roll of white five pound notes inside. He glanced around quickly. Everyone was far too intent on their work to notice what he was doing. Quickly he stuffed the money into the inside pocket of his jacket, then pushed the box back under a pile of broken bricks. Whoever it belonged to wouldn't need it now. If they'd been alive they would have been frantically trying to recover it. He might as well keep it rather than give it over to a scuffer to hand in. He shoved the twisted door frame aside and yelled, 'Anyone inside?' Upon hearing no reply he went back and picked up the discarded stirrup pump and was instructed by a policeman to give a hand in tearing down what was left of an end house.

It was Jimmy Townsend, exempt from National Service because of a weak chest, who found the second windfall of the night. He knew Jimmy well, he often used him in his 'business deals' as he called his nefarious trading.

'Eh, Eddie! Over here! Come over here!' Jimmy shouted.

'What for?' he yelled back.

'I need a hand with this beam, it's too heavy for me to shift!'

He was about to shout 'Bugger off!' when he saw Jimmy's head jerk significantly to one side and he clambered over a mountain of bricks, plaster and broken lathes. 'What beam?'

'There's no bleedin' beam. Look down there!'

They both squatted down and peered into what had been the cellar of a house.

'I can't see anything.'

An incendiary falling on the next street obligingly lit up the sky.

'Look, the gas and electric meters! They've burst open, it's like an Aladdin's cave down there!'

Eddie looked at Jimmy. 'Right. Fifty-fifty split,' before

they both eased themselves down into the hole and began to scratch around on the floor for the coins.

The light from a torch swept over them. 'Hey! What the hell are you two doing?'

'Jesus! The scuffers!' Jimmy hissed.

'Thought we heard noises down here, but there's nothing. Help us up mate, will you? I've got a gammy hand.'

Jimmy's weasel face registered total astonishment and admiration at Eddie's nerve. Fancy asking a scuffer to give him a hand, and him with a pocket full of loot! You had to hand it to Eddie MacGann all right!

It went on night after night after night until they were almost dropping with exhaustion. Even that razor's edge of terror that they'd all experienced during the first few days, had been dulled by the sights they'd all witnessed. Dogged courage and determination showed on everyone's faces as they struggled to keep things going. Firemen and policemen went for days and nights without even taking off their uniforms while wave after wave of Dorniers and Heinkels, like swarms of angry bees, tried to wipe the city and its people from the face of the earth.

On the 3 May, while Agnes Cooper and her three children cowered together in the shelter, their house was destroyed, leaving them with only the clothes they stood up in. Sall, Louisa and many other young girls and women battled alongside the men fighting the fires started by incendiary bombs.

In the grey, smoke-filled dawn Agnes wearily poked amidst the ruins of her home, trying to salvage what she could.

Sall, heavy-eyed, her face grey with fatigue, watched her for a few minutes before she went and took her arm. 'Leave it, Mam. You'll have to move in with me. We'll manage. At least we're all safe. We've got to be thankful for that.'

Agnes looked defeated. 'Just when I'd managed to get a few nice bits around me, too.'

'Never mind, Mam. It's only bricks and mortar and bits

of wood. We've still got each other and that's all that matters.'

On Sunday morning the city was silent. There were so many churches whose bells would never ring again, not even to signal invasion. The streets were blocked by fallen buildings. Pavements glistened with acres and acres of broken glass. Fire hoses, electricity cables and tram lines looked like giant snakes creeping through the devastated streets. As the day wore on the work of clearing up was hampered by people who had come in from the outlying suburbs just to see the ruins. They stood in shocked, bewildered silence.

At lunch time a convoy of lorries, presented by the Queen herself, rolled into the stricken city with food, water and blankets. The ammunition ship *S.S. Malakand* was still burning in No. 2 Huskisson Dock and from time to time explosions rent the air as her cargo continued to detonate.

Babsey did the best she could for Sunday lunch, despairing over a concoction known as 'Woolton pie' that consisted mainly of vegetables.

Jim, Eddie, Tommy and Louisa all dozed fitfully. Everyone had been up all night.

She roused them all and told them to be thankful for what they had. Food on the table and a roof over their heads.

Louisa pushed the unappetizing mess around her plate. Surely they would have to stop sometime? It just couldn't go on and on with such ferocity; they couldn't take much more. There would be nothing for her Da to come home to. She'd even forgotten about him for long periods over the last few days. But he was on his way home and she wondered if any of them would still be here to greet him.

She helped Babsey with the dishes and then everyone slept again.

Eleven o'clock came and went and the sirens were silent. Half past eleven and then a quarter to twelve.

'I'm afraid to say anything,' Babsey said quietly as the

207

hands of the clock on the mantel moved slowly towards midnight and the start of a new day.

'So far they've been overhead by now,' Jim said, hopefully.

'Oh, please let it be over! All I want is a night's sleep in my own bed! Another night like last night and I think I'll go mad!' Louisa added.

Jim patted her hand. 'It's all right, luv, everyone feels the same.'

Eddie said nothing, pretending to be asleep. He'd worked hard with the rest of them but he'd also been doing quite well out of the gas and electric meters and the odd bit of jewellery and money he'd managed to pick up. He looked on it as a sort of payment for the work.

The clock started to chime with tinny little thumps and then the inevitable happened. Louisa covered her hands with her ears and felt like shrieking along with the siren.

By two o'clock it looked as though the entire city was ablaze and fear and fatigue forgotten, with the aid of the tenants, she vigorously fought to douse the flames coming from the kitchen of a house. Dirt and sweat streaked her face and her hair, under her tin hat, was stuck to her head. She jumped each time there was another explosion that lit up a sky that was already as bright as day. Her whole body ached but she had to keep going.

They'd managed to get it under control when she turned and saw Sall staggering towards her, tears pouring down her dirty cheeks leaving white rivulets. She dropped the stirrup pump. 'Sall! Sall! What's wrong?'

Sall threw her arms around her and began to sob.

She tried to quiet her but it was useless, so in desperation she caught her by her shoulders and shook her hard. 'Sally Green! Pull yourself together! What's happened?' she shouted.

Sall choked. 'It's me Da! Me Da's . . . gone, Lou!'

Louisa let her arms fall to her sides. 'Where? How?' she stammered.

'Royal Street. A landmine! A bloody landmine! Your

Tommy came to tell me.' She raised a stricken face to the lurid sky where the sinister dark shapes of the aircraft could still be seen. 'I hate the bloody lot of you! You'll burn in hell! You killed my Da! You'll all roast, you bastards!'

Louisa caught her hands and pulled her to her. 'I'll take you home, Sall. Come on, your Mam will need you now!'

Sall pulled away from her, naked sorrow in her brimming eyes. 'No, Lou! You'll have to go home yourself. Your Uncle Jim was with me Da!'

She felt a wave of utter exhaustion and sadness wash over her and the tears welled in her eyes and spilled down her cheeks. Uncle Jim! Her dear, kind, peace-loving Uncle Jim! She groped blindly for Sall's hand and they clung together. Two frail figures etched against the inferno that surrounded them and of which they were both totally oblivious.

When she finally arrived home she found Babsey staring into the empty range and Evvie, her face buried in Jim's shop coat, sobbing brokenly. Tommy, his hands thrust deep into his pockets, turned towards her, mute misery and impotent anger in his eyes.

'I'm going to join up! I'm nearly eighteen and no-one's going to stop me! Not now!'

'Stop it! Stop it Tommy MacGann! Don't you think your Mam's taken as much as she can bear without you talking like that!' she cried.

Without answering her he stormed into the scullery and she knew he was crying. She wanted to go after him but what could she say that would help him? How can you console someone when your own heart was so heavy? She touched her Aunt on the shoulder and Babsey turned towards her.

'Louisa, you're home.' Her voice was steady and low. So steady it shocked Louisa. It was as though she'd just come in from a normal day's work. She didn't know what to say or how to react. She'd expected tears, hysteria or even silence.

'Aunt Babsey, is there anything I can do or . . . say?'

Despite her tear-streaked face and the catch in her voice, Babsey betrayed no sign of her own grief. 'Take our Evvie home. She'll do the baby no good crying like that. Tell Florrie to calm her down.'

'But what about you?'

Babsey's dark eyes were bright with incipient tears but she struggled to compose herself. She had to face the bitter, stark reality. She had to be strong now, she had to hold them all together. She *had* to do it. 'I'm all right, Louisa. Just get her home and tell Florrie to give her a drop of brandy, if she's got any.' She swallowed hard. 'I've always been a tough nut and I won't let them crack me! No, by God, they'll never break me!'

She looked at her Aunt with admiration that momentarily overcame her own grief. In that moment she doubted if there was anyone who would ever beat Babsey MacGann down.

She turned away and helped a distraught Evvie to her feet and took her to the Gouldsons. Then she went back to clean and tidy herself up, ready for work. She knew she could have taken the day off and no-one would have blamed her, but if Aunt Babsey could bear this sorrow with such fortitude, then so could she. There was no time for sleep and little enough for grief either.

On the Monday morning Tommy MacGann joined the Royal Air Force, two months before his eighteenth birthday.

They were spared any further tragedies for that Sunday was the last night of the blitzkrieg on Liverpool. Despite the worst bombing outside London, the port had remained operational and the city struggled on and in June the *Ceramic* came home.

Louisa stood on the patched-up Landing Stage and watched in the early summer twilight as she came in. Her hull was a mottled grey, there were patches of rust on her bows and anti-aircraft guns on her forward and aft decks. But she was home and home safely. This time she'd outwitted the wolf packs lurking in the north western approaches.

She flung herself into her Da's arms and hugged him, while he looked in horror at the ruins of his city. Nothing he'd heard had prepared him for a sight like this and he held his daughter closer. Dear God, what they must have gone through – all of them!

'Let's go home, Lou. Thank God we've still got one to go to, looking at this! Where's your Aunt Babsey?'

'She's in the shop. Da, there's something I've got to tell you!'

He looked down into her face and he knew. He couldn't explain it but he just knew. 'Jim.' The word was a whisper.

She nodded and clung to his arm tightly as they walked up the floating roadway in silence.

When they reached the Pierhead he sat down heavily on a bench and pulled her down beside him. 'How's she taking it?'

'She's better now. At first she was so calm that it frightened me and then she wouldn't even speak.'

'Shock.'

'She's strong, Da. She's always been strong.'

'I know, sometimes I think she's stronger than me. Was it very bad?' His gaze wandered towards Water Street. That was a crass question, he thought. There wasn't a building left standing for almost a quarter of a mile, except the Liver Building. Both the Cunard Building and the Dock Board Building were damaged.

'I never thought they'd stop. Every night it went on. Every night for a week, for hours and hours! There were hundreds and hundreds of planes and the bombs just kept on falling! We couldn't have stood much more Da! It gets worse the further into the city you get.'

'And I thought we'd had it rough!' he murmured, thinking of the four ships they'd lost on the way home. He looked at her again and he realized sadly that she'd changed. She was no longer a carefree, young girl. She was a young woman now and one who had seen things no woman should ever have to witness. There was a tracery

211

of fine lines around the corners of her eyes and a deep sadness in their depths. And he cursed. Again he'd let her down. When she'd needed him most he'd not been there to comfort her or, even better, to give her courage. She'd faced all this alone and bearing the additional burden of not knowing if he was safe. Yet there was nothing he could do about it and bitter frustration filled him. And Jim! The best brother-in-law and mate a man could have. Quiet, honest, hard-working Jim MacGann – gone.

'Sall's Da was killed, too. By the same landmine.'

He groaned. Frank, too! Another good mate. How many more? 'Isn't there any good news for me, Lou?'

She smiled bravely. 'Evvie's having a baby, but I wrote you about that. Tommy . . . he's joined up! He lied about his age. It was the day after Uncle Jim died and I think he felt he had to do something. Aunt Babsey was too shocked to say much. He's joined the RAF and after the way he was always going on about wanting to go to sea, too.'

'Poor Babsey, she'll not know a minute's peace now.' He got to his feet and picked up his case and kitbag and they walked towards the tram terminus.

'How long are you home for?'

'Ten days this time, Lou. We lost four ships and the escorts took a hammering, they need some repairs. Bloody U-boats!'

She remembered Mike Crowley and she felt guilty. She even wondered if she should tell her Da about their evening together but then she changed her mind. He'd had enough bad news for one day and she didn't want him worrying unnecessarily about her.

CHAPTER FIFTEEN

Those ten days were the shortest that Louisa had ever known, they seemed to fly by. On a beautiful evening, when a low mist hung over the river, obscuring its dirty, grey water, the *Ceramic*, along with eleven other ships and their escorts, left the Mersey. She watched them go with something akin to detachment. They appeared just to drift out into the estuary as though floating on a cloud. There was an evening haze over the sun, too, and if she ignored the flattened buildings on the Birkenhead bank she could really make herself believe that there was nothing unusual about this early July dusk. That there wasn't a war on and that out there, beyond the Irish coast in the grey-green waters of the Atlantic, there was no wolf pack waiting. A gull screeched mournfully overhead as she glanced along the waterfront. She was used to the vista of desolation now, but at the sight of the tower of St Nicholas', standing alone amidst the ruins, her heart lurched painfully.

She'd heard the incredible story of what the fire-fighters had found when the rubble had finally cooled down enough for them to get inside. Where the main altar had stood two blackened rafter beams had been deliberately laid across the floor in the shape of a cross. No-one had entered the shell and the rafters couldn't possibly have fallen in such a way for there had been no beams over that section. Someone or something had put them there. There were other stories, too, of other churches that had taken direct hits, where the only objects untouched had been those bearing a cross or even the crucifix itself. Some people

213

shrugged them off as pure coincidence, but she had to admit, it did make you think. Especially the story of St Nicholas'. Yet she wondered how God could allow such things to happen, but as Sall had said, it wasn't His fault. It was men who started wars and she'd remembered how all the young men she'd known had looked forward to it. She wondered how they felt now. Those who were still alive.

'If you closed your eyes you could really believe that none of this had happened.' The voice interrupted her deliberations.

She turned around to find Mike Crowley standing behind her. 'How did you know where to find me?'

'Easy. I knew when the convoy was due to sail and I found out that the *Ceramic* would be with it.'

'I hate to see them go, yet I had to come. Does that sound strange to you?'

'No.'

She smiled.

'What are you doing now?'

'I was going home.'

'This is my last night at home. Would you make a poor, lonely sailor happy and come dancing with me?' He wrung his hands in mock supplication.

'Poor, lonely sailor my foot! There's no such thing! I'm a sailor's daughter, remember?'

'That didn't work! Shall I go down on my knees?'

'Will you stop it! People are looking at us!'

'And they're saying "Ah, would you just look at that hard-hearted girl!"'

'Stop it!' she laughed.

'If I behave will you come?'

'All right but you've coerced me into it.'

'In the name of heaven, where did you learn words like that?' he joked.

'From working in an office. I'm not the ignoramus I used to be.'

'Joe told me where you'd gone.'

'I somehow thought he would. What else did he tell you?'
They were walking towards the trams.

'That he was very sorry to lose you and that you'd make a great city councillor, no less! He's full of grandiose plans is Joe.'

'He's mad! I told him I couldn't do anything like that! Could you just see me, a slip of a girl, arguing with all those old men?'

'How old are you?'

'Don't be so ungallant!'

'We're very touchy tonight.'

She chuckled. 'I'm nineteen.'

He looked thoughtful. 'By the time this is all over, I reckon you'll be old enough and you'd be good at it. You stood up to the dragon of Frisby Dyke's!'

'And got fired. A lot of use I'd be. Anyway, where are we going?' She didn't like to dwell on a future that may never materialize. Live one day at a time was her maxim these days.

'The State, if that suits madam?'

She laughed as she nodded.

'Don't you have to get a message home?'

She wasn't sure if he were joking or not. 'No. I do go out you know.'

They went upstairs on the tram and she looked out over the bomb-scarred city. He seemed to read her thoughts.

'I'm sorry about your Uncle.'

'How did you know?'

'These days everybody knows everything, especially the tragedies. I lost my Aunt and Uncle and three cousins. I was away but Mam said it was awful.'

'It was. I don't think I could go through that again.'

'Let's hope no-one will.'

'Where are you going this time?'

'Secret. Sorry, I can't even tell you and not on a crowded tram. Haven't you seen the posters?'

'Of course. I like the Squander Bug best, at least it's sort of funny.' She hadn't taken offence. She understood.

215

'Dare I ask if you'll be away long?'

'Don't know. Would you care if I was away for months and months?'

She turned her head away and looked out of the mesh-covered window.

'Louisa?'

'I . . . suppose so. I don't want to be too late home or they will worry.' She tried to steer the conversation into more neutral waters. She *had* to keep the tone light and not let him think he was anything more than a friend.

'Do you turn into a pumpkin after midnight, Cinderella?' he joked, but he took her hand as they alighted in Lime Street and she didn't pull it away when he placed it through his arm as they walked to the ballroom.

Again he left her at the end of the Terrace but he hadn't kissed her on the cheek. He'd kissed her properly, on the mouth, and she'd responded for an instant before common sense took hold of her and she drew away.

'No! I can't!'

He'd looked down at her. 'I'm sorry, I shouldn't have done that.'

A wild desire to clasp her arms around his neck and kiss him and hold him rushed over her and it took every ounce of self-control to fight it down. 'It's no use, Mike! It's no use!'

'I know, but if you ever change your mind or need a friend . . . I'll be here for you, Louisa, if it's possible!'

'It will never be possible, Mike! Never!' She'd pulled her hand from his and had run as fast as she could up the Terrace. She could never see him again – ever! It had to end now! But, as she'd opened the backyard door, there had been tears in her eyes.

Tad wasn't looking forward to his leave although it was the first since Sall's wedding. All he'd received from Doreen were infrequent, misspelt notes full of complaints. Did she think he was enjoying himself stuck up there on a gun site in the Orkneys! A cold, desolate, God-forsaken place inhabited by a few equally cold and dour people and sheep. Stupid, bleating sheep and nothing to do but scan the grey skies and the surface of the choppy, cold sea. All she could do was write and complain about how long she had to stand queuing.

He, too, was horrified at the scale of destruction. As his train had drawn into Lime Street and he'd walked out of the soot-blackened entrance, he'd stared at the city – his city – and thought he must have arrived at the wrong destination. It was as bad as London, if not worse. He thanked God his Mam and Dad were all right and their Alice, but he hated Doreen so much that he swore he wouldn't have minded if she'd 'caught it'. And what about Louisa, he wondered? Mogsey said she was becoming an obsession with him and hadn't he enough sense to stay away from her after that fiasco at Harry's wedding? But it hadn't deterred him. Maybe she was becoming an obsession, but he didn't care. He still loved her.

As he walked up the street, kitbag over one shoulder, most of the neighbours came out and called greetings to him and his mother greeted him with open arms and tears. Little Lotty hung back, clinging to Doreen's skirt. Afraid of this strange man that her Mam said she must call Da or Daddy.

Doreen hadn't changed, he thought, as she kissed him on the cheek. Lines of discontent were etched on her face, her hair was coarse and greasy and her cotton dress was stained and creased. How could he ever have thought her attractive, he wondered. He must have been seized by a fit of temporary insanity!

'Go on out and play, Lotty,' Doreen urged and the child toddled out obediently to sit on the doorstep and watch the older children at play. They never included her, she was only a baby.

Doreen sat down at the table beside him while Doris fussed around, trying to scrape a meal together.

'She'll get used to you after a bit. What have you brought?'

217

'Nothing. What did you want? I give you an allowance.'

'That measly few bob! You could have managed to bring something. All the others do!'

Doris pursed her lips tightly together to stop herself from interfering.

He began to get annoyed. He was hot, tired and hungry and he didn't need her nagging at him the minute he got home. 'And where do you think I'm going to get anything up there in the middle of nowhere? There aren't any shops, you stupid bitch!'

She got up. 'Don't you call me a stupid bitch, Tad Buckley!'

'If you're so bloody clever, why haven't you gone out and got work? Mam will mind Lotty, won't you, Mam?'

Doris nodded. She had no time for her daughter-in-law and would have been glad to have had her out of the house all day. The child was no trouble. 'She might have to. Married women with kids are being called up for war work now.'

'I'm not going to work in any stinking factory like our Sall! I had enough of that before I married him! That stuff they use turns your hands yellow and your hair green!'

'Only if you dye it!' Doris muttered. Doreen's attempts to give her hair more colour with henna had not been successful.

Doreen glared at her. 'I'm not going to slave like that again!'

'It wouldn't do you any harm. A great, strapping lump like you!' he shot back.

'You'd like that, wouldn't you? You'd like me to be wearing myself out!'

He ignored her and ate one of the cakes made from flour, dried egg and no sugar, that his Mam had put on the table.

Doris read the warning signs with accuracy born of experience. 'I'll go and see Florrie Gouldson and see what she can let me have, under the counter. It's not right that you should come home and have to make do with the few bits I've got.'

As soon as she'd gone Doreen started again. She hated her life just as much as Tad hated his. 'Oh, this is going to be wonderful, this is! She's in her element, fussing over you! All I get is complaints!'

'You probably deserve them.'

She placed her hands on her hips and glared at him with pure venom. 'I hate you! Why couldn't you have been killed, like those two lads from Cicero Terrace? At least I'd have got a pension and people would have felt sorry for me!'

'I've asked myself that question – about you!' He could be just as vicious he thought. 'When I saw the state of the city I wondered why you couldn't have been hit by a landmine or flattened by a collapsing building. Why does a fat, lazy, foul-mouthed slut like you have to be kept alive – just to torment me!' He shouted at her. 'Why did you have to pick on me to marry? It could have been half a dozen others? Or was it because you wanted to get at Louisa Langford?'

'Yes! Oh, she's so bloody prim and proper! So sickly sweet she'd make you puke! Yes, I wanted to hurt her and I did! She's never forgiven you for not turning out to be her knight in shining armour, has she?' She laughed cuttingly. 'Some bloody hero you are! Even at our Sall's wedding she'd have nothing to do with you, would she? Oh, I'd had a few but I wasn't that drunk. I saw the look on her face and I saw you looking like a stupid kid who's Mam has snatched his lollipop away! She hates you, just like I do and you'll just have to get used to that won't you?'

It was then that he hit her. His temper snapped and he caught her with the back of his hand across her face.

She screamed and then wiping the trickle of blood from her mouth she smiled fiendishly. 'You can hit me all you like but it won't change anything! She'll never even look at you again! And I'll tell you this, too. You married me

219

for nothing! Lotty's not yours! Are you so thick that you can't even see that?'

He caught her wrist and twisted her arm up her back. 'You bitch! You cheating, lying cow! Whose is she? Tell me, who's her father?'

'Let me go or I'll scream the place down! Let me go!'

He released her, pushing her roughly away from him.

'I don't know! That's the God's own truth! But I do know she's not yours, she couldn't be!'

'I'll divorce you! I'll kick you out — both of you!' he yelled.

'You can't. I've not deserted you or gone with other blokes and it's only your word against mine about Lotty!'

'I'll find a way!'

'There is no way! You're stuck with me and you'll have to support me for the rest of my life and her, too.'

'I'll kill you first!' he yelled as he stormed out.

Doris was walking down Northumberland Terrace as he walked up. 'Tad, where are you going? I've got a nice bit of cheese, we'll have it on toast. It's all I could get.' She caught his arm and stared hard into his face. 'She's been upsetting you, hasn't she, son?'

'No more than usual, Mam.'

'Where are you going?'

'To see Eddie MacGann.'

'Go easy, lad. Mr MacGann was killed in the May Blitz, same night as Frank Cooper.'

'I will,' he muttered, wondering why good blokes should die and bitches like Doreen survive.

Babsey greeted him with a smile. She'd forgotten all the trouble he'd caused. She laughed at herself when she thought about that. They hadn't known what real trouble was then.

'How are you, Mrs MacGann?'

'Not too bad. Can't really complain, Tad.'

'I was sorry to hear about . . . Mr MacGann.'

She sighed. 'Aye, it was a shock, but life has to go on, doesn't it? You'll know that only too well I imagine. Eddie's

220

in the back. He'll be glad to see you. When did you get home?'

'About half an hour ago,' he answered grimly, as he went through the shop and into the back.

Babsey raised her eyebrows to Dolly Unwin. 'I'm not surprised.'

'He'd not get much of a welcome from her,' Dolly concurred.

Eddie was sitting at the table with a black, leather-covered notebook in front of him and was nibbling a pencil between his teeth.

'All right there, mate! See you're hard at it.'

Eddie looked up and laughed, getting to his feet. 'Tad! Good to see you, lad! Is Mogsey with you?'

'No. He's minding the bloody sheep!'

'How long are you home for then?'

Tad's smile vanished. 'A week! A week of – her! Got anything to drink? I haven't had a decent bevvy in months.'

Eddie went to the dresser and drew out a squat bottle from the cupboard at the bottom. 'Hardly touch the stuff myself, it's like gold, but here . . .' He poured half a tumbler full and passed it to Tad.

Tad took a gulp and then coughed. 'That's good stuff, Eddie! Still got your contacts then? How's business?'

'Couldn't be better. If this war goes on I'll be a million-aire before I'm thirty.'

'As good as that? I should have got that bitch to belt me with the rolling pin or drop the iron on my foot and she'd have done it, too, with pleasure!'

'Things aren't any better I take it?'

Tad finished his drink. 'Worse. I didn't think they could be but they are. I bloody hate her! You know what she's just told me? That Lotty's not mine.'

Eddie looked wary. 'Then whose is she?'

'She swears she doesn't know.'

Eddie relaxed. 'Take no notice of her, lad, she's only trying to get you narked.'

'I'd divorce her if I could!'

221

'On what grounds?'

'I don't know. I'd have to see a lawyer or someone and that costs money. Give us another shot of that, Eddie.'

Eddie obliged. Tad obviously wasn't going to pursue the matter of a divorce. 'Get that down you and then come on out with me. I've got something to show you.'

'What?'

'Drink up first.'

They went up the back entry and into a yard attached to the back of the Northumberland Hotel.

'What have you got here?' Tad asked, openly curious.

'Davy Whale's letting me keep it here. We've no room in the yard at home.' He began to pull off the heavy tarpaulin sheets from a large object that took up nearly half the yard.

Tad gasped. Beneath the coverings was a big, black Bentley car. 'Is this yours?'

'All mine. I got it cheap from a bloke I know. He couldn't run it – no petrol.'

'And I suppose you've got your own petrol pump hidden somewhere?'

'No. It's an investment. This war can't last for ever and when it's over there'll be plenty of petrol and I'll have the money to buy it.'

'You're a crafty sod, Eddie MacGann!' Tad said, enviously. 'No sweating or dodging bullets for you. That Crowley did you a favour the way I see it.'

The look of pride vanished. 'Don't think I've forgotten him! I'll get him one day, if Gerry doesn't get him first.'

When they got back Evvie was sitting in the kitchen and, despite the fact that she was showing, she looked fresh and tidy in her print smock. She looked older, Tad thought, comparing her with Doreen. 'You're looking great, Evvie, how's Arnold?'

'He's fine, the last I heard. Although I don't know whether he's telling me the truth or not. So as not to worry me. I just popped over to see Mam. It's stifling in the shop.'

'What's your Louisa doing now?' Tad ventured, hoping he sounded suitably nonchalant.

'She's working at the Petroleum Board.'

'Isn't that dangerous?'

Evvie shrugged. 'They came through the Blitz all right.'

Eddie was watching Tad closely. So, he still hankered after Louisa. He was a fool if he thought she'd have anything to do with him now. But as long as it didn't involve him, he thought there was a way he could help Tad out of his predicament and pay Doreen back for the way she'd humiliated Louisa. He'd mention it later.

'I'd better get back. Mam managed to get some cheese for supper.' He laughed. 'When I think of the meals we used to have! Spare ribs and cabbage, a good pan of scouse, thick oxtail! Now we're lucky to get a bit of cheese.'

'I'll see you later, mate,' Eddie said, going to the door with Tad. 'I've got an idea that may help you out.'

'What?'

'Tell you tonight.'

When he got home Doreen wasn't there and Doris informed him she'd gone round to see her Mam who was living with Sall. 'But she won't be long. Once their Sall gets in from work, she'll be back. Sall can't stand her any more than I can. Here, eat this.'

She was proved right. Within an hour Doreen was back and she studiously ignored them both, sitting down and reading an old copy of *Woman's Weekly*.

'I'm going out. Eddie wants to see me about something.'

Doreen looked up. 'He's fine company! A real crook, that Eddie MacGann!'

Without answering, he got up and went to get washed and changed.

It was good to be back in the saloon of the Derby again, he thought as he waited for Eddie. He'd have to find something to do with himself all day while he was home. He couldn't take Doreen all day. It was bad enough that he was forced to share the same bed with her. Perhaps they needed volunteers to help clear up the place. There was nothing like hard physical work to keep your mind from dwelling on problems. It also tired you out so that you fell asleep as soon as your head hit the pillow. He'd ask Eddie. Eddie would know. He looked at his watch and wished he had a cigarette. Eddie would probably have some, even if he had to pay through the nose for them. He hadn't been joking when he'd said Crowley had done Eddie a favour. The way he looked at it Eddie had come off best of all, despite the bombing. He wasn't facing death every hour of the day and he didn't suffer all the torments of desert warfare. He had plenty of money and now that car! He'd never known anyone who owned a car. You thought yourself lucky if you owned a push bike.

Five minutes later Eddie appeared and surreptitiously passed over a parcel and was slipped some money in return. The barman even brought his drink over to the table.

'Got any ciggies, Eddie? I'm dying for a fag.'

Eddie duly produced a half-full packet of twenty 'Senior Service' and Tad took one, lit it and inhaled deeply.

'Keep the packet.'

'Ta. What's on your mind?'

'Doreen.'

'Doreen?' Tad echoed.

'Keep your voice down! You want to get rid of her, don't you? You don't want her hanging onto you like a leech for ever, do you?'

'Too bloody right I don't!'

'Then divorce her.'

'How? What for?'

'Adultery.'

'Jesus! Eddie! Who'd want that fat, smelly bitch?'

'There's this mate of mine. A real charmer he is, owes me a favour or two.'

'So?'

'So, I'll arrange it all. She's that thick she'll fall for his patter and I'll arrange photos, dates, times. All you have to do is go and see a solicitor.'

'They cost an arm and a leg!'

'Do you want to get rid of her or not?'

'Of course I do!'

'Then I'll pay. You can pay me back when you've got it. Call it a favour. Mind, I'll call it in one day.'

Tad was overcome. Suddenly there was light at the end of the tunnel. He'd be a free man again. He'd be rid of her and maybe in time . . . Louisa! He didn't even give Eddie's motives a thought. 'You're a real good skin, Eddie! I'll pay you back, you can count on me! When?'

'Wait until you go back. It will look better. Husband fighting for King and country, wife betraying him – all that stuff.'

'But what if anything happens to me?'

'Will you stop being so bloody morbid. Next time you get leave it will be all set up. Try and let me know before and I'll get an appointment with a solicitor. Look on the bright side, lad, you'll be a free man again!'

Tad slapped him on the back, gratitude exuding from him and Eddie grinned back. One day he'd find a way that Tad could pay him back and he'd sworn to deal with Doreen. Well, he'd make sure that the bitch would be out on her ear and no matter how much Agnes Cooper carried on, he knew that Sall wouldn't take her in. She could be as tough as nails when she wanted to be, could Sally Cooper, as he still thought of her.

The months dragged on. There were a few more raids but nothing as bad as those in May. The Luftwaffe had turned on other towns. Coventry, Hull, Southampton, Portsmouth and London again. In October, just after John Langford had sailed again, Evvie was safely delivered of a baby girl that she announced was to be called Julie Barbara and completely ignored all her mother-in-law's protestations that her name – Florence – should also be added. Seeing as the child had been called after Babsey.

She was a placid baby with Evvie's pale blue eyes and fair colouring and it soon became obvious that she was going to be dreadfully spoiled as both her grandmothers doted on her. Nothing was going to be too good for little Julie Barbara Gouldson and, despite the shortages, she had an elaborate christening at St George's with Louisa and Edith as Godmothers and Tommy, on embarkation leave, as Godfather.

Doreen Buckley had a boyfriend and it was the talk of the neighbourhood, though where she'd met him no-one seemed to know. Not even Doris who was outraged, and after demanding that Doreen give him up and had received a mouthful of bad language for her pains, had taken it on herself to write to Tad.

He'd written back and there was talk that Danny Buckley had gone with Eddie MacGann to see a solicitor. Doreen didn't seem to care. She seemed totally besotted. She wasn't doing anything wrong. Plenty of girls with husbands away had men friends. What harm was there in going dancing or to the pictures, she argued? She began to make an effort with her appearance. She got a job, leaving Doris with the added burden of little Lotty. She was always going into town to a dance or a club.

'She's a trollop, Mam, and don't you go defending her!' Sall stormed at Agnes. 'Everyone's talking about her and Tad off fighting!'

'Sall, not in front of the kids!'

Sall laughed, 'Who do you think first told me? They're growing up and she's the talk of the street! She's nothing but a tart! A cheap tart! She's always been a disgrace to us. I'm glad me Da's not here to see this, I really am!' It was Sunday and she and Lou were attempting to make two new dresses out of three old ones as they'd both used up all their clothing coupons.

The table had been cleared and pieces of material, pinned to bits of paper patterns, were spread over the room. On the table was the old, hand-operated, Singer sewing machine that Louisa had dragged out of Babsey's attic.

'I just don't want to hear her name mentioned again in this house – my house! Harry and me are paying the bills

– even the loan for our wedding. Oh, Mam, I wish you'd never borrowed so much. It was such a waste. We could do with that money now.'

'You got two dance dresses out of your wedding gown,' Louisa reminded her, somewhat thickly, her mouth full of pins.

'And they're still hanging up upstairs. Harry's never home to take me dancing! Have I got this the right way up? It doesn't look right to me.'

Louisa draped the tape measure around her neck and took the pattern from Sall. 'That's the facing for the bodice. It goes like this, cross-wise.'

Sall shook her head. 'I'll never get the hang of it! Why did I use all my coupons on those shoes and that coat?'

'Because you need them for work,' Louisa reminded her, deftly pinning the facing to the front of the bodice. 'Now you machine it and then turn it in, like this.'

'Can I turn the handle, our Sall?' Lily asked.

'No, it's my turn, Sall, you promised!' Joan wailed.

'Oh, for heaven's sake! If you can't agree on whose turn it is, I'll do it myself!'

'Go on then Joan or you'll start whingeing! Cry baby! Cry baby!'

Sall aimed a quick swipe at her sister who dodged out of the way and sat down, scowling.

'Now don't go mad, our Joan, it's not a barrel-organ, it doesn't play a tune and watch your fingers don't get under the needle. I'm not taking you to the hospital!' Sall carefully machined where Louisa had tacked. The tip of her tongue protruding as she concentrated. After she'd sewn several pieces she leaned back in the chair. 'Any chance of a cuppa, Mam? This is harder than filling shells.'

Agnes smiled and got up. 'You're lucky you've got Louisa to show you how to do it, otherwise you'd have just ruined a dress.'

'She'll get the hang of it in no time, you know how quickly she picks things up. She's good with her hands. She'll be making all your clothes soon.'

'Shut up, Lou, you'll be giving them ideas!' Sall studied the pattern. 'It's not exactly what I wanted but then I suppose it will have to do. Beggars can't be choosers.'

'Just exactly what did you want?'

'Something like this.' Sall picked up the stub of a pencil and began to sketch over the picture on the front of the pattern. When she'd finished she handed it to Louisa.

'I never knew you could draw like that. It's good, Sall. Really good.'

Sall looked blank. 'I can't draw. I've just stuck a few lines on it and a few curves, that's all.'

'You haven't. It's really good.'

Sall laughed. 'When the war's over I can sit back and draw, can't I? I'll send Harry out to work while I draw frocks and suits and things. Like hell I will! I want my old job back!'

Agnes cleared a space and set the teapot down on a ring made from coiled up 'bobbin work'. Something Lily and Joan both did, using bits of unpicked jumpers and empty cotton reels with four tacks stuck in the top. 'Let it draw. There's little enough tea in it as it is. Pour it now and it'll be like maiden's water.'

Sall held the half-finished bodice up against her. 'What do you think, Lou?'

'It looks good.'

Before anyone else could make a remark there was a loud hammering on the front door.

'If that's our Doreen tell her to clear off, Mam! I'm not having her here, it's my one day off and I want to get this finished!'

Agnes went to the door and returned with her hand behind her back, her expression apprehensive and fearful.

'Who was it?' Sall asked.

Agnes only shook her head.

Louisa got up and went to her side and took the official envelope from her. Her own hand shook as she passed it to Sall.

Sall looked at them both and then ripped it open. She

scanned the lines and then, with a cry, she swept everything off the table and buried her head on her arms.

No-one moved until Lousa at last picked up the letter from the floor where Sall had swept it. The words were so formal, yet in their way there was some compassion. It was from Harry's commanding officer.

Dear Mrs Green,
   It is with great regret that I have to inform you that your husband, Private Henry Green, was killed in action on the 2 December.

There was more but she couldn't read it. Harry! Happy-go-lucky Harry, who had idolized Sall! She passed the letter to Agnes. 'Get the kids out, Mrs Cooper, please?' she begged. 'I'll see to her and the mess.'

Agnes shoved the kids upstairs and went with them. It brought it all back to her, the night Frank had been killed, and she knew she couldn't help Sall. Not at the moment. Maybe later, maybe tomorrow.

Louisa put her hand on Sall's shoulder and Sall looked up. She wasn't crying but her face was flushed. 'Got to tidy up, Lou! Look at the mess I've made!' She bent down and started to scrabble around on the floor. Louisa knelt beside her. She didn't know what to say. What could she say that would help? 'Sorry, I understand'? But she didn't, she couldn't know how Sall was feeling! Anything she said would be so inadequate!

Sall stopped gathering up the bits and pieces and she sat back on her heels, clutching a piece of scrap material. 'Oh, Lou, we've never had anything! I've never had anything – not for long. Not before it was taken off me, one way or another! And now . . . Oh, why couldn't it have been Mogsey or Tad! No-one would miss them and I've missed Harry so much, Lou! Now I've lost him, too! Lou, help me! Help me!' She stretched out her arms and then the tears came as Louisa held her, the way she had done on the night Frank Cooper had been killed. It wasn't fair, she raged inwardly as the tears trickled down her own cheeks. Sall was right. Why were all the good ones taken when the likes of Mogsey, Tad and Eddie were left? But as she stroked Sall's hair she thought of her Da. No, not all of them. Not all of them.

Three days later the Japanese bombed Pearl Harbor and America entered the war.

CHAPTER SIXTEEN

Yet another dreary year had passed. A year of more short-ages, more work, more deaths, but after 10 January no more raids, at least for Liverpool. But there was no end in sight, even though there were now hundreds of American troops passing through Liverpool. The Battle of the Atlantic – as it came to be known – was just getting into its stride. In the desert the siege of Tobruk was lifted and Rommel and his armies were back at El Agheila, but not for long. German armies had penetrated deep into Russia and the Japanese were over-running South East Asia. The news was depressing on all fronts.

The only thing that brought a diversion from the daily grind was 'The Doreen Buckley Affair' as it was being called in the neighbourhood. And it was a scandal that both Agnes and Sall, still heartbroken and depressed over Harry's death, could well have done without.

Tad had been home on a very short leave and had gone straight to see a solicitor. He was filing for divorce, some-thing never heard of before in the decimated streets around Everton Ridge. Rich people got divorced: they didn't. And as if that wasn't enough he was filing on the grounds of adultery and he had photographs, times and places as well. The community was rocked. There had been drunkards, wife-beaters and gamblers as there were in other areas and not all of them poor; those wives suffered but they'd never got divorced. There were even some men, pitied by everyone, whose wives had 'gone off the rails' but rather than parade their dirty linen in public, they too had stayed married.

The shop was packed, for that morning Eddie had been fortunate enough to get quite a good stock of vegetables. He'd even obtained some oranges which were more precious than gold.

'She was never any good,' Flo Gaskell announced to all the waiting customers.

'Tell us something we don't know, Flo! I was heartscalded for Doris when their Tad married her,' Dolly Unwin concurred. 'But divorce! That's another thing! Any oranges, Eddie?'

'Got a green ration book?'

'No and you know it! My kids are grown up!'

'Sorry, but I can't go breaking the law now, can I?' Eddie grinned.

Dolly glared at him.

'I heard he's got pictures as proof, and times and places!'

The entire shopful of customers craned forward and even Babsey stopped serving and leaned on the counter. 'What kind of pictures?'

'Photos. You know, of her and . . . him.'

'Doing what?' Dolly asked, her expression avid with curiosity.

Flo cleared her throat and looked embarrassed. 'What . . . what she didn't ought to be doing, at least not with him!'

'Never!' Babsey cried as a simultaneous sucking in of breath caused a ripple to run around the shop.

Eddie was enjoying himself. They'd forgotten he was even there.

'The hussy!'

'Hussy! Tart more like!'

'That poor lad! When he was away an' all!'

'It's poor Doris I feel sorry for,' Babsey interrupted. 'It will all come out in court. All the sordid details and it will be plastered all over the papers, too! A respectable woman Doris Buckley! Never owed a penny in her life!'

'An' the way she's put up with that slut! She's a walking saint! I've said that many a time, haven't I, Mrs MacGann?'

'You have that, Flo.' Babsey resumed serving.

'What about poor Aggie Cooper and young Sall?'

'What about them?' Babsey asked.

'She's still Aggie's daughter and Sall's sister and Sall's not getting over losing Harry the way she should.'

'What do you expect, Dolly! She idolized that lad! She's not like that Doreen – never has been.'

'What I mean is, what'll happen after the divorce? I suppose she'll have to go and live with them. Where else can she go? I'll treat us to an orange, stick one in, Mrs MacGann. I'll cut it up and we'll have it for pudding! Pudding! That's a joke!' Flo pealed with ironic laughter as she waved the green ration book at Eddie. 'And then there's little Lotty. She'll have to bear that cross all her life. Mind you,' she lowered her voice, 'she doesn't look like him. Tad I mean. Not Doris or Danny and she did have to get married.'

'I'd watch that mouth of yours, Flo Gaskell,' Babsey warned.

Flo shrugged. 'Draw your own conclusions, all I'm saying is she doesn't look like a Buckley!'

'Then what you're saying, Flo, is that she could have trapped him into marrying her . . .'

'You're dead quick up on the uptake Dolly!' Elsie March called.

'And now he wants out!' Flo finished triumphantly. She had completely captivated her audience.

'Even if he gets his divorce he'll still have to pay for the upkeep of that child and probably her too. It would be cheaper all around just to put up with her.' Babsey stared, ever the calculating one.

'What if, and I'm only . . . surmising . . .'

'You that hard up for food in your house you've taken to eating the dictionary now?' Babsey interrupted.

'Surmising,' Flo repeated slowly, ignoring the barb, 'that Lotty isn't his. He wouldn't have to pay then, would he?'

'And just how can he prove that? She's not going to admit

something like that, is she? You're talking through your hat, woman! She'll have to go back and live with Agnes!' Babsey wrapped a few King Edwards and put them in Dolly's hemp shopping bag.

'I'll kill her rather than have her set one foot over my doorstep!'

There was an instantaneous hush and everyone turned to see Sall standing in the doorway. Her face was white and pinched but her eyes held something of the old fire. 'It's *my* house! Mine! You can talk about her as much as you like, but don't you dare to drag my Mam into it or me either! And how can you say such things about our Lotty? She's a child! A little girl! None of this is her fault! Her life's a misery as it is and you lot want to make it worse! You want her to pay for what her Mam's done and you call yourselves mothers!' She pushed through them all and went straight to the counter. 'I'll have an orange, Mrs MacGann, please. For our Lotty.' She slapped the ration book and the coins down hard. She was just like the rest of them, Babsey thought. Wasting money when they were desperately trying to make ends meet. God knows when the loan would be paid off – never at this rate. As Sall stormed out Babsey turned to her neighbours. 'Satisfied now?'

'We'll all club together an' buy you a wooden spoon, Flo! You're good at shit-stirring!' Elsie March called from the back of the shop. Babsey glared at her. She had a mouth on her like a sewer, did Elsie March.

Sall was shaking when she got home. When would Doreen stop tormenting them? Hadn't her Mam put up with enough without this divorce? They were all being pilloried, even poor little Lotty. Oh, that was wicked! Downright wicked, she fumed. She wouldn't put it past Doreen to trick Tad but surely even she wouldn't sink so low as to make her own child suffer the stigma of being called a bastard? Flo Gaskell must have heard something, some rumour. She wouldn't make up something like that. It was the worst possible insult you could level at anyone, let alone a three-year-old child!

She sat down wearily. She was getting fond of Lotty. She was bright and precocious; she reminded her of herself at that age. If only she'd had a child of her own. Hers and Harry's. It would have helped her to get through all the misery, all the despair. She would have had something to remember him by. Something she could touch and love, not just photographs and objects. She felt bone weary. Her Mam kept telling her she was young. That she'd get over it. That she'd find someone else, she had her whole life ahead of her. But she knew she would never love anyone else the way she'd loved Harry. There wasn't anyone who could take his place and the life that stretched before her was dull and grey and miserable as the patch of sky she could see from the window. She didn't even have any enthusiasm for her work now. When Harry had been alive her fingers had flown as she'd filled the shells and anti-tank mines. The more she made, the more could be used against Gerry and maybe that way the war would be over more quickly and Harry would come home. Now he would never come home, there didn't seem to be any point in working at such a frenetic pace.

She glanced around the room. Everything looked so shabby and worn now, constant use had seen to that. They were having a hard time making ends meet and her Mam had got a job cleaning offices in town. It was almost like the bad old days when she'd been a kid and her Da had been out of work. She looked at the orange, a bright splash of colour in the dismal room. She'd send her Mam round later with it. There was no way she was even going to speak to Doreen.

Agnes had gone and the kids had all disappeared and she was alone, sitting staring into the spluttering fire, when there was a knock on the front door. It wasn't locked. It was probably Lou, so she called for her to come in. It wasn't Lou, it was Eddie.

'What the hell do you want?'

'As if you didn't know! Don't tell me you've got no money either!'

'I haven't.'

'Oh, yeah! It looks like it!' He nodded towards the fire.

'So we're expected to freeze now, so you can buy fancy cars!' she shot back.

'I'm only asking for what's owing.'

She glared at him. He was a crook. A smarmy, sneaking, petty crook. Feeding on people's misfortunes. For the hundredth time she wished her Mam had never taken that loan and spent it on her posh wedding. 'You'll get what I can afford!'

'Don't come that with me! You can afford luxuries so you can afford to pay up! You still owe me a fair bit.'

'It's not you we owe, it's your Mam!'

'It's me, I've taken over the business now.'

'Congratulations! Now you can use the money to buy stuff to sell back to us at extortionate prices! Clear off, Eddie MacGann!'

He took a step closer, his demeanour menacing. 'You watch your mouth, girl.'

She stood up. She wasn't afraid of him. 'I said clear off! Get out of my house! I bet the scuffers would like to know a thing or two about you and your so-called business!'

He grabbed her arm and twisted it hard, making her yelp with pain and begin to struggle. 'You'll keep your gob shut or your Mam might just trip over on a bombsite one morning, on her way to work. Wouldn't that be a pity!'

She shrank from him as he released her. She was afraid of him and she had no-one she could turn to for protection. She fumbled in her bag for her purse and handed him five shillings. 'That's all I've got. I swear it is!'

Before he could reply, Louisa's voice came down the hallway and Eddie pocketed the money and turned towards the door as his cousin came through it.

'What's going on? What are you doing here?'

'I just came debt collecting, that's all.'

'Well, I've paid up so you can leave now,' Sall replied.

When he'd gone Louisa turned to Sall. 'Hasn't that been paid off yet?'

'No, all we seem to pay is the interest and we can't pay as much as we used to. Your Aunt Babsey doesn't seem to mind though. Don't worry, Lou, we're managing,' she said with a half smile, pushing her fears to the back of her mind.

At the end of November John Langford arrived home and Louisa was shocked by his appearance. He had lost weight and his flesh hung loosely on his big frame. His skin was an unhealthy greyish hue, his face haggard and there were deep lines in his forehead caused by constantly frowning.

'Oh, Da, you look terrible!'

'I'm tired, Lou. I'm getting too old for all this and she's getting past it, too.' He jerked his head backwards in the direction of the *Ceramic*. 'She's nearly thirty years old. The *Berengaria* was twenty-five when they scrapped her and it's about time they retired that old lady, too. And me with her! Those damned engines have played up all the way home!' He didn't add that it was the constant fear of the U-boats, added to the hours of sweated toil, that was turning him into an old man.

'How long this time?'

He managed a smile. 'You know, Lou, you ask me that every time I set foot in Liverpool.'

'I only want to know how long I'll have you for.'

'December 5th. Away for Christmas again, I'm afraid.'

She sighed heavily. 'It won't be much of a Christmas anyway.'

'How is everyone?'

'Aunt Babsey seems to be her old self. Evvie is coping quite well. Tommy's fine, he's been promoted, and Eddie's still making a fortune.'

He frowned. 'One of these days the police will catch up with him, although it will kill Babsey. How's Sall?'

'Not good, Da. She doesn't seem to care about anything any more. And I feel so helpless!'

'She will get over it, Lou. Believe me, I know. Her life will never be the same and she'll never forget him, but

she'll find someone or something to bring back the hope.'
He squeezed her hand. 'I had you.'

'She's fond of little Lotty.' She fell silent, wondering
whether to tell him about Tad and Doreen or wait for
Aunt Babsey to do it. She decided against that. 'Doreen's
in trouble again. It's the talk of the neighbourhood. He's
divorcing her.'

'Divorce!' Even to someone as broad-minded and widely-
travelled as himself, it was a shock. 'Who put him up
to that?'

She shrugged. 'Adultery. She's got a boyfriend and . . .
it's all so sordid and nasty! It's poor Mrs Buckley and Mrs
Cooper I feel sorry for.'

'Don't get involved, Lou.'

'Me?'

'If it comes off and he gets his freedom I don't want him
chasing after you!'

'Da, I wouldn't touch him with a ten foot pole! You'll
get all the details from Aunt Babsey, she's better than a
copy of the *Echo*,' she finished, drily.

'Have you seen anything of that Crowley lad?'

'No. The last I heard he was on a ship called the *Terrapin*.' She didn't want to think about Mike Crowley, it only
made her remember things she would sooner forget.

'Boats, Lou. They call submarines "boats".'

'I don't care what they call them, I hate them!' she
answered heatedly.

'Amen to that, luv!' he replied with feeling as they walked
towards the trams.

That Christmas turned out to be one of the worst in her
entire life. Eddie always insisted on tuning in to Lord
Haw Haw's 'Germany Calling' although she and Babsey
hated it. Babsey, on one occasion, had thrown a whole jar
of precious pickled onions at the set. It had dented the
wooden casing and made it all sticky but Babsey had been
more upset about the loss of the pickles. Louisa hated the
sneering, upper-class accent and agreed with everyone else

that everything that traitor said was a pack of lies, although sometimes they found events proved that theory wrong.

'This Christmas is going to be bad enough without having to listen to all that damned rubbish! Switch it off, Eddie, for God's sake, or change the programme!' Babsey demanded.

'It's good for a laugh, Mam, and we could all do with one! Besides, the more he spouts the more desperate they must be getting. Look at it like that.'

'I don't want to look at it any way, switch it off!'

Eddie continued to fiddle with the knobs, the voice was faint and there was quite a lot of static interference. Babsey continued to upbraid him but he ignored her. He'd caught a word, a name, he recognized. 'Shut up a minute, Mam, and listen.'

The voice became louder and clearer. 'Our gallant Kapitan-Leutnant Werner Henke of our beloved Fuehrer's glorious navy, wishes you all to know that he has claimed another prize. With the true precision of a man of the Masterrace, he states that west of the Azores, Latitude 40.30 North, Longitude 40.20 the merchant ship *Ceramic* was torpedoed and sunk! You poor, deluded people of Liverpool! There were no survivors.'

Babsey screamed and lashed out at Eddie who sat white-faced, his mouth half-open. As she had done once before when her world had crumbled, Louisa ran. Without coat or hat she ran out into the freezing, gale-swept night, her feet skimming the familiar path to the top of St George's Hill.

When she stopped she wasn't seeing the blacked-out, ruined city that stretched below her. She was seeing the river as she'd seen it that December day, so long ago. Then she'd cried out excitedly, pointing out to Sall the *Berengaria*'s black hull as she'd passed Perch Rock. But now . . . now she was straining to see a ship that would never come home. A ship that lay at the bottom of the cold, dark ocean and that had become her Da's grave! Her Da! Her poor, dear Da! He wouldn't have stood a chance in the engine room! The ghosts surrounded her.

Mocking, tormenting. 'Bloody indestructible they call me, Lou.' 'Don't worry about me, Lou.' 'Put me down Da! I'm too big for all that now!' 'Too big to give your old Da a hug, Lou?'

The wind tore at her hair and clothes and stung her cheeks but she didn't feel it. It screamed around the old church as though mocking her and she hugged her arms around her and began to rock slowly backwards and forwards.

Mike Crowley had also heard the broadcast. He listened to it like Eddie, to mock. Without a word to his parents, he snatched his uniform jacket off the back of the chair and ran out of the house. The sound of his pounding feet echoed along the quiet, deserted streets and at that moment he hated himself for what he did. There were other men now lying entombed in sunken hulls and he'd put them there.

Eddie opened the door in response to the loud hammering and then he staggered as he was gripped by the front of his pullover.

'Where is she? Where's Louisa?' Mike yelled.

Eddie flung off the grip. 'You stay away from her!' he yelled back.

Mike hit him and he staggered back into the scullery, colliding with a shocked Babsey. There was no sign of Louisa. Eddie lurched forward, his fist swinging, but Mike had already gone. He was a dim figure disappearing into the night. Only the sound of his footsteps ringing along the Terrace, evidence that he'd been there. Babsey dragged Eddie inside and shut the door.

He stopped as he saw the slim figure in the shadow of the church. He was panting and sweating but the way she stood, abject misery in every line of her body, tore at his heart. She was alone now. No mother, no father, only — those two. He walked slowly towards her and touched her on the shoulder, gently.

She turned and stared at him as though he were a stranger. Her eyes were dry, there were no tears on her cheeks.

'Louisa! Oh, Louisa!'

'It's not true! Tell me it isn't true, Mike!'

He couldn't answer her. He couldn't tell her it was just lying propaganda. Somehow he felt it was the truth. The details had been too exact. And the *Ceramic* would have been in those waters. Instead he put his arm around her.

'He used to say "Only the good die".'

He was disturbed by her calmness. She was too calm. 'He *was* a good man, Louisa.'

She sagged against him and shivered. 'Only the weeds are left now. Eddie, Mogsey, Tad . . .'

'And what about me, Lou?' he asked, gently. It was the first time he'd ever called her 'Lou' and it was as though the diminutive triggered off something in her mind. She drew back from him and her face contorted, her eyes held pinpoints of fire in their depths.

'You! You and your bloody U-boats! You murderer! Murderer!' she screamed, beating his chest with clenched fists.

He caught her hands and pulled her to him, holding her tightly until the rage gave way to wild weeping. He looked out across the city towards the river and he swore then that if he came through this war he'd take care of her. He'd marry her and to hell with the lot of them! She'd have everything he could give her. It was a promise to a dead man. A good man whose ship would never cross the Mersey Bar ever again.

PART II
'LOU'

CHAPTER SEVENTEEN

The world was a bleak place now. The toll of dead and wounded grew higher. The queues grew longer and still it went on with no glimmer of hope in sight.

At first they'd hoped against hope that the news, broadcast in that sneering, mocking, loathsome voice that she would never forget, wasn't true. That hope had died when the *Ceramic* had been officially declared lost.

She never went up St George's Hill these days and, if she could avoid it, she never went near the river either. Was it only three months she thought, as she stood waiting for the tram to take her home from work? It seemed a lifetime ago. Last year belonged to another life – almost to another person. She went through the motions of day-to-day living mechanically. Sometimes when she woke her first thoughts were almost happy – until she remembered. Then the weariness of grief descended and it was time to try to muddle through another dismal day.

She'd spent all Christmas in a state of bewildered shock, but on New Year's Eve when all the ships on the river heralded 1943 with a cacophony of sirens, klaxons and fog-horns, the shock had finally given way to a stark reality that had torn her emotions to shreds. If it hadn't been for Mike Crowley she knew she would have gone insane. Of all the people – family, friends and neighbours – who'd been so sympathetic and so kind, only Mike and Sall had really been able to help her. And Sall viewed him with suspicion.

Mike had met her from work, after she'd returned from bereavement leave and they'd walked the city streets for hours and they'd talked, and she'd found that in addition to a feeling of ease and solace, she was getting fonder and fonder of him. As Sall had remarked observantly, 'He seems to be the only one who can bring a bit of happiness into your face, Lou . . .'

She'd even told him of the reactions of Eddie and Babsey to the devastating news and of how she'd blamed Eddie at first.

'If he hadn't have insisted on having the radio on, I wouldn't have heard and then, maybe I would have had a few more weeks of happiness.'

They'd been sitting in the desolate, wind-swept gardens at the back of St George's Hall.

'You'd have heard it from someone else, Lou.'

'I suppose so. But it *had* to be him! Oh, I've never understood him, he's always been different from Evvie and Tommy. It's a terrible thing to say, but I . . . I don't like him, even though he's my cousin.'

'He's a crook. A crook and a coward. He thrives on the misfortunes of others.'

She'd looked away, across to the domed roof of the Picton Library.

'I'm sorry! I shouldn't have said that, he's family after all. It wasn't my place.'

'No. You're right. We've all closed our eyes for too long, even Aunt Babsey has!'

'Mothers and sons!' he said, sighing.

'She won't hear a word against him – not now! She's changed, she's become harder.'

'She's had to be, Lou. She's lost a husband and a brother.'

'It's more than that, Mike. She was always strong and she used to domineer everyone – including Eddie. I remember the way she carried on when he stopped going to church, but now . . . I think she almost looks up to him. She just ignores his "business" as he calls it. She leaves everything financial to him.'

'You mean the money lending?'

She nodded.

'I never liked her for that, Lou. Not just her – all of them! They're leeches! But if there was no poverty their sort wouldn't flourish, so I suppose you could say they're just opportunists.'

They'd watched a couple of pigeons fly down and strut on the edge of the unkempt grass almost at their feet.

'I shouldn't say these things. I have no right to and it certainly won't endear me to them.'

'They don't know about you. They think I work late.'

He'd leaned forward and rested his elbows on his knees. 'What are you going to do, Lou?'

'I don't know. I don't want to have to think about it, Mike, not yet.' She'd bent her head so he couldn't see her face. She hardly knew him and yet she felt she was closer to him than anyone else and the sudden memory of the last time he'd kissed her had brought the colour flooding to her cheeks.

'Can I write to you?'

'No!' The word was ejected vehemently but as she caught the look of disappointment that crossed his face, she put her hand on his arm. 'I mean how . . .?'

'I could send the letters to Sall's. Would she mind?'

'I don't know but I'll ask her.'

'Will you write to me?'

'Yes. When do you sail?'

'Tomorrow night, it's supposed to be secret.'

She felt as though she'd been asking that question all her life and the weariness had begun to steal over her again, but she'd managed a smile as he'd helped her to her feet.

'If they could be friends, then why can't we?' he'd asked, pointing to the two statues that looked down over the gardens.

Again she'd smiled. Canon Major Lester and Father James Nugent had been lifelong friends who'd worked side by side amongst the poor of Liverpool. In death and a city's memory they had not been divided. 'Maybe we should always come here – it might help us,' she'd answered, as

247

he'd slipped her arm through his and they'd walked down William Brown Street in the winter darkness.

As the tram arrived she pushed her way aboard. She never looked forward to going home now. There were too many painful memories. She'd have her supper and go and see Sall. Maybe there would be a letter waiting for her.

She forced herself to eat as she did each evening, under Aunt Babsey's forceful gaze that silently defied her to leave even a scrap on her plate. Because of Eddie's 'business' they fared better than most families. But that didn't make it any more appetizing.

Eddie was getting ready to go out and judging by his expression, he was in none too good a mood, she thought idly. Aunt Babsey never questioned his comings and goings as she once had. As she'd told Mike, Aunt Babsey appeared to expect him to take Uncle Jim's place. Something he could never do, she thought. There was no trace of his father's character in Eddie. Aunt Babsey just nodded as he muttered 'goodbye', to them both.

Sall had just stacked the dirty dishes on the table. Her Mam had gone to see Mrs Grierson further down the street who had just lost her only son at sea. Lily and Joan were out, probably hanging round on street corners with a group of lads, for they were growing up. She frowned. They'd have to make sure they didn't follow in Doreen's footsteps. She tried her best not to think about Doreen these days. The procedures for divorce appeared to be very slow and tedious and Doreen was still living with the Buckleys. Albeit under duress on their part. Her Mam said you could cut the atmosphere with a knife in that house and she often brought Lotty home. It was obvious that the child was confused and unhappy although Doris did her best with her.

Doreen's 'boyfriend' had mysteriously disappeared and she spent her time telling anyone who would listen that she hated all men. They were liars and cheats and only wanted a girl for what they could get. Then they left you high and dry. Many listened to this catalogue of woes, few had much sympathy.

Sall refused even to contemplate the scenes that were surely in store when the divorce was finally complete. Although she dreaded that day she was determined Doreen wasn't living with her! She just prayed that the legal system would grind on – slowly.

She left the dishes and sat down at the table to count out her wages and her Mam's. She put the coins into small piles. Each one representing a bill of one sort or another. Rent, gas, electric, food, tram fares. There wasn't much left over but she put three shillings to one side for the loan. They couldn't afford it but at least it was nearly paid off now. She gathered the coins up and put each pile in small tin boxes whose contents of face powder, Fuller's earth powder and cough sweets had long since disappeared. Then she placed the tins on the mantel beside the letter that had arrived that morning for Lou. She sighed and shook her head. Of all the men in this city Lou had to fall in love with *him*! Oh, she wouldn't admit it, but she knew. He was the only one who could bring a smile to Lou's face these days and she knew that in the dark days after John Langford's death, it had been to Mike Crowley that Lou had turned for comfort.

She turned away, wondering if she could fob Eddie off with some hard luck story. Joan did need new shoes. That's all life seemed to consist of these days, worries and more worries. She felt so old.

A frown creased her forehead as she opened the front door to the loud 'rat-tat' on the knocker. Eddie MacGann was standing there. The collar of his tweed overcoat turned up against the cold March wind.

'Don't tell me what you've come for, I know! You'd better come in.' She could tell by his face that it was no use trying the 'hard times' routine. Eddie MacGann had no sense of compassion and a heart like a block of ice.

He followed her into the kitchen and watched her as she reached up and opened a tin and counted out the coins. She flung them on the table. She would never hand them to him. It was a matter of principle.

'Here, take it and get out! At least you'll be off our back soon, how much is still owing?'

He picked up the coins. 'Another two pounds.'

'What? It can't be that much!'

'It is. Business hasn't been very good lately so the rates have gone up.'

'You can't do that!' she cried indignantly.

'I can do what I damned well like!'

'Just you try, Eddie MacGann! You'll only get the original loan out of me!'

'I warned you once before! Do you need another reminder?'

She stood her ground. 'You touch me again and this time I'll tell Lou!'

'You leave our Louisa out of this!'

'You can wait until the cows come home for your two pounds!' She turned away from him and replaced the tin next to the others. Her gaze alighted on the letter and she snatched it up and tried to hide it behind her back.

'What's that?'

'Mind your own damned business!'

'You've been claiming a pension haven't you? Let me see that! If you're getting any money then you can pay me!' He lunged towards her and she stepped backwards but caught her foot on the fender and lost her balance. As she staggered and clutched at the mantel, the letter fell from her grasp and before she could make a grab to retrieve it, Eddie had picked it up.

'It's addressed to our Louisa. Who's it from and why is she having letters sent here? The stamps are foreign too! What's going on?'

'I don't know!' she cried.

He caught her by her hair, forcing her head back. 'You lying bitch! Why is someone writing to Louisa here? Why doesn't she want us to know who it is?'

His grip on her hair was so tight that it caused tears to spring in her eyes and her neck felt as though it was being crushed. 'I don't know!' she screamed.

He hit her hard across the face, sending her sprawling against the table. The sharp corner caught her cheekbone and the pain jarred her whole face. She wasn't going to tell him! He could beat her black and blue but she wouldn't give Lou away. Slowly she got to her feet and backed away from him.

'She should have listened to Mam and never had anything to do with scum like you!' he snarled.

She screamed as with one swipe he knocked the entire contents of the overmantel to the floor where the cheap, plaster figurines and coloured glass vases smashed to smithereens on the floor. 'Who's it from?' he yelled.

She shook her head slowly, the movement was painful.

She shuddered and jumped as the dishes on the table were systematically smashed around her and then she started to scream. Surely someone must be able to hear her!

He caught her by the shoulders and shook her hard until her head snapped backwards and forwards like that of a rag doll. 'You'll tell me or I'll break every bone in your bleedin' body, you slut!'

She was terrified but she still refused to answer him.

The next blow caught her full in the face and the pain exploded in her nose and made lights dance before her eyes. She lay where she had fallen, her hands clasped over her head, her knees drawn up.

He raised his foot to kick the crumpled form but a sharp blow on the back of his head made him whirl around.

Louisa faced him, her eyes blazing, her whole body trembling. The broken umbrella in her hand. 'Touch her again and I'll go for the police!' she yelled.

Eddie was momentarily taken aback. He'd not expected her. On Fridays she usually called in to mind Julie while Evvie and Mrs Gouldson went to the cinema. Sall began to whimper and he waved the letter in Louisa's face. 'It's all your fault! Who's this from? Who's writing to you here?' he blustered.

She glared back at him, disgust and contempt showed

251

clearly in her face. Suddenly all the things she'd disliked about him over the years were compacted into a burning feeling of hatred. Her grief was forgotten in the hatred and outrage she felt. 'It's none of your business!' she replied in a voice cold with contempt.

His face twisted with rage and he began to rip open the envelope. He had a good idea who it was from but before he could get the folded sheet out of the envelope she snatched it away from him.

'It's from that bloody cogger, Crowley, isn't it? Isn't it? That red-necked, papist . . .' The torrent of abuse ended abruptly as she hit him hard across the mouth.

'Yes! Yes, it's from Mike! So go on and beat me up, too!' she screamed.

'You sneaking bitch! I'll kill him! I'll kill him for this!' He was beside himself with rage and humiliation.

'You tried that once, didn't you, and where did it get you?' she yelled back.

'You underhanded, cheating . . .! You're coming home with me, now, if I have to drag you all the way! You wait until Mam hears about this!' He lunged towards her but again she lashed out and caught him across the face.

'Don't you touch me! And don't you call me a cheat and a liar – you crook! You coward! While other men are risking their lives you're robbing people blind! Touch me and I swear I'll stand up in court and tell every single thing I know about you! I'll shop you and take pleasure in doing it! I'll see you in jail!'

At this threat and at the icy hatred in her voice he backed away. He'd always thought of her as being soft, pliable, sentimental. But this was a girl he didn't know. She could have been a stranger and yet the look on her face reminded him of someone. It hit him like a flash of blinding light, so strongly that he gasped. She looked just like her Da and for the first time in his life he was afraid of her.

'Get out! Get out and don't you ever set foot in here again and as for that damned loan, it's paid in full!' She pointed to Sall who had dragged herself upright. 'And if you so much as speak to her or any of her family again then "The Book" will be sent to the magistrates along with my statement!'

Eddie pushed his way past her, his face pale and set. They weren't idle threats, he knew that. She meant what she said. Mam would sort all this out! She'd soon put a stop to Louisa and Crowley. Louisa was fond of his Mam.

As soon as the front door slammed she ran to Sall and helped her to her feet. 'Oh, Sall! You should have told me! I'm not afraid of him!'

'He would still have belted me, Lou,' Sall muttered through swollen lips.

'Where's your coat, I'm taking you to the hospital! If you want to bring charges against him I'll back you up to the hilt!'

Sall shook her head as Louisa gently placed her coat around her shoulders. 'No. Only . . . bring . . . trouble.' It was painful to speak and her whole head felt as though it were on fire.

'I hate him! Now I realize that I've hated him for a long time! Mike was right, he's a coward and a vicious one! He's a leech, latching on to anyone unfortunate enough to get into difficulties! I hate him!' She was still trembling with the force of her emotions as she stuffed Mike's letter in her pocket and helped Sall down the lobby.

It was nearly ten o'clock when she got home. They'd wanted to keep Sall in hospital overnight, for observation, but Sall had refused point blank. She'd also stuck to her story that she'd fallen down the stairs. A tale which was so obviously a lie that it was pathetic. The cut on her cheek had needed a stitch and they'd done the best they could with her nose and had cleaned her up. Then they'd given Louisa a sedative to give Sall before she went to bed and had called a taxi to take them home, at Louisa's insistence. She'd calmed Agnes down and seen Sall settled comfortably in bed before she at last turned her steps towards Northumberland Terrace. She knew what was in store for her but she didn't care. She was still consumed with anger.

Aunt Babsey was sitting at the table and Eddie was seated in Uncle Jim's winged chair. The sight of him increased her rage. How dare he sit there! He wasn't even fit to live under the roof that had once sheltered her kind, honest Uncle. Aunt Babsey's lips were compressed in a tight line and her dark eyes glittered. She faced them both squarely.

'Is this true then? That that Crowley lad has been writing to you at Sally Green's house?' Babsey's voice was clipped and cold with suppressed fury.

'Yes, it's true and if he'd have asked me I would have told him!' She pointed a shaking finger at Eddie. 'I've been four hours in Stanley Hospital with Sall! He beat her up. Did he tell you that? And did he tell you that it's not the first time either? Oh, yes, she told me how he'd threatened to hurt her Mam! He's very brave – beating up on women who have no men to protect them! Men who died while this brave hero stayed at home!'

Babsey was still furious with Eddie for turning on Sall but she was far more horrified and outraged by the revelations that Louisa was now so openly admitting. 'That's not the point here!' she snapped. 'This has got to stop, Louisa! You are never to write to him or see him again, do you hear me?'

'It's not the point! You condone what he's done?' Her voice rose with outrage.

'I didn't say that! But you'll come to your senses my girl! You'll never see him again! I'd sooner see you dead, like your Mam and Dad, than mixed up with the likes of *him*.'

'Da knew he was my friend, so don't you drag him into it!' Her voice faltered at the mention of her Da, but she carried on. 'It's him you should be angry with! He's a crook! The biggest crook in the neighbourhood and all you've ever done is look the other way!'

'Don't you speak to Mam like that, you ungrateful bitch!' Eddie yelled.

She turned on him. 'Don't you ever speak to me again and don't talk about gratitude either! Why do you think

Da carried on going away to sea? Because he enjoyed it? No, he went so he could provide for me and for Evvie!'

'And Mam's provided you with a home!'

She turned to Babsey who was sitting ramrod straight, her eyes cold and hard. 'Yes, she did, and all the benefits and the luxuries we ever had were paid for by the sufferings of others! Bought with the interest they paid! We ate while they often went hungry! We had good clothes while they had no boots or shoes. They shivered while we had coal delivered every week! Oh, I've had my eyes opened at last and now I can see you both for what you are!'

Babsey's face turned scarlet and she rose, leaning heavily on the table for support. 'So, you've developed a conscience have you? And we all know who's been making the bullets for you to fire! That scum you worked with at the Union and . . . *him*! You'd never think like that! I'm hurt and disappointed in you, Louisa Langford! They've turned you against us!'

'Maybe they did show me the hypocrisy but it didn't take much to work out the rest, Aunt Babsey.'

'Give him up, Louisa!'

'No and I can't live here any longer, knowing you are both willing to go on exploiting people – poor people!'

'Then get out! Leave! You won't be missed!' Eddie shouted.

For a minute she thought Aunt Babsey was going to relent but then she sat down again. 'If that's the way you feel Louisa, if you're prepared to turn your back on us, to throw everything I've done for you back in my face, then Eddie's right. Go! Go!'

'Aunt Babsey . . . !' she cried, looking around the familiar room, her hands outstretched in a gesture of supplication.

Babsey looked away. She meant what she said. If Louisa insisted on seeing him and acting like this, then she would sooner see her dead.

'I'll pack my things.' She moved towards the stairs.

'Aye, get out and live with that slut you call your friend!' Eddie called after her.

She turned and stared at him bitterly. 'I'll see you in jail one day, Eddie MacGann!'

She sat down on the bed and looked around her. This had been her home for as long as she could remember. In this room she and Evvie had quarrelled and giggled and cried. Life had been so different then. It had been happy. That was before the war had come and changed her world so radically. Was she doing the right thing? What would her Da have said? Should she go down and apologize to Aunt Babsey? No, she couldn't live under the same roof as Eddie now. But *did* she love Mike Crowley? Was she strong enough to face what lay ahead? Right now she felt so drained that it was an effort to even try to dredge up the answers to those questions.

She thought again of Aunt Babsey. She'd brought her up! She'd been a mother to her, was she right to throw everything in her face? But Aunt Babsey had changed so much. She hadn't even berated Eddie for what he'd done to Sall! Babsey's heart had hardened but maybe circumstances had forced that upon her. It was too late to change all that now. Too much had been said.

She packed her things into the two suitcases and after glancing around the bedroom for the last time, she went slowly down the stairs.

CHAPTER EIGHTEEN

It was two years since the horror of the May Blitz had descended on Merseyside and Sall shuddered at the memory. It was an anniversary she'd sooner forget for that fickle lady – fate – had turned her back on her that day. The only good thing that had happened to her since that was that Lou had come to live with them. Even that she viewed as a mixed blessing.

She hadn't even known about it until the following day. The combined effects of shock and the sedative had rendered her almost comatose. At first she hadn't believed her Mam, but when Lou came home from work that evening she'd felt a mixture of joy and sadness. She was happy that Lou would be moving in with them but saddened that she had, by clinging stubbornly to her liaison with Mike Crowley, irrevocably cut herself off from her family. And family meant so much – especially now. It was two months since she'd come to live with them and she had never once mentioned either Eddie or Babsey and if anyone tried to broach the subject she would completely ignore them, as if she hadn't heard the remark. She had changed, too, Sall thought. She'd grown up so much. She'd become harder, more resilient – but hadn't they all? She often thought back to the party Babsey had thrown and compared the young, gentle, vulnerable Lou to the girl who now sat at her table in the cramped kitchen every night. The war had changed everyone. And yet Lou had always had a stubborn streak and a temper. If she believed in anyone or anything then she'd stand up for their rights or the principle. Sall sighed. Lou could have made life a lot easier for herself if only she hadn't fallen for Mike Crowley.

He was due home and Lou had gone into town to see what she could get with the clothing coupons she'd hoarded for this occasion. She'd asked Sall if he could call at the house. She wasn't ashamed of him, she'd said quietly. She wasn't going to sneak off to meet him. Sall hadn't been able to refuse the request, although she knew she, too, would have to bear the brunt of the gossiping and maybe even the openly vicious sneers.

She dusted the few bits of furniture and the odd ornament with care. There was little enough left after Eddie MacGann's wanton vandalism, but with Lou's help they were managing better now.

In her parlour there was a sideboard, two chairs and a rug, still in good condition because everyone was banned from using the room except for special occasions. She dusted everything with a gentleness that was almost reverent. She picked up the photograph of herself and Harry on their wedding day and a sad smile lifted the corners of her mouth. They'd just been a pair of kids but with such high expectations of life and all the optimism of that youthful generation. Well, she was back where she started now. She peered quickly through the piece of cotton lace curtain that covered the lower half of the sash window, then she stared harder. Mike Crowley was walking up the street towards the house and she could see the curtains twitching as he passed the other houses. Young children and toddlers were whisked in and the doors slammed shut after them, as though a leper were approaching.

He was early. Lou hadn't been expecting him for at least another two hours. She began to panic. What should she say to him? Should she speak to him at all? Should she pretend there was no-one in? No, she couldn't do that, it would be letting Lou down. She paused in the minuscule lobby, the duster clutched tightly to her, as he knocked sharply on the front door. She gulped and licked her dry lips and then walked to open the door. He couldn't eat her after all!

'You're Sall, aren't you?' he said quietly, with a smile.

She just stared at him.

The smile vanished. 'Mrs Green? I have got the right house, haven't I?'

She nodded, still clutching the duster.

'I know I'm early, but is Lou home?'

'No. Er . . . not yet.'

He looked down at his highly polished boots, a little embarrassed, and the gesture reminded her of Harry. She relaxed a little. 'She's gone into town but she won't be long.'

'Shall I come back then?'

He didn't look all that different, she thought. In fact, he looked quite smart and handsome. 'No. You'd best come in.' She opened the door wider and he stepped into the lobby. She closed the door quickly behind him. She could almost feel her ears burning with the remarks that would now be being bandied about behind all the closed doors. She indicated that he follow her into the parlour. 'You can wait in here.' She turned to go.

'I'm sorry if I'm embarrassing you, Mrs Green. I didn't mean to.'

She paused and shrugged. He was looking at her wedding photo.

'I never knew him, but I'm sorry.'

Again she shrugged.

'Tangled with his brother once or twice though.'

For the first time she smiled. 'Oh, aye, I heard about that. I had a good laugh about it at the time. Anyone who could blacken their Mogsey's eye . . .' Her words tailed off.

'You don't approve of me, do you?'

She'd never been one to mince her words. 'No, I don't. It's not you as a person, like. It's . . . it's what you stand for.'

'My religion?'

'You know what it's like in this city!'

'And isn't it about time all that was forgotten? Haven't

259

we got enough to do fighting the Nazis without fighting each other as well?'

She indicated that he should sit down and she sat facing him. She could now see what Lou found so attractive. He was handsome but his pleasant manner was more engaging and she sensed he was quick and intelligent. 'I suppose so, but it will be a long time before people here will accept each other, let alone be . . . friends.'

He twisted his uniform cap between his hands. 'Mrs Green . . .'

'Oh, will you give over with all that Mrs Green stuff! Call me Sall. You're making me feel about ninety!'

'Sall, I know what Lou has given up for me. Believe me I *do* love her and I'll do my best to make her happy – despite everything.'

'They're good intentions but your best might not be good enough. What about your family?'

He frowned and his expression changed. 'They're not happy to say the least!'

'Then why don't you both just . . . let go? It will be better in the end.

'Did you "let go" of Harry?'

She began to pick at the edge of the duster. 'It was different for me! Everyone approved!'

'Sall, I'm going to tell you something. Can you keep a secret?'

'That depends,' she replied, warily.

'If you tell anyone it will only hurt Lou.'

'Then I won't.'

'I'm going to ask her to marry me today. When I come back from my next trip I want her to marry me.'

She leaned back in the chair. 'Then you mean it. You really do love her.'

'I'd risk hell and high water for her.'

'You may well have to!' She rose. 'Would you like a cup of tea while you wait? She shouldn't be long.'

He nodded as she went towards the door.

''Fraid there's no sugar.'

He grinned. 'So, what's new?' If he'd won her over to his side then he'd overcome one hurdle. The others were not going to be so easy, he mused as he heard her moving about in the kitchen.

'He's here. I've put him in the parlour,' Sall informed Louisa perfunctorily as she came in the back way, carrying a brown paper carrier bag.

'Oh, Sall, I didn't want you to get too involved!'

'He seems nice. Not at all like I'd imagined he would be. I've given him a cup of tea.'

Louisa cast her a grateful smile as she took off her jacket and smoothed down her hair.

'Go on in and put him out of his misery. He's been here nearly an hour, the neighbours will have the stop watches out! Or they would have if they had any!'

He was sitting holding his cup when she entered the room, but he put it down immediately, stood up and crossed towards her. 'Lou! I've missed you!'

She took his hands and smiled up into his face. 'I've missed you, too.'

'I'm sorry I've been the cause of you leaving home and . . . everything. I never meant anything like that to happen!'

'Something would have happened one day, Mike. We can't hide for ever, and you were right about Eddie.'

'I'm sorry about that too.'

'Don't be. I never really liked him but when he beat Sall up I realized that I hated him! It opened my eyes to a lot of other things too.'

He took her in his arms. 'But I never wanted to split you up from your family.'

'That would have come too. Eventually.'

'Are you sorry?'

'In some ways I am.' She leaned her cheek against his.

'I love you, Lou. Will you marry me?'

She drew away from him, her eyes searching his face. 'What?'

'Will you marry me, Louisa Langford?'

'I . . . I . . .'

He placed a finger over her lips. 'Don't give me your answer yet. I know what I'm asking of you.'

She kissed the palm of his hand. 'I don't know if I have the strength . . .'

He gently pushed her down onto a chair and squatted down in front of her. 'It won't be easy, Lou. All your friends, your family and everyone who knows you will cut you dead in the street. Some may even curse you openly. They'll do the same to me but I'm used to that. I've always had to fight – literally sometimes – the insults. You've never been exposed to that.' He took her hands. 'And it won't stop there. You'll be insulted by Catholics too, and you'll never be accepted. Not even if the Pope himself commanded it! There's just as much bigotry, if not more, on their side. Do you really know what I'm asking of you? I won't paint a rosy picture for you, it wouldn't be fair.'

She didn't know what to say. If her Da had been here maybe it would have been different. Despite his views he'd always put her happiness first and he'd been more tolerant.

'And there are other things to consider. Where would we live? Where would we get married? What religion – if any – should children be brought up in? It goes on and on, Lou. You have to be strong! It's a special kind of love that can survive all that. That's why I won't press you for an answer now.'

The words formed slowly in her mind. 'All I know right now, Mike, is that I love you. That there's a war on and you'll have to leave me . . .'

'Lou, that's emotional blackmail! Do you think I'd use something like that against you?'

She smiled a little sadly. She did love him but was she strong enough to cope with the picture he'd painted?

'Give me your answer when I next come home.'

'And when will that be? How long do I have?'

'I don't know. Rumour has it that we're going out East. The Yanks are having a hard time of it out there.'

She felt the familiar fear rising. It was as if her Da were going away again. 'I don't need all that time!'

'No, Lou! You've *got* to think about it! It's something that needs so much thought!'

She slid from the seat until she was sitting on the floor beside him and she flung her arms around his neck. 'I don't need to think about it! I love you! I don't care about anyone else or what they think or what they'll do! I'll marry you, Mike! I love you!'

He kissed her gently then stroked her cheek. 'Oh, Lou! Much as I want to rush out now and tell everyone, I can't! I won't! You've *got* to have time. It's you I'm thinking of.'

'And it's you I'm thinking of! I couldn't stand losing you, too!'

He held her close, looking over her head to an uncertain future. A future that even if he survived the war, would be a struggle for them both. 'I'll come back, Lou! I'll come back for you and we'll be married – even if it's the registry office and we have to run the gauntlet of every bigot and fanatic in the entire city!'

At the start of another patrol, with the *Terrapin* making her way silently and stealthily down the Straits of Malacca and away from the Nicobar Islands, Mike thought, as he always did, of that promise. There had been times when he'd cursed himself for being so rash. How could he have made such a promise? What right had he to play God, for only God knew what lay ahead?

Over the years he'd sometimes wondered if Joe Doran's theories were the only sensible ones. He'd seen men who had once vociferously claimed to be atheists turn from that path and pray openly as they lay or squatted on the metal deck of the boat while the depth charges exploded around them. Each time they set out on patrol these thoughts hurtled through his mind and each time he uttered the same prayer. 'Dear God, don't let it end! Let me live to keep that promise!'

There had been times when he'd thought his last day had

263

dawned. They had been away from home for nearly a year now. Leave was spent in Ceylon. A paradise island where, apart from the ever-present flotilla of warships and supply vessels in the harbour at Trincomalee, it was possible to banish all thoughts of war and suffering and death. Their patrols lasted longer than a month and thirty-three days cooped up in appalling conditions were not guaranteed to boost morale. The air was always steamy, hot and foetid for to recharge her air tanks, a boat must run on the surface and that was dangerous and could only be done at night. Water was rationed so washing became an infrequent luxury, resulting in suppurating sores breaking out on all joints on the body. Sores that would only heal in sunlight.

Nerves were stretched to breaking point and 'obsessionals' were common. Superstition took hold of them all and they did everything in the same order as it had been done the day before; working on the principle that they had survived that way yesterday and would do so today. Put your left sock on first. Put on your shirt with your left hand, fasten it with the left hand. Count the cracks in the paintwork, the number of dinner plates in the rack until it became an obsession. There were times when he could murder his mess mates and he knew the feeling was mutual. Stupid things became blown up out of all proportion. If a knife or fork was dropped the insignificant incident would be the trigger for an explosion of rage. Rage that was hastily checked and suppressed. It was the only way they could work and live together.

As fresh food ran short, meals became appalling. Even the basest bodily functions were governed by time and latitude. Permission had to be obtained to 'blow the heads', the naval expression for flushing the lavatory. Sleep, when it was possible, was always disturbed and shallow. Thirty-three days at sea stretched everyone to breaking point and it was always a massive relief to return to Trincomalee with the Jolly Roger flying, complete with the bars that signified the ships they had sunk.

He'd been three hours on watch and was exhausted and

fell into one of the five bunks in the 8′ × 8′ mess that had just been vacated by the man taking his place. Then he groaned and staggered to his feet as the order went through the boat. 'Diving Stations! Attack teams fall in!' There was no panic but men were running in all directions, although it was impossible for two men to pass each other facing, they had to turn sideways.

'What now?' he asked the chief engineering officer, peevishly.

'Jap naval convoy ahead to starboard!'

He reached his station and stood waiting, watching for the first lieutenant checking his stop watch as the torpedoes were run out. All six of them. The sweat was trickling down his face and into his eyes and it was at times like this, in the silence before the explosions, that he thought of John Langford and all the men like him and that train of thought inevitably led to Lou. The seconds ticked by and the lieutenant looked at the captain with consternation. Surely all six couldn't have gone wide? Then there was an almighty explosion, so great that even the depth of water didn't muffle it.

Captain Mansell ran up the periscope. 'Jap cruiser badly hit and already listing to port! Shut off for depth charging! All unnecessary lights out! Rig for silent running!' The orders were issued in a calm, clipped, unemotional voice.

The main engines were shut down and the electric motor took over, powered by the huge batteries under the main deck. It took only thirty seconds for the boat to reach a depth of thirty feet. Five minutes to reach three hundred feet.

He tried to fill his lungs with air as the descent towards the ocean bed began. They would lie there until it was safe to ascend and surface. All auxiliary machinery was cut off, including the fans. The silence was all pervading as they lay on the deck not moving a muscle to preserve the precious oxygen and to guard against any careless movement that would cause an echo that could be picked up.

The sound of a number of surface propellers became

louder and louder. 'Jesus! They're not taking too kindly to that!' he thought as the sounds increased, then stopped, and he knew that the hunter had become the hunted. Within minutes the attack on the silent, unseen killer would begin.

He'd suffered depth charging before but nothing as ferocious or as prolonged as this, he thought. He was bathed in sweat, his head was thudding, his ears ringing until he thought he would go mad. No-one dared to move now. It would be fatal. It was as though he were in a metal barrel that was being repeatedly struck with a giant hammer.

Hour after hour it went on and the boat shuddered, her metal plates creaked and groaned in protest and leaks began to appear. He fought down the rising panic of being drowned, entombed in an iron coffin. 'Lou! Lou!' he prayed silently. 'Dear God let me live for her!'

Air was becoming increasingly short and many were already gasping as the bombardment continued without let up. Four hours passed, then six, then eight and conditions became unspeakably foul. There were times when he thought he was slipping into unconsciousness and he tried to focus his mind on one thought. He *had* to get through this for Lou. He couldn't let her suffer again.

They'd been submerged for almost twenty-three hours, although most of them had lost track of time. Some were already unconscious but he hung on grimly. Then he realized they were moving and he raised his head and peered up into the cavernous gloom. Dimly he heard Captain Mansell's order to the planesman. 'Bring her up to thirty feet!' Periscope depth! Thank God! It was nearly over! If only he could hang on a bit longer! His mind was as clogged as the pores of his sweat-drenched body but he heard the order clearly. 'Start the main engines!' He turned over on his back and stared at the mass of pipes and gauges that criss-crossed the bulkheads. The sound of the main engines throbbing into life was the sweetest sound he'd ever heard, knowing they would draw in high pressure air.

'Blow the main ballast!'

Dear God but he could have thrown his arms around Captain Mansell if he'd had the energy.

As the boat surfaced and the conning tower hatch was opened, a draught of sweet-smelling air rushed in and he struggled to his feet. His head began to spin and his legs felt weak as though he were drunk. He coughed, then laughed. He was drunk. Drunk on fresh air!

'Set a course for Trincomalee!'

He breathed deeply. They were going home! If he'd come through that he could survive anything, he thought. It was fifteen minutes later that he learned that two of his mates hadn't been as lucky. They'd suffocated.

CHAPTER NINETEEN

She'd had no letter for months now and she was worried, although she tried to be optimistic. Mail coming from so far away invariably took a long time. His other letters had arrived erratically. She'd once had three letters all arrive within days of each other, although he'd written them over a period of weeks. She re-read them all every night, feeling that it was the only way to keep in daily contact with him. But it was the end of May now and his last letter had been dated Christmas 1943.

'You're going to drive yourself round the bend, Lou, if you don't stop it.'

She looked up and realized that Sall had been watching her. Sall missed nothing. Her perception was only one of the things Louisa had come to admire. Sall had the rare talent of judging people's character almost as soon as she'd met them. She was hard-headed and yet she was very sensitive. She was practical yet there was a creative streak in her too. During the time she'd lived in Melbourne Street she'd learned more about Sall than she'd done over all the years of their friendship. 'Stop what?'

'Worrying about things that may never happen, that's what.'

'But it's been months!'

'Lou, he may write all those letters while he's stuck in that little iron tub, but how is he going to post them? They don't have a network of underwater post boxes, now do they? He has to wait until he gets ashore and you know how long it takes them to get anything done in those foreign places. Use your common sense and stop wearing yourself out fretting!'

It was so logical when put like that so she carefully placed the letters back in the Fry's chocolate box and tied it up with a piece of red ribbon that was now frayed and tatty with use.

'Oh, would you just look at this! It's all fat and gristle! Just wait until I see that Ernie Bower, palming me off with meat like this! I've a good mind to ask for my money and my coupons back!' Agnes was trying to carve up a small piece of neck end of lamb that was their meat ration.

'You should let me go, he knows he won't get away with palming me off with stuff like that!' Sall instructed as she drained the potatoes in the metal colander. 'If you slice that any thinner, Mam, we'll be able to see through it.'

'Not through all this fat you won't! Lily, go and get our Robbie in! He's always going missing at meal times and Joan, don't stuff yourself, you'll get indigestion and you'll be hungry again in half an hour and there's nothing else in the pantry! Oh, for a nice piece of sirloin!' Agnes's eyes took on a dreamy look.

Sall laughed. 'Mam, when did we ever have roast beef? We thought ourselves fortunate to have a turkey at Christmas!'

Lilly returned, dragging a scruffy Robbie by the back of his jersey.

'Look at the cut of you, Robbie Cooper! Go and wash those hands before you put them near food. You mucky little hooligan! Where've you been? I told you to be back in half an hour.'

The scowl left Robbie's face and he puffed himself up importantly. 'I've been watching the scuffers in Northumberland Terrace.'

'What were you doing hanging around the police?' There was a note of tension in Agnes's voice.

Robbie turned his attention on Louisa, ignoring his mother's question.

'I saw the scuffers go into your shop! They were in

269

there for hours and hours!' That was an exaggeration but Louisa hadn't noticed and neither had anyone else. He had captivated his audience. 'And when they came out they had your Eddie with them and Mrs MacGann was yelling at them to leave him alone. That he hadn't done nothin' wrong and that she was goin' to get a sol . . . sol . . . someone important who'd sort them out!' he finished triumphantly.

All eyes turned on Louisa.

'Do you think you should go round and see . . .?' Agnes began.

'No! He deserves to be in jail!'

'But what about your Aunt Babsey?' Agnes pressed.

'I'm not going! She's always thought the sun shone out of him, that he could do no wrong or at least be smart enough not to get caught. I won't go round there and say I'm sorry! I'm not a hypocrite!'

Agnes looked perturbed but Sall nodded her agreement. In her opinion Eddie MacGann had got his just deserts.

'Get that knife out of your mouth, Joan Cooper, you'll cut your tongue and it's bad manners!' Agnes snapped.

Louisa had lost her appetite. She wasn't sorry for Eddie but she hadn't entirely meant what she'd said about Aunt Babsey. For an instant she wondered if she shouldn't relent and go and see her. No, that would only lead to recriminations and arguments. Yet she knew just what kind of effect Eddie's arrest would have on her Aunt. She shook herself out of her reverie. Aunt Babsey only had herself to blame. She should have put a stop to Eddie's activities years ago but she hadn't and by her silence she had condoned them.

The meal was finished in silence and, after a short argument, Lily and Joan did the washing up between them. Then they clattered upstairs to prink and preen and squabble before trooping back down, ready to go out.

'I want you two back in here by half past eight at the latest!' Agnes stated.

'Ah, eh, Mam!' Lily protested. 'I'm older than her, can't

I stay out longer? Hetty Johnson can stay out until nearly ten o'clock!'

'And we all know where she'll end up – walking up and down Lime Street! You'll do as Mam tells you!' Sall interrupted. 'And you can stay away from the likes of Hetty Johnson too!'

Ignoring the derogatory remarks about her friend and tossing her head, Lily walked out, followed by Joan.

Sall supervised Robbie's ablutions in the scullery sink, which was no small task, while Agnes attacked the mending and Louisa half-heartedly scanned the *Echo*, her mind torn between the events at Northumberland Terrace and those taking place in the Pacific Ocean.

At half past eight they heard the key in the front door and Agnes gave a sigh of relief. She was too tired to be arguing with her younger daughters tonight. The key was attached to a piece of string that in turn was attached to the knocker and pushed through the letter box, so it hung on the inside of the door and could be pulled through. It was common practice which ensured that no-one was ever locked out.

Joan came into the kitchen but after whisking her clean nightdress from the slatted rack that hung above the range, went quickly back towards the lobby and the stairs.

'What's up with you?' Sall called after her. Usually there was a battle over bedtimes.

Before Joan could reply, Lily appeared in the doorway and behind her stood Doreen.

Sall jumped to her feet. 'What's she doing here?' she cried, her eyes narrowing.

Joan and Lily fled.

'You wait until I get my hands on you Lily Cooper!' Sall yelled after her sister.

'So, what have you come for?'

'Oh, that's nice! I *am* your sister!'

'More's the pity!'

'Sall!' Agnes laid a restraining hand on her arm.

Encouraged by this gesture Doreen began to unbutton her jacket.

'Don't take your coat off, you're not stopping! Say your piece and then get out!'

Doreen didn't look at her. Instead she fixed her eyes on her mother. 'I got a letter today from *his* solicitor. I've got to get out. At least that's what it means only they use long, fancy words.' She withdrew a creased and crumpled envelope from her bag and passed it to Agnes. 'I've nowhere to go, Mam!'

So, it had come at last, Sall thought. She'd prepared herself for this day. 'Hard luck! You should have thought of that before you started carrying on with lover boy! Go and live with him!'

'How can I? I don't even know where he is, the lying swine!'

'Well, you're not moving in here! I'd sooner burn the house down and put us all out on the street than have you here!'

Doreen began to cry. 'Where else can I go?'

'I don't know and I don't care! And you can turn off the waterworks too, it won't wash with me, I know you too well!'

'Sall where else can she go?' Agnes pleaded.

She'd prepared for this too. She knew Doreen would try to get round her Mam. 'She's working. She can get a room of her own. She can stand on her own two feet for a change, instead of sponging off others!'

Doreen glared at her after wiping her eyes with the cuff of her jacket. 'And just where will I get a room? Half the city's been flattened! People are all squashed in with relatives.'

'I know that, but don't think you're squashing in with us!' Sall turned to Agnes. 'No! This time, Mam, I mean it! I'm not having her! This is my house, mine, and I'm not having her bringing her reputation here!'

'Sall, she's your sister, your own flesh and blood. You can't see her thrown out on the street!' Agnes pleaded.

'Oh, Mam, you've got a short memory! What about all

the trouble and heartache she's caused. I'm just *not* having her and that's final!'

Doreen jumped up. 'You'll have her though, won't you! What about her reputation? Going around with a Catholic navvie!'

Sall saw Louisa stiffen. 'He's a damned sight better than the one you married or the one you were shacked up with! And you leave Lou out of this. She's here because I want her here! I don't want you and I'm not having you. You can stand on your own two feet for a change, you're getting what you deserve!'

'What am I going to do with Lotty? Even if I get the chance of a room, they'll soon change their mind when they know I've got a kid, won't they?'

'She's your child and it's about time you started to look after her!'

'How the hell can I do that when I've got to work?' Doreen yelled.

'I don't know!' Sall yelled back.

'Mam!' Doreen pleaded, turning again to Agnes who was biting her lip, incipient tears in her eyes.

'I've told you, it's got nothing to do with Mam! It's my house and you're not living here! Now clear off!'

'You bitch! You hard, sour-faced bitch! You're like a dried up old spinster, Sally Green! You'll never get yourself another man! It's a bloody miracle you ever got married at all! Mind I always thought Harry Green was behind the door when the brains were given out!'

The milk jug missed Doreen's head by inches and smashed against the wall. Little rivers of milk trickled down onto the lino. Doreen screamed, then turned and ran down the lobby, slamming the front door shut behind her. Leaving Sall shaking with anger and Agnes crying quietly.

Louisa appeared calm but that was an illusion. Inside she was trembling with temper. Doreen was a vicious, vindictive bitch! She got up and went into the scullery for the shovel and floorcloth and then began to pick up the pieces of broken glass and mop up the milk.

Sall bent down to help her.

'Leave it, Sall. I'll do it. You'll cut yourself.'

'I'm only sorry that it didn't hit her! I hate her! I hate her!'

'She's not worth upsetting yourself over.'

'I know but she's upset Mam. I knew this would come! I just knew it! She just thought she could move in here and begin to rule the roost, but I was ready for her.'

'Sit down and I'll make a pot of tea. That's the last you'll see of her.'

Sall sat back on her heels. 'I hope so. She's tormented the daylights out of us for too long.' Suddenly, she grinned wryly. 'I'll have to go out.'

'What for?'

Sall indicated the remains of the milk jug on the shovel. 'We've got no milk. I'll have to try and cadge some or buy some, on the quiet like. Damn the bloody rationing! Fancy rationing milk, I hate tea without milk!'

Louisa smiled. 'You should have thrown something else at her then.'

When she returned from her expedition everyone was much calmer but the news she brought with her made Louisa frown. Eddie had been released. Sall had seen him walking up the Terrace as though he didn't have a care in the world. She'd met Edith Gouldson who'd told her that the police hadn't enough evidence to hold him. He was too smart by half and he was a living disgrace to them all, Edith confided. Her Mam was mortified. Said she couldn't understand Babsey MacGann at all these days. She'd always been so proud of being a pillar of respectability. Even Evvie agreed that her Mam had changed. That she looked at life in a blinkered sort of way. Like the coalman's horse, only seeing ahead, unable to see right or left. Or right from wrong in Babsey's case. Evvie was ashamed of him, he lowered the tone of the neighbourhood. Despite his flash clothes, fancy foreign cigarettes and the roll of money he was always brandishing.

In a way Louisa was relieved, not for Eddie, but for

Babsey. Although she had cut herself off from her Aunt, a part of her still cared what happened to her. She wasn't interested in what Evvie thought. Evvie was an out and out snob.

'I could do with that tea, Sall,' Agnes reminded them. She was still upset. She could understand how Sall felt but it still upset her to see her daughters at each other's throats.

Sall had just poured out the tea when they heard noises coming from the lobby. A scuffling sound and then a loud thud, followed by another; as though two heavy parcels had been thrown in the hallway. They looked at each other in mystification and then Sall went and cautiously opened the door. Lotty stood in the hall, heavy-eyed with sleep, a faded pink blanket over her nightdress. Beside her was a case and a large bundle tied up with string to which was attached a note.

'Well, this is a surprise!' Sall knelt and put one arm around the child while detaching the note. It was in Doreen's untidy, childish scrawl.

'Seeing that you won't have me, you can look after her!'

'Where's your Mam, Lotty?'

The child began to cry. 'She . . . she said I had to come and live here now and my Granny Buckley and me Mam started yelling, and then . . .' The words ended in a choking sob.

Sall picked her up. 'Don't cry, luv, they were upset! You come in and see your Granny Cooper and Aunty Lou and I'll see what I can find for you. You can sleep in my bed tonight. You'd like that wouldn't you! Don't cry, Lotty, luv!'

'I want me Mam and me Granny Buckley and me Grandad!'

'You can see your Granny Buckley in the morning, I promise, and your Grandad, too. Come and we'll see what we can find for you, we might even have a biscuit.'

*　　*　　*

275

At first she cried frequently for her Mam although Agnes took her regularly to see Doris and Danny, who had agreed, after a bit of arguing, that she was better off with Agnes and Sall as she had Joan and Lily and Robbie to spoil her and play with her. Doreen had packed her case and gone and Tad had been away for so much of the child's short life that she had formed no strong attachment for him and she had pulled back and clung to Sall when he'd called round. He was home on a short leave.

'I'm sorry it turned out like this, Sall. I never meant it to. I never thought she'd dump Lotty on you.'

'She's better off here, Tad. At least she won't have to listen to all the arguments nor will she be shoved out in the street to play so as not to get on Doreen's nerves. And your Mam and Dad aren't getting any younger, it's not fair to land them with bringing up a child, they've done their bit with you and your Alice. Besides, she likes it here. Joan and Lily play with her and our Robbie looks after her at school, doesn't he Lotty?'

The child nodded but still clung to Sall's skirt.

'Look what your Dad's got for you. Chocolate! Real chocolate!' she enthused, her own mouth watering at the sight of the American candy bar Tad was holding out.

Lotty still wouldn't budge, so Sall took the bar and handed it to her. 'Say, Ta, there's a good girl.'

'Ta,' Lotty muttered.

He stood up and shook his head. 'It's all a bloody mess, Sall! I should never have married her.'

She could see he was on the verge of blurting out all his bitterness. 'Lotty, go and show your Granny what your Dad brought you and I'll take you for a walk later.'

The little girl smiled, glad to leave this man she had to call Dad but who she hardly knew.

'She tricked me into marrying her, Sall! Over Lotty. Then she told me I'm not Lotty's Dad.'

'Who is her father then?'

'I don't know and she swears she doesn't either but I don't believe her.'

'So she's a . . . bastard? Oh, dear God!'

'But no-one will ever know that, Sall. It's my name on her birth certificate. I couldn't do that to the poor kid, things are bad enough for her as it is. Or at least they have been.'

Sall relaxed. 'She'll be happy here, Tad. I love her as though she were my own. She'll want for nothing even if I have to work my fingers to the bone.'

'You won't have to do that. By law I have to support her and I won't mind giving you the money. I'd sooner have gone to jail than give that bitch a halfpenny!'

'That's good of you, Tad, but she's my niece. She's family, so I'd have kept her anyway.'

He looked uncomfortable and embarrassed. 'Is Louisa in?'

Sal nodded, her expression changing to one of mistrust.

'Do you think she'll see me?'

'You're wasting your time, Tad!'

'Maybe, but can I see her?'

'I can only ask her. Wait here.'

He stood staring into the black-leaded grate where the ashes of the fire still smouldered and wondered if he could stir the ashes in Louisa's heart. Could he rekindle that flame of love? He'd try. He'd try his damnedest. He'd dreamed of this moment for years. Long, lonely, bleak years.

He turned as she entered the room and his heart began to race. She was beautiful. It was so long since he'd seen her and the picture he'd carried in his mind was that of a pretty, young girl with a cloud of rich brown hair. Now she was a woman. She was twenty-two and the sweet freshness of youth had given way to the ripe bloom of womanhood.

'How are you, Tad? I hear Lotty was a bit shy with you.'

All he could do was nod. All the flowery speeches he'd planned had fled from his mind as soon as he'd set eyes on her.

She smiled. 'She'll be all right as she gets older. I learned

277

to cope with my Da's absences and she will too. I'm sorry about you and Doreen.'

'I'm not! I should never have married her!' Suddenly the dam burst and he caught her hands in his. 'It's you I wanted! It's you I should have married! I still love you, Louisa! I always have and I always will! Soon I'll be a free man again, can't we put the past behind us and start again, please?'

She snatched her hand free and backed away from him. 'No! No! I told you once before that I just don't love you!'

'You could learn to love! You could try!'

'It's no use, Tad! There's someone else. I've promised to marry him when he next comes home.'

The light in his eyes died and the colour drained from his face. 'Who?'

'It doesn't matter who.'

'It does to me!'

'Oh, I suppose you'll hear soon enough. He's the reason why I'm living with Sall. I thought your Mam would have told you about him.'

'She told me you were here, that you'd left home, but she didn't have time to tell me the reason why. I dashed straight round to see you – and Lotty.'

She felt sorry for him. He'd wasted so much of his life and she didn't want to hurt him. She'd have to be cruel to be kind. 'I'm going to marry Mike Crowley.'

He stared at her as though she'd struck him. Crowley! Crowley! Maybe he could have understood if she'd named any of the other lads he knew, but Crowley! 'You can't marry him!'

'I can and I will!'

'It won't work! You can't marry one of *them*!'

'I'm going to. I love him,' she said gently.

'Then I hope I don't come back!'

'Oh, Tad! Don't say things like that! You've come through so much!'

'But only because I thought I had you to come back to!'

'You'll find someone else! You will! Don't tempt fate, Tad!'

'I'd sooner be dead than see you married to him!' he stormed, before turning on his heel and leaving her biting her lip. Feeling as though she'd just handed out a death sentence.

CHAPTER TWENTY

It was over. After six nightmare years it was all over. Lily brought the news, dashing into the kitchen followed by Nancy Gillow from next door and both of them screaming at the top of their voices. Laughing and crying at the same time.

'It's true Aggie! It's the God's own truth! It's over! They've surrendered!' Nancy threw her arms around Agnes and whirled her around the room. Lily and Joan and Lotty joined in the impromptu dance as, for the first time in six years, the church bells rang out all over the bomb-scarred city. Both banks of the river Mersey reverberated with the sound of ships blasting away on their fog-horns until the very air seemed to vibrate with exhilarating jubilation.

The neighbours were out in the street, throwing their arms around each other and laughing and crying. The entire Cooper household joined the throng as Mr Selby and three other men were pushing and shoving the Selby's piano out into the street. The older women were already starting to organize a formal celebration. Kids of all ages, Lotty and Robbie amongst them, ran yelling and whooping in and out of the groups of people, swinging each other around.

'Nancy, get them flags out! The ones you 'ad for the Coronation, an' we'll all find bits an' pieces to do up the street! Nelly, have you still got that big Union Jack or did your Maureen cut it up an' dye it to make that frock she 'ad on when she got engaged to that Yank? You need 'ors-whippin' if you let 'er desiccate it!'

Sall and Louisa collapsed with mirth. Mrs Selby was well known for her malapropisms.

'Bring all your chairs out, an' the tables. We'll put them end to end down the middle of the street and we'll all club tergether and 'ave a do! I said ter you, George, didn't I, that that bloody 'itler will meet his match one day! And by God 'e has! May the evil bugger burn in hell! An' that'll teach 'im to bomb our chippy! Come on, now, let's be 'avin yer all!'

Mrs Selby fired directions at everyone and she being something of a tartar, everyone rushed to do her bidding.

'Eh, the lights'll be back on ternight, Nelly an' the lads will be coming home soon!' Nancy called to her neighbour.

The activity became frenetic as cupboards and drawers were searched for anything that could be used as bunting. Chairs and tables were manhandled out into the street and cupboards, larders and food presses were raided for anything that would provide a celebration 'tea'.

After the first initial burst of exuberance was over, Louisa and Sall stood in the parlour watching the activity outside.

'Look at them Lou! Just look at them! They've fogotten all they've suffered.'

Louisa laid a hand on her arm. 'No, they haven't. They're just hiding it. You can't blame them for celebrating.'

'But what have we got to celebrate, Lou? I lost Harry and my Da. Mam lost a husband and her home, and you lost your Da and Uncle Jim. Oh, the lights will go on again, but they'll be lighting up a different world. One that's never going to be the same again.'

'No, Sall, it's not ever going to be the same and for me . . . it's not over yet.'

Sall grasped her hand, contrition in her eyes. 'Oh, I'm sorry! I forgot about Mike, but surely it must be nearly over out there, too? The Yanks are pushing forward now, it can't be long, and you keep getting his letters so he must be all right!'

281

Louisa nodded as she gazed mutely at Sall. Six years ago they'd both been so different. A couple of kids, not knowing what to expect. They'd been forced, by events over which they had no control, to grow up quickly. All that youthful innocence had been stripped from them and she wondered what kind of life faced them both. So many men and boys lost. So much damage and so much hardship. How would they cope? After all they'd endured was there any strength left in them to face peace? Families had been devastated, torn apart – her own included. How were they going to pick up the pieces? They both stood wrapped in their own thoughts until Agnes bustled in.

'So this is where you are! What's up with the pair of you? You've got faces like a wet week! Come and enjoy yourselves! It's over!'

Sall turned to her mother and smiled sadly. 'Mam, it's been over for me for years. All the flags and singing and dancing can't bring Harry back, or Da either.'

The joy disappeared from Agnes's face. 'No, luv, it can't. But would he want you to be standing here as miserable as sin? Of course he wouldn't! Don't you think I miss him? I miss him every day, but if he were here he'd be out there with the rest of them!'

Louisa tried to push away the depression. They owed it to all the men and boys who'd made these festivities possible. She smiled at Mrs Cooper. Today they should enjoy themselves. Remembrance would wait until tomorrow. 'Your Mam's right. Your Da and mine would be out there heaving furniture around with the rest.'

Suddenly, the ghost of her impish smile crossed Sall's face. 'This will put paid to your Eddie's business!'

Louisa smiled back. 'It will, won't it. Mind you, knowing him, he'll find some other way of squeezing money out of people!'

Louisa wasn't the only one who was thinking about Eddie and his business. Babsey sat in her kitchen listening to the bells, the klaxons, the shouting and the laughter.

Eddie was out in the Terrace doing most of the organizing for the street party.

'You should be out there, Mam. They need someone like you to get things going,' he urged.

'They don't need me to make fools of themselves! I'm not going out there with that rabble and I'm not having my good furniture dragged out into the street either!'

He started to coax her but she'd remained obdurate and in the end he'd given up and left her to her thoughts, informing her that Mrs Gouldson and Evvie were helping to hang the bunting and that Mary Wills' treasured piano was already parked on the corner of Neil Street. She'd ignored him. She'd never mixed socially with her neighbours and she wasn't starting now. Even if the Wills and the Gouldsons had forgotten their status.

The news had left her with a deep sense of loss and it wasn't just because of Jim and John. Everything had changed and she hated change. She'd lost the world she'd known and loved. She'd been secure in those days. Quiescent and sure of her position in society and family. Now things would never be the same again, but she blamed everything on the turmoil of the last six years. It was the war that had caused Eddie to indulge in petty crime. He wasn't bad, just misguided. He was a good son although she'd never really approved of his 'business transactions'. Especially after he'd been arrested, falsely of course, but she'd been hard put to hold her head up after that. That was because of the war and the fact that he was unfit for military service, like his friends. How could she blame him for trying to make the best of things? She'd always encouraged them all to seize the opportunities life offered. You seldom got a second bite of the cherry.

She felt old and very, very tired and her shoulders sagged as though she were carrying a great burden. She leaned back in her chair and closed her eyes, listening to the noise outside. The fools! Didn't they realize they were celebrating the loss of their world? She'd never been one to dwell on things for long. That was a negative attitude and she opened her eyes and sat up. Now Eddie could carry on his business legitimately. Tommy would come home and they could start to rebuild their lives. They'd come through it all very well compared to others. She still had the shop and her home and they weren't short of a bob or two. Things would soon get back to normal. Her shoulders straightened. Old and tired indeed! There's plenty of life left in you Babsey MacGann, she told herself. She'd sort everything out. When Tommy came home he could run the shop if Eddie wanted to carry on his own form of retailing. She had Evvie and Julie just over the road and . . . the animated light in her dark eyes died as she thought of Louisa. Louisa had become another victim of the madness of the war years. For it must have been madness that had driven her into the arms of that Crowley lad! Now it was all over. Louisa would see sense. She'd see how foolish she'd been and then she'd come home, too.

She got up and went into the shop and pulled back the window blind. 'Utter bedlam!' she said aloud, tutting, watching the boisterous preparations while trying to pick out Evvie amongst the crowd. There was nothing for it, she'd have to go and find her.

Her appearance was greeted with cries of, 'Ain't it great, Mrs MacGann! We'll 'ave a good knees up ternight, Mrs MacGann! Your Eddie's got us a barrel of beer! A whole barrel! And he's giving it buckshee! A good skin is your Eddie, Mrs MacGann!'

She smiled imperiously as she walked across the street, her back straight, nodding regally as though she were favouring them with her presence. She caught sight of Evvie who was halfway up a lamp-post. Clinging on with one arm and trying to drape some red, white and blue paper flags around the cast-iron cross-bar. Edith Gouldson was keeping her eye on Julie while directing Evvie's efforts.

'What do you think you're doing, Evvie! Get down from there! Making a show of yourself, showing your suspenders and you a married woman!'

'Oh, Mam! Don't be so stuffy!'

'Here, Ernie Howard! Put your eyes back in their sockets and make yourself useful! Put those flags up before she falls and breaks her neck!' Babsey commanded one of her passing neighbours.

'We're going to have a party to end all parties! Our Eddie's gone stark, raving mad and promised a barrel of beer – free!' Evvie was flushed and laughing and Babsey thought poignantly of the young girl she'd been just six short years ago. 'I heard. I want you to do something for me.'

'What? Julie, get up off the cobbles you'll get your knickers dirty!' Evvie laughingly admonished her small daughter.

'Come inside, I'm not having the whole street listening to my business.'

Evvie shrugged and handed the remaining bunting to Edith and followed her mother back into the shop.

'What's so important?'

'I want you to go and see our Louisa.'

'What for?'

'I want to talk to her!'

'I thought you'd washed your hands of her?'

'I can change my mind, can't I? Now that the war's over I want us – as a family – to get back to normal.'

'She won't listen to you. You know how stubborn she is, and I don't particularly want to go traipsing round there.'

'Evvie, do you want to see her married to . . . *him*?'

'Of course I don't!'

'Then go and tell her I want to talk to her!'

Evvie could see she was fighting a losing battle. 'All right, but don't blame me if she won't come.'

'She'll see sense now, I know she will!'

Evvie frowned before going out. Unless she was very much mistaken, they'd only end up having another row and that would be a good start to peace.

She didn't need to go knocking on Sall's door for everyone was out in the street and she was greeted as a long-lost friend, being showered with hugs and kisses from the inhabitants of Melbourne Street. Sall and Louisa were helping to set the tables with a motley collection of plates and cups and even a few glasses that had come unscathed through the Blitz.

'Mam sent me to ask you to go round and see her. She wants to talk to you,' Evvie announced flatly.

Louisa paused, one of Nancy Gillow's treasured tea cups in her hand. 'What about?'

'Something about "getting back to normal". It's nothing to do with me. I'm just the messenger.'

'Does she want me to go back?'

'I don't know. Will you come or not? I haven't got all day, we've got a street party to organize, too.'

Louisa put the cup down carefully and looked at Sall. 'Do you think I should go?'

'Lou, you have to make your own decision.'

'I think you should go. It won't do any harm and after all we should let bygones be bygones now,' Agnes interrupted.

'Mind your own business, Mam. It's between Lou and her Aunt Babsey,' Sall rebuked her mother gently.

Evvie tapped her foot impatiently. 'Are you coming or not, because I'm not waiting any longer?'

That sense of sadness descended on her as she thought of what her Da would want her to do. She nodded. 'All right. I suppose I owe it to her to listen to what she has to say.'

Louisa apprehensively pushed open the scullery door and walked through into the kitchen. Aunt Babsey was sitting in Uncle Jim's winged chair and she suddenly noticed how small and shabby the room looked and how much her Aunt had aged.

'Hello, Aunt Babsey,' she said quietly.

Babsey looked up and for an instant she was startled before she mentally shook herself. Somehow she'd expected to see a young girl of fourteen standing there. Her memory was playing tricks on her. 'Sit down, Louisa.'

She pulled out a chair from beside the table and sat

facing her Aunt. Evvie stood in the doorway. 'I thought you would have been out in the street.'

Babsey shook her head. 'That's never been my way and you know it.'

'But it's all over and even though we've all got our grief, we should at least celebrate today. We've all been to hell and back together. Now we should enjoy ourselves together.'

'That's what I've been telling her,' Evvie put in.

Again Babsey shook her head. 'Maybe later on.'

'Why did you want to see me?'

'Because I want to get everything back to normal. I was sitting here thinking, that although everything has changed so much it doesn't have to be for the worst. Eddie can now earn a respectable living, Tommy will be demobilized soon and you . . . you can come home.'

She was taken aback by the softening in attitude and the fact that Aunt Babsey was admitting that Eddie had been guilty of criminal activities – although she would never put it directly into words. 'Does this mean that you've changed your mind about me and Mike?'

Babsey's expression changed. Her face hardened. 'I meant give him up, Louisa! Stop being a fool! Stop deluding yourself, you can't love him! You don't love him, you only think you do!'

'I do love him! You don't know him, really know him!'

'I know enough about him and I don't want to know any more! He only wants one thing from you, Louisa! Their kind always do! Can't you see it? Are you blind? It's as clear as a pikestaff to me. He'll string you along, promising the earth and when he's done with you he'll go off to confession and then marry one of his own kind!'

She jumped to her feet, clenching her hands tightly, but Evvie forestalled her protestations.

'Mam's right! Remember that Lucy Ayres? Remember how she finished up – in the river!'

She turned on Evvie. 'That was years and years ago,

before we were born! She was no better than a common tart! Mike's not like that. He'd never abandon me! He'd never use me like that!'

Babsey tried reasoning. 'Come to your senses Louisa. Can't you see that you only turned to him for comfort after your Da was lost? It was the war. A crazy, upside down time!'

'You still don't understand, do you? I love him! I don't care what religion he is!'

'You should care!'

'Mind your own business, Evvie!' she snapped at her cousin.

'You'll end up hating each other if he does marry you! You'll rue the day! You'll curse the day you ever met him!' Babsey's voice rose higher with anger.

Before Louisa could reply Eddie barged in, looking a bit worse for drink already. 'Now what's going on? What's she doing here?'

'I sent for her. I'm trying to talk some sense into her over that . . . that Crowley lad!'

Eddie glowered at Louisa but he remained silent, it was Evvie who interrupted.

'For God's sake, Louisa, can't you see what you're doing? Can't you see the disgrace, the fingers that will be pointed, the jangling that will go on?'

'Oh, I'd expect that from you, Evvie! You're so high and mighty! But I don't care about anyone! I don't care what *they* say!'

'Well you should! He's no good! Bloody red-neck!'

'I'm warning you Eddie MacGann, any more of that and I'll smack your face, like I did once before! And don't you dare say I'm disgracing you! You're nothing but a common crook! A vicious, cowardly crook! I'll never forgive you for what you did to Sall!'

Anger flooded Eddie's face. 'You'll regret this, Louisa! You'll regret it!'

Her eyes narrowed. 'If you're threatening me then it'll be you who regrets it.'

'Oh, stop it both of you! This is leading nowhere and half the street can hear you!' Evvie intervened.

'Never mind the bloody neighbours for once. That bastard crippled me! Crippled me for life!' Eddie thrust his deformed hand towards Louisa. 'And she's going to marry him!'

Evvie had had enough. With her lips compressed in a tight line she stalked out.

'Now look what you've done! You won't be satisfied until you've torn this family apart!' Eddie yelled.

Babsey was holding her temper firmly in check. 'He's right, Louisa. That's just what you're doing.'

'I'm not! He's always hated Mike and he needn't go ranting and raving about his hand. That was his own fault and you both know it.'

Babsey tried another approach, determined not to give in. Her expression became softer, her eyes reproachful. 'What would your Da have said, God rest him? Do you think he'd have given his blessing to this lunacy?'

She was just as determined. 'Yes, I think he would. All he wanted was for me to be happy and he wasn't like the rest of you! Even Uncle Jim might have understood.'

'Indeed he wouldn't! He wasn't a church-going man but he was a good Protestant just the same!'

'Aunt Babsey, I love Mike Crowley and I'm going to marry him. You'll have to accept it.' Her anger was abating. 'And it's not over yet for him. He's still out in the Pacific fighting the Japanese.'

Babsey turned away. 'Then maybe it would be for the best if he never came back.'

The flame of anger burst forth again, accompanied by a deep hurt. 'May God forgive you, Aunt Babsey! How can you say such a thing after Da, your own brother, was lost at sea. It's a wicked thing to say! Evil and wicked! Oh, I knew I should never have come.'

Babsey's voice was cold and her dark eyes hard. 'If you go out of that door again, Louisa Langford, you go for good this time and if I see you on the street, I'll cut you dead – and I won't be the only one!'

She stared at her Aunt for a second before shaking her head, then turning on her heel she left Northumberland Terrace for ever.

CHAPTER TWENTY-ONE

On a cold, damp November morning she stood beneath the big clock in Lime Street Station and watched the train pull in. The engine emitted an ear-splitting whistle, accompanied by an out-rush of steam that added to the murky gloom of the station.

All around her were little groups of people, dressed in their best clothes, now all shabby. There were girls like herself, who paced up and down, alone, nervously clutching handbags. Waiting, glancing towards the platform, searching for one special figure amongst the crowds of men who were now spilling from the train and pressing towards the ticket collector's gate.

'Under the clock at Lime Street Station,' she'd written when she'd received his letter, telling her he was coming home.

Aunt Babsey's words had hung over her like the sword of Damocles until VJ Day, although Sall and the rest of the Coopers had tried to keep her spirits up. She would never forgive her Aunt for those callous words.

Over by the barrier she'd caught sight of Pat Crowley and his small, dark-haired wife. He'd glanced in her direction and she'd thought she'd seen a hint of a smile hover on his lips, before Maggie had pulled him towards the barrier. It was only right that he greet them first, she thought, but she felt a little frustrated and her joy at seeing him again would be overshadowed by the knowledge that now bigotry would rear its ugly head. They would both need every ounce of strength, courage and love to face the future.

She stood rooted to the spot as she watched him embrace

his mother, then his father. Her eyes greedily drinking in the sight of him, noticing how much thinner he was and that, despite the tan, there were fine lines etched on his face and an air of tautness in his movements. Then he looked up and saw her and she forgot everything and everyone. Pushing her way through the crowds she flung herself into his arms.

'Lou! Oh, Lou! I've missed you! You can't know how much I've missed you!'

She was laughing and crying at the same time and her heart felt as though it was bursting. 'I can! I've missed you just as much! I was so frightened you'd be killed! My nerves have been stretched to breaking point!'

'It's all behind us now, Lou!'

'Well, it's fine manners you have, Michael Crowley!' his father interrupted.

With his arm around her shoulders he turned towards his parents and it was with an inward sigh of relief that he saw that his Da was smiling. 'Mam and Dad, this is Louisa. Lou, I call her.'

Pat Crowley smiled at her. 'You've grown up since I gave you that toffee!'

'I didn't think you'd remember that!' she smiled back.

So, this was the one! This was the bold Protestant piece who'd lured her son away from his own kind, Maggie Crowley thought as she looked up at Louisa. She'd gone to mass every day and benediction and said so many novenas that she'd lost count, all so that this day would never arrive. But her prayers hadn't been answered. Well, they had in part. He was home safe at last.

'Mam, haven't you got anything to say?' Mike prompted.

'If I said I was pleased to meet you I'd be lying and I'm no hypocrite. I don't approve of you,' came the terse reply.

Although she'd expected it, she still felt hurt but Mike's grip tightened. 'I'm glad you're so honest Mrs Crowley. I know it must be hard for you. It's hard for me, too, but I won't give him up and we do have something in common. We both love him.'

Oh, hardfaced with it, too, Maggie thought. Uppity, but then wasn't she one of those MacGanns? The ones who thought themselves so high and mighty. 'If you love him, you'll leave him alone!'

'Maggie, that's enough! We're not having a confrontation here with half of Liverpool listening!' Pat said firmly, seeing the anger in his son's eyes. He knew he was in for a tirade about 'sticking together' from Maggie but he wasn't having a slanging match here. Of course he would have been happier if his son had chosen a Catholic girl, but you had to be thankful for the fact that he'd come home in one piece and that she was a respectable girl. 'We'll go home,' he announced.

He felt his wife freeze and he looked helplessly at Mike.

'I'll take Lou home first, if you don't mind. We've a lot to talk about.'

'No, you go ahead, lad,' Pat said quickly before Maggie could comment. 'Here, give me your things. I'll take them.' And picking up Mike's case he began to walk away, followed by his wife.

'You made me look a right eejit, Pat Crowley! Didn't we agree we'd tell them straight!'

'But did you have to start the minute you set eyes on him, woman? There he is with his feet barely on the soil of his native city and you start!'

'And what did you expect me to do? Say, "It's pleased I am to meet you," or "Hello there! Isn't this just grand?" Sure, the Almighty would have struck me down where I stood for the lies!'

'Maggie Crowley, you're a terrible woman, that you are!' he replied with a smile, hoping to placate her.

'Have you changed your mind? Do you want your son married to an Orangeman's daughter? Do you want us disgraced throughout the parish? Do you want Father Maguire round by the minutes . . .'

'Jesus, Mary and Joseph! Will you give it a rest, Maggie! She's an orphan! From what I've heard her Da was a good man – tolerant – and she's a decent enough girl!'

293

'Holy Mother! Would you just listen to him! You turn-coat! You traitor! You'll be buying a bowler hat and singing "The Sash me Father Wore" next!'

'Oh, get off with you, woman! You take things to extremes! If you don't give your tongue a rest I'll be getting off the tram in Scotland Road and going to the Throstle's Nest for more pleasant company!'

Maggie sniffed disdainfully. 'Don't think that's the end of it!'

Pat raised his eyes to heaven and whispered under his breath, 'I'm under no illusions about that!'

'That was a good start,' Louisa said quietly as they waited for the tram.

'Take no notice,' Mike sighed.

'She doesn't even seem to want to get to know me.'

'She's bitter, is Mam. Have you changed your mind?'

'No, it only makes me more determined. I had pretty much the same from Aunt Babsey. They can all cut me dead, I don't care – just as long as I have you.'

Oblivious to the smiling glances of the women in the queue, he kissed her again. 'Let's get you home, at least Sall won't slam the door in our faces.'

'No, she won't. But everyone else in the street will.'

Sall didn't disappoint them. She greeted them with a smile and showed them into the parlour, saying that maybe now she'd get some peace and quiet. That for the last six months Lou had almost driven her to distraction.

He stood holding her at arm's length and smiling. 'You've changed, Lou.'

'So have you. You're thinner and you look . . .'

'Older? Well, I am older. I'm twenty-eight. Just the right age to settle down.' He drew her into his arms and kissed her and she clung to his lips, wishing he would never stop kissing her. If she'd had any doubts they all fled now. No-one could take him from her now or ever again.

'I think we should get married as soon as possible,' he whispered in a voice gruff with passion. 'I've waited too long for you, Lou.'

She drew him towards the sofa and they both sat, arms entwined. 'So do I, but where . . .?'

'We'd need a dispensation and you'd have to take instruction and sign forms and then we could only be married in the vestry – that's if Father Maguire would marry us at all! Lots of priests won't.'

'I don't think I could go through all that . . . it's . . . Oh, I suppose I'm bigoted in a way! I don't want to be but . . .' She shrugged helplessly.

'I know how you feel. It's something that's so deep-rooted inside us, that no matter how much we may love each other, it will be hard to erase.'

For the second time that day she felt hurt but she shrugged it off. The testing time was just beginning. 'So, where?' she smiled wryly. 'Your Mam would burn St George's down before she'd see you set foot inside.'

'Let's upset everyone! The registry office?'

It was the only possible solution and she nodded her agreement, sealing it with a kiss. She'd long ago realized that the sort of wedding Sall and Evvie had had was not for her.

'As soon as we can?'

'As soon as we can,' she repeated before his lips cut off her words.

Maggie placed his meal before him. She'd cooled down a little but she still hadn't given up hope of talking sense into him. 'It's good to have you home, son.'

'Aye, Mam, I can't tell you how good it is to be back and to get back to your cooking. There's no-one can make scouse like you! I dreamed about your scouse, with the potatoes so soft they'd almost become part of the gravy and good pieces of mutton.'

'You'll have to hunt for the meat! We're still on nine ounces a week! Pat, will you put that damned *Echo* down and come and get your meal! Oh, wouldn't it be just grand if you were coming home to a nice Catholic girl.'

'Mam, you're just going to have to accept it. I love

Lou and I'm going to marry her just as soon as we can arrange it.'

Maggie stared at him beseechingly. 'No! Don't do it, Michael! Don't endanger your immortal soul!'

'That's Father Maguire speaking – not you.'

'I've lost him! Holy Mother of God, I've lost him!'

'Don't you think you're being a bit hysterical?'

'No! I'm bitterly hurt and disappointed in you! How can you throw everything back in the faces of those who love you by marrying that . . . Protestant! Don't expect me to come to the wedding or to have her in this house! She's lured you away from us, from your family, your church . . .'

Pat flung his spoon down. 'For the love of God, Maggie, there's no need to carry on like that and the lad only just home!'

'It's all right, Dad, I expected this. We both did. Lou has had all the same arguments with her family. We're going to get a couple of rooms and we're getting married at Brougham Terrace.'

'The registry office! That's no marriage at all in the eyes of the church. You'll be living in sin with her!' Maggie cried.

Mike pushed his dish away and stood up. 'You can call it whatever you like, but by the law of the land we'll be married and besides, I thought it would have been preferable, from your point of view, than me getting married in a Protestant church!'

Maggie crossed herself and uttered a silent invocation.

'But quite honestly Mam, I don't care much what either you or Father Maguire think about it. I've seen too much, I've suffered too much to believe that God is so narrow-minded that he allows only Catholics into heaven! I saw good men, Methodists, Anglicans, Jews all suffer and die and I don't believe they can all be sentenced to burn in hell, just because they happened to be born and brought up in a different faith to me. You must have seen the pictures of Belsen and Auschwitz? That's where bigotry leads! To evil so great that it defies description or comprehension! Attitudes have to change!'

'They won't change that quickly!' she replied, shaken.

'Then I'm sorry for you, Mam. You might just as well have lost a son.' He grabbed his jacket and pulled it on, then slammed out without another word.

'He's right, Maggie. Is that what you want, to lose your son?'

'I lost him the day she got her claws into him!' she replied bitterly.

Sall opened the door to him. 'It's started already then?' she said drily. 'Come in.'

Louisa took one look at his face and got her coat and hat while Agnes poked the fire to hide her embarrassment. It wasn't only Louisa who would be shunned and criticized. They all would for even allowing him into the house.

'Just going for a walk,' Louisa said.

'You'd better take your umbrella, it's raining,' Sall called after her.

A steady drizzle had set in and the streets were deserted, except for the occasional stray cat hunting amongst the rubble of the bomb sites.

'So you told them?' she said quietly.

'Yes. Da took it well but . . .'

'But your Mam didn't. Oh, well, at least she and Aunt Babsey have that in common.'

'I'd hoped that she would have unbent enough to have let us live with them, just for a while.'

'Then you're a fool, Mike Crowley! We might have all stuck together during the bad times when there was a common enemy but things haven't changed that much.'

'I'd hoped they had. While I was away religion didn't seem to matter so much. We all prayed to the same God to get us all through.'

'We can't live with Sall. There's no room and, besides, it wouldn't be fair on them. They'd be shunned because of us.'

He kicked at a piece of broken kerbstone. 'After all

they've been through together, Catholic and Protestant alike, why can't they see how bloody stupid and futile it all is?'

She squeezed his hand. 'I'll start looking for somewhere for us to live. It's not going to be easy, we may have to accept just one room, but we'll manage.'

'That's no way to start married life! Is this what I fought for?'

'Lots of people are having to start like that, the housing shortage is so great. It won't be for ever, Mike.'

'No. I'll build you a house, Lou. A big, fancy house and then they'll all be jealous and sorry.'

She laughed. 'Just a small house would do.'

'Here I am talking about building you a house when I've only just got home! But I've got plans for us, Lou! I want to start my own business. I always swore that one day I would. There's going to be a building boom and I want to get in at the start! I have a few contacts and Joe Doran will help. I know a couple of good lads, too. I'll only be able to afford a couple to start with, but . . .'

'Will you have enough money?'

He grinned. 'No. I've got my savings and that's all.'

'I've got a bit. Not much, just what I've saved and what Da left me and we'll try and manage on my earnings so we can put everything into the business.'

'We won't fail, Lou! I promise! We'll call it the Crowley & Langford Construction Company.'

She pealed with laughter.

'What's so funny? Don't you like it?'

'Yes. But don't you see you will have publicly united the orange and the green!'

'And there'll be no discrimination either. I'm going to change all that!'

She reached up and kissed him. 'I love you, Michael Crowley.'

'And I love you, Louisa Langford. My Liverpool Lou.'

Her eyes were suddenly bright with tears. 'That's what Da used to call me . . . from the song.'

He smiled and began to sing, 'Oh, Liverpool Lou, lovely Liverpool Lou . . .' His voice carried clearly along the empty, rain-washed street and she thought she heard the echo of another voice, a voice from another time and another place.

Her best green wool coat had been refurbished by trimming the collar and cuffs with black velvet ribbon and Sall had spent hours with the remaining scraps, fashioning tiny rosettes which she stitched in a cluster on one side of Louisa's green, velour pillbox hat. She was going to stand for Louisa and Joe Doran was going to be Mike's best man. No-one else would attend the ceremony.

Louisa had reluctantly rented the large attic of a house in Faulkner Square. She'd spent nearly all her time answering advertisements, only to find when she arrived at the address that the accommodation had already been let. As she'd looked up at the flaking brickwork and peeling paint she'd almost turned away, but things were getting desperate.

The houses were all large, four and five storeys and had once been the homes of the wealthy merchants and bankers in better times. Some were still occupied by middle-class tenants who strove to keep up their pre-war standards, but there were few girls and women now who looked on a life 'in service' as desirable. Those houses exuded an air of faded gentility in a rapidly declining area. Even the park in the centre of the square was overgrown, its railings rusted. The other houses appeared to be occupied by tenants of all nationalities, creeds and colours.

Mrs Dean-Swifte, with an 'e' she stressed upon Louisa on showing her into a lofty but dingy hall, was a widow who was obviously of genteel stock who had fallen on hard times.

'My dear departed was a frivolous man. A gentleman, of course – but improvident. Debts! Debts! Debts!' She had waved a plump and none too clean hand in the direction of the incongruously grand, sweeping, staircase that was devoid of carpet or lino.

Louisa had followed the plump figure, swathed in black draperies that floated after her, emitting a faint odour of lavender water, perspiration and cats. By the time they'd reached the top floor her prospective landlady was wheezing and spluttering and had gone very red in the face.

'Are you all right?' she'd asked.

Mrs Dean-Swifte nodded and motioned with her hand that they wait. 'I don't often come up here. My heart!' she at last gasped, before throwing open the door with a flourish.

Her heart had sunk even further as she'd walked into the room. The lino was dirty and torn. The skylight window let in only a minimal amount of daylight and was fly-speckled and curtainless. There was a small fireplace and a gas ring, encrusted with soot. Two rattan chairs, dusty and fragile-looking, were set each side of the fireplace. A huge, old-fashioned wardrobe took up one wall and an equally ancient wash-stand another and an iron bedstead with a stained mattress, the third wall. It was the most depressing room she'd ever seen, she'd thought miserably.

'It's a snip at the price, but that doesn't include the gas or electric. I could let it three times over!'

Louisa knew she was right. 'Where are the meters?' Sall had warned her about the usual practice of 'fixing the meters'.

'They've not been tampered with!' The black draperies fluttered over a bosom out-thrust with indignation.

'I'm sure they haven't but I'd just like to try. Just to see how much I'll have to budget for, you do understand?'

There was an intake of breath but she'd ignored it. Inserting a penny into the meter she lit the gas ring and watched it burn. She did the same with the electric before switching on the one, naked bulb that hung from the centre of the sloping ceiling. She hated it. It reeked of decay and damp and dirt. 'I'll take it.'

Mrs Dean-Swifte smiled as she held out a grubby hand

300

for the advance rent. 'You can keep your coal at the back of the cellar and the bathroom is on the landing below, you can inspect it on the way down Mrs . . .?'

'Crowley. Louisa Crowley, or at least I will be when we move in.' She thought how strange it sounded. Louisa Crowley. Such fancies were instantly banished when she saw the monstrous, Edwardian bathroom and she had a good idea of what Mike would say when he saw their first home.

On the way home on the tram she'd begun to think that it might not be too bad once it was cleaned up. With some curtains, lamps, rugs, a new mattress, a table and maybe some pictures it could look cosy, except for that bathroom. Although she'd never lived in a house with a proper bathroom that one was not what could be called a desirable feature. She'd have to use gallons of Jeyes Fluid in there! And then there would be all those stairs, carrying coal, shopping, water and washing. Apparently there was a garden at the back. At least they would be on their own and they would both be out at work all day. It wasn't what she was used to, or Mike either come to that, but they would just have to make the best of it and it wouldn't be for ever.

It was raining when she got off the tram. A misty rain and, looking up, preparatory to crossing St Domingo Road, she saw Mike waiting for her. Her heart sank when she thought of the house in Faulkner Square.

He kissed her on the cheek as she tucked her arm through his and held the umbrella over both of them.

'I thought you were working?'

'Rained off. Well, what was it like? Are we going to have a roof over our heads or not?'

'I said we'd have it. It's just one room. A big attic room but there's a gas ring and fireplace and a bathroom.' She tried to sound enthusiastic.

'Can we afford it?'

'Of course we can and with a few bits and pieces, rugs and lamps, it'll look really cosy.' Her forced, optimistic tone hadn't fooled him, she could tell by the look on his face.

'It's a dump.'

She sighed heavily. 'Yes, it's a bit of a dump but I was getting desperate. Beggars can't be choosers and it *will* look much better after it's cleaned up and we've got a few things of our own around us. It's a fairly respectable house and she seemed very nice, in an odd sort of way.'

'I wanted better for you, Lou.'

'Don't let it get you down! It will be ours! Our first home and we'll laugh at it in years to come.'

He sighed and nodded. 'I've bought you something.'

'What?'

'I was going to keep it until we were married but I think you need cheering up a bit.'

'What is it?'

He looked around at the narrow, darkening streets, aware that they were being observed. 'Not here! Come on, there's a tram coming!' He caught her hand and pulled her along.

'Have you gone mad! Where are we going?'

'The Pierhead.'

'In this? You are mad!'

'I've just suddenly thought that it's the most appropriate place!' he laughed as they sat down on the long seat by the conductor's platform.

'Will you stop teasing me and tell me what it is? And why we have to go to the Pierhead in weather like this!'

'You'll see.' And they were the only words she could get out of him until they reached their destination.

The cobbled setts glistened like pewter. The Birkenhead bank of the river was obscured by the misty rain. The lights of the ships feebly penetrated the gloom and she was reminded of all the nights she'd spent at the top of St George's Hill, looking down on all this.

He placed his arm around her shoulder and drew her closer.

'There was a time when I hated the river,' she said

302

softly. 'It took Da away. But then, it brought you home to me.'

'I don't think anyone could hate it for long. It's too much a part of us all. It's the life blood of the city.'

She nestled closer to him and fingered the locket that she treasured so dearly now. 'Are you going to tell me why you've dragged me down here?' she wheedled.

He reached into the inside pocket of his coat and pulled out a small box. 'Are you wearing your locket?'

She looked puzzled but she nodded.

'I saw this in a jeweller's window. Open it.'

She took it from him and lifted the lid. Inside was a small gold ring to which three charms were attached. The kind you saw on heavy gold bracelets.

'I couldn't afford the bracelet but I thought you could slip this on your locket chain. The girl in the shop explained it all to me. The cross symbolizes Faith, the anchor Hope and the heart, Charity. It was just so apt. You've got all three virtues, Lou, and your Da had them, too. That's why I brought you here – it just seemed the right place.'

She felt a lump in her throat and tears stung her eyes. 'Oh, Mike! I do love you!' she choked as she closed the box and drew closer to him.

'And I love you! No regrets, Lou? No doubts?'

She looked up at him and smiled. 'No regrets, no doubts, just a few nerves.'

He smiled and touched her cheek gently. 'I've a few of those myself, but we've got Faith, Hope and Charity to help us along now . . .'

'And love,' she murmured as his lips caressed her.

At ten o'clock the following morning, in the austere surroundings of Brougham Terrace, Louisa Mary Langford became Mrs Michael Joseph Crowley and she'd repeated her vows as solemnly as if she'd been standing in front of the Archbishop of Canterbury himself instead of the superintendent registrar.

Sall, with tears in her eyes as she remembered her own wedding, kissed them both, and Joe Doran pumped Mike's hand and kissed Louisa on the cheek. The registrar, a stiff-looking bureaucrat in a starched, winged collar and dark suit, unbent sufficiently to smile and wish them happiness, while wondering at the wisdom of the match after noting the mixed religions on the marriage certificate.

As they all walked out into the pale, watery November sunlight, a young policeman was coming up the steps. Louisa stopped and clutched Mike's arm, while Sall's mouth formed an O of astonishment.

'I'm too late! Never mind. Congratulations, Louisa!'

'My God! Tommy MacGann! A scuffer!' Mike cried.

Tommy stretched out his hand. 'Pax, from one family outcast to another?'

Mike grinned and shook it while both Louisa and Sall just stared at them both, bemused.

'Does Aunt Babsey know?' she asked at last.

'Of course she does.' He frowned, remembering the scene his announcement that he'd joined the Liverpool City Police had caused. She'd accused him of getting big ideas, of bringing disgrace on them. He knew what people thought of the police, they were to be avoided like the plague and the war hadn't changed that attitude. She'd gone on and on about how would Eddie feel and how she'd have to keep it from him. He'd replied angrily that he didn't give a damn how Eddie felt, he'd thought she would have been proud of him. His Da would have been, he'd stormed. And why did she now suddenly think the world revolved around Eddie? What had Eddie ever done except think about himself? He was the one who had disgraced the family – even getting arrested! Well, Eddie would have to watch himself now. 'And when they finally nail him, don't come crying to me Mam!' had been his parting shot. He still hadn't got over the hurt of being rejected. He didn't understand her any more. The war had changed her or maybe it had been his Da's death.

'Does Eddie know?' Mike asked.

'I don't know. Mam swore she wouldn't tell him.'

'But where've you been?' Louisa was still mystified.

'Bruche. Training School. I'm on probation now, stationed at Rose Hill. I live at the station house.'

Sall finally found her tongue. 'What made you join, you know scuffers aren't liked around our neighbourhood?'

'My mate from the Air Force joined when he was demobbed. It's a good career and they were pretty short, so I thought, why not? It's better than serving in a shop!'

'Look, we're off to the Exchange Hotel for a quiet meal, come with us?' Mike asked.

Tommy shook his head. 'I'd like to but my sergeant will have my guts if I'm not back soon. He's a decent enough bloke. Gave me time to nip up here.'

As the little group made its way towards the tram stop on West Derby Road, Sall laughed. 'Can't you walk ahead a bit? It looks as though we're all under arrest!'

'Give over, Sall Green!' Louisa interjected. 'I'm not ashamed of him. In fact I'm proud of him!'

'And I'm proud to have him as a cousin-in-law. He's better than the other one!' He turned to Tommy. 'He'll find out sooner or later and you never know, you may have to lock him up one day. Would that bother you?'

Tommy grinned. 'I'll face that when the time comes but I think he's got enough sense to stay well clear of me. I nearly didn't get in because of him. He was locked up once but they didn't have enough to hold him or charge him.'

'They know you are brothers and that he is a villain and they still took you on?' Sall said.

'I told you, they're short of men and, besides, if you come clean with them, you get treated fair and then there's your war record.'

'And yours was pretty good?'

Tommy nodded but shrugged. 'I was only doing my bit. There were others braver than me. Here comes the tram, yours anyway.' He seemed glad to escape the questions about his war service.

'Come and see us soon. Number 16 Faulkner Square. Top floor!' Louisa called.

'For a while anyway, until I build her a decent house!'

Mike shouted and Tommy gave them a smart salute, then looked quickly around to see if he'd been observed. A constable was only supposed to salute a senior officer or the civic dignitaries.

On his way back to the station he thought about Mike's words concerning Eddie. They were firmly on the opposite sides of the fence now and he wondered if the day would ever come when there would be a confrontation. He turned his thoughts to Louisa. He had nothing against Mike Crowley. Like Mike, his time in the forces had broadened his outlook and during his training it had been stressed that neither creed nor colour should be allowed to interfere with duty.

He turned the collar of his cape up as it had started to rain. Sergeant MacLean had asked him home a couple of times for a meal, after he'd explained his position, and his daughter, Jean, was a good-looking girl. He wondered if he should ask her out.

CHAPTER TWENTY-TWO

Under a Labour government led by Clement Attlee, the country was struggling to rebuild and Liverpool was not the only city that was faced with a desperate housing shortage. Slowly the bomb-sites were being cleared, houses were being patched up and to ease the chronic overcrowding, single-storey, prefabricated houses were being erected on the outskirts.

Mike had ploughed every penny he had into his business and worked as hard, if not harder, than the handful of men he employed. Through Joe Doran's good offices he'd obtained contract work at first but in the summer of 1946 he'd landed his first big contract.

Louisa had gone back to work at the offices of the Union. Life was hard and it wasn't easy to live on just one wage but Babsey had brought her up to be thrifty, so they managed. But at least they were moving from Faulkner Square to a small, terraced house in Anfield.

She'd nearly finished packing and Sall had come straight from work to help.

'I won't be sorry to leave here!' she said emphatically, as she wrapped the last few pieces of china, bought from Great Homer Street market, in old editions of the *Daily Mirror* and placed them in an orange box.

'I don't blame you. The black widow downstairs gives me the creeps – all those floating bits of black chiffon she has attached to her!'

'She's not bad really. She's never bothered us. But it will be heaven to have a kitchen and a privy of our own!'

'That bathroom is a disgrace, you should inform the

public health! Even our privy in Cicero Terrace was better than that! You seemed to be the only one in the house who ever cleaned it!' Sall was folding the bedding and putting it into a large, cardboard box.

'And have them come and throw us all out?'

'I could have cried at times, Lou, watching you scrubbing that floor. You aren't used to this!'

'I am now!'

'I'm glad you're getting out and I'm glad that business is booming. God knows, you both work hard enough. You'll have that big house one day.'

'I'll be satisfied with a small one. Have you thought any more about what we were talking about last week?'

Sall shrugged. She'd returned to her old job at the match factory when the munitions factories had closed down. 'I don't see much point in it, Lou, going to art school in the evenings. What use will it be to me?'

'You enjoy drawing and sketching, don't you? You could get a job in fashion design or something.'

Sall eyed her sceptically over the top of the box into which she was packing the jug and basin set. 'Don't be daft, Lou! People like me don't get jobs like that!'

'Why not, there's always a first time. You must have a dream, Sall.'

'Oh, I had dreams once. Now all I've got is plain, old-fashioned common sense.'

'Then go just for the enjoyment. It will give you an interest in something other than that house and that factory.'

'I'd feel a fool! I wouldn't even have the right pencils or paints or whatever they use.'

'They'll tell you what to get. Try it! You don't know what you can do until you try!'

'You mean like you joining that political party thing?'

'Something like that. Mike and I have made new friends. Friends who don't care about what religion you are.'

'The people who go to those meetings are like you and me, working class.'

'And how do you know the people who go to evening classes aren't the same? You don't until you go and find out.'

'I wish you'd stop bullying me, Lou Crowley!'

'I promise I'll stop when you go to evening classes, now give me a hand and we'll get all the stuff down into the hall. Tommy has arranged for a carter he knows to come round and pick it up in the morning.'

'If she comes out and starts hovering and wafting those black crêpe scarves I'll scream, I swear I will!'

'She won't. It's not as though we're doing a moonlight flit. We've always paid the rent on time.'

'How's your Tommy's romance with Jean MacLean going?'

'Quite well, I think. He was saying the other day that they might get a police house or flat if they get married.'

'And that's another wedding your Aunt Babsey won't be going to either, I presume, even though Jean is the "right" religion?'

'I don't know if she'll go or not, but I will!'

'Mam was only saying the other day that she thinks your Aunt Babsey's going a bit "strange". She hardly ever goes out now, unless Eddie takes her in the car. Your Evvie seems to have taken over the shop and what with Arnold taking over from his Dad, they can't be short and she's giving herself all kinds of airs and graces again. Now I hear she's talking of taking Julie away from St George's and sending her private. Private! Does she know how much that costs?'

Louisa grinned as they staggered down the stairs laden with boxes and parcels. 'She always did have big ideas, did our Evvie.'

'And Eddie's encouraging her, now they're on speaking terms again. He's doing all right, too, although no-one seems to know exactly what it is he does do. He's got both Tad and Mogsey working for him and the pair of them all done up like dog's dinners! That Mogsey's so sharp he'll cut himself one day!'

'You never did like him, did you, Sall?'

'No and I've not changed my opinion. Oh, blast! I've caught my stocking on that broken spindle and these are my only decent pair! Isn't it about time they scrapped all the ration books? The war's been over for a year now!'

'Sometimes I think we'll have ration books when we're sixty! I've forgotten what it's like just to go into a shop and buy whatever takes your fancy without having to count up to see if you've got enough coupons left! There! Put them by the door but not too near in case someone falls over it all.' She pressed her hands into the small of her back. 'I think we deserve a cuppa after all that.'

Sall clapped a hand to her mouth.

'Now what?'

'I've packed the kettle and all the pans and cups!'

Louisa started to laugh. 'You never change Sally Green! You're still as scatty as ever!'

'What will you do about Mike's dinner?'

'We'll have to have fish and chips, out of a newspaper, and I'll get blamed!' she grinned.

'I'll leave you to it. Mam will have kept my dinner warm.'

'So, will you go?'

'Go where?'

'Evening classes!'

'I might. I'll see how I feel.'

Louisa feigned a lunge at her and Sall screamed in mock dismay. A door along the hall opened and Mrs Dean-Swifte appeared.

'Oh, Lord! It's the black widow, I'm off!' Sall laughed.

The following week Sall walked apprehensively through the doors of the Liverpool College of Art in Hope Street and enrolled for evening classes. She was surprised to see a motley collection of people of all ages and classes in the room to which she'd been directed by a pleasant woman who had helped her fill in the necessary forms. She was to start with a foundation course, whatever that meant.

310

She slipped into a seat at the back of the room and watched a tall, thin man with a greying beard and moustache speaking to the other students in turn. When he finally reached her he smiled.

'And who is this little mouse hiding at the back?'

'Sall Green, Mrs,' she said.

He referred to his list. 'Ah, yes.'

She didn't like the tone in which this was uttered. 'I've never done anything like this before.'

'Never? Not even at school?'

'Not really.'

He smiled and she felt a little more at ease. 'We'll start you off with still life just to see how you shape up. I want you to give me your impression of that collection of objects on the table there.'

'I . . . I didn't bring anything with me.' She felt so embarrassed as he placed a large sheet of paper and a soft leaded pencil before her. 'You want me to draw that jug and that cup and that half-dead flower?'

'You're very direct Mrs Green but I have to agree. It does look rather wilted, but we have to make do with what we can find these days.' He walked away, leaving her staring blankly at the objects.

She wasn't at all pleased with her efforts. The jug looked too narrow and out of proportion. The goblet was too squat and the flower looked even deader than it really was. 'I give up! It's awful!' she said flatly, handing it to her teacher.

He examined it carefully while she wished the floor would open up and swallow her, for she'd caught glimpses of the other students' work. 'It's not that bad. You have a certain degree of talent and I'm sure we can build on that and improve your style. You'll never be a Leonardo da Vinci or a Raphael but . . .'

'If I had that kind of talent I wouldn't be here, would I? I'd be living in some foreign country in a big house with servants, wouldn't I?'

He smiled again, she definitely wasn't his usual sort of

311

student. 'What do you want from your art, Mrs Green? A career, a pastime, the fulfilment of a desire or ambition?'

'I don't know what I want – yet. But I think I'll enjoy coming here, if nothing else.'

'I hope you will and who knows, there may be a career opening later on.'

'Not in my line of work, unless they want me to design a new matchbox cover.'

He looked puzzled.

'I work in a match factory. I'm a chargehand.'

'Oh, I see. You never know though they just may want a new design for their boxes one day.'

'I could do that. They've had that same picture of a bloke in a sou'wester clutching a ship's wheel, for ages!'

'You see! You might think of a career in commercial art.'

'Designing box lids?'

'Not only box lids, as you put it. Commercial art covers a wide field and it's becoming more and more popular. And it's very lucrative.'

She began to look interested. 'What shall I bring for next time? What kind of stuff will I need and where will I get it?'

He scribbled some items down on a pad, plus the name and address of a couple of suppliers. 'You won't need everything just yet. It's quite expensive, if you can get it at all. You can build your equipment up, bit by bit. I take it we'll be seeing you again, Mrs Green?'

'Oh, aye. I've paid my money!' she smiled impishly.

Louisa was hanging out some of Mike's work clothes in the back yard when he came home earlier than usual. He opened the yard door quietly and stood watching her, a smile on his lips. In the nine months they'd been married he'd never regretted a single day. There had been times when he'd missed the bickering between his parents that had been part of the fabric of his early home life. The cheerful waves and greetings of the neighbours, the convivial atmosphere of the pub. Yet he knew he would have felt a much deeper sense of loss for that former life, if it had not been for the war.

Attitudes were changing, slowly, amongst the younger generation who had had more on their minds than religious differences. They'd both made new friends and not all the old ones had deserted them. He worked hard. They both worked hard. It was no easier for her and yet she never complained. There was always a meal on the table and a smile. But he'd learned that she was a complex woman. She could be gentle, submissive, sometimes even shy and yet there was a strong, obdurate and aggressive side to her nature that came to the fore when confronted with injustice and discrimination. And when faced with the pompous obstinacy, patronization and tyranny so beloved of minor civil servants and council department heads, she became as stubborn and imperious as them and there were quite a few who had already borne the brunt of her sharp, sarcastic wit that deflated their egos and defeated their bombastic blustering.

She turned and caught sight of him. 'You're early, what's the matter?'

'Nothing. It's half past six. I thought I'd come home early for a change and take you out.' He put his arm around her waist. 'I neglect you too much, Lou.'

She touched his cheek gently. 'No, you don't. You don't hear me complaining, do you? But you do work too hard, Mike. Come in, your dinner's ready.'

'I hope I'll be able to ease off a bit soon. As soon as we get the last of those prefabs up I can afford to hire a foreman and that will take some of the work load off my shoulders.' He hung his jacket on the peg behind the scullery door and washed his hands.

'Have you got anyone in mind?'

'Aye, my Da.'

'Will he accept? Your Mam hasn't forgiven you for marrying me.'

'I think he will and he's as honest as the day is long and that's just why I want him. I know he won't be robbing me blind.'

He sat down at the table as she placed his meal before him.

'I think I'll go round and see him later.'

'Ay, so you didn't come home early just to take me out? There's a method in your madness!'

He pulled her down onto his knee. 'Do you ever regret marrying me, Lou?'

'Don't be stupid, of course I don't. We're happy, aren't we?'

'But it's all bed to work. All work and no play and I promised you'd have the best that I could provide.'

'When did you promise me that?'

He shook his head. 'I didn't make it to you. I made it on the night we heard that the *Ceramic* had gone down. A silent vow to your Da, Lou.'

She touched the gold locket around her neck. 'And you've kept it.'

'No, I won't have kept it until we have our own house, filled with new furniture and you've got good clothes and jewellery and we've got a car and money in the bank.'

'And how do you know that I want all those things? I don't if they separate me from my friends. I'm not a social climber, Mike. I'm happy just as we are and soon I'll be even happier.'

He looked up into her face and saw the soft, translucent glow in her eyes. 'Lou . . .?'

She laughed and nodded. 'I went to the doctor's this afternoon. There'll be three of us next March! You're going to be a father!'

He couldn't take it in, he just shook his head and then he let out a yell and holding her tightly in his arms, he whirled her around the kitchen. 'Me a father! I can't believe it, Lou!'

'You'd better believe it and you'd better put me down or you'll have me dizzy!' she laughed.

314

He instantly became solicitude itself, gently easing her down onto a chair and taking her hand and patting it.

She pealed with laughter. 'Stop that! I'm not an invalid! I intend to carry on working for as long as I can.'

'Oh, no, you're not!'

'Now don't start that! We need the money.'

'To hell with the money!'

'No! You won't be able to ask your Da to work for you, will you? And I'd like our baby to see its father more than just for half an hour a day and we want it to have a good life, a good education.'

Reluctantly he agreed.

'So, will you go and see him?'

'We'll both go! Mam can't ignore this!'

She was feeling more than a little apprehensive as she stood on the doorstep of the house in Beacon Lane, her arm through Mike's.

Pat Crowley quickly covered his surprise at seeing them by grinning and shooing them into the kitchen.

'Hello, Mam. You look well,' Mike said quietly.

Maggie's smile vanished as she caught sight of Louisa and Louisa's heart sank. Mike held her hand tightly in his.

'We thought we'd come and tell you the news – you're going to be grandparents!'

There was silence and then Maggie closed her eyes and crossed herself.

Louisa felt all the elation drain from her. Why did some mothers hate the women who took their sons? It wasn't just religion with Maggie Crowley, she sensed something deeper, more complex. 'We shouldn't have come, Mike,' she said softly, but Mike's expression was grim.

'No. We're not leaving until we've had this out once and for all!'

'Maggie, the lad's right! It's time all this bitterness was put aside. There's a baby on the way – your grandson or granddaughter – and didn't Jesus Christ himself say "Suffer the little children to come unto me"? Are you setting yourself above Him now?'

315

Louisa clenched her hand tightly in her pocket. She wanted to go home. This woman hated her, she could feel it.

'And what religion will he . . . or she . . . be?'

Oh, they were never going to get away from it, Louisa thought.

'Does that matter now? We've not even thought of it!' Mike cried.

'Of course it matters! Will you let your child grow up a heathen, steeped in Original Sin?'

Louisa had had enough. 'Mrs Crowley why do you hate me so much? Apart from being brought up in the Protestant faith, what is it that you hate so much? I didn't take your son away from you and I won't take your grandchild, unless you force me to! After all we've been through, isn't it time we stopped fighting each other?' She'd made the first overture, she thought, now it was up to her mother-in-law.

Maggie's gaze flitted from the face of her husband to that of her son and finally that of her daughter-in-law. She had to admit that what the girl said was true, although it hurt her to do so, but basically she was an honest woman. She had hated her for taking her son but she had been the one who had suffered because of it. And now, was it right to involve an innocent new life and deny herself the joy a grandchild would bring? She bit back the retort that had risen to her lips. Maybe if she relented the girl might agree to the child being brought up in the Catholic faith? Slowly she nodded her head. 'Maybe it's . . . time.'

Mike let out his breath slowly. The first crack in his mother's armour had appeared.

'Sit down the both of youse, I'll whet the tea.'

'Aye, sit down, girl, you have to take care of yourself now!' Pat, openly relieved, pulled a chair forward. 'Me! A Grandad! Won't that be grand! You'll be able to rename the business. Crowley, Langford & Son, if it's a boy that is.'

'I wanted to talk to you about that, Da.'

'Talk away!'

Maggie raised her eyes to the ceiling as she handed Louisa her tea in one of her best china cups. 'Work! Sure, he talks of nothing else!'

Louisa sipped the tea, picking her words carefully. 'Mike's got plans . . .' she began tentatively, feeling she was treading on very thin ice.

'He always had plans, even before the war. Said he'd be his own man one day.'

She took her courage in both hands. 'You're proud of him, aren't you?'

'That I am, in the circumstances,' came the abrupt reply.

She smiled. She had to keep trying. 'Then we have that in common, too.' It was a start but she knew she had a long way to go before she could break down the barriers between this woman and herself.

It didn't take much to persuade Pat Crowley to accept the job of foreman. Mike's was one of the few construction firms who employed both Catholic and Protestant alike and treated them all the same and he openly encouraged them to belong to a Union and was gaining the reputation of being a fair employer. In fact he could have trebled his workforce overnight, if he could have afforded it.

With his father in charge he was free to pursue contracts and follow up contacts and as there were never any stoppages due to industrial action, the work was finished on schedule and sometimes even before. He was aware that there was graft and corruption within the industry, it had always been there, but he'd managed to keep his business clean until he walked into the site office one afternoon and found Pat looking troubled and grim.

'What's up, Da? Problems?'

'Not with the lads, or the work or the suppliers, son.'

'Then what?'

'Had a visitor about half an hour ago.'

'Who?'

'Said his name was Smith! Jesus! He must think I came over on the last boat!'

'And?'

'He beat around the bush a bit, but the top and bottom of it is he's after protection money!'

'Is he, by God. He'll get none out of me!'

'You'd better have a word with the lads, Mike, he may try to put the wind up them. Threaten them or their families. He more or less said we could expect trouble. Fires, damaged materials, things like that. I told him to sod off or I'd be damaging him!'

'What did he look like! Seen him before?'

Pat nodded. 'I've seen him around but never in any of the pubs I've been in. Big, ugly looking bloke, although I'd say he was past his prime. Looked a bit like an ex-boxer to me.'

'Jed Leach! I'll bet it was him! And I know who's backing him!'

'Who?'

'Eddie MacGann!'

'Lou's cousin?'

Mike nodded. He'd heard that Eddie was into all kinds of villainy these days. He turned towards the door.

'Where are you going?'

'To see MacGann!'

'Hold on a minute, me and a couple of the lads will come with you.'

'No! This is between me and him! I don't want anyone else getting involved.'

'Take care then.'

'I will.'

'Corner a rat and it'll go for your throat!'

'Not if you get it by the throat first!' came the grim reply.

It was Babsey who opened the door to him. At first she looked puzzled and then she glared at him.

He was shocked by her appearance. She seemed to have shrunk and her hair was almost white.

'Get off my doorstep!'

'Where's your son? I've got some business with him.'

'He'd have no business with you, clear off!' She made to slam the door but he was too quick for her, thrusting his foot in the steel-capped working boot into the doorway.

'Send him out or I'll have no hesitation in forcing my way past you!'

'You'll not set foot in my house, you dirty papist!'

'Then send him out or is he so afraid he has to hide behind his Mammy's skirts?' he shouted.

It worked. Eddie appeared behind Babsey. 'What do you want, Crowley?'

'Outside! You!'

Eddie stepped into the yard while Babsey stood, her arms folded, glaring at them both.

'You sent Jed Leach to the site this afternoon, didn't you, looking for protection money? Don't deny it! Too yellow to come yourself! You don't change, do you? Well, I'm here to tell you that you'll get nothing out of me and if you touch a single piece of timber or even speak to any of my lads or their families, I'll break your neck the way I broke your hand!'

Eddie laughed scornfully. 'That doesn't scare me any more, Crowley! I've enough men who would be only too willing to see you lying in a jigger with your head cracked open!'

'Grown to be the big man now? Plenty of fools to do your dirty work! Oh, you think you're smart not to get caught but I'm sure that between them Lou and Tommy could build a case strong enough to convict you.'

Eddie laughed again. 'For what?'

'Your activities during the war!'

'That's history!'

'And history has a way of repeating itself, except that this time your brother's on the other side!'

'You'd never make any of that stick and you know it, now get out!'

The bluff had failed but Mike wasn't one to give in easily nor was he averse to stooping to Eddie's own level. 'I'm warning you, MacGann, come near me, my men or my property and you'd better stay with your Mam day and night or something nasty might happen to her! This house could suddenly catch fire, with her in it! Or your precious car might suddenly get in the way of one of my diggers. You might even meet with a very nasty accident! Do I make myself clear?'

'You wouldn't dare, you bastard!'

'Try me! I can sink as low as you if I have to or pay others to do it for me – like you! I know men who would chuck a can of petrol in there and set fire to it for a couple of fivers. Men who'd think the loss of that old bitch a blessing! Don't say I haven't warned you, MacGann!'

The yard door shook on its hinges while Eddie just stared at it, ashen faced. That bastard had meant it, he hadn't been bluffing. There were just as many hard men working for Crowley as there were for him. He'd have to back off – for now. He couldn't risk his Mam or himself or his car. But his day would come, even if he had to wait ten years it would be worth it in the end.

On a wild, windy March day Sall called in to see Louisa and tell her her news.

Louisa was sitting on the sofa with her feet on a stool for lately her ankles swelled. She was heavy and she tired easily now. She was struggling with a half-finished bootee. 'Oh, I'll never master how to turn a heel! Look at it! I'll have to buy some, if I put him in these his feet will be deformed!'

'Don't say things like that, it's tempting fate! Anyway, how do you know it's going to be a "he"?'

'I don't, but I can't call him "it". Besides it was Mike who first said "he".'

'Then I hope he's not disappointed. Guess what?'

'What have you been up to now, Sall Green? You've got that look on your face.'

'I entered a competition to design a new chocolate box lid, for Cadbury's. The old Queen – Queen Mary – had graciously offered to judge them. We all entered, half the country entered!'

'She must have gone right off chocolate! If she's had any that is.'

'Don't interrupt! That's what it was for – when they come off the ration and I think someone must have sorted them all out first or she'd have been buried under piles of artwork!'

'Well, get on with it!'

'I am! I won!'

Louisa dropped the knitting, gave a shriek of joy and tried to get up.

'Sit still! I can't believe it! I keep pinching myself! Me! Sally Green from Cicero Terrace who once had no stockings, no decent shoes, nits, bugs!'

'You see! I told you you were good! Oh, Sall! I'm so pleased and so proud! Is there a prize or anything?'

'What more do you want? A Queen picked *my* design! Mr Cheltenham said every commercial art company will be after me now! I can go anywhere, do anything! He was going on about London but I soon shut him up about that! I'm staying put!'

'But the opportunities . . .!'

'I'm not leaving Liverpool! But I will be leaving the match works. Just think, Lou, I'm going to be paid and paid really well, for doing something I really like doing!' Her eyes misted. 'Oh, Harry would have been over the moon, Lou, and Da, too.'

A grimace chased the smile from Louisa's face as a pain stabbed low in her abdomen.

'Lou! Oh, now look what I've gone and done!'

'Go and phone for the ambulance Sall, and my case is in the bedroom.' She relaxed as the spasm passed.

'What about Mike?'

'He's on the site, you'll have to get word to him.'

'I'll send our Robbie!' Sall rushed upstairs for the small suitcase.

She could feel the next contraction coming, stronger than the last. 'That will take hours. You'd better go for his Mam!'

Sall stared at her. 'Maggie Crowley?'

Louisa nodded. 'She is his Mam and it is her grandchild – it may even help!' She bit her lip as the pain seared through her and in its wake came fear. What was she going to have to go through these next hours? What was going to happen to her?

Sall shrugged. 'I'll go down to the phone box on the corner! I'll come with you in the ambulance! Just don't go and have it while I'm gone or "Mother MacCree" will beat me to death with her rosary beads!'

It was eight long, agonizing hours later when the doctor came out of the delivery room and smiled at the assembled group. Mike, his nails bitten down to the quick, Pat surrounded by cigarette butts and Sall and Maggie tense and anxious, their initial animosity forgotten.

'Mr Crowley?'

Mike rushed forward. 'Is she all right? Is the baby all right?'

'Everyone's just fine. Your wife is tired and a little bit sore. We had to use forceps for the second one, but she's young and healthy . . .'

'The "second" one?' Mike echoed.

The doctor laughed and extended his hand. 'Congratulations, Mr Crowley! You have two fine, healthy boys!'

Suddenly Sall began to laugh and she caught Maggie's arm. 'That's Lou Langford all over – she never does anything the easy way!'

PART III
'LIVERPOOL LOU'
1954

CHAPTER TWENTY-THREE

The years of austerity appeared to be over and standards of living had risen for many, but there was still a housing shortage and there was still poverty in Liverpool. Although Crowley, Langford & Sons had prospered and grown to four times its original size, Louisa refused to move from her home in Stonehill Street.

'I don't want to be stuck out in the wilds of Woolton or Croxteth Park, away from all my friends. What use would a great big house be? It would only become a barrier between us and everyone we know and love?'

'Sall's moved her family to Newsham Park,' Mike persisted.

'And she spends most of her time here and Mrs Cooper has practically moved in with the Gillows. She hates it there. She says it's too quiet and no-one ever speaks to her and she's sick of looking at trees! No, Mike, we've been happy in this house and I want to keep it that way!'

'I want the boys to have somewhere to play other than the yard or the street.'

'There's Breckside Park and they've all their friends here and at school. And what would your Mam say about you moving her grandsons miles away from her?'

He sighed. She was right – as usual. Ever since John and Patrick had been born and both he and Lou had decided that they should at least be christened as Catholics, Maggie's attitude had softened. Her grandsons were the apple of her eye and they could do no wrong in her eyes. The fact that they'd been sent to a state primary school had caused a row, but now that they were to make their first communion at St Matthew's, where the Parish Priest was a very ecumenical man, far in advance of his times, had placated her. Even though they were always in scrapes of one kind or another and were usually the ringleaders, did nothing to alter the fact that to her they were as pure as the driven snow. He knew she was storming heaven's doors that Lou would be converted but he knew she was wasting her time there. Lou had gone as far as she would go. In fact he had been surprised that she had given way on both the christening and the communion.

The conversation was interrupted by two very grubby seven-year-olds who were as alike as two peas in a pod. A fact that they had soon learned to use to their advantage, although their mother could tell them apart without even seeing them, just by their voices.

'Mam, have you got any old rags? The rag and bone man's round the corner and he's got fishing nets!'

Louisa laughed. 'I could give him you two! Just look at the pair of you, you mucky little hooligans! What have you been up to?'

'Grid fishing, we got tuppence!' John said before Patrick jabbed him in the ribs and scowled.

'Mike, will you speak to them! I'm sick of telling them that poking around in filthy grids in equally filthy gutters will make them ill! They could catch anything!'

'Big mouth!' Patrick hissed at his brother.

'You heard your Mam – no more grid fishing!'

'Have you got any rags, Mam?' John persisted.

'Indeed I have not! Go and get washed, you're to go with your Granny for instruction tonight.'

'Off with you both, here . . .' Mike slipped a coin into each grubby hand.

'You spoil them. They'll have to learn the value of money!'

'I remember being dragged off for instruction myself. It's no fun!'

'Hush, they'll hear you! What kind of an example is that?'

'I'll take them round myself in the van. Mam's not getting any younger and traipsing them down to Queens Drive is exhausting, although wild horses wouldn't make her admit it. Nor has she forgiven Father Maguire for not letting them make their communion at Our Lady Immaculate's. Told him he was a narrow-minded old man and was he prepared to lose two souls because of his sin of pride! I never thought I'd see the day when she'd argue with him! I don't know whose sin of pride it was – his or hers! She really wanted to parade them through the neighbourhood. Her grandsons, above other mere mortals. No-one else has twins! She's going soft in her old age.'

'Get off with you! And make sure those two are clean!' she laughed.

After they'd gone she began to tidy up. Straightening up with an armful of assorted papers, books and toys, she caught sight of herself in the oval mirror that hung above the modern tiled fireplace. Just one of the improvements Mike had made to the house. He'd built on at the back and they now had a good-sized kitchen and a bathroom upstairs.

She didn't feel any older than the day she'd been married and yet she was thirty-two. I'm middle-aged, she thought and scrutinized her face for wrinkles! She didn't look *that* much older, she thought, or was that just wishful thinking? Her hair had been cut in the Italian style of short layers and feathery kiss curls that were supposed to fall onto her forehead but the natural wave in her hair had a perverse way of flicking the curls up instead of down. Her dress was of a fine wool, the skirt longer than she used to wear them but considered very smart for the mature woman. She sometimes envied the young girls with their wide, full skirts and nipped-in waists. She'd had neither the money nor the freedom they had when she was their age. Her generation had missed so much. She sighed. She was turning into a staid, middle-aged woman. Most evenings she and Mike sat and listened to the wireless, occasionally they went to the cinema.

Sall usually called three or four times a week and tonight would be no exception, she thought as she went to open the front door.

'Have you had your dinner?' she greeted her.

'I had it before I left home. Mam virtually threw it at me she was in such a rush to get to Nancy Gillow's.'

'I don't know why you moved them all out there, you know she hates it and you don't spend much time there yourself.'

'I know. I'm beginning to agree with you, but it seemed like a good idea at the time. I've always wanted her to have a nice home and I wanted somewhere where our Lotty could make decent friends.' She looked wistful. 'I had the money – for the first time in my life I had plenty of money!'

Louisa smiled at her. Sall hadn't changed much either. Oh, she dressed more smartly, she spoke better and she'd gained confidence ever since she'd been snapped up by the Thomas Bond Commercial Art Studio. To look at her now, a senior member of their staff and paid, as she put it, more money than it was decent to earn, it would be hard to find the scrawny, little waif who'd run the streets of Everton Brow barelegged and in plimsolls. 'Mike's been harping on at me about moving to a bigger house but I've told him I'm staying here. I've got the example of you living in splendid isolation to hold up to him.'

'Where is he? I wanted to ask his advice.'

'He's taken the boys and Maggie to St Matthew's.'

'Will he be long?'

'No, he's gone in the van. He doesn't wait, he'll go back for them later.' She laughed. 'I think he's scared of Father Hayes. What's the matter?'

'Nothing. It's all to do with the house and my job and you, too.'

'Me?'

'I was talking to Joe Doran yesterday and . . .'

'Don't you start! I know what you're going to say! Joe's been after me to go back to work, to take charge of the welfare department.'

'Why don't you? How do you stand it, stuck here all day with just the boys and they're at school all day? It's not like before the war, Lou, when women only went out to work because they were forced to. Lots of women have carried on working because they enjoy it. And I agree with Joe, you're far too intelligent and skilled in sorting out all the red tape to be stuck at home.'

'I happen to enjoy it and besides I'm not having the boys become latch-key kids. Maggie would kill me!'

'It's not like you, Lou, to be worried by what she says.'

'These days, Sall, I find it easier to give in a little, mainly for the sake of peace. Oh, I know it's not always the right thing to do but she's not that bad when you get to know her. I think she forgave me for "stealing" her son when I gave her two grandsons, but she'd never forgive me if I let them run the streets and they would. Especially in the school holidays.'

'She'd look after them, you know she would! If you put it the right way, and you're good at that, she'd jump at the chance. It may mean that she'd have more influence over them though, in religious matters.'

'I'm not starting another war with her over that! I've made my concessions because I thought they were right, but this first communion is as far as it goes. Quite honestly I think seven is too young. They don't really understand the deep significance of it and how can they? They're little more than babies. But she says they do, that's what this instruction is all about. So who am I to argue? I never got confirmed or went to communion.'

'Neither did I.'

They heard the key in the door and Mike came into the room.

'She's come to discuss some grand plan,' Louisa laughed.

'What's she up to now?'

Louisa shrugged.

'Come on, Sall, out with it! Don't keep us all in suspense.'

'I want to start my own business.'

'Doing what?' Mike asked.

'I got the idea when I was buying things for the house. You know the trouble I had finding materials at a price I could afford. I needed yards and yards, those windows are so big. Everything was so dull and old-fashioned and so expensive that I told them they had a nerve charging prices like that. So, I want to design my own and get them manufactured at a decent price and sell them myself. I'd do cushions and curtains and maybe lampshades to start with. And braids and trimmings to match.'

Mike looked thoughtful. 'It's a good idea but what will you use for capital?'

'I'll sell the house. Pay off the mortgage and have a clear profit. Everyone hates it, so I won't be upsetting them. Mam keeps saying if she sees another tree she'll scream! We'll get a small terraced, like we used to have.'

'You'll need more than you'll get for that house, Sall, and it will be hard work. You'll have to sort out contracts with the mills, find your markets, find suitable premises.'

'I know all that. I was talking to Joe Doran and he said he'll help me – with the mills anyway. He thinks there's going to be a slump in the textile industry soon with all the cheap stuff coming in from abroad. That's when we got to talking about Lou.'

'Joe's been recruiting Sall for his campaign to get me back to work.'

'I can't see why she shouldn't. Your Mam will look after the boys. She'd be in her element and you'd know they were in good hands.'

Louisa looked at Mike who returned her gaze quizzically.

'You know what I think, Lou. Joe's right, you're wasted at home.'

'It's a conspiracy!'

'Think about it!' Sall urged.

'All right, I'll think about it! But that's not a promise.'

'Seeing as she won't move house, the capital I'd put by for a house I could lend you, Sall, and I'd do up any premises you find.'

Sall shook her head. 'I didn't come here on the cadge.'

'We know that. Don't be a fool, Sall. Take the loan, you'll need it, won't she Mike?'

Sall bit her lip. She was quite prepared to sink all her money into this venture but Mike's money – that was different.

'If you take the loan then I'll go back to work for Joe!'

Sall hesitated, then nodded slowly.

Mike threw back his head and laughed. 'You walked right into that Sally Green! Shrewd business woman though you are, this one takes some beating! I have plans for her.'

'Now you've started him off on his pet subject! I'll never hear the end of it!'

'I'm going to see her on the city council if it's the last thing I do! She's just the person we need. She's stubborn, dogmatic, honest and fair and she'll stand up for the ordinary people and that's what's needed!'

'I've told you, Mike Crowley, if you're so interested in the welfare of the people of this city, then get yourself elected to the council! I'm going to have enough to do now as it is, with the house and the boys and now the welfare department. What are you trying to do, the pair of you? Kill me with work. What's wrong with Sall standing for the council? She'd be better at it than me. Underneath that frail, helpless-looking exterior she's as tough as old boots!'

'You watch who you're calling an old boot, Lou Crowley, or when I've got a chain of shops all over the country, I won't even speak to you!'

When Agnes heard that Sall intended to move back to the old neighbourhood she was overjoyed, although she wasn't quite sure about all Sall's other plans. She thought Sall was over-stretching herself and said so, but all she received in return was a pained look and the stubborn set of her daughter's chin. She knew she might just as well have saved her breath. Sall never ceased to amaze her. She'd been flabbergasted when Sall had won that competition and got the job of commercial artist. She'd been totally bemused when they'd moved to Newsham Park. Although it hadn't taken her long to realize that to dream about a big house in a park and to actually live there were two different things. She didn't know where Sall got her talent from. It certainly wasn't from her and none of the others showed any aptitude in that direction. In fact Sall was always commenting, acerbically, on the total lack of taste her sisters showed. And as for Doreen . . . The less said about Doreen the better! She was living in a run-down house in Toxteth with a sailor. She said they were married but Agnes doubted it and Sall openly scoffed. 'She's living over the brush with him, Mam! He's probably got a wife and kids somewhere, maybe even grandchildren. He looks old enough and he must be half blind to see anything attractive about our Doreen!'

Agnes sighed. Life had changed so much and she was getting old, too old to cope with all the changes Sall was thrusting on her, but moving back – that was different. She'd enjoy that. You could keep your fancy houses, give her her own donkey-stoned doorstep to stand on and good neighbours to jangle with any day!

Joan was not so delighted. 'All we seem to do is move! You've dragged us all over this city, our Sall!' That was a bit of an exaggeration but it only emphasized her point. 'I was getting used to it here and now I suppose I'll have to share a room with our Lily and Lotty!'

'It won't be for long. She's been talking of getting engaged to Pete Higgs.'

'That won't solve anything, will it? The waiting list for council houses and flats is as long as my arm. They'll probably want to move in with us!'

'They can move in with his Mam if they have to.'

'And what about Lotty? She's been to more schools than I've had hot dinners! She's that confused that she doesn't seem to have learned much at all.'

'Don't exaggerate! She's only been moved twice!' Sall

glanced at her niece who had grown up into a quiet girl who resembled neither the Coopers nor the Buckleys.

'I don't mind. I'll be going to commercial college soon. I want to be like Aunty Lou.'

'Louisa Crowley never went to commercial college. She worked in a shop before she worked in the Union offices,' Joan commented.

Both Lotty and Sall glared at her. Sall had encouraged Lotty's admiration of her friend and her desire to emulate her. She'd also been relieved when Tad had finally given up making his monthly visits. He and Lotty had nothing to say to each other and the hours he spent with her were strained and tense for both of them. Sall smiled at her. She loved Lotty as though she were her own daughter. She didn't care who her father was, she loved her. Yet there were times when she caught a glimpse of something familiar in Lotty's expression, about the way she turned her head, but not wishing to probe the subject she'd deliberately put the matter out of her mind.

'Mike is going to look out for a property for me as well as a house, and he's going to do it up. I'm going to be busy at first. I'll have to go and see people, so I'm relying on you, our Joan, to keep everything in order here.'

'Why me?' Joan asked peevishly.

'Because Mam is not getting any younger and she hasn't been looking well lately.'

'So I'm supposed to go to work and run a house as well?'

'Stop whingeing! You don't moan when you get money for clothes, do you? And you buy enough of them! We could have a stall on Paddy's Market with all the stuff you've got!'

'Give it a rest you two! All I want is a bit of peace and quiet. Sall's right, I haven't been feeling well lately and I've had a lifetime listening to you lot rowing! I want to listen to the radio. It's Victor Sylvester.'

'I don't know why we can't have a television set,' Joan grumbled.

'I'm not a bloody millionaire and I'm going to need every penny I can get my hands on!'

'If you two don't stop it, you'll get the back of my hand – big as you are!' Agnes snapped as Sall returned to her columns of figures and Joan flounced upstairs to get ready to go out.

CHAPTER TWENTY-FOUR

Eddie sat at the table counting the notes and making suitable adjustments in his notebook. Things were going very smoothly, he mused. He felt good when everything went to plan and, over the past few years, it had. Now he was the owner of two clubs, legitimately, as well as his other 'sidelines'. He'd wanted to move house. He could afford it, but Babsey wouldn't hear of it. She wanted to stay near her grandchildren and Evvie. She was too old to be moving, she liked it here.

'You mean you like having all the things no-one else has got. A radiogram, a washing machine. Someone to do the heavy housework, a fur coat and a big car to take you out and your two weeks at the Imperial Hotel in Llandudno.'

'What if I do!'

He'd laughed. She hadn't changed in that respect. She was older and her tongue and her temper were less acerbic but she relied on him so much these days. Still, she was his Mam and he wasn't going to upset her, he'd told Marge, his fiancée of three years' standing. She was a stunner was Marge Roberts but she was definitely lacking where brains were concerned, which was part of her charm – for him. She never questioned anything he said. Marge, too, liked all the luxuries his money bought, although he had no plans to marry her – not yet anyway.

His Mam had stood by him all these years, even when Tommy had come poking his nose into his affairs. He'd never forgotten the shock he'd received when he'd learned that his kid brother was a scuffer. And he'd never have known until he'd come round one day with that detective

335

sergeant. How Babsey had kept it quiet he didn't know. He had been labouring under the assumption that Tommy was working down south somewhere. The excuse she'd given him. But he'd always made sure he'd covered his tracks and it would take more than a couple of flat-footed 'jacks' to nail him.

He folded the money and closed the book then put them both into his pocket.

'You going out?' Babsey asked.

'Only for a few hours. There's some property I want to see. I'm thinking of opening a coffee bar. A posh one, like. Not like some of the dumps I've seen. I'm thinking of giving it a foreign name and doing it up with cane seats and plants.'

'Don't let them cheat you over the price.'

'Do I ever? The place I've got in mind is at the top end of Bold Street, handy for the art college and the university. It's a run-down dress shop, so I should get it cheap.'

'You take care, Eddie.'

He frowned. She always said that and it irritated him. It was as though he were still a kid. 'Shall I send Evvie over to sit with you?'

'No. She never shuts up! She talks like a ha'penny book! The latest thing is Julie is going to stay on at school and maybe go to teacher training college or even university! I said to her, Evvie why waste all that money educating her when she'll only up and get married? You'll get no benefit from her. Now if it was young Arnold, that would be different. I'd even offer to help out so he could make something of himself but she says he hasn't got the brains! Hasn't got the brains! He'd run rings around us all!'

'I'll bring you a drop of Harvey's Bristol Cream in then,' he called, shutting the door on the muttered tirade. He couldn't care less what either young Arnie or Julie did. They were like Evvie, snobs the pair of them, and Arnold did what Evvie told him to do.

He collected Mogsey on his way into town. Not that he wanted Mogsey's opinion, just a bit of company.

'So, what are you going to call this coffee bar?'

'Something foreign. Italian or Spanish.'

'You don't know any Italian!'

'You'd be surprised at what I know.'

'I picked up a few words in the Army. How about "El Cabala"?'

Eddie mulled it over for a few minutes and repeated it once or twice. It sounded good. 'What's it mean?'

'Haven't got a clue! Just saw it painted on a sign, but it stuck in my mind, like.'

'Check it out! It could mean anything knowing you! Could be a bloody brothel for all I know and a right bleedin' fool I'd look then!'

'Then stick to something English like you did for the clubs.'

'I want something foreign, it's got more class! It'll be more appealing to all the arty-farty types from the art school and the university.'

'And that typing school round the corner and the shop girls from the posh shops.'

'Oh, you're finally getting my drift now, Mogsey. Dead quick on the uptake!'

Mogsey wasn't sure whether that was a compliment or not but he decided to take it as such as they drew up outside an empty and rather dilapidated shop at the top end of the city's most fashionable street.

'Is this it? It's not up to much is it? A right dump! It'll cost millions to do it up!'

Eddie wasn't listening, his gaze was fixed on the three figures inside the shop.

'What the bloody hell are they doing here?' Mogsey cried as he caught sight of them too.

'I've got a good idea but I'm going to find out. Come on!'

'Good God! If it isn't Liverpool's answer to Al Capone and his side-kick!' Sall remarked caustically, glaring at them both.

'That'll do youse!' Mogsey snapped at his sister-in-law.

Mike and Eddie eyed each other warily.

'What brings you here?' Sall asked.

'I could ask you the same question!' Eddie shot back.

'I'm looking around with a view to buying it.'

'You! What do you want it for?' Mogsey was openly derisive.

'A furnishing fabric shop. I suppose you want it for a gambling den?'

'He wants it for a high class coffee bar.'

'Oh, aye, given up selling dodgy cars and knocked off stuff now, Eddie? Going to sell frothy coffee instead?'

Mike placed a hand on her arm while watching Eddie. 'Nothing to say, MacGann?'

Eddie looked at the estate agent. 'Only that I'll up anything they offer!'

'Er . . . Mr MacGann, was it! I think we should all have a proper discussion about this. I wasn't informed that there was any other serious offer in hand.'

'Well there is!'

'I'm not discussing anything with *him*!' Sall cried.

'We won't have to. You've heard our offer Mr Bradley, it's as much as this place is worth taking into account what will be required to improve it. If Mr MacGann wants to waste his money . . .' Mike shrugged. 'I've had a survey done, as you know, and there are structural faults, caused by the bomb that hit St Luke's church up the road. If he wants to pay out having them put right, that's his affair. I can do them at virtually no cost to myself or Mrs Green.'

'What structural faults?' Eddie snapped. 'Your office said nothing about that!'

'Oh, nothing drastic, Mr MacGann, I can assure you!'

'Only cost you a couple of hundred to get them done, "Mr MacGann"!' Mike was enjoying Eddie's annoyance.

'I still want it!'

'You'll be chuckin' money away!' Mogsey muttered. 'If he knows nothing else, he knows about the building trade.'

Eddie ignored him. He felt sure Crowley was up to something.

338

Mike shrugged. 'Come on, Sall. We'll leave "Mr Mac-Gann" to have a look around his new property.'

Sall made to pull away but Mike tightened his grip.

'I'd take care going upstairs! Most of the treads need replacing!' he called after Eddie as they left.

'What did you do that for? It's just the right place, we won't find anywhere else like it!' Sall exploded when they were outside.

'I'm taking a calculated risk. If he thinks we don't want it that much and he thinks he'll have to spend a lot of money on it structurally, before he starts fitting it out, he'll turn it down.'

'What if he doesn't? He might just buy it to spite you and me!'

'When it comes to money, Eddie MacGann's not that stupid.'

'But if it needs that much spending on it we'll have to spend it!'

Mike laughed. 'We won't. There's hardly anything wrong with it! Come on, I'll treat you to lunch at the Adelphi.'

'I'd sooner go to Lyons or the Kardomah. Those posh places make me feel awkward and I always end up dropping something or spilling something and that only makes things worse!'

He laughed again. 'If you're going to be dealing with "posh" people as you always insist on calling them, you'll have to get used to it.'

She managed a smile. 'They won't be that posh. I'm not designing and selling stuff for the disgustingly rich!'

They began to walk down Bold Street towards the Kardomah Tea Rooms when they heard someone calling after them and turning saw Mr Bradley hastening towards them. Eddie's Bentley was drawing away from the kerb and heading towards Hardman Street.

'Mrs Green! Mr Crowley! A moment please!'

They stopped and waited until a red-faced Mr Bradley reached them. 'Glad I caught you both! Er . . . Mr

MacGann and his associate have decided against the property. It was a rather er . . . sudden . . . decision. Are you still interested?'

Sall grinned up at Mike. 'Yes, I think we can say we're interested. At the original price of course.'

'Oh, of course! Shall we go back to the office?'

'I was just about to take Mrs Green for lunch, so perhaps we can join you at say three o'clock?'

Mr Bradley was effusive in his agreement, having nearly lost two purchasers which would not have endeared him to his employers.

'Mr MacGann and his associate! Mogsey Green an associate! I could hardly keep my face straight! The only "associate" he'll ever be is of the Derby Arms saloon bar!' Sall laughed.

'I wonder how long it will take "Mr MacGann" to find out that there was hardly anything wrong with the place? I rather thought Mogsey would put his twopennyworth in! When he finds out he'll be mad as hell!'

He found out the following month and it was Tad who unwittingly informed him. They did still meet in the Derby Arms, although now they had their own 'corner' that no-one else dared to use. Eddie wasn't in a particularly good mood. He was having difficulty finding a property that matched the shop in Bold Street. The location was wrong or the price too high, or the building too small or too large. The Green Parrakeet had been raided the night before and the 'jacks' had gone in mob-handed, which meant he'd had to close it and spend more money replacing broken fixtures and fittings, besides the loss of business.

'Who got you up? You look like something out of Hepworth's window!' Mogsey greeted Tad who was sporting a new and obviously expensive suit.

'There's a sale on at Austin Reed in Bold Street, picked it up cheap. It's really sharp – hand-stitched lapels!'

'I'm paying you too much if you can afford to buy your gear there!' Eddie remarked caustically.

'And when I got to the top of the street, doing a bit of window shopping, who should I see dressing the window of a shop that's been done out, but Sall. Your Harry's Sall. She dragged me inside to have a proper look. It's dead smart. A bit too fancy, like, but high class gear. I reckon she'll do well. She's designed it all herself too, calls it Evergreen. Dead classy that!'

'I thought the place was falling down! That feller said it would need all kinds of building work done on it and she couldn't have had that done already!' Mogsey voiced Eddie's thoughts, while slowly realizing that Tad had just dropped him right in it. He'd been the one who had persuaded Eddie not to have it.

Eddie smashed one balled fist into the palm of his hand. 'That feller didn't say it! Crowley did and I believed him, with some encouragement from you! The lying, cheating bastard's got the better of me again! He's done me out of a prime site! You and your bleedin' gob, Mogsey Green! "He must know what he's talking about Eddie, he's built half the new houses in the city! And you can't trust these estate agents either!"' he mimicked Mogsey's arguments.

'Maybe he got the work done double quick!' Mogsey tried to calm him down.

'You soft get! How could he in four weeks and get it fitted out! But this time I've had enough! It's time to pay him back for all the old scores! This time I'm going to finish him!'

Mogsey and Tad exchanged glances. They'd both done well out of Eddie but if they thought he meant what he did! Tad shook his head. 'Christ! Eddie, you'll not get away with . . . topping him!'

'People have accidents all the time on building sites.'

'You'd not get within a mile of one of his sites!'

'I wouldn't but I can plant a man. He can get me all I need to know and then we can arrange an accident!'

They both paled. He meant it.

'It's not worth it, just for a bloody shop!'

'You never were very bright, Mogsey, were you! It's not

just that bloody shop, it's . . . everything! Ever since the day he broke my hand I swore I'd get him – one day! That day's arrived!'

'Eddie, I'm not sure about this!' Tad ventured.

'You're sure! I've got enough on you to put you away for a bit!'

'I've only been helping you out! You wouldn't shop an old mate, Eddie . . .!'

'Wouldn't I? Anyway, look on the bright side. With him out of the way you can go chasing our Louisa again, can't you? She might have you this time and you'd be marrying a wealthy widow. You'd never have to work again! Look at it like that!'

Tad didn't want to look at it any way but he was too afraid to say so. He knew now that Eddie was mad. He had to be.

Sall was just about to close when Louisa walked in.

'How's business?'

'Great! I think word is getting around, but my feet are killing me. I must be mad to wear these heels!'

'It looks really smart, Sall, and your designs are so different! They're unique.' She turned over the ticket attached to the end of a bolt of material. 'And reasonably priced.'

'My head is just bursting with ideas! If this takes off I want to open another shop in, say, Chester or Southport and then I want to go into wallpaper, china, kitchen and bathroom stuff – all to match!'

'You'll be in competition with Lewis's and George Henry Lee next! You're crazy Sally Green!'

'I'm not! I don't want big shops like that. They're too impersonal. I want to keep them small and . . . homey. Anyway, I've got to make this one pay first and pay off my debts! How did your day go?'

'Hectic as usual. Sometimes I get so mad, so frustrated! You can't get anything done in this city unless it's written out in triplicate, wrapped in miles of red tape and signed and sealed by the mayor and the entire watch committee!

342

Things could be done in half the time if only I could get past the petty, little men who think they have the power of the Almighty Himself! The housing department is the worst! You'd think with all the overcrowding that they'd rush to get things moving, but, no! Dead slow and stop are the speeds they work at!'

'You've got the answer in your own hands, Lou!'

'What?'

'If you can't beat them, join them! Get onto the council!'

'And would I be able to do more for people then or would I just become like them? Taking myself so seriously that I'd trip over my own dignity!'

'You'd never be like them!'

'You'd make a better councillor than I would!'

'No, I wouldn't and besides,' she grinned, 'I'm too busy being a capitalist!' She became serious as she glanced around her. 'I suppose all this is in some way to take the place of Harry and the life we never had. To sort of . . . compensate. There was never anyone else for me, you know that. So, now, this is my life, my dream. You've got Mike and John and Patrick.'

'Don't you get lonely, Sall? Isn't there anyone . . .?'

'No, there's no-one. I do get lonely sometimes, but then I think about all this and Lotty. I want her to have everything I never had. She's like a daughter to me, Lou, you know that.'

She nodded. All the love and affection that Sall would have lavished on Harry, she had transferred to Lotty. She just prayed that Doreen would never come back into their lives or Lotty's father – whoever he was. 'Lock up and we'll get home. My pair of devil's imps will be driving Maggie to distraction by now!'

CHAPTER TWENTY-FIVE

He'd thought about it day and night, virtually to the exclusion of everything else. Brooding for hours on the past. On the sequence of events that had cumulated and compacted the now all-consuming hatred.

The first time he had tangled with Crowley. The fight he'd been so sure would have stopped Crowley once and for all. Three to one and it had been himself who'd been left maimed. That had been Louisa's fault. In fact the more he thought about it, the more he realized how Louisa seemed to be the cause, directly or indirectly, of every misfortune that had befallen him.

It all led back to that fight. The loss of his job on the docks. His exclusion from military service that had robbed him of the experiences and camaraderie of his mates, like Tad and Mogsey. Thick as planks the pair of them, yet they'd been to places he'd never see; done things he could never do and had been treated as little tin-pot heroes when they'd come back. Even his kid brother, Tommy, who he'd always looked on as a bit of a dope, had been decorated for his war service. He'd been a navigator on a Lancaster bomber. A survivor of the raids on Dresden and Berlin itself. A bloody hero and now a bloody copper – worse a 'jack'. He scowled. With his brains he could have done just as well, if not better. He could have been decorated too – except for his hand.

Then there was that row that had sent Louisa off to live with the Coopers. Crowley's letter had sparked that off, but he'd already been poisoning Louisa's mind against them and luring her away from her family and her religion.

He couldn't give a damn about religion, it had been the principle. She'd betrayed them. It had also been Crowley who'd put the idea of working for the Union in her mind. Crowley and Louisa. The names haunted him. And she'd threatened to 'shop' him and sworn she'd see him in jail.

Crowley had crossed him in business too. Threatening his Mam and himself and there had been that episode over the shop. Crowley had cheated him out of that and because of it Sally Green looked set to make a fortune. What would be next?

He lit another Gold Flake, leaned back in the winged armchair and stared into the fire. Crowley was dangerous. He was getting too big for his boots and people were starting to listen to him. Important people. He'd heard it rumoured that either he or Louisa would stand for the city council and then they would start up some sort of crusade. They were just that sort. Louisa had always been different, even though his Mam had tried to make her conform. Look at the way she'd determinedly clung to her friendship with Sally Green. The way she'd stuck up for that girl she'd worked with and lost her own job because of it. She'd been a fool, yet her Da hadn't been angry with her. Oh, aye, they were the kind who would campaign for the working man and promise to stamp on everyone who exploited them. That would include himself. He saw everything he'd worked, schemed and lied for over the years disappearing and himself being held up to ridicule, scorn and hatred. His Mam being deprived of all the luxuries he'd provided and openly reviled by the neighbours who'd respected her for years. No! By God! He'd have to stop Crowley once and for all. Louisa would cause him no trouble after that. A widow with two kids to bring up. That would keep her fully occupied.

He smiled sardonically. Maybe after a decent interval she'd be glad to have Tad to relieve her of some of the burdens and Tad could be relied upon to do as he was told. One day, using Tad as a go-between, he might even get control of Crowley's business. He smiled again at the thought. He'd still have his own business interests and he could expand, and when Mam finally 'snuffed it' he'd marry Marge and they'd have a big house in Woolton and every luxury.

He'd plan it all so carefully, so meticulously, that no-one would ever suspect that it was anything but an accident. They'd never be able to prove a thing. He'd laugh in the face of his brother who'd turned against him. He knew just the bloke to send in to spy out the ground. Not too bright but with enough sense to know which side his bread was buttered on. Then he'd get him out of the way and nothing could be traced to him. He leaned forward and poked the fire, then poured himself a whisky. Crowley's days were numbered.

He wasn't the only one whose mind was filled with the proposed 'accident'. Tad couldn't sleep. He stood at the window and stared out over the darkened rooftops. He'd done some things in his life that didn't bear too close a scrutiny and some he never thought of at all, if he could help it. He'd had to kill in battle, when it was kill or be killed, but to take part in this! Even though the room was cold the sweat trickled down his neck. Eddie would never get away with it. He was a fool even to contemplate that he would – or would he? Eddie was crafty, always had been, even as a kid. He had a kind of animal cunning, a devious mind and an aptitude for planning detail, be it with figures or situations.

He remembered Eddie's joke about Louisa. Was his love for her as obsessive as Eddie's hatred of her husband? Was he so besotted that he could take part in an act that would crush her and yet leave her free – for him? Would she have him? She'd be devastated at first, but women like Louisa had an inner strength. Look at what she'd already suffered and survived. He remembered her standing in the moonlight in the yard behind the community hall on the night of Sall's wedding. A young girl in a pink dress, her hair falling in thick waves around her shoulders. She was so beautiful that the memory hurt him. Could he see her bowed down by grief and stand by and say nothing? Could he see that lovely face haggard and drawn with sorrow and shock and try to comfort her as though he'd had no part in her misery? Could he live out a lie for her sake? Would she ever love him? Would she even contemplate marrying him – in time? And if he warned her, what then? He would lose her for ever and Eddie would be furious. Would an 'accident' befall him, too? At best he was looking at a jail sentence.

He flung himself down on the bed. Cold now, he hugged the quilt to him but the questions hurled themselves at him, making sleep impossible. What if they were caught? What if some miscalculation or misfortune that even Eddie's careful planning couldn't control or foresee? Murder and accessory to murder were punishable by death! His throat constricted as though he could feel the noose around it. He wanted no part of all this! Yet he *was* a part of it! There was no way out and he couldn't confide in anyone either. Or could he?

He got up again and began to pace the room. Could he send an anonymous letter to Crowley? No, eventually Eddie would find out. It would only be a matter of time, a process of elimination. Should he pack his bags now and do a bunk, but where would he go, and what would he do when he got there? He spent money as quickly as he earned it. He'd never been a saver. And it would mean leaving Louisa for ever. He could never come back. Oh, God! What a mess he'd made of his life! All he'd ever wanted was to marry Louisa and live contentedly. Why had fate conspired against him? Why had he ever got mixed up with Doreen Cooper in the first place? For a few minutes of youthful pleasure he'd paid dearly and, by the look of it, he'd go on paying for the rest of his life! Why couldn't Doreen have been killed in the Blitz? Why couldn't Crowley have been lost at sea instead of Big John Langford?

He kept a bottle of whisky on top of the wardrobe and now he knew that the only way he would be able to block out the despair was to drink himself into oblivion.

* * *

Eddie smiled at the burly labourer who stood before him, twisting his cap between his hands. 'Shorty' Osbourne was the typical gentle giant. His powerful six-foot two-inch frame belied a gentle, guileless nature. He was a good worker and would slave away for hours on end without complaint. He lived quietly at home with his widowed sister, next door to Jimmy Townsend.

'Jimmy said yer might have a job for me, Mr MacGann?'

Eddie nodded and smiled expansively. 'Sit down, Shorty.'

The big man sat down gingerly on the edge of the chair Eddie had indicated.

'Jimmy's been telling me about you. How you look after your Mary. It's not many who'd do that, Shorty.'

'Aye, but she's not strong, isn't our Mary. The last thing Mam said before she died was "You see you look after our Mary" and I couldn't let Mam down, could I, Mr MacGann?'

'You're a good bloke. There's not many who'd do that, they'd be too busy having a good time with the girls. I'd like to help you.'

'Help me?' The bovine face took on an air of dazed bewilderment.

'But in return I want you to do something for me.'

'Anything, Mr MacGann!'

Eddie held up his hand to stem the enthusiastic burst that he knew was imminent. 'It's going to be a bargain, Shorty, between you and me. Understand?'

'A bargain?'

'Jimmy tells me you've got a brother out in Australia. George, is it?'

'Aye, he stayed out there after the war. He got something wrong with his leg in the jungle and was in hospital. He married a nurse. Our Mary said it was due to him staying there that finished Mam, but I don't blame him.'

'How would you like to take your Mary out to see him? Stay with him, for good – if you liked it?'

348

Shorty's expression became totally dazed and his mouth dropped open.

'Well?'

'That would cost a fortune, Mr MacGann! Where would I get money like that from?'

'From me. I'd pay your fares. Yours and Mary's.'

'You! But . . . but . . .'

Eddie was enjoying himself playing the generous benefactor, but only because it suited him. If everything went to plan, two tickets to Sydney would be cheap at the price. 'In return for the job I want you to do.'

'I'll do anything for that!'

Eddie leaned forward. 'All I want you to do is get yourself employed by Crowley, Langford & Sons. I hear they're taking on labourers.'

'But I thought I was going to work for you Mr MacGann?'

'You will be, in a round-about sort of way. I want you to keep your eyes open on the site. Tell me what time the lads knock off. If anyone stays behind and, if they do, until what time? Tell me where the site office is, where the watchman's hut is. Where all the equipment is kept and if it's locked up. Things like that. But what I don't want is you telling anyone, not even your Mary, that you're really working for me!'

'You mean spy out the land, like?'

Eddie nodded, smiling. 'That's exactly what I want and after a month, maybe two, you'll be off to see your George.'

The big man shook his head in disbelief. 'Is that all, Mr MacGann?'

'Except that you don't tell anyone that you're going.'

'Not even our Mary?'

'Especially not your Mary!' From what he'd heard Mary Kelso had a mouth like the Mersey Tunnel. 'It's to be a surprise and if you go and tell her then it won't be a surprise, will it?'

Shorty looked uneasy. 'But I tell her everything, she

worries you see. And she'll want to start packing and things like that.'

'Then tell her you've been saving up to take her to Blackpool or Llandudno for a few days. A bit of a holiday, like. My Mam goes to Llandudno.' He felt relieved when he saw the grin on the other man's face.

'You're dead smart, Mr MacGann! But that's all I've got to do? Tickets cost a lot of money and I'll be getting paid by them, too.'

Eddie nodded slowly. 'I told you Shorty, I like you. You're a good skin. One in a million and you deserve a chance. But it's a secret so make sure you keep your side of the bargain or there won't be any trip to Australia.'

'Wild horses wouldn't drag it out of me, Mr MacGann!'

'Good. Now get over to Crowley's while there's still jobs on offer.'

Four weeks later Tad and Mogsey were sitting in their usual places in the Derby and neither of them were at ease.

'He's mad! He's gone off his head!' Tad muttered.

'All right, so he's off his rocker! He's always had a bee in his bonnet about Crowley but what the hell can we do about it? We're not as pure as driven snow and he knows it. He'd put the finger on us if we welshed or did a bunk now! Besides, he may be cracked but he's not daft. He's always been smart. They didn't have enough to hold him that time they nicked him, did they?'

'But that Shorty Osbourne! If you ask me he's not the full shilling. What if he blabs to that sister of his?'

'He's sound is Shorty. So would you be if you were getting a free ticket to Sydney. For Christ's sake shut up, here he comes!'

Eddie joined them and signalled the barman to bring over his usual drink. 'You two all right?'

Mogsey nodded.

'I asked if you were all right.' Eddie looked pointedly at Tad.

'I suppose so,' Tad muttered.

350

Eddie's eyes narrowed. He'd have to watch Tad. 'I've paid Shorty off, in three days he'll be on his way to Australia.' He laughed. 'That Mary's been packed up for a week, she thinks she's going to Llandudno. I told him not to tell her anything until they were on the ship. That I'd see to their stuff – have it sent on. Stupid sod was nearly in tears.'

'You got everything you wanted from him?' Mogsey asked in a tone that was barely audible.

Eddie nodded. 'Drink your ale and smile, you look suspicious!' He raised his glass and smiled at a group of men sitting in the opposite corner.

'So, when . . .?' Tad asked. He had no stomach for his beer.

'Next week. When I'm certain Shorty's well out of the way.'

'How?' Mogsey muttered.

'He's always the last to leave. He checks everything personally before his watchman comes on at nine. There's one block of maisonettes nearly finished. The roofers were working on it yesterday. If he sees a light up there, moving around, he'll go to investigate won't he? He'll think someone's nicking something.'

Tad felt the bile rising in his throat but it was Mogsey who asked the question. 'So, who's going to be up there with the light then?'

Eddie nodded to another acquaintance and smiled. 'Me.'

'You!' They both uttered in unison.

'I want this done properly so I'll do it myself. Besides, I want the satisfaction of seeing his face before his brains are splattered all over his bleedin' site!'

Tad was forcing down the vomit, his face a sickly white.

'You won't be needing us then.' Mogsey sounded relieved.

Eddie groaned. 'God knows how you ever got into the Army! You've got your brains in your arse! I'll need you to keep a look-out for me, and you,' he stared straight at Tad, 'to wait in the car. When it's done I want to get away as quickly as possible – understand?'

351

Tad understood only too clearly. Eddie wasn't giving him any opportunity of backing out. If he were to drive away in Eddie's car, leaving them in the lurch, Eddie would pick up the nearest phone and call the police. He'd tell them his car had been stolen and then . . . Beads of sweat formed on his forehead and he got shakily to his feet. 'Got to . . .' He rushed from the room, unable to keep down the contents of his stomach.

'What's up with him? Shit scared?'

'No. Just a bad pint, he'll be all right,' Mogsey answered with a confidence designed more to bolster his own spirits than Eddie's.

'It'll go like clockwork, you see. We'll be away before the watchman gets there and raises the alarm. And there'll be nothing to trace anything back to us. We'll be home and dry, Mogsey!'

'Home and dry,' Mogsey agreed gloomily.

The weather the following Wednesday couldn't have suited Eddie's purposes more if he'd ordered it. It was cold and windy with intermittent bursts of heavy rain. The sort of weather that made people stay indoors and men want to get home from work quickly, or seek the warmth of the pub.

It wasn't weather that suited Mike at all for it held up the work and was turning the site into a quagmire. As he closed the door of the site office, his boots quickly became sticky with the cloying mud and he pulled his cap lower over his forehead and turned up his collar.

His nocturnal tours of inspection had arisen from the day Jed Leach had threatened trouble and they had become a habit. They acted as a deterrent too. Would-be vandals and thieves knew he was around and then Charlie would be there all night and the beat copper would stop off for a chat and a brew. The poor sod would need it on a night like this, he thought. In a quarter of an hour he'd be on his way home to a hot meal and a warm fire. Charlie would sit in his hut before a roaring brazier with his thermos of tea. The poor coppers had to walk the streets until the end of their shift, occasionally sheltering in doorways and warming themselves up with visits to the likes of Charlie. He didn't envy them.

Things were going well. If the weather didn't hold them up too much, they'd be finished on schedule. But you could never bank on the weather. Strange that Shorty Osbourne leaving like that, he mused. He'd been a good worker. Probably been offered something better. Still, labourers came and went on construction sites. His place had soon been filled.

He scanned the first storey of the first building with his torch, then turned and let the beam play over a pile of timber and beyond a stack of roofing tiles. He trudged on through the mud, the beam stabbing the darkness, revealing materials and half-finished buildings. The rain became heavier and more persistent and he shrugged. It was turning into a pig of a night and everything seemed to be in order. Picking his way between the puddles he made his way back towards the small site office. He'd just check he'd locked up and then he'd get home. It was then that out of the corner of his eye he caught the glimmer of light. He turned back, peering into the storm-lashed darkness. There it was again, in the upper storey of an almost complete building. He switched off his own torch. It couldn't be the reflection of the moon or a star, not in this weather. The beam of light moved onwards. There was someone up there! They were taking advantage of the weather, thinking he'd gone home and were probably removing the copper piping or the lead flashing.

In the darkness it was hard to pick his way across towards the building, but he didn't want to risk the light of his torch being spotted. When he reached the ground floor he paused, looking upwards and listening. He could hear nothing but the wind. Cautiously he climbed the staircase to the first floor. He could no longer see the light but he thought he heard the sound of someone moving around.

He groped his way towards the second flight of stairs, using the wall to guide him. Again nothing. He climbed slowly up to the next landing. Although the building was almost finished there was no glass in any of the windows and the wind howled through the gaps. He reached the top storey and reversed the torch in his hand, making it usable as a weapon, for he had no idea how many were up here, but it would take at least two to remove and carry lead or copper. The new, unseasoned floorboards protested beneath his weight and he stopped, his back towards a window frame. Suddenly he was blinded by a large torch being switched on, its beam shining full in his face. Instinctively he raised his arm to shield his eyes. 'What the bloody hell's going on here!' he yelled, twisting his head to avoid the light.

A voice full of venom answered from the darkness. 'Hell is just where you're going, Crowley!'

He lunged forward as he recognized the tones. Eddie MacGann! He still couldn't see anything for the beam was blinding him. He felt himself being shoved roughly backwards and he lashed out with his own torch but met only empty space.

'I swore I'd get you one day and that day's arrived!' Eddie's voice had risen with excitement as the adrenalin pumped through him, increasing his strength. With one powerful thrust he pushed Mike backwards, towards the window. He heard the sound of splintering wood and then a cry that ended abruptly.

He only stopped once when he reached the ground floor, just to check that there was no sign of life in the body that lay face down in the mud. The head and one leg twisted at awkward angles. Then he whistled once and stumbled and foundered towards the gates and the car beyond.

He reached it almost the same time as Mogsey. 'Get in!' he snapped, jumping into the passenger seat beside Tad.

'Is he . . . ?' Tad's voice shook as did his hands that gripped the steering wheel.

'Of course he bleedin' well is! Now drive! We'll drop Mogsey off, then I'll drop you off at the Derby. Go in and get a round in, you're the only one who's no covered in mud! We'll get changed and follow as quickly as we can.'

'Bloody hell! I'm covered in mud, we should have got rid of this stuff! Mam's going to see the state of me!'

'Use your head for once in your life Mogsey! Tell her you cut across the bombsite. We can get rid of the stuff tomorrow. Slow down you maniac! Do you want the scuffers after us!' he yelled at Tad, who was racing through the mostly deserted streets.

Tad's insides were in knots. His throat was dry, his eyes burning and his heart pounding, but Eddie sounded excited. He was mad – they were all mad! Mike Crowley was lying dead back there and Louisa . . . Oh God! Poor Louisa! He swerved sharply to avoid a cart and thankfully pulled up at the bottom of Everton Valley and got out. He stood in the rain and watched the car pull away. Every instinct told him to run. To get as far away as possible, but it was too late to run now. He had to act normally, as though nothing untoward had happened. He needed a drink. He needed a few drinks, in fact he knew he'd need at least half a bottle before he could sleep. Gingerly he pushed open the door of the saloon bar and stepped inside, nodding to the barman with a smile that was more a grimace.

CHAPTER TWENTY-SIX

'How long will you be in London for?' Louisa asked Sall, placing a cup of tea on the table. Then she carried on wiping and putting away the twins' dinner dishes. She always waited for Mike to come home and they had their meal together.

'About three days. I've got so many people to see. Do you think I'm over-stretching myself, Lou? Mam says I'm mad!'

'Isn't there a saying, "You've got to speculate to accumulate"? I think you'll do well if you get a franchise to supply a couple of the big stores.'

'But that wasn't my aim!'

'I know, but it will provide the money you'll need to open more of your own shops. It will get your name and designs known in a bigger market place so that when you do expand it will be easier. People will already have heard of Evergreen.'

'Oh, I'm just tying myself up in knots! Do you know something, Lou?'

'What?'

'I'm scared stiff.'

'What of?'

'I've never been to London.'

Louisa laughed. 'Neither have I!'

'I'm terrified of meeting these people. I start thinking of all kinds of daft things.'

'Like what?'

'Will they understand me – my accent I mean? Or will they look down their noses at me and think I'm some kind of eejit, as Maggie says.'

'Will you stop that! I've never known you to back away from a challenge and you're one of the shrewdest women I know. They'll have to be pretty quick off the mark to get one over on you Sall!'

Sall shrugged. 'Maybe Mam's right,' she said, gloomily.

'She's not! Look, you've come this far, you can't stop now and, besides, everything is arranged. I don't know why you pay for business advice if you won't take it.'

'Well, what about you?'

'Don't change the subject.'

'I'm not! If I've got to go out and conquer the world, why shouldn't you?'

Louisa looked at her quizzically. 'Now what are you going on about?'

'The council, that's what. Are you going to stand at the next election?'

'You have to be elected to stand.'

'You have to let people know that you *want* to be elected to stand.'

'Don't you think I've got enough on my plate at the moment? A full-time job, a home to run, two young boys to bring up and not forgetting a husband and his business!'

'Where is he anyway?'

Louisa looked at the clock and frowned. 'He's late. He always checks everything himself before Charlie comes on. It's a foul night so maybe he stopped off for a drink.'

Sall finished her tea and rose. 'I'd better be going. I've a hundred and one things to do before I go. Our Joan's that dozy you have to leave her a detailed list of everything. It's no use leaving Lily to cope on her own, all she can think about is her wedding and that prefab they're hoping to get! When she's gone Mam might get some peace although I doubt it. There'll be no peace until Joan finds herself a husband and I think I'll have to pay someone to take her off our hands!'

Louisa handed her her umbrella in the hall. 'Have a good

trip and don't let anyone take advantage of you. Just you remember you've built your business from nothing and you didn't have all the advantages they've had, so you've every reason to hold your head high. Never mind their Oxford accents, it's what's up here that counts.' She tapped her forehead with her finger before opening the door.

'Will you look in a few times, just to see everything's all right?'

'I've said I would. Now go on before we're both soaked, it's blowing inwards. I don't think you'll have much luck keeping that brolly up.'

As she battled her way up the street Sall cursed. Lou had been right, for the wind had ripped the umbrella inside out. Now she'd be soaked to the skin before she got home. In the distance she saw a black taxi coming towards her. Damn the expense, she thought, waving her arms to catch the driver's attention. If she couldn't afford a little luxury now and then there wasn't any point in working so hard. As she closed the cab door behind her she felt a stirring of guilt at the extravagance. She'd been brought up the hard way, she came from a world where people didn't use taxis. She'd have to make him stop at the corner of the road and walk up. If her Mam saw her there would be hell to pay for wasting money.

She walked into yet another quarrel between her sisters, over the colour of the bridesmaid's dress Joan was to wear.

'This is Lily's wedding, it's her choice! When it's your turn – and God help the man that gets you – you can choose!' She hung her sodden coat over the back of a chair and took off her shoes and put them on the hearth.

'I hate yellow and she knows it! That's why she's been dithering about it. Why can't I have blue or pink or peach or even lilac? The others look all right in yellow, I'll just look like death warmed up!'

'I'm paying for it and if Lily wants yellow, then it's yellow! If you don't like it then you don't have to be a bridesmaid at all! Now shut up the pair of you, I've had a hard day and I've still not finished and I don't want any quarrelling while I'm away! Can't you both have a bit more consideration for Mam?'

'She's listening to the radio in the parlour,' Lily announced with a triumphant gleam in her eye.

'I don't blame her. It's like living in a madhouse here! I'm actually beginning to look forward to this trip, just to get away from the pair of you! Oh, who the hell's that!' she snapped as the sound of the door knocker echoed down the hallway. 'Don't just stand there gaping, go and see who it is!'

Lotty's footsteps were heard on the stairs and she called that she would open the door. Then there was silence.

Sall looked at both her sisters and then at her brother who was absorbed in a glossy magazine advertising motor bikes and who appeared to be oblivious of everything. Before she could speak Lotty entered the room, consternation in her eyes.

'What's the matter? Who is it?'

'It's the plainclothes police.'

Sall's gaze instantly alighted on her brother and with a quick movement she plucked the booklet from his hands. 'What have you been up to, Robbie Cooper? If you're in trouble you can say goodbye to any motor bike!'

He wasn't listening to her, he was looking straight past her. She turned to see Tommy MacGann standing in the doorway and her hand went to her throat. 'Tommy! What's wrong? Is it Lou . . .?'

'You'd better get your coat, Sall.'

'I've only just left her! What's the matter with Lou?' She almost screamed the question.

'It's not Lou. It's Mike.'

Sall's shoulders sagged with relief. 'What's happened?'

'An accident on the site. The local police sent for me, because of Lou.'

She was pushing her feet into her damp shoes. 'Is he badly hurt?'

359

'He's dead, Sall. He fell and broke his neck, the watch-man found him.'

She pressed her hand against her mouth to stifle the cry. Oh! Dear God! Poor Lou!

It was worse than when Louisa had fully realized that her Da was never going to come back. Then she'd had Mike to comfort her. To ease the hurt and the shock. Now there was no-one. None of it seemed real. It was happening to someone else. It hadn't been she who had been led, in a daze, by Tommy and another policeman, to identify him. It hadn't been she who'd sat dry-eyed and still while Pat had tried as best he could to explain to the twins, while Maggie had sobbed quietly on the bed upstairs.

She'd wandered around the quiet house touching things. Picking up articles and staring at them as though she were a stranger in her own home. She'd slept fitfully on the sofa while Sall had watched her from the fireside chair. She'd remembered, briefly, how they'd clung together in their grief, in the middle of an air raid, on the night Uncle Jim and Frank Cooper had been killed. But now she couldn't reach out and grasp Sall's hand. Something inside stopped her.

She'd refused the help of Dr Hardman but she had a strange feeling that between them Sall and the doctor had managed to sedate her. It was the only explanation she could think of for the leaden drowsiness and the periods of darkness that overcame her, despite the fact that she fought against them.

Her world was dark and empty and silent. Sometimes she would look at the clock and wonder where Mike was. Why he was so late. Then she felt worried and that feeling would be replaced by panic and she'd start to call his name. Then Sall would be there with a cup of tea. Tea that tasted bitter-sweet and she would feel her limbs becoming heavier and the darkness would close in again. But it was all right. Sall was there. Sall was with her.

Sall was exhausted. Exhaustion that sprung not solely from physically going without sleep. It stemmed from anxiety, frustration and grief. The anxiety of watching Lou and trying to keep her sedated. The frustration of being utterly helpless to do anything to ease Lou's pain and the grief that her friend's plight evoked. She, more than anyone, understood what Lou was now going through and would continue to have to face for months and years to come. Sall, too, was shocked and miserable. She'd been fond of Mike Crowley.

Her initial suspicion of Robbie being in trouble was now almost laughable. She couldn't believe what had happened and it had happened so easily, Tommy had told her. The slippery mud on his boots, the pools of rain water that had collected on the floor beneath the unglazed window. He'd slipped, fallen hard against the window frame that had splintered. But at least it had been quick and painless, they had to be thankful for that. And they'd had a good look around, there was nothing suspicious. There was mud and footprints everywhere, the men had still been working on the building. Mike had just been checking as he always did, but just the same it was a tragedy. Tommy himself had been upset.

She glanced across at the figure on the sofa. Lou was asleep again, thank God. She looked at the clock. She should have been in London but none of that was relevant or important now. Maggie had taken the twins home with her. She'd composed herself enough to collect their things and lead two white-faced, bewildered seven-year-olds, hand in hand, into the waiting taxi that she had ordered. It had been left to her to see to the friends and neighbours who were calling to offer condolences and it was she who opened the door to Tad.

'I . . . I . . . heard. I've just come to say I'm sorry.'

'It was good of you to come, Tad.'

'Can . . . can I see her, Sall?' He knew he shouldn't have asked by the expression on Sall's face. He shouldn't have even come but he'd forced himself to make the short journey. If life had been bad before, it was a living hell now.

'There's no point. She's asleep. Dr Hardman left me some powders to sedate her. Somehow we've got to help her get through the next few days. The funeral, the inquest. They had the post-mortem early this morning.'

'A post-mortem?' He'd never thought of that.

'Broken neck, leg and internal injuries. They said at the coroner's office that the inquest will bring in a verdict of accidental death.'

He gulped. 'When is the funeral?'

'The day after tomorrow. At Our Lady Immaculate's, he was baptized there and Maggie wants the requiem mass there.'

'You're going?'

Anger sparked in her eyes. 'I am and so is all his workforce, Catholic and Protestant alike! Don't you dare start that, Tad Buckley!'

'I didn't mean it to sound like that. Will you tell her I called, Sall, please?'

She nodded slowly as she watched him walk away. Would he be the only one or would this bring Babsey to her senses and Evvie, too? She didn't hold out much hope of Eddie showing his face.

Somehow Louisa had got through it all. The mass with its eulogy, hymns, candles, tinkling altar bells and the pungent smell of incense that reminded her of the only other time she'd been in a Catholic church – when the twins had made their first communion, such a short time ago. Then the church had been bright. The flowers, the colourful robes of the priest, the little girls in their long, white dresses and veils. The boys in crisp white shirts and new trousers and there had been pride and happiness on everyone's face and in everyone's heart, hers included. But all was now sombre, dark and dull and sorrow filled every heart.

He'd been laid to rest in Anfield Cemetery and she'd been touched by the size of the crowd of mourners. Old friends and neighbours. Men in their working clothes, delegates from the Union, even a few men in the uniform of the Royal Navy and the police. Now it was all over and she was alone. She'd even sent Sall home. She wanted it this way.

Automatically she began to tidy up. Taking the newspapers out into the scullery her hand brushed against one of the coats hanging on the back of the door . . . It was one of his old working jackets. Dropping the papers she buried her face in it and all the smells she associated with him exuded from the fabric. Bitumen, asphalt and cement dust from the site. The faint aroma of Fairy soap. He'd always washed his hands even before taking off his coat. Aniseed and liquorice, there was seldom a day when he hadn't brought sweets either for her or the boys. And the unmistakable odour of – him. Fragments of his life trapped in the fibres and he was close to her. He was with her again. 'Mike! Oh, Mike! What am I going to do? How can I face the future without you!' she sobbed into the old, stained jacket.

'Be strong. Be strong. I haven't left you. I'll always be with you.'

She wasn't sure she'd heard the words at all. Had she longed so much to hear them that she'd imagined them? Was it her own heart and mind playing tricks on her?

'There's work to do. You've years ahead of you, don't waste them, Lou.'

'Work! What work?' she cried aloud, but there was no answer. She stood alone in her cold scullery clutching his jacket to her as if it were made of gold.

The wild, wet weather of March and April gave way to a gentler, but still unseasonably chilly, May. The first days of June were damp and not much warmer. Sall had finally agreed to take her postponed trip to London and she'd persuaded Lily to put back her wedding, not without some arguments. But she'd been adamant. She had too much to do at the moment without having all the frenzied activity of a wedding as well and as for the new prefab, well he could go and live in it couldn't he? She knew what Lou was going through and so did Agnes. Mike's death had brought back to them both all the shock and grief of their own losses and had reopened wounds that had never really healed.

'If only I could reach her, like I could in the old days! I could help her, Mam! She's building a wall around herself and I don't know how to break it down.'

'Maybe it's the only way she can cope, Sall. Everyone is different.'

'I've tried and tried but she changes the subject and manages to turn the conversation around to me. It's not like her! We used to be so close! Closer than most sisters!'

Agnes sighed. 'All you can do, luv, is to keep trying and be there when she does want to talk. But don't forget, Sall, she's a lot like her Da and, in a funny way, like Babsey MacGann.'

'Babsey MacGann!'

'They were both strong, inside where it matters. Oh, I know Babsey's gone a bit odd now, but it was she who held that family together.'

'Ruled them with a rod of iron, more like.'

'Aye, but what I'm saying is that Lou's got that same inner strength. She got over her Da's death. She battled both Babsey and Maggie Crowley to get her man. She openly defied all the bigots. She'll be all right, Sall, eventually.'

'I'm going to try once more before I go to London, Mam.'

'Don't be too disappointed or upset, Sall, if it turns out to be a wild goose chase.'

'I thought I'd just come and see you before I go. I'm off to the big city the day after tomorrow,' she informed Lou as she sat down in the kitchen. She'd passed John and Patrick playing in the street and had marvelled how resilient children were. They were just two eight-year-olds laughing and yelling with the rest. She'd smiled. Mike wouldn't have wanted them to be miserable and withdrawn.

'You really should have gone weeks ago. I told you I don't want you losing business because of me.'

'And I told you to hell with the business! Oh, Lou, can't you talk to me about it? I know how it feels, remember!' She caught Louisa's hand. 'It's me, Sally Green, not just *any* friend or neighbour making polite enquiries. I'm worried about you. You've lost weight and you're too quiet. You should let it all out, Lou!'

Louisa squeezed her hand. 'Sall, let me cope with it my own way. I'm fine, really I am, and I've got something to tell you. I'm going back to work for Joe Doran. Only part-time. Mike's . . . accident has taken its toll on Maggie and I need to spend time with John and Patrick.'

The concerned look left Sall's face. 'I'm glad, Lou. I really am! It will do you good to get out again and mix with people.'

Louisa smiled. That was the argument Joe had used to cajole her into agreeing to go back. The period of shock and unreality had passed. She'd even begun to sleep all night lately. Sometimes she still found herself listening for his footsteps, for the sound of his voice and occasionally she would turn to ask him a question – before she remembered. Those were the worst times. 'Life has to go on, Sall. I'm learning that. Oh, I've heard people say it so often but I never really understood what they meant. Time doesn't stand still and you have to face things eventually. You have to make decisions.'

'I know, Lou, and it does get better as time goes on. Time does heal, it's not just an idle saying. Take my word for it.'

'I was thinking of Da last night. Thinking of all the things he taught me. It can't have been easy for him having to leave me.'

'But he did it because he loved you and wanted the best for you.'

'And that's what made me agree to go back to work for Joe. I have to carry on for John and Patrick. I have to bring them up and do the best for them.'

For the first time in months the anxiety left Sall's eyes and she felt a weight being lifted from her shoulders. Lou was going to be all right. Her Mam had been right, she was strong. That had been John Langford's legacy.

CHAPTER TWENTY-SEVEN

Tad waited in the doorway of the corner shop, pretending to read the advertisements written on pieces of card that were displayed in the window. From the corner of his eye he watched Sall leave and walk down the street and turn the corner. Then the door opened again and Louisa called the boys in. He looked at his watch. He'd have to leave it another half hour, he didn't want them there when he told her. He walked slowly down to the pub and ordered a pint and stood in the corner of the bar. He was taking the biggest gamble of his life and his hand was shaking so much that the beer slopped over the glass. What if she refused to believe him? What if she refused him? What if . . . He'd been over this ground a hundred times!

''Ere, you all right, mate?'

He looked at the barman and nodded. 'Just had a bit of a shock,' he lied.

'Oh, aye. Anything I can do, like?'

He shook his head and muttered a thanks.

'It's a short you need, lad. 'Ave a tot of the hard stuff?'

Again he shook his head. He wasn't going over there reeking of rum. 'Ta, but I'll stick to the ale.'

He hadn't seen her since the day of the funeral and that was a day he'd rather forget. Why he'd gone he'd never managed to explain to himself. Eddie had commented that it had been a smart move. A remark that made him hate Eddie even more.

She looked surprised to see him but at least she looked better than she'd done that day.

'Tad!'

367

'Can I come in, Lou? I've got to talk to you!'

She gripped the door tightly. Had he no compassion? 'Tad, please . . .'

'I've not come to . . . upset you. I've *got* to talk to you! Will you hear me out, please, it won't take long?'

Reluctantly she opened the door wider and he stepped inside. She showed him into the parlour, hoping that the formal atmosphere may serve to remind him of her situation.

He stood before the empty firegrate and shivered. The room was cold and almost dark but she made no attempt to switch on the light. She stood facing him, her arms folded as though protecting herself.

'Well, what is it?'

He shivered again feeling that there was another presence in the room, watching him from the darkened corners. Mentally he shook himself. He was becoming superstitious. He swallowed and ran his tongue over his dry lips. 'It wasn't exactly true, about not upsetting you.'

She turned quickly towards the door.

'No, Lou! It's nothing like that, not really! I mean, it's to do with Mike's death!'

She turned back to face him. 'What about it?'

How was he going to tell her? He'd had it all worked out but now all the well-rehearsed explanations were forgotten. 'I don't know how to say this without sounding hard and calculating! But there's something I want from you . . . in return.'

'Tad, what are you talking about? You're not making any sense. What *is* it? What have you come here for?'

He sank down in a chair and gripped the arms tightly. 'It wasn't an accident!' His gaze was riveted on her face as he watched her sink slowly onto the sofa.

'What do you mean? There was an inquest!'

'Lou, I'm putting my own neck on the line for you, don't you understand?'

'No. I don't understand! You're talking nonsense! Have you been drinking?'

'One pint, that's all! Lou, he didn't fall . . . he was pushed!' It was out. His words echoed around the room and he watched her shake her head incredulously, her eyes widening as understanding and horror dawned. He cringed. He had to go on, he had to finish it. 'It was Eddie! He set it up! He did it!'

'How? Why?' The questions were whispered.

'Because he always hated him. He's mad, Lou! He's crazy!'

The cold blue eyes were piercing him like shards of ice. 'How . . . how do you know all this?'

He looked away. 'I . . . I was there. Waiting in the car.'

She didn't utter a sound but he still couldn't bring himself to look at her. The moment stretched on, seemingly endless, and then, in a voice that turned his heart to stone, she said quietly, 'I'll see you both hang for this!'

'Lou! I had no choice! I couldn't stop him! If I'd have tried he would have had me silenced one way or another, and he would still have killed him! You've got to believe that, Lou! But I can help you now. I can make sure he gets what he deserves! That way I can try and make it up to you! I couldn't live with it any more. I went to see a solicitor. I couldn't tell him, I had to beat around the bush. He called it a hypothetical scenario, whatever that means! But if I give myself up and turn Queen's Evidence, tell them everything, he'll hang!'

'You were as bad! How could you do it?'

'Lou, I'd give anything to turn back the clock, but I was afraid. I admit it. He's mad! Can you understand that?' He paused for breath but rushed on, unable to stop the torrent of words. 'I want to make it up to you. I want to help you get justice or revenge . . .'

'How can you do that if they hang you, too?' Feelings that had lain dead for months were beginning to awaken and the anger and outrage were so intense that she felt her whole body begin to tremble.

'They won't. I'll get a short sentence or maybe none!' He couldn't take this controlled conversation any longer and he jumped up and caught her hands. He'd put his neck on the line for her. 'Lou, you know I've always loved you! I never wanted to do anything to hurt you! Let me help you now? I'll testify against him, I swear. Just let me look after you. Try to ease some of the pain and grief. Marry me and let me take the burden off your shoulders? Life isn't easy for a widow with young kids to bring up. Let me help, Lou? Let me try to make amends, please? I'd be a good husband. I don't expect you to love me, but maybe in time . . . Lou, are you listening to me?'

She wasn't. Her mind was crammed with images. Mike's beloved face so cold in death. Mike laughing as he played with his sons. The love and tenderness on his face the day they'd been married. Then the images changed and she saw Eddie twisting the knobs on the radio the night they'd heard of the loss of the *Ceramic*. Eddie with his sly, sardonic smile. Eddie, his face contorted with fury the night he'd beaten Sall up and she'd hit him. Eddie! Eddie! Eddie! She pushed Tad away. 'Get out! Get out and leave me alone!'

'Lou! Think about it, please?' he begged. 'I've always loved you and isn't this proof enough? I'd die for you, Lou!'

'You'll both die! I'll go to the police!'

He became desperate. 'It's my word against yours! They had an inquest. There was no suspicion of foul play! Please, Lou! Think about it! Just think about it! Marry me and get revenge or justice!'

She threw open the parlour door with such force that it banged against the wall. 'Get out, Tad Buckley!'

He tried to catch her arm but she wrenched herself away.

'I love you, Lou! I love you! It would be justice, an eye for an eye!'

She pushed him forcefully into the hall. 'Get out and leave me alone!'

He'd gone and she leaned against the closed door. She couldn't think straight. Everything was so confused. But she *had* to think. She *had* to sort it out, the whole tangled mess! She pulled her coat from the hallstand. She had to get out, she felt stifled here. There were too many memories. She had to go somewhere where she could walk and think. Mrs Jessup from next door would keep her eye on the boys.

All the way into town on the bus she could hear those words. 'He was pushed. He was pushed. It was Eddie. He set it up. He did it.' She got off in Lime Street and crossed over towards St George's Hall. She had no predetermined destination or route, she just kept walking until she found herself in St John's Gardens. Looking around she wondered why she'd come here. The last time had been with Mike, before they'd been married.

The fury had subsided a little as she sat down on a bench. Around her the lights of the city shone brightly and the sound of the ships on the river carried clearly. The river that was so much a part of everyone's life. The river that had taken her Da away. Why was she thinking of him now and not on the events of the past hour? Her Da always said 'Do what you think is right, Lou. Make a decision and stick to it.' She had to think positively. She had to try and make a decision. A terrible decision. With a great mental effort she recalled every word of her conversation with Tad. And each word she mulled over and over in her mind until she lost track of time. He'd given her a choice, that's what it all came down to in the end. If she would marry him then he would turn Queen's Evidence and Eddie would be brought to justice. Could she go through with it? Should she go through with it? Would she be betraying Mike if she agreed to marry Tad? But what was more important to her, her own future, her own feelings or justice? If she refused Tad could she live with herself, with the knowledge that Eddie had got off scot-free? That *would* be a betrayal of Mike.

She got up and began to walk backwards and forwards between the statues. 'Vengeance is mine, sayeth the Lord.' Did she believe that? Why should Eddie be left in peace to go on preying on people? To go on wrecking lives. He

371

deserved to be punished. 'An eye for an eye,' Tad had said. That, too, was from the Bible. Round and round the thoughts and questions flew, like birds of prey swooping and darting to attack her stunned and defenceless mind. She pressed her fingers hard against her temples. What if she agreed to Tad's proposal, how would she cope in the months and years ahead? A memory jarred her forced concentration and she heard the whispered words again. 'There's work to be done. You've years ahead of you, Lou. Don't waste them.' Work! She seized on the word. She could do it if she could throw herself into work of some kind. She stopped pacing and looked up at the statue of Father Nugent, his arm around a ragged waif. It had been Mike's dearest wish that she stand for the council. She made up her mind. She'd do it. She would marry Tad and then she'd work. Every hour of the day she would work. Not just for herself and her family but for Mike and everything he had believed in and had worked to put into practice. And she would work for the people of her city so that men like Eddie MacGann would never thrive and prosper.

She didn't go straight home. There were two things she had to do first.

Doris Buckley looked at her in astonishment when she opened the door. 'Louisa!'

'Would you give Tad a message for me, please?'

'Com on in, luv, you look worn out.'

She shook her head vehemently. 'No! No, thank you. I'm fine. Just tell Tad that the answer is yes. Tell him I won't go back on my word. Good night.' She turned abruptly on her heel and walked away, leaving Doris standing on the doorstep, staring after her.

She did accept Jean's invitation and was thankful to learn that Tommy was at home.

Jean took one look at the pale face, the over-bright eyes and immediately went into the tiny kitchen to put the kettle on.

'Louisa, what's wrong?' Tommy, so confident in dealing

with people, was momentarily disturbed for she looked so shaken.

In short, unemotional sentences she told him.

'You don't have to marry him! Why should you keep your word to scum like that?' He'd had some shocks in his life but he'd never expected to experience anything like this. Estranged though they were, Eddie was still his brother. He didn't stop to think about his Mam. He couldn't.

'Because if I broke it then I'd be as bad as them! I'll manage. I have my plans.'

'Just bear it in mind, Louisa. Will you stay here with Jean while I go and see Tad?'

'No. I just want to get home now to my boys. When will you go for . . . Eddie?'

'Some time tonight.'

'I want to be there, Tommy! I want to go with you when they arrest him.'

'Then we'll leave it until morning. I'll sort out the warrants and go for Tad about eight o'clock, unless he comes in himself before that. When he's made his statement I'll pick you up and we'll go together.'

She rose. 'I'm going home now. I'm tired. So tired.'

'Wait while I call you a taxi. You're not walking home or even to the bus stop.'

Much to her own surprise she slept soundly and it was seven o'clock when she woke. The sun streamed in through the window for she'd forgotten to draw the curtains. It was a beautiful day. Too beautiful for all the ugly things that would happen, she thought. For all she knew Tad may even now be under arrest and Doris and Danny Buckley would experience yet more sorrow and shame. And then . . . She thought of Evvie and her neat, respectable, secure world that was about to crash around her and Aunt Babsey. A bitter, withdrawn, old woman who would reap what she had sown. And Eddie. She wanted to see the look on his face. She'd show him no pity, he'd shown Mike none.

She got the boys up and gave them their breakfast and

their dinner money, telling them that they'd have to stay at school today, she had important business to attend to. She silenced their protests by reminding them that they'd soon have to stay every day when she went back to work. She must see Joe Doran today, too. When the worst was over.

She was waiting, wearing the dress she had worn for Mike's funeral, when the police car drew up outside. Tommy took her arm and helped her in and they both ignored the avidly curious faces peering from behind curtains and half-open front doors.

'He came in himself and he's made a full statement. They've gone for Mogsey, too.'

'Mogsey?'

'He tried to deny it, I'll say that for him, but he's a frightened man and they make mistakes. Mogsey was the look-out.'

She closed her eyes, thinking of Mr and Mrs Green. Two more lives that Eddie had wrecked. Sall had never liked Mogsey but he was still her brother-in-law and Sall was fond of her in-laws.

As they drew up outside the shop she gripped Tommy's hand. 'I'm sorry, it's going to be hard for you. I should have gone to someone else, I just never thought.'

'It's all right. They asked if I wanted to be taken off the case and I refused. I know he's my brother but anyone who deliberately takes a life . . . Oh, let's get it over with!'

She caught a quick glimpse of Evvie's startled face behind the shop window as two uniformed constables ran around the back.

'Tommy! Louisa! What's wrong?' Evvie cried, her hand going to her throat while her customers stood transfixed.

Tommy ignored her but Louisa shook her head sadly. 'You'd better close up, Evvie,' she said quietly.

Evvie darted in front of them and through the door into the living room behind.

Babsey was just putting Eddie's breakfast on the table he wasn't an early riser. She peered at them both over her spectacles. 'What do you two want?' she snapped. 'To say you're sorry?'

Neither of them was listening. Both were staring at Eddie whose gaze flitted over them both rapidly.

'So! What's all this about then? Must be important for a deputation!' Eddie blustered.

'Edward James MacGann, I'm arresting you for the murder of Michael Joseph Crowley. I must warn you that anything you say may be taken down in writing and used as evidence against you.' Tommy's tone was flat and without a tremor as he recited the often used caution.

Eddie leapt to his feet as Evvie uttered a scream and clutched Babsey's arm.

'He wasn't murdered! The inquest said accidental death, so who do you think you're kidding? Get out of here!'

'It's no use Eddie. Tad's given himself up and made a full statement and by now Mogsey will be in the nick, too.'

She'd thought that this moment would have brought triumph, relief, even a sort of happy satisfaction, but it didn't. Eddie's suddenly haggard face and wild, staring eyes made her feel sick. She looked away but then she was pushed hard against the wall and Babsey, her eyes as wild as Eddie's, was screaming at her.

'It's all lies! Lies! It's all your fault, Louisa! You went and married that swine who broke Eddie's hand! It's your fault! It's all lies!'

Tommy pulled her away. 'Stop it, Mam! Stop it! It's not her fault! You'd never see it, would you? He's always been bad! Rotten!'

Like a small, white-haired fury she turned on him. 'What kind of a son are you? What kind of a man are you, coming here to arrest your own brother! Your own flesh and blood!'

'I'm ashamed! Ashamed of this family! And I'm glad Da's dead so he doesn't have to see this shame and degradation!' Tommy said gruffly.

'Ashamed! You're ashamed! What about me and Arnold

375

and the kids?' Evvie screamed. 'You were always different, Louisa Langford! You always attracted trouble! Why couldn't you leave things alone?' Evvie was near to tears.

'Evvie, don't blame me! He murdered my husband! He left my children fatherless! He waited and deliberately pushed him, can't you understand that!'

'You've torn this family apart, Louisa! The day you took up with Mike Crowley was the day our troubles started! Oh, God! The disgrace!' Evvie sank onto a chair, sobbing.

'Take him out!' Tommy instructed the uniformed men who had come in through the scullery.

Louisa looked at her Aunt and her cousin with pity. Aunt Babsey still couldn't see where she'd failed. She would never believe Eddie had done wrong and all Evvie seemed to care about was the scandal. 'I'm going home,' she announced wearily. Suddenly there was a bitter taste in her mouth. Whoever said revenge was sweet was wrong, she thought.

The scandal had rocked the city, for Eddie had never been known for his loyalty or courage and he had talked. In fact he had talked a great deal and the police had been busy rounding up all his associates and acquaintances.

Louisa hadn't been able to bring herself to attend the trial. To expose herself to the speculation of the curious or the incessant questions of the press. She'd sent the boys away with Maggie to visit Maggie's relations in the peaceful countryside of County Wexford. Pat had stayed and had grimly attended the Crown Court in St George's Hall every day. Today was the last day. Today the jury would give their verdict and the Judge would pronounce sentence. Sall sat with her in the parlour, waiting. Pat and Joe Doran would bring the news.

Sall sat watching her old friend and knew what was going on in her mind. After today Lou would put the past behind her and try to pick up the threads of her life. She just wished she could have talked her out of marrying

Tad. She'd tried. God knows she'd tried, as had Tommy and Jean and Pat and Maggie. Even Danny Buckley had tried, telling her not to throw away her life on a criminal like his son. Lou had faltered then, touched by his gruff plea, knowing how much it had cost him to make it. But she'd stuck to her promise. She'd replied that if she broke her promise to Tad, how could people ever trust her in the future. She was determined to stand for election and she'd argued that if she went back on her word then everything she promised people who would support her would be viewed with suspicion and scorn.

'But they'd never know, Lou!' Sall had tried reasoning.

'It would come out in time, Sall. Do you think that Tad would go through all this and then keep quiet about something like that? He'd be so hurt and angry that he'd shout it from the rooftops, then the press would have a field day at my expense and how would that look? In his own way he cares.'

'How can he when he stood by and let Eddie . . .'

'He was afraid of Eddie. Eddie would have had him killed too. No, Sall, I've got to go through with it.'

'But either way it won't reflect well on your nomination! If you do go through with it they'll point the finger and say, "Can we trust a woman who's willing to marry a man who helped murder her husband. A man who grassed on his partners, even though they are criminals."'

'I've thought about that too. Tommy reckons he'll get a long sentence. Mr Justice Harper-Seaton is a hard man. Tommy doesn't think he'll get off lightly. By the time he comes out everyone will have forgotten the . . . circumstances and I will have proved that I can be trusted.'

She'd had no answer to that.

'Shall I make another cup of tea or shall we have something stronger?' Sall asked, getting up and trying not to look at the clock.

'I couldn't drink any more tea, I'm awash with it, and don't feel like anything stronger. You have something if you want to.'

Again her life had taken on all the aspects of a dream. Was all this real? Was she sitting here in her own home waiting for news that should uplift her heart and spirit? All she felt was a queer numbness. She'd tried to imagine what her life would be like in the future – with Tad – but she couldn't. In a strange way she pitied him. If only she'd believed him all those years ago when he'd said he never loved Doreen Cooper. If she'd gone on loving him how different life would have been and how much sorrow she would have been spared. But she'd come to believe that one's life was mapped out by a higher hand and that, although you had some choices, the course was set. Destiny was predetermined.

She glanced at Sall sitting restlessly in the chair opposite her. Who would ever have believed all those years ago when they'd left St George's school, that Sall's life would have changed so drastically. All Sall had been interested in then was getting a job – any kind of a job. Sall had believed that she'd get married, have children and live a quiet, maybe hard and undistinguished life. But Sall's destiny had also been charted. She was now starting to build her business, a business that she had no doubt would expand until she was a successful and wealthy woman. She sighed. Soon Lily would be married. One day Lotty too would marry. Agnes would die, Joan and Robbie would marry and Sall would be alone and maybe lonely.

'You've heard that the shop's up for sale or lease?' Sall asked.

Louisa nodded. 'Dolly Unwin told me they're moving away from Liverpool. Going down south. She said Edith Gouldson told her that Babsey has become even stranger. Sometimes she doesn't even know who Evvie is.'

'It will be the end of her. Oh, I wish things could have been different. I feel so sorry for her.'

'She could have stopped him, Lou. Oh, I don't mean recently. Years ago she could have stopped him if she'd tried. Anyway, Edith told Dolly that they just couldn't stay here. It wasn't fair on Julie and young Arnold, having that stigma attached to them. And Evvie herself doesn't think she could stand it when . . . well, when the final day comes.'

'I understand how she feels.'

'I wish I understood you, Lou! What's happened to you?'

'I suppose you could say I've made up my mind about what I will do with the rest of my life.' She paused. 'Mike and that part of my life are over. Like you, I'll never love anyone else, even though I will marry Tad and try to be a good wife. Like you, I'll devote my life to my work. It's just that my work and yours are different. Da always said, "make a decision and stand by it". It's no use looking back, Sall, on what might have been. We've both got to follow the paths we've chosen.'

Sall did understand that. 'Everything changes, Lou. People change. Attitudes change, places change.' She smiled. 'Thank God that dirty old river will never change and the Liver birds will never fly off!' she sighed. 'Evvie will find it hard adjusting down south.'

'Evvie will cope. She's got her family to think of and they are precious to her. It's best that they make a fresh start, but I wish things could have been different.'

Sall jumped up. 'I can't stand this waiting! We're both going to have a brandy, for medicinal purposes!'

They'd had two brandies by the time they heard the footsteps in the street outside. Sall went and opened the door, for Louisa seemed rooted to the chair.

Pat and Joe entered together and both women turned questioning eyes upon them.

Pat cleared his throat but then shook his head, unable to speak.

'They found him guilty,' Joe said flatly.

'And?' Sall put in.

'I'll never forget Lord Justice Harper-Seaton's words as long as I live, or his tone. As cold as ice water it was. He's going to hang.'

She leaned back in the chair and closed her eyes. Those

words were more terrible than any feelings she'd had of outrage or revenge. She felt Sall's hand on her shoulder and she looked up at Pat whose throat muscles were working.

'And Tad?'

'He got three years. Some thought that harsh after turning Queen's Evidence. I didn't. He should be punished. Mogsey got five years.'

'Thank God it's all over!' Sall said.

Three years, Louisa was thinking. In three years she would have to keep her promise. But during that time she could begin to build up her strength, begin her work. Three years may ease the grief and blur the sharp edges of painful memory. And she would need strength, a great deal of strength, but she'd find it.'

'Before I go, there's something I have to tell you, Lou. I think it will help you,' Joe said.

'What?'

'We had a meeting the night before last. All the local party members attended. We agreed that we want you to stand for the council. The official candidate for this ward. All this has been hard for you but your integrity and courage has shone through. Mike Crowley was a much loved and respected man and people will be willing to accept you because you have the same qualities he possessed. You didn't publicly bay for Eddie's blood as many would have done. You won't publicly gloat or glory in his . . . downfall. We want you to do this, Lou. Not only for us but for Mike and for the twins, but most of all for the people. Your people, Lou!'

She looked around at them and she felt very humble and touched. It was what Mike had always wanted her to do and now it seemed that others wanted her as well. Suddenly she felt a strength flow through her. She could do it! She would do it – for him! She smiled as those whispered words came back to her. 'There's work to do. You've years ahead of you, Lou. Don't waste them.' She knew now that she'd never waste one single minute of them.

EPILOGUE

On a freezing cold day in January 1976 the crowds that surrounded St George's Church at the top of Everton Ridge shivered in the icy wind that was blowing in from the Mersey estuary. The rows of terraced houses had gone and in their place stood tower blocks. Grey, impersonal, soulless towers of concrete bearing names like 'St George's Heights'. They dwarfed the church that was filled to capacity with civic dignitaries and politicians as well as family, friends, neighbours, colleagues and the ordinary citizens of Liverpool. They'd all come to pay their respects to the woman who'd devoted her short life to them. Louisa Mary Buckley or Lou as most of them called her.

In the front pews were her family. Tad, grey-haired and a little stooped. John and Patrick Crowley. Grown men who had kept their father's name and had taken over the business when their grandfather, Pat, had died. Maggie Crowley, a frail, silver-haired old woman. Detective Inspector Thomas MacGann, his wife Jean and their son and daughter-in-law.

In the pew behind them sat Robbie Cooper and his wife; Lily and Joan and a tall, strikingly beautiful woman, known professionally as Charlotte Buckley QC but to her friends as 'Lotty'. Beside her stood Sally Green, a small, fine-boned woman, dressed in a fur jacket and matching hat over a black wool dress. She was only fifty-four but her name and her designs were known in households all over the country and parts of Europe, and she'd taken the first steps to turn Evergreen into an empire. But she would willingly had given it all away to have her dear friend alive and well.

With a small hand, encased in finest black kid, she wiped away a single tear. 'Oh, Lou, we came a long way together, didn't we? Do you remember the gloves you bought me that Christmas? The first pair I'd ever had. I'll miss you, Lou,' she said silently, seeing in her mind's eye a pair of woollen gloves with a Fair Isle pattern on them.

Tad looked down at his feet, unwilling to raise his eyes and see the plain coffin. She'd undermined her strength, they'd told him. She should have had more rest, less stress. Her heart just hadn't been able to cope with it all. And she'd had such a big heart. She'd given so much of herself. Less stress, he mused sadly. He'd been married to a woman who had appeared to thrive on it. Elected first as a councillor, then a Member of Parliament, she had often berated other MPs, Cabinet Ministers and the Prime Minister on the behalf of the underprivileged people of her native city.

He'd loved her for nearly forty years and for the last twenty he'd been as happy as any man could have been. She'd been a good wife and a good mother, although they'd never had any children. But John and Patrick were like sons to him and he knew he'd need them in the months and years ahead. The strains of Handel's Largo throbbed quietly through the church but the words of the old ballad were running through his mind.

'Liverpool Lou, lovely Liverpool Lou.'

She'd never behaved like other women or girls and his poor heart had followed her – in vain. She'd never really loved him the way he loved her. But he had his memories and they were good ones.

The service was over and the coffin, covered in flowers, was carried out into the churchyard. People began to surge forward and the police on duty tried to hold them back.

''Ere, lad! Let's through!' A small woman, her face wrinkled and weather-beaten, her white hair scraped back into a tight bun, looked up at the police sergeant.

He smiled. 'Come on then, Ma, we don't want you gettin' crushed.'

She brushed away a tear with a red, work-roughened hand. 'I want ter give 'er this.' She held out a shiny, red apple and he recognized her as one of the barrow women from Clayton Square. She'd been selling fruit there since he was a lad in short pants and years before that, too.

'Go on, Ma, be quick.'

She gave it a last polish on the sleeve of her coat, then placed it reverently amongst the flowers and stood back. 'She liked a nice apple, did our Lou.'

The sergeant felt a strange stinging in his eyes. 'Aye, she did, didn't she,' he answered quietly.

THE END

A SELECTED LIST OF FINE TITLES
AVAILABLE FROM CORGI AND BLACK SWAN
BOOKS

☐	13600 X	THE SISTERS O'DONNELL	Lyn Andrews
☐	13482 1	THE WHITE EMPRESS	Lyn Andrews
☐	13230 6	AN EQUAL CHANCE	Brenda Clarke
☐	13556 9	SISTERS AND LOVERS	Brenda Clarke
☐	12887 2	SHAKE DOWN THE STARS	Frances Donnelly
☐	12607 1	DOCTOR ROSE	Elvi Rhodes
☐	13185 7	THE GOLDEN GIRLS	Elvi Rhodes
☐	13481 3	THE HOUSE OF BONNEAU	Elvi Rhodes
☐	13309 4	MADELEINE	Elvi Rhodes
☐	12367 6	OPAL	Elvi Rhodes
☐	12803 3	RUTH APPLEBY	Elvi Rhodes
☐	13413 9	THE QUIET WAR OF REBECCA SHELDON	Kathleen Rowntree
☐	13557 7	BRIEF SHINING	Kathleen Rowntree
☐	12375 7	A SCATTERING OF DAISIES	Susan Sallis
☐	12579 2	THE DAFFODILS OF NEWENT	Susan Sallis
☐	12880 5	BLUEBELL WINDOWS	Susan Sallis
☐	13136 9	ROSEMARY FOR REMEMBRANCE	Susan Sallis
☐	13346 9	SUMMER VISITORS	Susan Sallis
☐	13545 3	BY SUN AND CANDLELIGHT	Susan Sallis
☐	13299 3	DOWN LAMBETH WAY	Mary Jane Staples
☐	13573 9	KING OF CAMBERWELL	Mary Jane Staples
☐	13730 8	THE LODGER	Mary Jane Staples
☐	13444 9	OUR EMILY	Mary Jane Staples
☐	13449 9	TWO FOR THREE FARTHINGS	Mary Jane Staples